THE LAWMAN AND THE LADY

She clasped her hands in front of her, hesitating. "Shall I help you undress?"

As if he couldn't bear for her to think him weak or hurt, he reached for his collar button. His fingers twisted, fumbled, slipped. With a sigh he took his hand away. "I'd be much obliged."

A little embarrassed, she began to unbutton his shirt. She stopped when she came to his belt buckle.

"You don't have to do this," he murmured huskily.

She could feel her cheeks burning and didn't dare look at him for fear she'd lose her nerve. The shirt slipped off his right shoulder and she stifled her cry of horror so that it came out in a gasp.

"Pretty ugly, isn't it?"

She couldn't stop herself. She put her hand and then her mouth to the spot. "I'm so sorry. I'm so sorry."

"Don't," he croaked.

With her mouth still pressed against the scarred flesh, she murmured, "Oh, Will."

He groaned. "You'd better get out of here if you know what's good for you."

She didn't realize her hands had clutched him tighter until he tried to pull her arms from around his waist. No! She couldn't let him go.

She was on fire. Dazedly, she looked up into his face. "I think I do know what's good for me."

His head came down as she turned up her mouth to fit his . . . .

BOOK YOUR PLACE ON OUR WEBSITE AND MAKE THE READING CONNECTION!

We've created a customized website just for our very special readers, where you can get the inside scoop on everything that's going on with Zebra, Pinnacle and Kensington books.

When you come online, you'll have the exciting opportunity to:

- View covers of upcoming books
- Read sample chapters
- Learn about our future publishing schedule (listed by publication month *and author*)
- Find out when your favorite authors will be visiting a city near you
- Search for and order backlist books from our online catalog
- Check out author bios and background information
- Send e-mail to your favorite authors
- Meet the Kensington staff online
- Join us in weekly chats with authors, readers and other guests
- Get writing guidelines
- AND MUCH MORE!

Visit our website at
http://www.zebrabooks.com

MY LAWMAN

Deana James

Zebra Books
Kensington Publishing Corp.

http://www.zebrabooks.com

ZEBRA BOOKS are published by

Kensington Publishing Corp.
850 Third Avenue
New York, NY 10022

First Printing: November, 1998
10 9 8 7 6 5 4 3 2 1

Printed in the United States of America

For
Janice Pace
Dearest friend and traveling buddy
Coffeyville was cold as the North Pole that December
afternoon, but you never faltered.

Love you—

Chapter One

"We're gonna spend Christmas in Brazil!"

Bob Dalton lifted his foaming glass of beer in a toast to his two brothers. With a sly grin of anticipation, he leaned forward to drink. "Gonna leave Coffeyville with a whole lot more than we had when we got here. Gonna start 1893 in Ree-oh."

"Shut up, Bob," Grat rumbled.

Peach Smith wished he'd shut up too. The Daltons hardly ever had more than a couple of dollars among them. How they were going to get enough money to go to Kansas City was the question. Thousands of miles away to Brazil was ridiculous. Unless they were going to do something terrible.

"Ree-oh day Ja-nay-re-o," Bob insisted. He smiled widely at Peach before leaning back and practically pouring his beer down his throat.

At least the middle Dalton brother couldn't talk while he was drinking, Peach thought. Bob's loose mouth was going to get him in real trouble someday. She looked around uneasily, but nobody seemed to be paying any attention.

As a matter of fact, nobody was close enough to the table to hear anything. The saloon of Scurlock House was deserted except for poor old Will Wesley, who usually sat at the end of the bar at three in the afternoon. Lord knew he was harmless—crippled up and drinking like he was.

Was there anybody in the dining room? Peach took a step backward to peek through the swinging doors. Old Neddy Barnes, the swamper, was leaning on his mop handle, half asleep. His haystack hair fell over his forehead. Between it and his tangled beard, his face was nothing more than a big red-veined nose and a pair of loose lips.

She could smell the odor from his sour mop. She'd have to speak to him or get their boss to. Luke Scurlock ran a clean establishment. He wouldn't cotton to stuff like that. She was about to look away, when she realized Neddy's eyes were staring at her. His mouth twitched into a leer. She wondered how much he'd heard.

She wrinkled her nose and pointed to the mop.

He shrugged his shoulders and went back to swiping the gray, ropy rags back and forth over the floor.

Setting his beer down, Bob Dalton swiped the foam from his upper lip and motioned her back to the table. "What you think about that idea, sweetheart?"

He'd called her sweetheart. Conflicting emotions sent a little ripple up her spine. Bob Dalton was trouble, but she was human and getting old fast. What she wouldn't give for somebody to call her sweetheart—and mean it. What she wouldn't give if handsome Bob Dalton meant it. She could feel her face melting into what she was sure was a dying-calf look.

Bob swung the glass in her direction. "Hey, tell me what you think, Peachy?"

The name snapped her face back into shape. Bob had been calling her Peachy since he'd first met her more than three years before. He knew how she hated to be called that, but her protesting only made him more determined to do it.

"Sounds like fun, Bob." Then she curled her lip in the sneer she used to keep the fresh drummers and rowdy cowboys away. "Not much!"

"Hey! Give a guy a chance!" He cut a two-inch-square bite off his steak and stuffed it in his mouth.

Peach tucked her tray under her arm. "Will that do it, boys?"

Grat Dalton's mouth was full, but Emmett, his baby brother, smiled politely and nodded.

As she turned away, Bob shot out his hand and grabbed her butt.

She froze. Absolutely nothing made her madder than for some drunk to do that. She jerked the tray from under her arm and swung it in a vicious circle. The edge crashed into Bob's wrist.

"Hey!"

She stepped out of reach and turned back. "Yes?" she inquired sweetly.

Bob still chewed, but he'd dropped his fork and was nursing his wrist. His automatic anger faded into a know-it-all grin.

She hated men who grinned like that. They didn't believe she was serious.

His brother Emmett laughed out loud and slapped the table. "You gotta watch Peach, Bobby. She don't like that stuff."

Bob managed to swallow the enormous bite and assumed an air of grievance. "You didn't need to take my arm off, Peachy. You knowed I was just being friendly."

Peach rolled her eyes. *That* friendly she could do without, especially since it was so far from the friendly she longed for from Bob Dalton. "I take it you've got all you're going to need for a while, boys."

"Bring us some more beer," Grat demanded without raising his eyes from his plate.

"Coming right up." She went behind the bar and began to draw a pitcherful. In the mirror she met the enigmatic stare of Will Wesley as he bent his elbow on the bar and nursed his beer through the afternoon.

Their eyes held as she filled the pitcher. An understanding passed between them. Not sympathy. Neither of them had any need for sympathy. Instead, they looked at each other with resignation bordering on boredom. They'd heard it all before.

Their lives were what they were and not likely to change.

She cooked and cleaned for Scurlock House, a drummers' hotel by the L.L.& G. Railroad track. She worked from before daylight till long after dark, making beds, sweeping floors, washing linens, and cleaning the bathrooms at each end of the halls. For breakfast and lunch and supper she cooked the meals and waited on the tables. In the evening after the dining room closed, she made meals out of the leftovers and took them to the prisoners in the Coffeyville jail.

At night Will walked the halls as the house detective in the same hotel. In the morning he swept out the jail and emptied the slops. Even though he was supposed to be Connelly's deputy, he was pretty much useless with that busted shoulder. His in-between hours he filled by staying quietly drunk.

"Top it off, Will?" she asked softly.

"Much obliged, Peach." His voice was just as soft, his southern drawl mellowing it and stretching out the syllables. He'd drifted up from Arkansas, but Louisiana or maybe Mississippi had left its print in his speech.

The Daltons weren't looking as she refilled Will's glass to the brim from their pitcher.

He hadn't shaved in a week. His eyes were bloodshot and the way he dropped his head between his hunched shoulders let her know that he was trying some of the "hair of the dog" to get himself in shape to go to work. She probably shouldn't have encouraged him to drink.

"Hey, Peachy!" came the rude shout. "We're dying of thirst."

"Coming, Bob."

As she slipped out from behind the bar, Charlie Connelly pushed in through the swinging doors. The marshal of Coffeyville blinked, waiting for his eyes to adjust to the dim interior.

He scowled at the Daltons, who ducked their heads and pretended great interest in their food. He sneered at Peach, who walked by him with her chin in the air. His eyes narrowed as he found his quarry.

"Wesley! I need you right now."

Will didn't move immediately.

"Wesley! Are you deaf too?"

Will took a swig of his beer before he slid off his stool and came around the bar. Face-to-face he could look down into Connelly's angry eyes. "Not deaf," he replied softly. "And not *too* either."

Bob Dalton turned a snigger into a cough when Peach glared at him.

Connelly glared around him. "You'll get yours, trash."

"Not from you," Bob predicted under his breath.

Connelly jerked his thumb in the direction of the jail. "Need you right now, Wesley. If you want to keep that badge, you'll come."

Will acknowledged. "Right behind you."

After Connelly strode out, Peach smiled sympathetically at Will. "I'll hold your spot for you."

"Much obliged." He hooked his right thumb in his belt loop and followed the marshal.

The silence that followed was broken by Grat's calling for some ketchup for his steak.

* * *

Peach was adding water and bacon grease to the beans when the door of the cookshack swung open. The chilly wind lifted her skirts and blew greasy strands of hair forward around her cheeks. She shuddered. Sometimes she thought she couldn't stand being the way she was a minute longer.

"Close the door," she called over her shoulder.

"Sure thing, Peachy."

She spun, spoon uplifted, splattering pot liquor on her skirt. "What do you want, Bob?"

Grinning, he stuck his hands in his back pockets and shuffled his boots in the dirt. "Just came to see if you'd like to walk out for a spell."

She almost dropped the spoon. A sudden spurt of raw emotion made her tremble all over. Bob Dalton. Handsome Bob Dalton wanted to walk out with her. She'd dreamed of this moment for—

She looked at him narrowly. "You're kidding."

"Naw! Me? Would I kid you?" He shook his head. His grin was even wider. "Nary a bit. Me and Grat have got a proposition for you, Peachy. One you're gonna like the sound of."

So much for romantic dreams. They had a proposition. She took a firmer grip on the long-handled spoon and folded her arms tight across her chest. "I don't like the sound of it and I haven't even heard it yet."

To her surprise, he didn't come closer. Instead, he folded his arms and lounged back against the door. She could feel his eyes sweeping her. "You'd clean up pretty good, Peachy. I remember when I first laid eyes on you. I said you was one pretty girl."

"Oh, come on, Bob!" She rolled her eyes. She knew what she looked like, knew what she'd always looked like.

She was thin and plain. Plain blue eyes, straight blond hair the color Sister Agnes Mary had called dishwater.

Behind her, the beans began to bubble again. She needed to stir them, but she didn't want to turn her back on him.

"No. I mean it." He smiled at her with all his teeth. "How long ago has that been? Two years? Three? We go way back."

She lifted her chin. "Yeah! I heard Minnie Johnson finally got married."

As her remark sank in, Peach grinned at his sheepish expression. He'd been bragging about Minnie Johnson when Peach had first gone to work for Scurlock's.

Minnie had been as pretty as a Pears Soap girl. Bob and Charlie Montgomery, a whiskey peddler and small-time crook, had both been sweet on her. She'd stepped out with Charlie a few times. Then his body had been found over across the railroad tracks on the far side of town.

No one had ever been arrested for the killing. However, it had happened when Grat was the deputy U.S. marshal, so he probably hadn't looked too hard.

After that Minnie and Bob had gone at it hot and heavy for a while, but he'd never proposed marriage. She'd finally given up on him and run off to St. Louis.

Peach swiped back the stray hairs sticking to her cheeks and waited. She knew she wasn't much of a catch. Bob Dalton surely wasn't going to marry her just because he'd let somebody like Minnie get away.

Bob kicked at a greasy spot in the dirt floor. "Hell! Minnie and I hadn't been getting along for a spell. I knew it was all over. To tell the truth, I'm just as glad she's gone."

And pigs can fly, Peach thought. Turning halfway around, she managed to give the pot a twirl while she kept her eye on Bob.

"The fact is, Peachy—" He clamped his jaw tight when she glared at him.

"Er—Peach, the boys and me was wondering if you'd be up for helping us with a job."

A chill trickled down her spine. The Daltons had wild reputations. For all they'd been deputy marshals for Judge Isaac Parker's court in Fort Smith, they were a rough bunch. She was starting to shake her head, when Bob held up his hand.

"Listen, Peachy—er—Peach. I can see you're busy right now. But I've got a real good deal for you. That's if you don't want to sling hash for the rest of your born days."

She hadn't realized Bob Dalton had ever thought much about anybody else's job but his own. She didn't think he'd had an ounce of feelings for another human being anywhere—Minnie Johnson excepted, of course.

Ever since she'd known him, he'd ridden high, wide, and handsome and damn-you-all-to-hell-and-gone-if-you-don't-like-it. Now, out of nowhere, had come this comment that struck at the heart of what she'd been feeling for quite a while.

She felt herself softening. Bob was the man Peach had fallen in love with the first time she'd ever laid eyes on him. He was tall and handsome. He shaved every morning, bathed when practical, and dressed well. He had good manners when he chose to use them. He'd teased and flirted with her when he was twenty and she was a blushing seventeen and new in Coffeyville.

He'd broken her heart without ever knowing it. She cocked her head to one side. Or did he? Did he know more than he'd let on?

He met her gaze steadily as he straightened away from the door. "This is gonna be big, Peach. We need one more person in on it. Someone who wants to get out of here as bad as we do."

"I don't know what you're talking about, Bob." He was

right about her wanting out of Scurlock's, but something big with the Daltons wasn't the way. She was dead certain about that.

He stared her up and down. Not the way he usually looked at her, but with a critical eye. He looked serious somehow and a little sad. "How old you figure that dress is, Peach?"

She stiffened. She didn't remember when she'd gotten it. It'd been left behind in one of the hotel rooms. She'd tucked it away, waiting for someone to come back for it. When no one did, she'd started wearing it.

She'd washed it Saturday night, so it had been clean when she'd put it on on Sunday. She had three left-behind dresses. Fortunately, she was skinny and could take them in at the waist and turn up the hems. They worked just fine.

She didn't need pity from the likes of him. She bent closer to the boiling beans, hoping he'd think the heat was causing her face to turn red. "None of your business."

"How long since you've had a real bath?"

"Now, that is strictly none of your damn business." She was blushing for real and she didn't care if he knew it or not. She'd known when he walked in he was trouble. Now here he was asking all sorts of rude personal questions and upsetting her. Bob Dalton being serious was making her feel a hell of a lot worse than Bob Dalton raising hell and grabbing her butt.

She peered at him through the steam and haze of the cookshack. He looked older than his twenty-three years. Like maybe the last four years of raising hell and letting Grat lead him from one bad time to another were beginning to get him down.

He put his hand behind him and pushed the door open. "If you're interested, meet me over behind Kloehr's Livery Stable after you take the meals down to the jail. I'll be waiting."

"You may have to wait a long time."

He shrugged. Just before he closed the door behind him, he threw out a last word. "Better think about it, Peach. This might be your last chance."

As Bob strode out of the cookshack, he collided with Will Wesley. Both men staggered and righted themselves. The younger Dalton scowled as the older man's face twisted and he wrapped his left hand around his right shoulder

"Hanging out in alleys these days, rummy?" Bob snarled as he started to push on by.

Will set his jaw tight enough to make a muscle jump in his hollow cheek. He dropped his hand away from his throbbing shoulder and tucked both thumbs into his belt loops. "Just waiting around in case a lady needs assistance when some lowlife sneaks in to bother her."

Bob's eyes narrowed. He lowered his head between his shoulders and clenched his fists. "You calling me a low-life?"

"If the shoe fits—"

"You better step back, you old drunk—" Bob raised his fists.

"As it happens, I'm not drunk right at the moment." Will stared hard at Dalton. Bob was a brawler when he had his brothers to back him up, but he didn't like to face a man on his own. Will waited. "You go first."

Bob scowled harder. Slowly he lowered his fists. "I think I'll just walk away from this one, old man. I wouldn't want to hurt you. Tal Karnes might want to come back and finish the job."

Will smiled faintly. "But you wouldn't mind hurting someone else—like Peach Smith."

Bob hesitated. A faint color rose in his cheeks. "I ain't gonna—"

"Peach is a good girl," Will interrupted. "She was raised

in a convent with all the convent rules. She's worked like a field hand ever since. She'd lose her job if Luke Scurlock found you sniffing around back here."

Bob kicked at a stone in the path. "Hey! This ain't any of your business. I've got a proposition for her—"

Will's expression turned thunderous. His voice turned silky, belying the words he spoke. "Why don't you just git, like the dog you are, Dalton? Any kind of proposition you'd make wouldn't be fit for a nice girl to hear."

Those were fighting words, all the more insulting because Will's southern drawl dripped contempt. They made Bob bristle, but the desire to fight had clearly left him. Will Wesley had been a no-nonsense peace officer and a dead aim with a gun before Tal Karnes had shot him up.

The middle Dalton took a step backward. "What'd you know about nice girls, you rummy old cripple?"

Will merely dropped his left hand to his gun butt. His stare never wavered. He didn't think Bob knew whether or not he could pull off a left-handed shot. It didn't make any difference. He knew from long experience as a lawman he'd made his bluff.

When Will continued to stare at him, Bob Dalton seemed to remember business elsewhere. With a virulent curse he brushed hard against Will's injured shoulder and strode down the alley. When he was out of sight, Will allowed himself to relax. He hadn't taken much of a chance with a bully like Bob, but an armed man always had the means to kill another.

He pulled off his hat and swiped his forearm across his brow. His sweat stained his blue linsey-woolsey sleeve. His arm was hurting from neck to elbow, and he needed a drink. He didn't get paid for doing stuff like this. But he'd wait around for a while to see whether Bob Dalton tried to sneak back.

* * *

Peach Smith thought she was most likely twenty years old, three years younger than Bob Dalton. The reason she didn't know for sure was that she'd been reared in a Catholic orphanage near Westport Landing northwest of Independence, Missouri. The nuns had named her Patience, but when she'd left at sixteen, she'd changed her name to something sweet. There'd been little enough sweetness in her life up till then.

By fits and starts she'd drifted over to Coffeyville, Kansas. She'd heard there was money to be made where three railroad lines criss-crossed. There was money all right. But not nearly enough of it had come her way. She still hadn't had to sell herself, but she'd come close a few times. So she'd ended up cooking and working in a drummers' hotel.

The job meant that she wouldn't ever go hungry. Since Luke Scurlock didn't mind her bringing in her blanket and curling up on top of a bed if any room went empty, she usually had a soft place to sleep. And she had a cot in the cookshack when the cattle buyers were in town.

Still, she'd given some study to Bob's words about slinging hash for the rest of her born days. She'd been thinking about that herself especially as she started on the mound of dirty dishes she had to wash morning, noon, and night seven days a week. She was still thinking about it.

Of course, she did have an extra job that Will Wesley had gotten her. With checkered napkins over the tin plates, she carried beans and corn bread to the prisoners in Marshal Connelly's jail. For this service the town paid a dollar apiece, seventy-five cents of which went to Luke Scurlock, who owned the hotel. The twenty-five cents was hers.

She'd get fifty cents tonight for the two prisoners in the cells. That was exactly half of what her wages were for the week.

When Connelly let the drunk out the following day,

she'd get only twenty-five cents. On Saturday, when they transferred the other prisoner to Judge Parker's district court at Fort Smith, she wouldn't have that income until someone else was arrested.

The uncertainty of her life had made her think a little longer about Bob Dalton's proposition. Rio de Janeiro had such a romantic sound. So far away. A chance to start over as Bob's girlfriend. Would she be any worse off?

Of course she would be. It would be about the worst thing she could do. She wasn't stupid. Someone would be arrested in Coffeyville before the night was out. It was a tough little town with trash moving through all the time on the railroads. Connelly was strict. Mean but strict. He'd throw people in jail at the drop of a hat.

It was full dark when she stepped out of the door of the jail. Will Wesley came up behind her. "Walk you back to the hotel, Peach?"

She hesitated. She was lucky to have an escort. Kloehr's Livery Stable was just down the alley from the jail, but Coffeyville wasn't all that safe to walk around in at night even with the two new electric streetlights over on Walnut.

She knew she ought to go with him. She was safe with Will. Even though he was a drunk, he was a nice drunk. As a matter of fact, she couldn't smell liquor on his breath tonight. She walked beside him to the end of the block. Then she stopped.

"Thanks, Will, but I've got something to do before I go back. I'll see you later on."

He caught her arm, his grip tight enough to scare her.

She froze. Surely, not Will Wesley. He wouldn't try to get fresh with her. Why, he must be a lot older than Grat Dalton. "What do you think you're doing, Mr. Wesley?"

"Peach. I—"

She jerked her arm away and turned on him, bristling, fists digging into her hips. "I most certainly am surprised.

I thought better of you. But I guess I was wrong. Sooner or later, every man I run into gets fresh.''

''Sorry,'' he muttered. He pushed his coat aside and hooked his thumbs in his belt loops. ''Listen, Peach. I don't think you ought to be listening to anything Bob Dalton says. He's rotten to the core.''

She gaped at him. An odd chill trickled down her spine. How could Will know she was meeting Bob? Not that Bob ever kept anything a secret. He'd probably spilled it all over town that she was meeting him at the livery stable. *Darn it! Why did somebody so handsome have to be such a blabbermouth? And have to have a bad reputation to boot!* Now she wanted to march right over to Kloehr's and smack him good. She looked around her. If Bob were suddenly to appear, she'd tell him a thing or two.

''Peach—?''

''You go on, Will,'' she said. ''And thanks for the tip, but believe me, you don't have to say anything. I've known Bob Dalton for years. He's everything you say and then some.''

Leaving Will to stare after her, she hurried away. She'd intended just to listen, tell them politely to count her out, and go on her way. Now she was so mad, she wouldn't be so polite when it came time to tell Bob to stop spreading her name around.

''It ain't never been done before,'' Grat was insisting. ''Even Jesse and Frank didn't never do two banks at once.''

Peach froze in the doorway of the livery stable. She hadn't heard what she thought she'd heard. She shook her head and listened some more.

''It's double dangerous,'' Emmett protested. ''We'd have two sets of guns banging away at us. We could get caught in a cross fire.''

The feeble light of the kerosene lantern lit their avid

faces. She'd heard it all right, and Emmett was the only one who wasn't drinking Grat's words in like a catechism.

Three of them sat listening as if he were delivering high mass—Bob and his friends Dick Broadwell and Billy Powers.

She started to back quietly away, but the stable door creaked. Bob looked up and saw her. "Peachy!"

"Goddamn." Grat lumbered to his feet and tossed his head like a bull. He drew his gun and waved it in her direction as he turned his angry glare on Bob. "What's she doing here?"

Bob grinned at his brother. "She came to see me. I asked her to come."

"Oh, no!" Peach didn't wait to see how Grat felt about that. She fled the stable. She would have disappeared in the darkness if she hadn't blundered over a rut in the alley and turned her ankle.

She stumbled when she tried to put her weight on it. The stable door opened wide and Bob found her in the light. "Come on back in," he urged. "Grat's just stubborn. He don't like women much."

"Let me go." She tried to twist free. Her ankle was hurting, but not so bad that she couldn't walk away fast. "I heard what he said. You all are planning something like your worthless cousins."

"They ain't worthless," Bob declared.

"Ha!" Peach dug in her heels and refused to move. "They're all in jail. You can't get much more worthless than that."

"Frank's not," he argued doggedly.

"No, he's not. And Jesse's not either. He's dead." Peach punched her finger into the center of Bob's chest.

"Well, that's why we're getting out of the country." Bob pulled her firmly back into the stable.

"Let go of me."

"Just listen, Peachy."

"What in hell did you bring her in on this for?" Grat was bigger than Bob and eight years older. He had a ferocious mustache that completely covered his upper lip. He claimed it was to strain his beer, but Peach guessed it was to hide his nasty, crooked teeth.

Bob crossed his arms over his chest. "I ain't going to Brazil without someone to cuddle up to. Peachy's gonna help us, and then me and her are going to get married."

"What?" Peach couldn't believe her ears. "I'm not marrying you."

He flashed her a devilish grin. "Fine with me if you want to tag along without a license. Just goes to show, a feller never can tell. I figured a good girl like you—raised in a convent and such—wouldn't settle for a roll and a tickle."

"A roll and a tickle. Listen here, Bob Dalton—"

"She's not tagging along." Grat's big shoulders swelled. He lowered his head like an angry bull.

"She's gonna hold the horses for us."

"The hell I am." Peach was sure Bob had lost his mind.

"The hell she is." Grat *knew* Bob had lost his mind. "She ain't in this."

"Belle Starr—"

"That whore didn't ride with Cole. She just claimed she had," Grat snarled.

"She's dead too," Peach added.

"Peachy. Peach." Bob let his hand slide down her arm to take her hand. Gently he swung it back and forth. "You've thought about what I said, or you wouldn't've come here."

"That's not so." Of course it was—along with that stray remark that Will had made, but she wasn't going to admit that to Bob. Besides, she wasn't up for bank robbery now. And she wouldn't ever be.

"Sure it is."

She glared at him. "Bob Dalton. Why would you think I'd be willing to rob a bank? You know I'm honest. I'm not going to steal from people."

He looked over his shoulder at Grat. "Just give us a minute." He took her outside again. "Listen. I didn't mean for you to carry a gun. I just thought that you could hold the horses. Then we could duck out of this hick town forever."

"Oh, sure." She'd never thought Bob was stupid until then. "That's just what would really take me out of this hick town forever. Carried out in a pine box. I'd be the first one shot dead on the street."

"Listen. We're gonna plan it so you won't even be on the street. We're planning escape routes and everything."

She put her hands over her ears. "Shut up! Shut up! Shut up! I don't want to hear it. If I don't know anything, then I can't be in on it."

He stopped. "Well, dammit, Peachy—"

She turned and hobbled off. Over her shoulder she yelled, "And don't call me Peachy!"

She was hobbling worse than ever when she got back to Scurlock's. Luke, the boss, gave her the fish eye. "Got your spoonin' done, Peach? We got some people in on the late train, waitin' for their suppers in their rooms."

"Yes, sir." She was out of breath and shaking. If Luke said it, then it was all over town that she'd met Bob Dalton in the stable. She'd wasted time and energy and hurt herself and ruined what little reputation she had. She should have known nothing good would come from Bob Dalton. She closed her eyes.

But, oh, she wished it had.

"Found you a room, Peach." Will Wesley pressed a key into her hand at midnight. "Number ten's not taken."

"Thanks, Will." Even though she'd been running from morning till night, she gave him a big smile. She was sorry for the way she'd spoken to him in the alley. He'd just been looking out for her best interests after all.

Too bad he was so old. She was lucky to have a friend like him who cared about her. With him as the house detective, she wasn't in any danger of stumbling into an occupied room and getting in trouble. Will always took a look at the book to see who rented what. That way he could be near the ones that looked like trouble.

He heaved a sigh. "Did you get your business taken care of?"

"Yes."

He waited. But she wasn't going to give him any more of the story. If it were just Grat Dalton, she'd tell Will Wesley what she'd heard quick as a flash. But Bob was her friend. Unfortunately, he wasn't ever going to be anything more, but she wasn't going to squeal on them.

Besides, she didn't have anything to tell. Just talking about doing something wasn't against the law. They could talk themselves out of something just as easily. And she didn't know any of the details—like which banks and when. She didn't really have anything to tell Will.

"You didn't get yourself into any trouble?" he asked softly. "I notice you're favoring your left leg."

"I tripped in the alley. You were right, Will. I should have stuck with you. But I'm lucky enough to've come out of it all right."

He nodded. "You're sure."

"I'm sure. It's all over and done with." She held up the key. "Thanks a million, Will."

Wrapped in her own blanket on top of the bed in the empty room, she tried to think of why Bob Dalton might have wanted her in on this deal. He couldn't be in love with her. Everyone knew he'd loved Minnie Johnson for a long time, but he'd never popped the question. Maybe now that Minnie had run off, he wanted to show her that he didn't care.

Peach touched her callused palm to her slicked-back hair tied in a greasy knot. As if Minnie Johnson would be impressed if she ever met Peach Smith! Bob Dalton didn't have much common sense. She sighed.

Of course, she'd had dreams about him suddenly seeing her and falling in love and asking her to marry him. She'd say yes. Then she'd tell him that she'd always loved him since the first moment she saw him. They'd settle down. He'd be the town marshal and she'd work for Luke or someplace else until the babies started coming. She hated to give up on those babies with handsome Bob Dalton as their father. She sure did want a couple of pretty babies.

She wouldn't give up, she told herself. Even though she couldn't have Bob, there had to be someone else for her. If Minnie Johnson could run away and get married after being fought over by a lowlife like Bob Dalton and Charlie Montgomery, a whiskey peddler, then there sure had to be hope for Peach Smith. On the other hand, maybe she ought to try to find a couple of galoots to fight over her. Maybe the trick was that if somebody else wanted her, she must be worth more.

Bob Dalton was waiting in the cookshack the next morning. When she saw him, she tried to back out the door, but he caught her by the arm. "I need to talk to you bad."

He looked hung over and miserable, and he smelled like the inside of a saloon. She wondered if he'd been to bed at all.

"Well, I don't need to talk to you." She cocked her head to one side, studying him. "But I can give you a cup of coffee."

"Much obliged."

While she stirred in sugar but no cream, just the way he

liked it, he sat down gingerly beside the butcher block. The silence grew between them. This must really be serious. She couldn't ever remember seeing Bob quiet.

He took a sip of coffee. "That's good. Thanks."

"You're welcome." She counted out a dozen potatoes from the gunnysack and began peeling them.

He stared into the dark brown liquid as if it held an answer to an important question. At last he thumped his fist down on the table. "We ain't none of us been worth a plugged nickel since Franklin died."

She ran water into a cast iron pot. "Your brother Franklin's been dead four years, Bob. And you and Grat have been deputy U.S. marshals nearly that long."

"That don't pay nothing," he shot back. "Why, hell, Peach, it don't pay but two dollars a head on outlaws we bring in."

She'd heard this complaint before, but Will had told her how they really made their money. "Don't you get to turn in all your expenses?"

Bob nodded, a little surprised that she knew.

She kept on going. "Plus you get whatever they've got with them—their horses and guns and clothes and such. And of course any money that isn't written down on the warrant. Isn't that right? Seems to me—"

"Peach," he interrupted. He drank deep from the coffee cup and set it down with a sharp clack. "It was us robbed the Katy."

Again she looked around her hastily. Someday he was going to say something like this at the wrong time. The Katy train robbery in July had gotten the whole state in an uproar. "You shouldn't be telling me this."

"I just gotta tell someone. We been accused of a lot of things that we never done. You know they couldn't prove a lick at that trial last year."

"Bob—"

"But we done bad in July. Hell. That old son of a bitch

down there in Fort Smith wouldn't pay us what he owed us—" He turned up his coffee and gulped it down as if it were a shot of whiskey. Then he strangled and sucked in air with his mouth open. "And we was thinking how Franklin got shot trying to do his job. It just made us all so mad."

She hoped he'd scalded his tongue but good. "So you robbed a railroad to get back at Judge Isaac Parker. Good job, Bob. Real smart."

He nodded his head. "I know. I know. And now we're wanted—for real. We gotta get out of here, or we're going to jail."

She wiped her hands on a rag and pumped water over the potatoes. "They said you got forty thousand dollars from the Katy. Why don't the three of you get on out while the getting's good?"

" 'Cause we didn't get forty thousand. The damn railroad lied, probably to collect on their insurance." He let his head sag between his shoulders. "We got four thousand."

He was practically crying over the injustice of it all. She would have laughed if it hadn't been so stupid and so pathetic.

"We can't get far even in Brazil on that."

She folded her arms across her chest. "You could get honest work."

He looked at her with hopeless eyes. "We're Daltons. We've got a bad reputation. We haven't done hardly a thing, but we're blamed for every damn thing that happens in this whole United States of America."

She could see his point. And it was the truth. The stories had been told from as far away as California about the Daltons robbing trains and rustling cattle.

Sometimes they were said to be in the company of their cousins Jesse and Frank James and the Youngers. Newspaper accounts still reported their adventures even though the word had flashed from coast to coast eleven years earlier that Jesse had been shot dead in his own home.

Frank now worked as a bouncer at a saloon in St. Louis, and the Youngers were in the Minnesota state penitentiary for life. Still, when people were robbed, they liked to say they were robbed by Jesse James.

Peach left off peeling potatoes and dried her hands. Walking to his side, she touched his shoulder. "Bob," she said gently. "You could get out of here. Go down to Texas, get a job. You're young."

He shook his head. "We're going to Brazil."

She knew right then, it was hopeless. It was like talking to a brick wall. With a shrug she turned back to her chores. She needed both hands to lift the heavy pot of potatoes onto the big wood-burning cookstove.

He came up behind her and put his hands on her shoulders. "Come with me, Peach." His voice sounded a little choked. "I ain't never coming back, and I want to take someone besides Grat and Emmett to remind me of home. Someone to speak English to me when she loves me."

He almost sounded like he was begging. Her insides turned to water. She loved Bob Dalton even though she'd done her best to hide it from him and from herself. Why, oh, why, couldn't this proposal have been an honest one? Bitterly, she acknowledged that he was thinking only of himself. He didn't love her. He just wanted someone to speak English to him.

It was true he was as close to a steady fellow as she'd ever be likely to have. She wondered if he would come to love her. The thought tempted her. "We could go to Texas."

"No!" He slapped his hand down on the butcher block. "No, we'll go to Brazil. Ree-oh day Ja-nay-re-o."

She spun around. She could feel the color drain from her face. It left her weak with wanting and not wanting. "Then I can't go with you. I won't go with a bank robber."

His expression hardened. "You'll change your mind." He thrust his hand into his pocket. "Here. We're gonna pull this job and then I'll come back and get you. You be ready."

She shook her head and backed away, warding him off as if he pointed a gun at her, but he came after her and caught her by the wrist. Holding it tightly, he pressed a leather poke into her palm.

"Here. Hold this for me. It's twenty-nine fifty. It's all the money I've got in the world. It's honest. I earned most of it bringing in that last Injun for Judge Parker. He had a real good horse and a pretty good gun."

"Bob, I don't want this."

He smiled his biggest smile. "That's so you'll know I'll come back for you. It's a promise. You be ready."

"Bob Dalton."

"You be ready, Peach," he repeated. He caught her by the shoulders and dragged her in against him. Her mouth was still protesting when his came down on it. She tasted coffee and sugar that completely masked whatever he tasted like. Still, excitement stirred in her breast.

His kiss was the first real one she'd ever had. She gasped and started to protest, but his tongue slid into her mouth. His chest heaved and pushed against her breasts. Even though he was rough, he didn't hurt her. All she felt was excitement and heat and the desire to snuggle closer.

Holy Mother! Before she knew what was happening, she *was* pressing closer. She should be trying to push him off her. She should be slapping and fighting. Instead, she turned her face and fitted her mouth tight against Bob Dalton's. With a groan she kissed him back.

When he let her go, he was grinning from ear to ear. "You're going to be the best thing that's ever happened to me. You be ready. I've gotta go."

She shook her head, too dazed to know what she was really shaking about.

He laughed like a boy and then he was gone.

Her hand closed tight around the purse. It was a lot of money to her. It was probably a lot of money to Bob, but he wouldn't admit it. Nearly thirty dollars was more than she earned in half a year.

She wondered why he couldn't be satisfied with it.

And she wondered what banks they intended to rob.

Through the upstairs window of Scurlock House, Will Wesley watched Bob Dalton leave. So much for warning the scalawag off. Will ran his hand around the back of his neck as he stared hard after the swaggering figure.

He liked Peach a lot. She was a good girl.

Even though she was grown, she acted like a little girl most of the time. He'd never doubted her when she told him she was reared in a convent. She kept her eyes to herself. She didn't flirt or lead a man on. She worked harder for pennies than anybody he'd ever seen for much more.

Damn Luke Scurlock! If Bob Dalton was able to get Peach roped in on some nasty scheme, the owner of the hotel would be indirectly to blame.

Will shook his head. Once upon a time, he would have been able to lean on the man and get him to give Peach a decent wage. Now he was just as bad off as she was.

He felt the burning in his gut. His eyes watered and he smothered a cough. He'd been without a drink for nearly eight hours. He could feel his insides beginning to quiver. The tremors were running along his arms and down his legs under the skin. Like red ants they scurried along the muscles, itching and stinging him.

With a curse he put out his hand against the wall and steadied himself. He needed a drink, but he needed to get after Bob and find out what was going on. When he'd heard Bob shouting about going to Brazil for Christmas, he'd known something was up. Probably a robbery. The word was out among lawmen that the Daltons had probably robbed the Katy. They'd gone bad just like their cousins.

Poor little Peach! He was sure she didn't know anything about any of that. She was too innocent. She believed too much good in people. And she worked so damned hard.

Too damned hard.

His eyes were burning. He squeezed the bridge of his nose between his thumb and forefinger, then wiped his hand across the lower half of his face. God! He hadn't shaved in so long, he could feel his beard beginning to curl.

He needed a drink. He thought about stopping by the taproom and pouring just a tot to steady himself. He needed to get on after Bob.

He should have called Grat Dalton's hand four years before and arrested Bob when Charlie Montgomery was killed. But he'd given his fellow lawman the benefit of the doubt, and now it was too late.

Sometimes the last three years seemed like a bad dream. Sometimes he really thought he might wake up and find that it hadn't happened. Not to him at any rate.

He coughed again. Best not think about that.

He'd have just one jigger. Scurlock's whiskey was watered anyway. It would be just enough to steady him.

With exaggerated care, keeping his fingertips skimming the wall, he walked down the hall to the staircase.

Chapter Two

Peach couldn't help worrying.

As she ironed sheets and tablecloths behind the stairs, her hands moved slower and slower until they stopped their job.

Old Neddy ambled by and stopped short in his tracks. Suddenly, her nose told her that she'd scorched the sheet beneath the flatiron.

Aghast, she jerked the material off the ironing board and scowled until he'd gone on his way. Luke Scurlock was going to have another reason to scowl at her, as he'd done that morning when she got the breakfast orders mixed.

Darn Bob Dalton! This was all his fault. She couldn't put him and his crazy plans out of her mind.

She'd never thought much about banks for the simple reason that she'd never had enough money to bother with an account. A leather snap purse smaller than the one Bob had pressed into her hand served for her bank. She had about five dollars in it instead of thirty. It was buried deep in the bottom of the barrel of dried beans in Scurlock's cookshack. After Bob had left, she'd buried his beside it.

She thought about that money. He must really be planning to come back for her. A man might tell all kinds of lies to a girl about love and such, but if he gave her his money, that was real. He must be serious.

She closed her eyes as a hot blush flooded her cheeks. Bob Dalton surely knew how to kiss a girl. She just couldn't let him ruin his life. She had to put him on the straight and narrow. Sister Agnes Mary had talked often about saving the sinner. She began to plan what she'd say when she went to him and begged him not to go through with his crazy plan.

She tried to imagine what towns would have two banks worth tackling. Fort Leavenworth had two banks, but they also had a heck of a lot of law enforcement, plus the soldiers. If she were going to rob a place, she wouldn't pick one where every other body on the street had a sharpshooter's medal.

Grat was probably thinking about Independence or Kansas City or maybe even St. Louis, although they'd have to take the train to get there. But those were cities. She couldn't imagine the Daltons in cities. Knowing Grat, he'd probably get lost trying to find the places. The oldest brother was one Sister Agnes Mary would say was hiding behind the door when the brains were passed out. Why was Bob listening to him?

She was sweeping the porch in the early afternoon, when the three brothers and their friends trotted out of the alley behind Kloehr's and rode down Walnut Street. Peach saw them coming. She clutched the broom harder, then relaxed.

Thank heaven they were leaving town! That meant that whatever they did would be over and done with before she even heard about it.

Grat scowled.

Much I care, trash, she thought.

Emmett touched his hat politely as they rode on by.

She nodded and smiled. Emmett was only a few months older than she was. He was just a kid, tagging along with his brothers.

Only Bob slowed his horse and headed it in so that it was parallel to the neatly painted railing. Peach came around the rocking chairs and leaned against it.

They stared at each other for a minute. Her eyes dropped to his mouth curved in a smile. It made her remember his kiss, which in turn started little flutterings in her belly.

She clutched the broom a little harder. "You sure you don't want me to give you back that purse?"

He shook his head. "It's a damn sight safer with you than it would be in a bank."

She frowned at his remark. If he was talking like that, the robbery must still be on. She opened her mouth to say the words she'd rehearsed to beg him not to do it.

Suddenly, he broke into a broad grin. "What I'd really like you to do is lean over this here railing and give me a sweet kiss good-bye."

She backed up a step, hitting the rocking chair and setting it in motion. "Shame on you. Right here before God and everybody. Not on your life, Bob Dalton. You get on out of here."

He pretended to look crestfallen. "You're a coldhearted woman, Peach." Then his devilish grin broke out again. "Peachy."

She raised her broom. "Get on out of here. Your brothers are getting ahead of you."

"Yes, ma'am, Peachy Smith. But I'll be back." With that, he spurred his horse. It broke from a stand into a gallop. The fine dust of Coffeyville's main street rose behind him, so Peach had to start sweeping again.

"And good riddance," she muttered. She wished she meant it.

A week passed.

Trains came and went over the railroad tracks. A passel of Texas drovers herded their stock into the pens at the edge of town, sold it, and paid off their hands, who promptly set out to lose it all before they headed back home. The jail was full every night with drunk-and-disorderlies.

Peach made more money than she could remember. One day she was actually paid three dollars when Marshal Connelly had to break up a fight over at the Red Rooster on the other side of the tracks. Unfortunately, she was cooking for more people than ever. The hotel was full with the owners, trail bosses, and cattle buyers.

She dropped down on a bench beside Scurlock's back door. Leaning back with her eyes closed, she fanned herself with her apron and wished something bad would happen to Luke Scurlock. She'd asked for the afternoon off to take some of her money and have a bath at the bathhouse.

Luke had said he couldn't spare her. Ordinarily she would have shrugged and gone on about her business as if nothing could be done. This time she'd flared back at him. He'd better pay her more money, because he'd have to hire two or three people to do the work she was doing.

She'd surprised them both and scared herself with her daring. Then she'd tensed her shoulders waiting for him to fire her.

Luke had blinked and jerked his head back as if she'd slapped him. Then he'd surprised her by saying he'd think about it.

Oh, she'd gone back to work, but for the first time since she could remember, she had a little hope. With the possibility of getting more money, she'd sat down while

the pies were baking and begun to think about money in
general. With all the traffic at the jail, she'd doubled her
stash in a week. Of course, it was a long way from being
as much as Bob had given her, but added to his—

If she could just talk to him for a few minutes, maybe
he'd see that they could make a go of it in Texas. The
state sounded so much better than Brazil.

"Are you still mooning over Bob Dalton?"

She opened one eye. Will Wesley was standing in front
of her. The one good thing about his being there was that
he was blocking the sun. She was too tired to be mad—
which she ought to be. She was too tired to tell Will to
mind his own business—which he should. After all, she
didn't have to do what he said.

"What if I am?"

"He's bad to the bone, Peach. That's what."

She knew he was right, but he still made her angry. She
was taking practically the first rest she'd had in five years.
She was thinking some really important thoughts. And Will
had to come along and spoil them.

She defended Bob. "His cousins have the bad reputation. He gets tarred by the same brush."

Will shook his head. He dropped down beside her on
the bench. "Did you read the paper?"

She closed her eyes and fanned herself some more.
"When would I have time to read?"

That shut him up. He was silent for so long that she
opened one eye to check his reaction. He was sitting with
his elbows on his knees, his hands laced between them.
His head hung between his shoulders in that hangdog way
he'd had ever since he'd been shot.

He'd been a handsome man in his time. He still had
sharp, regular features and warm brown eyes that could
be kind or threatening, depending on what he was doing
as a lawman. Now his hair, dark chocolate-brown and thick,
flopped over his forehead and curled untidily over his shirt

collar. It had a lot of white running through it, just like his four-day growth of beard.

He didn't shave but once a week now, and she guessed he'd just gotten up. She was a little surprised he'd come out to find her. Usually, he'd be finding a drink in Scurlock's about then.

She knew he drank to kill the pain from his right shoulder. She'd overheard Luke tell the story to one of the Pinkerton detectives who frequented Coffeyville because of the three railroads that criss-crossed there. Some bandit had gotten off his shotgun first. She shivered at the thought of how that must have hurt. Then she realized he was staring at her.

"I guess you don't have much free time."

"Not much."

He heaved a sigh. "The Dalton gang is supposed to have robbed a bank in Wyoming."

She sat up straight. "Wyoming? *A* bank in Wyoming." Grat had been talking about two banks.

"That's what the paper said."

She thought for a minute. "Were they caught?"

He shook his head. "And the robbers wore masks."

"They didn't do it." She made her voice sound absolutely positive. She told herself she was pretty sure. They'd never have gone so far away from home.

To her surprise, he agreed with her. "But don't you see? They're already marked men. Anybody who strings along with them, any"—he cleared his throat—"good girl that takes up with them is going to be sorry for the rest of her life. They've got a bad reputation. It's just a matter of time till they try to live up to it."

"They're law officers," she pointed out.

"Not very good ones. They're just bounty hunters. What's more—they're thinking about it." His brown eyes met her own and held. Will Wesley might have a voice that was soft as honey dripping from a comb, but his words went straight as a bullet to the target. The only thing was, he hadn't specified what *it* was. She stirred uncomfortably because she knew.

Will's prophecy lay between them like a judgment. No matter how much she wanted to believe in Bob Dalton, she knew she was betting on a terrible long shot.

She couldn't stand to meet Will's clear-eyed gaze a minute longer. She stood up and smoothed her apron. "Got to check on the pies. The drummers don't like burned crusts."

He caught her hand and held it. His hands were warm and hard—the kind of hands a girl could depend on. Still holding her, he rose to look down into her face. He was taller than Bob Dalton and his shoulders were broader even though his bones poked against the material of his shirt.

His face was gaunt too, and permanent creases cast their shadows between his eyebrows and around the corners of his mouth. He looked like he was hurting right that minute. A muscle flickered in his jaw as he set it. He was dead serious.

She waited for him to speak, but he didn't. He just shook her gently before he let her go.

She stepped back. Her hand was tingling. She pushed it down into her apron pocket. "I have to go."

"You think about it," he called as she hurried into the kitchen.

"You leave that stuff alone," Connelly snarled at Will. He gestured toward the bartender. "Scurlock, I'm ordering you as of now not to sell any more drink to my deputy until this is over."

Scurlock shrugged amiably. "Sure thing, Marshal. Whatever you say." He looked amiably at the glass of beer in front of Connelly. "You want me to pour that out?"

Connelly's mouth snapped closed.

Farther down the bar, a couple of citizens laughed. Cornelius Dahlerheidt and Lee Ketcham hunched their shoulders when Connelly swung around to glare at them. They kept their heads well down to hide their quivering mouths.

When he turned back, they pretended to explode in silent fits of laughter.

"We've all got to be alert. Got to be ready." Connelly addressed Will again. "I can't do it all. I expect you to be available at light tomorrow." With that, he strode out.

"Can't do it all." Luke Scurlock nodded. "Can't do much if any." He drew Will another beer and passed it to him.

"You heard the man," Will objected.

"He said not to sell you another beer. He didn't say anything about giving you one."

When Peach asked Luke Scurlock for the money for a new coffeepot, he didn't say anything about a raise, but he didn't object when she told him she was taking an hour off after she bought it. She'd promised herself that she was going to take a half dollar and treat herself at the bathhouse. Morning would be the best time. Hardly anyone would be there, and she could be sure the water would be clean.

Feeling almost happy, she walked into Henry Isham's Hardware. The three men grouped around the cash register stopped talking when they saw her. As one, they stared at her, then looked away.

She blinked. She could almost feel the tension in the air. In an uncomfortable silence she walked past them. "The bottom on the hotel coffeepot burned out, Mr. Isham," she told him, more to break that silence than anything else. "I'm going to get a speckled enamel one to replace it. It cooks better than bare metal."

They were staring at her as if something were wrong with her. She patted her hands against her skirt and pulled out the silver dollar Luke Scurlock had given her. "I've got the money."

"Why, sure! Right this way, Peach." Henry Isham came down the counter and led the way into the cookware department. His expression serious as a judge's, he pulled out what she needed and carried it to the cash register. "Everything all right with Luke, is it?"

The other two men stepped back out of his way.

"Just fine." Peach smiled at each of them as Isham handed her the change and the coffeepot. She knew them by sight but not to speak to out in public. One was Art Reynolds who'd been in Scurlock's taproom many a night. He knew her name and had once slipped her a fifty-cent piece. Today he didn't speak to her.

The other was Lemuel Mungerson, a member of the town council and a real nasty customer. He and his wife, Edna, ate in Scurlock's dining room every Sunday. Nothing ever suited either one of them. He scowled at her and muttered something to Art.

"Shhh," came the hasty reply.

They must have been discussing something terribly important, she thought as she hurried out of the store.

"It's them. They're a-coming." Bert Ayers dashed into the taproom. His face was white. "They're a-coming, Will."

Wesley rose from a chair by the window, took a deep breath, and checked his gun. He'd had time to get over the shakes, and now the once-familiar feeling of deadly calm settled over him. He'd all but forgotten it, but now it felt good. He welcomed it. In some strange way, he felt more alive than he'd felt in a long time.

"They got fake mustaches and beards, but they musta

put 'em on in the dark, 'cause they look like hell.'' Bert's youthful laugh had a hollow ring.

Will glanced hastily through the swinging doors to the dining room. Peach was nowhere in sight. Thank heaven for small favors. He tugged his hat down tighter on his forehead. ''Let's go.''

In the bathhouse Peach poured the tub full of water as hot as she could stand it. Shivering with pleasure that was mixed with pain, she stepped in and lowered herself. As the water came up around her neck and shoulders, she breathed in the steam.

She tilted her head back in the water, held her nose, and sank under. Again and again and again. Coming up at last, she reached for the soap, but changed her mind.

She wanted to savor this feeling. Shifting around, she hooked her knees over the edge of the tub and let her body float. Her hair swirled around her as she made idle paddling motions with her hands. The water was like a nun's cowl covering her entire head except for her face.

The first thing had gone wrong. Bob Dalton glanced at Emmett uneasily. They had planned to hitch their horses on Union Street between Condon's Bank and the First National. They hadn't counted on the street's being torn up. The hitching posts were down.

He looked to Grat. Dick Broadwell could hold the horses between the two buildings, but he'd be a prime target. Bob thought about Peachy saying she'd be the first one shot.

Grat just shook his head and hunched his shoulders. Stringing their horses out, they rode single file around the back of the bank and down by Kloehr's Livery Stable. At the end of the alley they finally found a hitching post they could use.

"Well, at least we won't have far to walk if they catch us," Emmett joked as they walked past the back of Connelly's jail, where Peach brought the meals.

Bob hunched his shoulders. Things didn't feel right. He knew he'd seen at least one man's head duck back into the hardware store. He tried to tell himself that even if they'd been spotted, nobody would have any idea what they were going to do until they'd gotten the bank money and started for the horses. Maybe not even then if the bankers were chicken-hearted.

Still, he looked around with a suspicious eye. It was fairly early in the morning, but more people should have been up and about.

"What're they waiting for?" Bert whispered in Will's ear.

"The bank needs to open officially." Will checked his own watch. "The vault has a time lock that keeps it from being opened before nine."

"But the door's already open." Bert was leaning way out into Walnut Street. He looked at the men standing in the entrance to the alley and then into the bank. "I can see Mr. Condon in it plain as can be."

Will caught the boy by the back of the neck and hauled him back into the cafe. "If you can see them, they can see you, sprout."

"Why don't Marshal Connelly arrest them?" Bert growled in disgust. "They're just standing around out there. He could get 'em easy."

"No law against standing around," Will said patiently. He wished this kid hadn't been in on the deal at all. He made so many quick moves, he was going to be hard to protect.

Will shook his head in exasperation as the youth got

down on his hands and knees and poked his head around the edge of the door again. He was going to get them both killed. He caught hold of Bert's collar and dragged him back. "If you don't get on your feet, I'm going to lock you in a closet."

"But they're just standing there," Bert whined.

"We can't do a thing until they actually make a move." Will hooked his thumbs in his belt loops and leaned against the wall beside the door. "If you want to scare 'em off, go right ahead. Just keep on bobbing your head out where they can see you and act real interested in what they're doing."

The boy stepped back with a frustrated sigh.

Peach inspected one hand. Her fingers were getting all wrinkly in the hot water. She sighed. No matter how much she wanted to, she couldn't stay there forever.

She reached for the soap. Lathering it between her palms, she tipped her head back and sank her fingers into her hair. In a matter of seconds she was washing away soil and grease that she hadn't been able to brush away in weeks.

It felt so good. She groaned with pleasure. She treated herself to hot baths like this only twice a year. She'd always taken cold baths at the convent. Someday she was going to have a house with a bathroom, and she was going to take baths as often as she liked.

Plan big, Peach, she counseled herself. *Big plans can come to nothing just as easily as little ones.*

Grat checked his big pocket watch. " 'Bout nine, boys. Time to scare them bankers out of a year's growth." He laughed at the thought and clicked the watch closed. "You ready, Emmett?"

As the youngest Dalton nodded eagerly, the sick feeling

in the pit of Bob's stomach grew until it seemed to fill the whole cavity. If he'd eaten any breakfast, he'd be puking it up just then. He opened his mouth to say "Let's forget it." Instead, he cleared his throat. "Let's go."

Together he and Emmett walked across Walnut Street past Condon's Bank toward the First National on Union. With the feeling that a thousand eyes were watching him, he heard Grat's boots thump the boardwalk a minute behind him. Then Dick's and Bill's. They were only a few seconds behind as they made for the Condon.

"There they go. Things are going to get right interesting." Will put his arm out to halt Bert when the kid would have charged by him. "I want you behind that rain barrel across the street."

"Oboy, oboy, oboy!" Bert would have burst through the cafe door and run like a jackrabbit.

Will caught him by the collar and shook him like a child. "Walk. Walk! Condon's Bank got glass doors. If they see you acting like you're playing hide-and-seek, they'll start shooting."

Bert did the best he could to look casual, but Will shook his head at the slow stroll toward the bank, the leap off the sidewalk, the giant steps across the dusty street, the duck behind the barrel. Their only hope was that the men inside the bank were all facing the other direction.

Peach ducked under the water and rinsed her hair. This time the soap stung her eyes, but she decided she didn't care as she pulled her hair back from her forehead. She tried to imagine how long she'd spent in the tub. The water was still plenty warm.

She had lots of time for another lathering. She reached for the soap again.

* * *

The contents of the First National's two cash drawers slid into Emmett's bag. He laughed excitedly at the weight of the cash and silver.

The door to the safe was standing open. Bob pushed his hat back on his head and motioned the cashier inside. Two packages of paper money lay in plain sight.

He lifted one and fanned it. It was rich. He dropped it and its companion into his sack.

"We got enough," Emmett called. "Let's get out of here."

"Not nearly enough." They were going to Brazil. Bob wanted them to travel in style. "Where's the gold?"

The cashier hesitated. His eyes flitted to a strongbox on the floor.

"Come on. Come on," Emmett called. "We can't carry it."

"No! Dammit! I want it all." Bob grabbed for it. It damn near jerked his arm out of its socket. It must have weighed a hundred pounds. He couldn't tuck it under his arm. Another mistake.

His mind raced. Stupid! Stupid! Why hadn't he thought about the weight of the gold and silver? For the simple reason that he'd never had enough of it to weigh much. So much gold in his hands, and he couldn't carry it. He wanted to curse and cry at the same time.

Instead, he stabbed the gun at the cashier. "You! Get on out of here."

The man backed out, his face white and pasty.

Bob took a firmer grip on the handle and dragged the strongbox out. "We can make it," he snarled to Emmett. "We can make it."

The three customers and the three employees stared at the brothers. Bob's mustache had slipped. Sweat was running down his face. He swiped at it with his forearm.

The false hair came away on his sleeve. Cursing, he gestured with the gun again. He'd use the customers for cover.

"Get on out ahead of us."

He threw the money sack to Emmett and gestured again. Then he could have wept with anger and frustration.

"Don't shoot," one of the customers begged. "Please don't shoot. You know me, Bob. Don't shoot."

Motioning to Bert to stay behind the water barrel, Will started moving up the street. He pulled his coat back from his gun belt, ready to draw if either bank door so much as cracked.

He walked slowly, his eyes sweeping the scene, his mind calculating whether he had time to circle the block and come from the back. He'd been given the worst possible position to move on the banks. The plaza where Union and Walnut streets converged was an open area with a bandstand, a flagpole, and one small shade tree.

If Grat happened to look out through Condon's windows, Will would be a good target for a snap shot.

His eyes narrowed as he saw the men coming out of the First National Bank. A glance told him there were too many of them, bunched too close together to be casual. They were being herded. He darted behind one of the timbers that supported the bandstand. He had to turn sideways for it to offer him any cover at all.

Then he froze.

Beyond the First National he could see George Cubine had stepped out of the door of Cubine's Boots. He was leveling his rifle. The other men who worked in the shop had come out with him to watch the spectacle.

The fools! Double damned fools! "Wait!" Will yelled. "Wait! Nooo!"

George had his cheek against the stock. Will could almost see his trigger finger tighten.

Cursing, Will ducked for cover.

Peach ducked under the water and rinsed her hair again. When she came up and ran her hands over it, she could hear it squeak. She was clean. She hated to get out while the water was still the least bit warm, but now the surface was so scummy that she didn't want to sit in it any longer.

She stood up in the tub. Water sluiced off her. She rubbed her hands down the sides of her body and reached for the bucket of rinse water. She poured it over her and stepped out onto the mat.

Flinging her hair forward, she wrapped it in a towel that covered her from nape to forehead and began to twist to wring the water out.

Bob grimaced and jerked the remaining hairpiece from his face. So much for these damned fake beards and mustaches. Emmett had been right to grow his own. Why hadn't they remembered that Grat was dumber than dirt? The mistakes were piling up now.

"Just get out and walk across the street." He stabbed his gun into the cashier's back. "We'll all walk together and we'll all be fine. Get your hands down. We wouldn't want nobody to think you weren't just taking a stroll."

In a packed, stumbling group, they moved across the sidewalk. Bob followed them, trying to tote the unwieldy strongbox and still keep a pistol trained on his hostages. It slipped, and he had to make a grab for it. Emmett was still in the doorway, when a Winchester thundered. The bullet carried Bob's hat away and almost parted his hair.

The customers and employees scattered like chickens.

Bob jerked the strongbox back inside the door and sprawled backward on the floor. Glass shattered around him.

He closed his eyes for just a second. When he opened them, Emmett was staring down at him, too stricken to move. "We're done," he whispered. "We been spotted. How'd they know so fast?"

The cashier, and the teller too, had jumped back through the door. Now they crawled across the floor and flattened themselves behind the counter. The Winchester boomed again. A revolver from out across the plaza joined the Winchester. If they ran out, they'd be caught in a cross fire.

"There's a back door!" Emmett yelled. "Let's go."

Bob jerked so hard on the strongbox that he thought for the second time he'd dislocated his arm.

"Leave it. Come on." His younger brother jumped to the back door. "You can't carry it."

"Goddamn. They think they've got us running. I'll give 'em something to think about." Bob wrenched himself away and jerked open the bank door. He pulled a second gun from his coat pocket.

In a single quick movement he stepped out and faced the street. Pointing in both directions, he snapped quick shots at the fellow hiding somewhere across the plaza and the man with the Winchester. One man in a knot of three standing under the Cubine's Boots sign fell over backward. His rifle went flying.

As the other two scrambled to help their fallen friend, Bob hollered like a wild Indian and ducked back inside.

"Now, let's go!" he yelled to Emmett.

At the first shot, Peach jumped nearly out of her skin. Her breath caught in her throat. She tried to swallow, but suddenly her mouth was dry. "Please," she whispered, her voice like a rasp. "Please, please, please, let it be a stray shot."

Another and then another and then more and more.

And she knew—as if the bullets had voices—who was firing.

"Holy Mary, Mother of God." She crossed herself. She had never really been a Catholic, but it was the only way she knew how to pray. "Please, don't let anybody get killed. Two banks. Two banks. Coffeyville. Oh, Bob. You idiot. Oh, you fool!"

A bullet struck the wall of the bathhouse next to her head. The wood splintered, but nothing came through. Better safe than sorry, she dropped to her knees behind the cast iron stove. Flattening herself on the floor, she dragged her clothes to her and began to pull on her dress.

Another bullet thudded against the wall. She ducked and squeezed her eyes tight to hold back the tears. "Holy Mary, Mother of God, pray for us sinners now and at the hour of our deaths . . ."

"They've lost us," Emmett panted as they sprinted across Walnut Street. "They don't know where we are."

The pair had dashed around the row of buildings containing the First National and along the street behind Condon's Bank. The bullets were coming from Condon's Bank now, and men were firing into it from buildings all along the plaza.

"Grat's trapped," Bob yelled. He vaulted the corral fence at the front of Kloehr's Livery Stable and ran for the alley. "Get to the horses."

"We can't leave him!"

"We can't help him!"

They climbed between the corral bars in time to see Grat blunder into the alley.

"He's hit!" Emmett screamed.

Blood ran from Grat Dalton's shoulder and his side. It made a trail in the dust behind him. Bullets spanged off the brick wall above his head. Emmett's gelding tied at the end of the alley screamed like a woman and fell over on its side.

Bob pushed his younger brother away. "Get our horses. I'll get him."

Ducking low, he started for Grat. Billy Powers ran past him, bleeding, his eyes wild. Bob looked back in time to see a shot from Isham's Hardware catch his friend between the shoulder blades. Bob saw the dust spray from his coat. Billy threw up his arms and fell flat.

In front of Billy, another of their own horses neighed shrilly, reared, and buck-jumped away. Blood spouted from its haunch.

Bob swung his head back in time to meet his older brother's eyes.

"Grat! Grat! This way!" Bob straightened. Aiming his revolver, he shot one of the men in the door of the hardware store.

Grat took another step, then staggered as an answering shot hit his shoulder. His eyes were glazing, but he managed to grin at his brother.

Bob reached for him, but a blow cut his leg out from under him. He fell sprawling. Fear ripped through him, but he couldn't feel any pain.

As he rolled over, Grat came toward him, staggering, shooting, shooting. Bob raised his head in time to see the town marshal, Charlie Connelly, fall facedown over the corral fence.

Aw, shit! he thought. He managed to get one knee under him. "Grat!"

Another shot from the corral caught the oldest Dalton in the throat. His blood sprayed out in a fountain.

"Grat!" Bob flung himself forward to catch his brother

as he fell. Another bullet struck him. He couldn't tell where. He let his brother's body go and turned around.

John Kloehr stood behind the fence, his rifle barrel resting on the topmost rail. He jacked another shell into the chamber, then lowered his cheek to the stock.

Bob had time. He could see Kloehr's eye line up with the sight, could see the barrel moving down. His own gun wavered. Wavered up.

Kloehr fired. Bob Dalton felt a blow like the kick of a mule. It threw him backward, but he never hit the ground.

Peach ran smack into Will Wesley's arms. She pushed herself off and stared up at him. She was trembling from head to foot, cold and hot by turns. Her voice shook. "What happened? Tell me what happened."

He pulled her in against his chest. "You don't want to know."

She shuddered. "I don't. But I have to find out."

"No. You don't."

She hung in his arms, her knees weak. He could feel her heart thumping frantically. Her breasts heaved with her rapid breathing.

Across the plaza he could hear cheers. They made him sick. Why didn't Connelly take charge?

Peach tried to look past Will, but he spun and held her tight with her back to the alley across from Condon's Bank.

Bert Ayers had dashed into the alley as soon as the shooting stopped. Now he came running back. "You gotta come, Will. Marshal Connelly's dead. Someone who knows what he's doing needs to come."

"Oh, no. Who killed him?" Peach cried.

"The Daltons!" Bert exclaimed. "But they're dead. Every dadblamed one of 'em. Excepting Emmett, and he's shot in the back. He's not like to make it." The young man brandished his gun over his head and did a little stomp dance in the dust. "By golly. We got 'em all. They didn't get nothing from our banks. No, sir. They bit off more'n they could chew when they tried to rob Coffeyville."

Peach's knees gave out completely. Will knew that if he hadn't been there to hold her, she would have fallen flat right in the middle of the street. He stooped to pick her up, but she steadied herself. "No."

He was torn between the need to calm the frantic, furious townspeople and to take care of Peach. Just then she was experiencing the symptoms of someone who'd been in a fight herself. He didn't have any trouble guiding her to the bench underneath the shade tree.

He glanced around him. Had only minutes passed since he'd heard the first shots? Had the Daltons been alive only a few minutes earlier? He helped her to sit. On the bench next to her skirt was a fresh scar.

He stared at it, recognizing the tiny round of lead. The wood had been deeply grooved and splintered and the bullet was still there.

He thought of the Daltons, every one of them younger than he was. He put his hand over the scar. She didn't need to see any of this.

As he stared at her bent head, he realized with a start that her hair wasn't twisted up into a greasy knot at the back of her head. It was loose, flowing down her back to her waist. Still damp.

She must have been at the bathhouse. Morning light filtering through the leaves glinted off the strands. It was blond, the color of honey. He closed his eyes as his heart gave an unfamiliar thump.

Behind him, he heard a chorus of cheers, then loud applause and laughter. He had to get over there before something terrible happened.

She raised her head and tried to push herself to her feet.

Bert came dashing back. He clapped a hand on Will's shoulder. "Oh, wow! They're bringing the bodies out of the alley. Come on. You gotta see this."

Peach sank back against the bench and covered her face with her hands.

Will knelt in front of her. He took hold of her wrists and gently made her look at him. "Promise me you'll stay here."

She didn't answer.

"Promise me."

He wasn't sure she knew what she was promising, but she nodded her head.

He had to take that as a promise. He squeezed her hands. When he rose, his knee joints creaked. For a minute he'd forgotten how old and beaten up he was. All he was fit for was to comfort someone as pretty as Peach. "I'll be back as soon as I can," he told her huskily. "Wait for me."

As he crossed the plaza, the clock on the pedestal in front of the First National Bank struck ten. It had taken the Daltons less than an hour to die.

Chapter Three

Will was afraid Peach would follow him. He wanted to stay by her side, but if Connelly was dead, then the respectable townsmen needed someone in charge before they started doing things they'd regret later.

He was pretty sure he'd seen at least two men fall in front of Cubine's Boots. Their friends and neighbors would be wanting revenge for their death.

He'd seen dead outlaws strung up and shot to pieces by outraged citizenry. Then later he'd heard good men talk about the nightmares they suffered because they couldn't get the bloody deed out of their minds. He didn't want the Daltons to cause any more trouble. Six maybe seven dead men was a high enough price for Coffeyville to pay.

He hurried toward the milling, shouting crowd.

Luke Scurlock saw him coming. "You men clear a path there," the portly hotel owner shouted. "Deputy Marshal Wesley will take charge now."

"That drunk," someone howled.

Will flinched as he pushed past the speaker, then set

his jaw. He wasn't drunk now. In fact, he was so sober, he felt as if he'd never had a drink in his life. Over the heads of the crowd he could see what was about to happen. On the sidewalk in front of Condon's Bank, God-fearing men were trying to wrestle a rope around Bob Dalton's bleeding, stiffening body. Someone had taken the marshal's handcuffs and locked them on his wrists.

"Let him be!" Will shouted.

"Just want to take some pictures for the paper." John Tackett, the town photographer, had already set up his camera.

"I said, let him be." Will tried to push his way forward.

"Naw! You let 'im be!" Someone punched his crippled shoulder. The blow spun him half around as agony lanced through him.

He ended up facing John Cubine, who cradled his rifle in his arm. The old man's eyes were red. "Keep out of this, Wesley. They killed my poor George. Let 'em have their way."

The crowd closed ranks around him. Will found he couldn't move.

Men from the banks, from the hardware store, and from the boot shop all were turning out the robbers' pockets and stuffing the contents into their own.

Still facing the bootmaker, Will jerked his head toward the sidewalk. "Your neighbors are robbing the dead."

"Let 'em take what they can." John's breath smelled of whiskey.

He's already drinking to deaden his conscience, Will thought. "John, listen to me. The bankers might have had some reason, even though the outlaws didn't have time to pocket any money. The rest are just damned souvenir hunters. Get out of my way, or I'll have to arrest you."

The bootmaker didn't exactly step aside, but Will managed to push his way past and mount the sidewalk. "Dammit. Let those boys alone."

No one listened to him. Two men grabbed him from behind and held him back while Tackett took his pictures. Then the men holding the ropes let go. The robbers' bodies tumbled down in a heap. The photographer took a picture of that.

At last he was finished. While Will watched in helpless frustration, he carried his camera into the alley to take pictures of the Daltons' dead horses.

Finally, John Cubine called, "Let 'im through, fellas."

At the elderly bootmaker's command, the crowd pulled back and let the deputy marshal through. Finally able to protect the corpses, Will stood above them, swallowing hard. Grat's head had slipped sideways to rest against Bob's shoulder. They might have been asleep—except for the bright red rivers of blood now drying on their clothing.

Peach edged her way through the crowd. If she could have made herself invisible, she would have. Her ears were burning. She could almost feel the men staring at her. Did they know Bob Dalton had asked her to run away with him? Did they know she had been asked to hold the horses for this awful thing?

"Poor George is dead," she heard one man growl. "Bob Dalton shot him down like a dog."

She winced. George Cubine had been handsome and young with a fine handlebar mustache. She'd waited on him in Scurlock's.

"They got old Charlie Brown in the eye. He didn't even have a gun on him."

"I hear Lucius Baldwin's fighting for his life. Poor boy. Poor boy."

Only a couple of broad backs were between Peach and the sidewalk in front of Condon's Bank. Over their shoulders she could see the bullet holes in the glass doors. And blood. Splatters of blood.

She swallowed hard. Maybe she should have kept her promise to Will. If Bob were truly dead, looking at him wouldn't make him come alive. She felt hollow inside. Her eyes were burning, but she couldn't cry. Someone bumped against her, staggering her off balance into another man.

"Here now." His voice sounded far off. It echoed in her mind.

Bob had been alive just a few short days ago. He couldn't be dead. Not handsome Bob Dalton. He was going to Brazil. He was going to spend Christmas there. She started to turn and run, but movement behind her pushed her forward.

"Oh." She couldn't believe her eyes. "Our Father, Who art in Heaven—" she began.

The Dalton gang had been heartlessly dumped in the dusty street in front of Condon's Bank. There they lay like rag dolls, limbs tangled, heads on one another's chests. Filthy, bloody, obscene, stinking from the release of their body wastes.

She covered her mouth. Closest to her, so close that she could have gone down on her knees and touched his body, was Bob. Blood had flowed over his dark shirt and pants from the hole dead center in his chest.

But his handsome face was unmarked. Her tears started with a gush. His jaw hung slack, his lips pulled back from his teeth in a travesty of his grin. She had the odd feeling he was going to open his eyes and tell her this was a joke. He'd call her Peachy and make her mad.

She closed her eyes. She was swaying, falling.

"Here, girl."

"What's she doing here?"

"She was in on it," an angry voice yelled. "She was. She was Bob Dalton's gal."

"No, she wasn't." Will stepped off the sidewalk and lifted her in his arms. Even her slight weight wrenched his shoulder and made him smother a gasp, but he managed to hold on to her. "She wasn't in on it," he denied loudly. "She didn't know a thing about it."

"But she was sweet on Bob Dalton," John Kloehr yelled. "She was meeting him in my livery stable."

The crowd pushed and shoved. Several muttered among themselves.

Will realized a few more minutes of this kind of talk would turn the crowd nasty. Four citizens, including the town marshal, were dead or dying. The violent death of the potential bank robbers had been too swift. It wouldn't be enough to satisfy them. They wanted a measure of revenge. They wanted to see someone suffer.

He pitied poor Emmett being worked on by the town's three doctors. When the last Dalton got his strength back, they'd probably lynch him.

"She was taking food to the jail," Will argued. "That's what the town pays her to do. She walks down that alley every evening. You know that, John."

The livery stable owner didn't seem convinced. He looked around, trying to gauge whether he should accuse poor Peach again. The crowd stirred and muttered.

Will searched for and found Luke Scurlock. Fortunately, the hotel owner recognized the silent plea in Will's urgent stare. Luke stepped up on the sidewalk and raised his hand. "Great shooting, John. You got 'em both. Three cheers for John Kloehr! Hip-hip-hurray!"

The crowd instantly joined in. This was a good idea. This was better. "Hip-hip-hurray!"

"Hip-hip-hurray!"

With the cheers still echoing, Scurlock gestured toward the hotel. "Come on over to my place, men. John, you drink free today."

Will carried Peach's unconscious body to the back of the hotel. He didn't know which rooms were empty, and he didn't want to go down to the desk to find out. He knew his little cubbyhole definitely was.

She'd probably pitch a fit when she woke up in his room, but he couldn't put her out on her little cot in the cookshack and let her wake up alone. He knew within reason Scurlock, as well as every other hotel owner, would be renting every room in town within hours. Already the telegraph was carrying word of the shootings to Joplin and Springfield, to Kansas City and Topeka, to Fort Smith, Arkansas, and to Tulsa and Oklahoma City. Reporters and curiosity seekers would start arriving by rail within hours.

Gently, he lowered Peach to the rumpled bed. It almost never got made up, and the sheets were none too clean, but it was softer than the narrow cot in the kitchen. Nobody could find her here. She wouldn't be disturbed.

That glorious honey-colored hair was surely a surprise. It pooled and rippled over the pillow. He'd never even had a clear idea of the color. Now he lifted her head and pulled the skein over her shoulder and down over her breast. It reached almost to her waist. His hand trembled slightly as he pulled his blanket up over her and adjusted the window shade.

In the dimness he closed his eyes and tried to take stock of his own situation. He couldn't believe it was barely noon. He felt exhausted, as if he'd fought the whole day long. The truth was that he'd never gotten off a shot.

In some strange way, the whole world had changed for him. He caught a glimpse of his face in the shaving mirror on the washstand. His expression surprised him. He looked the way he used to look when he'd been a marshal.

He pulled his hat from his head and raked his fingers over his lank hair. It had been hours since he'd had a drink. The thought made him thirsty, but he wasn't sick for it. In fact, he was more thirsty for water than for anything else. Or a cup of hot, strong coffee.

Behind him, Peach moaned.

He turned slowly, not wanting to frighten her.

She looked up at him, through the muted light from the shaded window. Her eyes were blue, like pools of clear water in the sunlight.

Quietly, he watched those eyes fill with horror and with tears.

"Oh, Will."

He sat down on the bed beside her. He supposed he shouldn't sit like that. She might be frightened, and she wasn't thinking straight.

"They're all dead, aren't they?"

He nodded soberly. "Emmett's still alive, but he's pretty much shot to pieces. Doctors are working on him, but they don't hold out much hope. The rest of them are dead. Nothing to be done for them. And the town's celebrating."

She bit her lip and covered her eyes. "How can they be celebrating death? Those men were so young."

"So were some of the men they killed."

She didn't say anything, but she began to sniffle. Silently, he pulled a handkerchief from his washstand drawer and handed it to her. She pressed it into her eyes and then rolled over on her side, looking out the window. Her drawn-up knees brushed against his hips. He shifted.

"Poor Bob. He'll never get to Brazil."

Will shrugged. He had never been impressed with the outlaw's stories of South America. Maybe a few Confederate veterans had made a new and successful life down there, but he'd be willing to bet a whole lot more ended up working in bad situations or dying of jungle diseases. "He should have gotten a job."

She looked at Will sharply. "That's what I told him."

He nodded. His gaze focused on a bar of bright light thrown on the floor from behind the ill-fitting window shade. "Good. Then you did the right thing. It's not your fault that he didn't take your advice."

She pressed the handkerchief to her eyes again. Her tears were almost gone.

"If you loved him, I'm sorry he's gone." Will put his hand on her shoulder. His fingers tingled. It had been a long time since he'd set his hand gently on a woman's shoulder. He felt a faint stirring in his blood.

Peach drew a deep breath and let it out on a tremulous sigh. "I'm sure he didn't love me. I think if he loved anybody, it was Minnie Johnson."

"Missed his chance on that one," Will observed quietly. He noticed she didn't say whether or not she loved Bob. It really wasn't any of his business, but he hated the thought that she might be sad.

Peach nodded. "He knew it. I think that's why he wanted to go to Brazil. He didn't have anything here. He wanted me to go with him so he'd have a girl who'd understand English, someone he could talk to."

Will kept his face impassive through her mournful tale. From a lawman's point of view, Bob Dalton had gotten what he deserved. He hoped Peach was telling the truth that she wouldn't be mourning for the outlaw as if he were her lost love. Peach was too much a lady to weep more than a few decent tears over someone as bad as Bob.

She frowned. "Where am I?"

Will swallowed. "You're in my room."

"What?" She sat up quickly, then fell back down with a groan. Her eyelids fluttered closed.

He rose, his knee joints protesting noisily. Hoping she hadn't noticed, he stepped back and hooked his thumbs through his belt loops. "Now, don't get excited. Nobody knows."

She rolled her head on the pillow. He'd expected her to get upset, to spring up and hurry out, but she didn't move. Was she hurt?

"It doesn't matter," she whispered.

He frowned. He didn't know how to take that. Cautiously, he sat back down. "Are you all right?"

"I suppose." She rolled half over. The light fell full on her face. "Everybody thinks I'm a bad girl anyway. What difference does it make where I spend the night?"

Will vowed to have a serious talk with John Kloehr first thing the next day. "Don't be silly," he said harshly. "Nobody thinks anything of the sort. You never encouraged Bob Dalton. Every man in town has talked to you more than he did."

She shook her head. "But Bob probably told everybody."

"He didn't have anything to tell, did he?"

"No."

"And anyway, it's broad daylight outside. You're just taking a short rest."

She stared at him, trying to gauge the truth. Her eyes glazed, her eyelids drifted closed. He recognized the signs. She'd seen too much. The sight of those boys stacked up like slaughtered goats had left her wounded. She needed to heal. As Will watched, she slipped into an exhausted sleep.

He tiptoed to her side and pulled the bedspread up over her. As he straightened and stretched, he heard his back pop. Lord! He was feeling every one of his thirty-five years. His shoulder was giving him the devil. He might look like he'd once looked, but he knew the look was all there was to it.

He gazed down at the sleeping girl. Peach Smith had beautiful skin and a sweet little mouth. He felt that stirring again.

Slowly, slowly, his conscience telling him to behave himself and his mind castigating him for his foolishness, he bent from the hips.

When his mouth was only a few inches from her face, he hesitated. Just one, he argued. Just one. He touched his lips to her cheek.

* * *

Where was the forty thousand dollars the Daltons had stolen from the Katy railroad?

A knot of men discussed it loudly over their drinks. They cursed and thumped the table and said it was lost forever.

All those gangs had hidden treasure. He'd heard stories about it all his life. The James boys. The Youngers. Bill Doolin. Even Belle Starr.

But the Daltons were from around there. It must have been buried right close.

This was his chance.

He hunched his shoulders over his beer and scanned the room, a little alarmed that his thoughts might have communicated themselves to someone else—someone who'd try to get there ahead of him.

Peach knelt beside the barrel of beans. Tears trickled down her cheeks. In each hand she held a leather pinch purse. As she turned one and then the other over, the coins inside jingled faintly. Bob Dalton's last words came flooding back.

You're going to be the best thing that ever happened to me.

Poor boy. Poor wild, wild boy. She thought about his kiss. The first kiss she'd ever received from him. And the last. She was terribly afraid she'd remember it till the day she died.

She pushed her own purse into her pocket and opened Bob's. Plenty of money to make a new start. He'd had it. And he hadn't used it. Sister Agnes Mary had talked about irony. Peach had never understood what that was until now.

Bob could have been riding free, high, wide, and handsome on his way to Texas instead of lying cold and stinking on a knocked-together table of rough one-by-twelves in the marshal's jail.

John Kloehr was selling a nickel a look through a hole he'd cut in the back of his livery stable. The newspaper reporters and photographers were crowding off every train that came through and paying money to anyone and everyone who had a story—or a lie—to tell.

She poured the coins out into her hand. Four silver dollars, a tiny five-dollar piece, a larger ten-dollar one, some paper money, some change.

She supposed by rights this was Emmett Dalton's. Or Bob's mother's. She didn't know the woman's name or whether she still lived in the neighborhood. She should find out.

But how? She didn't dare ask too many questions.

Peach pictured herself walking up to the mayor or even to Will and saying, "Bob Dalton gave me nearly thirty dollars to hold for him. What should I do with it?"

If Will didn't believe she was Bob Dalton's woman until that very moment, he'd certainly believe it after he heard that. Everyone would know and she'd lose her job for sure.

On the other hand, she didn't want the money. It wasn't hers. It was Bob's. She closed her eyes, picturing his still face lying against Grat's chest. She drew a controlling breath and opened her eyes to concentrate on the money. She didn't want to think about Bob again.

She pushed her purse back into the beans and tucked Bob's into the pocket of her skirt underneath her apron. She'd keep her ears and eyes open. Maybe Bob's mother would come back to town to bury her sons, and Peach could slip it to her.

"There she is. That's Bob Dalton's girlfriend. She was going to Brazil with him."

Peach had wondered why three of Coffeyville's ladies

dressed in hats and gloves had come into Scurlock's dining room for lunch. The meal was always steak for half a dollar or meat loaf for a quarter with mashed potatoes and whatever vegetables were available. The drink was coffee. Not at all a lady's fare like Miss Hannah's Boardinghouse and Tearoom over on Second Street.

The woman spoke in a voice just loud enough for Peach to hear her and freeze in the act of setting the plates in front of a reporter and a photographer from the *Dodge City Democrat*.

The men's heads shot up.

The reporter whipped out his notebook. "Are you Bob Dalton's girlfriend?"

Peach's hand trembled as she set his meal in front of him.

"No."

"I can pay two fifty for your statement," he went on eagerly. "Has anybody else talked to you? McCluskie could take your picture. I'd send you a copy of the story."

"No." Peach set the coffee down so fast, it sloshed into the saucer. She tucked the tray under her arm. "No."

"Okay. Three."

"No!" As she started away, he caught her by the back of her skirt. "Listen—"

Quickly, she snapped the tray around her body—as if he were a drunk in the bar, as if he were Bob Dalton trying to grab her butt.

The reporter yelped and grabbed his wrist.

Luke Scurlock, busy at the cash register, looked up. The ladies gasped. Every customer stopped eating and stared.

She took a deep breath and smiled sweetly at the reporter. "Oh, I'm sorry. Did I hurt you?"

He looked deeply injured, but he too was aware that he was part of a scene. The big-bellied man at the cash register was scowling.

The reporter knew tempers were short in Coffeyville.

Something very unpleasant could happen. Now that he looked at his waitress, she didn't look like a floozy. He managed a pained smile. "Just an accident, ma'am. No harm done."

She nodded. "Will that be all, sir?"

He nodded.

She threaded her way among the tables until she stood beside the woman who had spoken. "Meatloaf or steak, ma'am?"

The woman looked at her companions. All three had seen her snap the tray into the reporter's wrist. She could tell by their expressions that they didn't know what to say.

Had they expected her to be crying and carrying on because Bob was dead? Had they expected her to be wearing a red taffeta dress and showing her bosom? She smiled as she tried to picture herself in a getup like that.

One leaned across the table and whispered something she didn't quite hear. The three put their heads together. Then the lady who'd spoken sat back.

"Er—I believe we'll go elsewhere. That is, we just remembered that—er—Lucille forgot—" She gave up entirely. Her face turned quite red. She pushed her chair back from the table. The others did likewise. In silence they hurried out, their heads bent.

Behind them Peach glanced at Luke Scurlock. He shrugged and went back to counting the receipts. Four drummers who were regulars took the vacant table immediately.

When she went back to collect the plates from the *Democrat* reporter's table, she was amazed to find that he hadn't given up. He laid a silver dollar on her tray. It was an extravagant amount. If she was tipped at all, it was usually a nickel or sometimes a dime.

"If you don't want to talk about yourself and Dalton," the man murmured, "maybe you could give me a clue as to who tipped their hand."

"Tipped their hand?"

"How'd the town know they were coming?" The reporter leaned forward, watching her intently. "Was it you?"

"Me?"

"You know. **Was he going** to leave you behind?"

"I don't know what you're talking about."

He raised one eyebrow and leered at her. "Did you want revenge? The woman scorned, deserted?"

"I didn't have anything to do with anything."

"Where'd all those guns come from?"

She frowned. "I—I don't know. What guns?"

"Where'd all those men come from with their guns? How'd they know?"

"Th-the hardware store," she stammered. "Mr. Isham runs a hardware store. They sell—er—guns."

"What about the bootmaker? He doesn't sell guns. What about the drugstore across the street from Condon's Bank? What about the livery stable man? Why was the marshal waiting for them in that alley?"

She shook her head. "I don't know anything about it. Believe me. I don't. Please leave me alone." She laid the dollar back down on the table.

He tapped his finger beside it. "Keep it. You might remember something. I'll be here till noon tomorrow."

Peach dropped down at Scurlock's kitchen table. Her knees had been so weak, she'd barely made it out of the dining room. She wrapped her arms around her ribs and held on tight as her mind whirled.

Had someone tipped the sheriff? Had the whole town known about the robbery? Of course, Bob had told *her*, but she hadn't suspected that they were planning to rob Coffeyville. But who knew what he might have said elsewhere? Had an acquaintance of Bob's—or a friend—or someone here in town whom he'd trusted betrayed him to his death?

The more she turned the idea over in her mind, the more angry she became. Who was the traitor? The no-good scalawag who'd betrayed a friend.

No! She brought herself up short. Somebody had spotted them riding into town. That had to be it. She was just letting her imagination run wild. Sister Agnes Mary had said she was good at that.

The reporter had to be wrong. Surely if the marshal had known beforehand that a robbery was being planned, he would have arrested the Daltons in the bank. Then all those people wouldn't have died.

She tried to think, to remember the story as Will had told it to her. Suddenly, it all made a terrible kind of sense. The marshal couldn't have known about the robbery. He'd been killed himself. Maybe those men had seen the Daltons and just run into Isham's to borrow new guns. Probably the Cubines had suspected something and tried to help stop the robbery. They'd probably had a Winchester under the counter somewhere.

The marshal might have been running through the alley, taking a shortcut to the bank, and gotten there too late. What if he'd stepped right into Grat's guns instead of coming up behind the Daltons and arresting them in the act?

On the other hand, if the citizens had been deputized and had started shooting early, then one thing was sure as Sunday. Someone had tipped them off.

The reporter could be right. Someone could have told the marshal along with everyone else in town—and everyone had been armed and ready.

She shook her head and tried to think who might have been the one. More than likely, another outlaw had spilled the beans. Bob and Grat had been marshals. They weren't well liked. Maybe someone they'd arrested had gotten wind of it.

But who? Who had told and caused the death of eight men?

She clenched her jaw. Remembering Bob's bleeding body made her sick to her stomach. The Daltons shouldn't have died. They should have been captured and gone to jail. They should have served their time and come out reformed. She hugged herself against the painful memories.

Now the reporters were trying to scavenge any story they could, whether it was true or not. Coffeyville was full of souvenir hunters who'd pay good money for anything that had come in contact with the Daltons. How she wished they'd all go away!

Emmett Dalton lay facedown on the narrow bed in Doc Shandlin's attending room.

He couldn't feel much of anything, just a buzzing in his head and recurring nausea. That was from the ether. He'd had a lot of it. They'd worked on him for hours, taking out the buckshot in his back and the slugs in his hip and arm.

He tried to move his cheek out of the wetness where he'd drooled. Nausea roiled inside him. He swallowed hard. If he puked, how would he get his face over the side of the bed?

He heard a sound behind him. Someone had come in.

If it was the doctor or his nurse, why didn't he come closer? The sour feeling in his stomach grew worse. He was going to puke. He needed help.

"Where'd you bury it?"

He forgot about the nausea. He couldn't believe he'd

understood, couldn't believe he'd heard correctly. Oh, Lord, who was back there behind him? Had someone come to kill him?

"Tell me and I'll go get it and split it with you. I'll even help you get away."

The voice was closer. He wasn't delirious. He couldn't be imagining it. He tried to lift his head.

Pain flashed from his neck and back to his brain.

It swept him back into the blackness.

Peach could hardly believe her eyes.

Will Wesley looked like a different man. Why, he was handsome! He'd bathed. And gotten a haircut. His hair was actually sandy brown and wavy and thick! What she'd seen of it hanging out from under his hat had been lank and dark.

He'd shaved so his strong jawline showed and complemented his cheekbones. She'd never seen a man's face look so wonderful.

He was wearing a new shirt. She could tell by the fold marks in it. His boots were polished and he had pinned the marshal's star to his shirt pocket.

His eyes were clear too. He didn't look like a drunk anymore. He was standing straighter than she remembered ever seeing him. His head wasn't hunched down between his shoulder blades any longer.

She smiled at him, and he joined her beneath the shade tree next to the bench. The white scar was still there in the wood, but some souvenir hunter had dug out the bullet. She hoped he thought it was fired by one of the Daltons. The chances were good that it had been fired by one of the Coffeyville Defenders, as they were being called.

She refused to let that bother her. She put her hand on his arm. "You look good, Will."

He smiled down at her. She could see his shoulders straighten even a little more. "You do too, Peach."

She could feel a little heat rise in her cheeks. She hadn't thought about herself. She was wearing her best "left-behind" dress, a dark blue faille with pockets and lapels trimmed in black grosgrain. The hem was stained, and she'd had to mend a tear in the skirt, but neither one showed in the evening shadows.

Will cleared his throat. "Your hair looks nice down your back like that."

That remark did startle her. She hadn't ever had a compliment about her hair before. She'd fastened the sides up at the crown of her head with a black grosgrain ribbon, another "left-behind." She stifled an impulse to touch them to be sure they were in place. "Thank you," she murmured.

The bandstand was draped with red, white, and blue bunting, and the mayor was already on the bandstand, as were members of the town council. Coffeyville's electric streetlight shone grandly down on the proceedings.

"You should go up there too," Peach whispered to him.

He shook his head. "No, they don't want me."

She stared at him. "For heaven's sake, why not?"

"Seems somebody reported that I didn't fire a shot during the raid. They said I was hiding behind the bandstand."

Peach couldn't believe it. "You were not." Then she realized that she didn't know. She'd been taking a bath. "I mean, even if you didn't fire a shot, that doesn't mean you were hiding. It probably means you were smart. Some of the men who fired shots are dead."

He nodded, his gaze moving over her. A slow smile curved his mouth. He had a beautiful mouth.

"Besides," she whispered, "I know you wouldn't have wanted to kill Bob or Grat. They were your friends. And fellow marshals."

His smile died. He looked away. "Peach, I—"

"Ladies and gentlemen," the mayor began, "and you, gentlemen of the press, you're welcome to our fair city of Coffeyville. The city of heroes."

He paused for applause. The townspeople clapped. The reporters and photographers looked generally bored and restless. "We've gathered here this evening to honor the names of those gallant gentlemen who defended us so— er—gallantly against the dastardly attack of the notorious Dalton gang.

"Each member of the town council is going to read two names. If each of you will step forward when your name is called. Then we'll read the names of those four who cannot step forward, but who will remain forever in our hearts and minds."

Peach frowned. She leaned toward Will. "That doesn't make sense."

He looked down at her, a little flicker of amusement at the corners of his mouth. "The mayor doesn't make many speeches that do."

Peach had to cover her mouth to keep her giggle from escaping.

The ceremony began.

As it progressed and each man took a bow, Peach became more and more resentful. As the names of the four fallen were read, she could feel her temper slipping away. "They should call your name," she whispered to Will. "Why, Lucius Baldwin and old Mr. Brown didn't fire either. Old Mr. Brown was just standing on the sidewalk, and Lucius never drew his gun. You shouldn't be blamed because you didn't shoot before you had something to shoot at."

"Peach, it's all right," Will whispered.

"I'm going to tell them."

"No. Don't—"

She dodged his hand when he tried to stop her. Working her way through the crowd, she reached the bandstand.

She tugged at the mayor's trouser leg. "You forgot Deputy Marshall Will Wesley."

He looked down, startled at her interruption.

"You forgot Will Wesley," Peach repeated.

The mayor shook his head. His affable smile disappeared. "I haven't forgot a thing."

"He's your town marshal now," Peach kept on. "And he ought to be up there with you."

"Young lady, who are you?"

She looked around her for support. People were staring at her. If she couldn't get the mayor to see reason, maybe she could get the crowd to listen.

Before she could say more, John Kloehr's voice sounded loud and clear. "I'll tell you who she is. She's Bob Dalton's girlfriend. She was in on it from the beginning."

She spun around. "I was not."

"Sure you were. Meeting him in the stable."

"I never." It was not strictly the truth, but near enough.

"She knew all about it," Kloehr insisted.

She shrank back against the latticework of the bandstand. People were frowning. They began to mutter among themselves.

"We oughta throw her in the jail right now," someone opined loudly.

Councilman Mungerson nodded in the direction of the speaker. "I say arrest her," he said loudly. "She was probably in on it somehow."

"Put her on the next train," a woman called. "Good riddance to bad rubbish."

Corny Dahlerheidt jostled against Peach's shoulder as she spun around to face the crowd. "How's about you takin' up with me?"

The noise grew as more and more people added their opinions.

Corny grinned at some of his companions. He threw a fat arm around Peach and tried to drag her against his side. "Bob Dalton ain't gonna be scratchin' your itch no more."

His whiskey breath almost made her eyes water. Peach couldn't help herself. With all her strength she pulled back her arm and slapped his leering face.

Chapter Four

Will dragged Peach away from the bandstand into the covering darkness. "Have you lost your mind? They'd have lynched you in another minute."

He would have continued to berate her, but she stumbled against him. He realized she was shivering. The chilly night couldn't account for her chattering teeth.

"Peach," he murmured. How right he felt when he put his arms around her and hugged her to him. "Peach."

"Why were they so angry with me?" Her voice was a soft wail. He could feel her lips move against his chest. She shook her head in disbelief. "I've never done any of them any harm. A lot of them have known me for three years. I've cooked for them and waited tables and drawn their beers."

He cupped the back of her head, stilling her helpless movement. "Don't think about it."

"I don't understand." She pushed her hands inside his coat and clasped his waist. Her palms were cold, her fingers like ice. Her forehead was cold against his throat.

"It's all right," he whispered. "It's all right."

"Why?" Her single word was just a puff against his neck.

"Blood," he told her. He felt her shudder and cursed himself for being so blunt. What a thing to say to a convent-bred girl! Not only was he older than she in years. He was infinitely older in experience.

He hesitated, pondering whether to explain. She needed to see that she was in real danger. "Once it's shed, it's like a dam bursting. Blood calls for blood."

"But they killed Bob and Grat and Dick Broadwell and Billy Powers. Isn't that enough?"

She tried to lift her head, but he held her against him, forcing her to take more time to steady herself. She was all soft and warm and her woman's shape was pressed against him in places that he'd just about forgotten he had.

He thanked the Lord that Peach wasn't given to weeping. His own feelings were in such turmoil, he doubted he could handle a weeping woman.

"Their own blood is what I mean. It's up. They're just boiling inside. Those men grew up hearing stories about how their daddies and granddaddies fought the Civil War and Quantrill's raiders. Truth to tell, they loved this fight. Spying, knowing the raid was going to happen, storing the guns. The way they'll tell it to their children, it was Lawrence all over again, except this time the good men of Kansas were ready for 'em."

She reared back in his arms. "Five country boys," she scoffed. "Some raid."

"Eight people were killed." He reminded her. "And it was all over too soon. They wanted it to go on and on. They wanted a charge down Main Street. They wanted to chase the Daltons out of town and shoot them off their horses. It was their chance to make their mark. They just didn't get to carry it far enough."

He held her a little tighter against him, savoring every

minute of it. His body was hardening and heating even while his mind was preaching sense.

He closed one hand around her shoulder and tucked the other under her chin to tip her head up. He stared into her face eye to eye. "They didn't get to hang somebody."

"Oh."

He hated to scare her, but he'd told her the truth. Fortunately, she didn't argue. She'd felt the crowd's anger. He'd bluffed them and held them back, but she had to be very careful to stay out of sight. The town needed time to cool down.

"Me?" She sounded about five years old.

"Probably not. I think they'd stop short of hanging a woman, but you wouldn't want to live here anymore after they were done with you. And something like that can get out of hand before you can blink."

As if to punctuate his statement, a staccato shout echoed from the direction of the bandstand. A horse, ridden hard, thundered past the alley.

He needed to get back to his new job. He also needed to get her off the streets and safe, but he couldn't take her directly back to Scurlock's. The crowd was dispersing in that direction. Some of them had already had too much to drink. They might turn ugly.

Keeping her against his side, he led her off into the darkness.

Gradually, she stopped shivering. Her hands and face began to get warm. She pulled away from him. "I'm all right," she said in a normal voice. "I can head back to Scurlock's on my own."

"I'll take you back." He was startled at how the cold air rushed inside his coat. She had kept him warm. He wanted to keep her against him.

Far from the tenderness he'd felt yesterday when he'd kissed her without her knowing, he felt an urgent tightening in his groin. Sobriety had returned to his body and with it other basic urges. So long drowned in alcohol, they now reasserted themselves with powerful insistence.

Peach was a good girl, he reminded himself. He buttoned his coat and took her arm. As sedately as a husband and wife on their way to church, he escorted her down the sidewalk.

They were halfway down the alley beside Scurlock's, when he heard a cough. He half turned in time to take a crushing blow with his right shoulder. A scream of agony burst from his lips. His knees turned to water as his mind blanked out before the excruciating pain.

"Will!" Peach yelled. Then, "Oh, stop! You've hurt him."

Her hands clutched him even as she was pulled away.

"Let 'im be," a man's voice grunted. "He'll get his legs back soon enough. You're the one we want. Like I said afore, how's about givin' us some of what ol' Bob Dalton was gettin'?"

Even in pain Will could smell the whiskey. Good. Drunks were easier. He forced himself up to his knees. He put one hand down and ducked his head, ready to lunge.

Peach stepped in front of him. "I wouldn't give you the time of day!" she yelled as she doubled the man over with a roundhouse swing. "You drunken sot!"

"Ooof!" The attacker lost his breath in a great gasp.

Will recognized the motion as the one she usually used to swing her tray into some fresh yahoo who'd tried to torment her.

"Bob Dalton wasn't getting anything!" she yelled. "And neither will you!"

She was drawing back for a second swing, when another figure joined the first and grabbed her around the waist from behind. "Come on! Catch her feet, Lee. Hurry!"

Letting go of his middle, Lee Ketcham made a game try, but Peach reared back and kicked out with both feet. Her heavy shoe made a satisfying thud against his nose.

"Ow! Damn, Corny!" Lee fell to the ground, clutching his face. "Ow! Ow! She boke m'node."

"Let me go!" she screamed. "Lemme go! Lemme go! Lemme go!" The alley reverberated with the noise.

"Like hell," her captor growled. "We don't need Bob Dalton's whore in our town. Damned—"

"Let her go." Will could feel the red haze of anger gathering at the corners of his vision. Peach's writhing body was between him and the attacker, who Will knew was Corny Dahlerheidt.

What in hell did these loafers think they were doing? Drunk and disorderly was one thing, but this was assault and possible rape.

He couldn't lunge into the fray with Peach in the way. Climbing to his feet, he drew his pistol with his left hand. "Let her go, I said. Dammit! Lee! Corny! I know you. Let her go!"

"So you know us! That don't mean nothin'. Just back on down the alley, Marshal," Peach's captor warned. "This don't concern—"

"One." Will thumbed the hammer back. Even with Lee whining and grunting in the background, the mechanism clicked ominously. For a moment everybody froze.

"Hey," Corny protested, "This whore—"

"Two." Will's left arm came up. The moonlight ran along the metal barrel. He hoped that the darkness covered how it wavered. He needed his right hand to steady it, but his right shoulder wasn't functioning at the moment.

"Oh, Jesus. Oh, glory," Lee moaned. He didn't even try to climb to his feet, but scuttled away on all fours like a crab. In the darkness he collided with the side of the building, where he pulled himself to his feet and stumbled away.

Silence fell among the three figures in the alley.

"Thr—"

Simultaneously, Peach drove her elbow into her captor's

ribs and kicked back with all her strength. The blow connected with Corny's shin. He grunted. His grip loosened. She twisted in his arms and scratched at his face.

"Goddammit!" Shoving Peach into Will, Corny took off running, disappearing into the darkness.

Breathing a silent prayer of thanksgiving, Will let the weight of the pistol carry it down to his side.

"Are you all right?" Peach threw her arms tight around his waist. Her breasts pressed against his chest. Her head tilted back to find his face in the darknesss.

With a weary sigh he holstered his pistol. Pain was running down his arm and all across his chest. His imagination conjured up a picture of steel shot rattling off shards of bone. He shook his head. "I'll do."

"They were after me," her voice shook. "And they hurt you. I'm so sorry."

He wrapped his good left arm around her and herded her down the alley. "You can't spend the night in the cookshack. They're liable to come back."

"Oh, d-do you think so?" Her nerves, strung tightly as piano wires, set her body vibrating against his side.

"I know so."

"You scared them pretty bad," she suggested.

"Not so bad as you did." Will chuckled. He couldn't help but marvel at the way she'd fought. He'd seen plenty of men who wouldn't have acquitted themselves so well. "If I hadn't recognized his voice, Lee Ketcham would still be pretty easy to pick out tomorrow with his nose spread all over his face. I promise I'll take care of him."

"I'll be all right," she insisted, but her voice quavered.

"I'll take you to my room."

"I've already been there," she argued. "I don't want to impose. Besides, they were just a couple of drunks. They didn't really care about getting back at anybody. They were just—" She hesitated. He could see she was thinking fast and coming to the same conclusions he had reached. Still, she straightened her shoulders. "I can take care of them."

Before he could argue further, she hurried away in the dark. He followed her and saw her open the door to the cookshack, then stop.

"Oh." Her hand rose to her mouth. He came up behind her. By the light of a fire blazing in the big iron stove, he could see her dismay.

Her little cot had been destroyed. The rails had been broken, the crosspieces smashed, the canvas ripped. The sheets and pillow were gone, undoubtedly accounting for the flames blazing away behind the grate. Corny and Lee or some others just like them had come here first.

Dazed, she went down on her knees beside the broken pieces of wood. Her hand trembled as she reached out.

He couldn't bear it. He could *not* bear it if she wept. She'd been so brave. He bent over her, his mouth against her ear. "Don't cry about sticks and rags," he whispered urgently. "Don't give it a moment's thought. Luke Scurlock should do better by you than this anyway. Now he'll have to. Come on."

He lifted her despite some unintelligible protests. He didn't want her there a minute longer. "Come on. Come with me. Hurry."

He'd almost gotten her out the door, when she balked. "My things."

He closed his eyes. "Where?"

She twisted away and darted into the shadows. He heard the lid of a chest creak open. She sighed. "Oh, thank heaven. They're all right."

He sighed too. At least she wouldn't cry about that.

She emerged from the shadows holding a dress over her arm. Her cheeks were wet. "My clothes are all right."

"Don't you start bawling," he commanded.

She managed a pitiful smile. "It's just for joy. These are all I have."

He heard a shot. He had to get back out there on the streets. "Get them and let's go," he ordered gruffly.

She'd heard it too. She nodded. Darting back into the shadows, she emerged with a small ladies' traveling trunk, not much bigger than an apple crate.

It was too bulky for her to manage easily. Once it would have been no problem for him to take it from her and carry it down the street on his shoulder. But now he had only one good shoulder. He didn't dare tie up his gun hand. Gritting his teeth, he hooked his right hand under one end. She took the other and led the way across the alley. Together they manuevered it through Scurlock's back door and up the stairs.

The good citizens of Coffeyville were feeling wild and woolly. Scurlock's saloon was a miniature version of hell. Through the blue haze of cigar smoke came the loud voices, the curses, the cheers and boasts of men who at last felt they were part of the tradition of danger, destruction, and death that had eluded them all of their lives.

The beer and whiskey flowed like water as they tossed back one great swallow after another and wiped their mouths with the backs of their hands. They grinned and hiccupped and slapped each other on the back.

Up until October fifth they'd been thinking they'd been born too late. The bushwhackers and Jayhawkers were old or dead. The James gang was gone—killed, jailed, reformed. The old days of glory and battle, of protecting the town against warring battalions and outlaw raids, were memories as Kansas hurried toward the twentieth century. They'd settled down to become dirt farmers and stockmen and shopkeepers and drummers.

And then the Daltons rode into town.

Those murdering sons of bitches! They'd killed them

all. Yes, they had. Except Emmett, who most likely wouldn't last the week.

Now they were part of history, just like their grandfathers.

The piano player's hands were a blur over the keyboard as he beat out "Seein' Nellie Home." With his left foot he rhythmically stamped a pedal that beat a small drum fastened to the piano leg. Appreciative customers had bought a line of beers to keep him playing.

From his post at the end of the bar, Luke Scurlock saw Will come in. The two men exchanged nods across the room. Luke looked of two minds.

Will hooked his right thumb into his belt to support his arm. His left arm swung loose at his side. He could get his weapon out and into action in just a few seconds, probably fast enough to level it at anyone in the room. Still, he hoped the star on his shirt pocket was enough.

A swath of silence followed him as quite a few of the customers stopped their bragging to stare balefully at him as he walked between the tables.

The piano player finished with a cascade of arpeggios and a final bang of his drum. Curious at the quietness of the room behind him, he glanced over his shoulder. His eyes widened but he caught Luke's nod. He swung into "Wait for the Wagon," banging the drum with extra force.

"Marshal," the saloonkeeper called, "have a drink on the house."

Will stepped up to the bar. A low growl rose as men turned to each other. He could hear his name pass among them. Tonight was a test. If he showed the least bit of weakness, they'd throw him out into the street and hurrah him till they broke him.

He'd kill for a whiskey, but he knew he didn't dare. He needed every ounce of wit and courage he possessed to get through this next twelve hours.

"Whiskey?" Luke uncorked the bottle.

Will almost licked his lips. His whole body shuddered with desire. A few days before, Luke wouldn't have offered it. And Will wouldn't have turned it down. "Just some sarsaparilla. And much obliged. I've got to be making rounds all night."

He turned and leaned back against the bar shoulder to shoulder with the saloonkeeper. "Got to keep things orderly." He let his gaze sweep round the room. He pitched his voice above the music. "Drunks and such won't be tolerated."

At his words, some of the men hunched over their beers. One raised his head warily, then ducked it, but not quite before he met Will's intense stare.

Too late! Will moved to his side. "Corny Dahlerheidt!" he boomed. "Well, well, well. Ribs smarting pretty good? How about your shin? Those scratches on your face look pretty fresh."

Corny said never a word. His shoulders twitched.

"I guess Lee's run home to Mama Ketcham. She'd be sure upset if she knew you fellows were assaulting a girl in a dark alley."

The bar quieted as men leaned forward to hear the latest doings. Luke Scurlock carried Will's drink to him. His thin mouth curled in a sneer. "You been a bad boy again, Corny?"

The man swung around so suddenly, his beer slopped on the floor.

"Hey, Corny! You're wastin' it!" somebody jeered.

Like the drunk he was, Corny swung back around and slammed the mug down on the bar. "What's a feller got to do to get a drink in peace and quiet around here?"

"Treat all women like ladies and stay out of dark alleys," Will suggested.

Corny gaped for want of sense to defend himself. At last he gave up and contented himself with a glare.

"Finish up and get on out," Scurlock muttered in his ear. "Don't come back."

As Corny stomped out, Will took his usual spot at the end of the bar. The smells of whiskey, beer, and cigar smoke were tempting him mightily. He tipped up the sarsaparilla, swallowed, and almost gagged. His eyes watered with the effort to keep it down. He managed a weak grin at Luke. "Much obliged."

"I'd sure like to shake the hand of the man that warned us." Bert Ayers stood in the middle of a circle of admiring young men. As usual, his mouth was running. This time he was boasting. "We knew for more than a week that they was coming."

"That so?" His cohort wondered aloud who it could be. "Who you reckon could of told?"

"I don't know that. Marshal Connelly only told me to get ready. I'm his junior deputy, y'know. Why, we knew which banks and everything nearly as soon as the Daltons did."

"Don't that beat all?"

"Yep. Nobody's owned up to it, but we was ready for 'em. Even took the hitchin' posts down in front of the banks so they'd have to tie their horses up somewheres else. No question about it. The fella's a hero. A gen-u-ine hero." Bert regarded his rapt listeners with evident satisfaction. "A gen-u-ine hero."

Will scanned the crowd, then stiffened.

Peach Smith stood in the door connecting the dining room with the saloon. She'd put her hands up to cover her mouth. From the expression on her face, she'd done so to keep from screaming. Her face was white with shock as she stared at Bert Ayers.

Luke Scurlock saw her at the same moment. He shook his head and motioned. She stepped back into the shadows.

Will felt his gut twist. She'd come down to work and heard that loose-lipped young fool. She'd seen a heap of dead bodies, some of whom had been friends of hers. She'd been accused and frightened; she'd been attacked and her bed had been destroyed. And now she'd learned that the Daltons had walked into a trap.

Convent-raised as she was, she probably thought that the Daltons should have been given a slap on the wrist and a good talking-to.

As he watched, she clenched her hands and brought them down to her sides. Her face looked as if she were about to charge out into the room. And he realized he didn't have the strength to rescue her. His hands were shaking as he clenched them over the bar.

Bert's audience grew as he stretched the truth to its utmost limits. "Them hitching posts was Marshal Connelly's idea, don't you know? He wanted 'em to have to leave their horses in the alley, where we could shoot 'em dead. Once they was in it, they couldn't get out. He was waiting for 'em. It was just like he knew it would be. Just like a turkey shoot. That's the way Coffeyville takes care of outlaws."

The talk ran on.

Will watched the figure in the shadows. He thought twice about going to her side, but both times he'd had to rest easy as Bert told about himself and Marshal Wesley hiding in the store across the plaza as the Daltons rode by.

"I'd've jumped right out and gunned them down," the boy declared, "if Marshal Wesley hadn't stopped me."

"Damned coward," someone muttered.

The figure in the shadows started forward.

But Bert Ayers showed a grain of sense. "Now, that's just where you're wrong." He faced the man who'd spoken and the rest of the room as well. His voice had a ring of truth. "Marshal Wesley wouldn't let me make a fool of myself. The Daltons hadn't done a thing but ride up the street."

"They had on fake mustaches and beards," someone pointed out.

"No law against that," Bert insisted. "No, he was right. They had to pull something first. And when they did, we was ready for 'em."

"We was too smart for 'em!" somebody yelled.

"Yeah!"

"Goddamn right!"

"They didn't get a nickel," Bert boasted.

Luke Scurlock carried a tray of foaming mugs out from behind the bar and wove his way across the room. Nobody but Will noticed him stepping out of the saloon. He spoke to Peach, who shook her head at first. He put his big hand on her shoulder and turned her around. She disappeared in the darkness as Luke came back to wait on a table of customers.

"Too bad they're all dead," someone in the crowd opined loudly. "Now nobody'll ever find what they stole from the Katy."

"Emmett's still alive," someone else remembered. "Maybe—"

A shot and then another penetrated the din caused by the loud talk over the piano and drum.

Will pushed the sarsaparilla back and pulled his hat down over his eyes. He nodded to Luke Scurlock and strode across the room.

"Go get 'em, Marshal," Bert called.

A few halfhearted cheers followed him into the night.

Halfway up the back staircase, Peach gave out. Sinking down on the riser, she rocked her forehead against the oak railing.

She'd come down to see if she could spot the men who'd roughed them up in the alley. She was sure she knew who they were, and if one of them had a broken nose and the other scratches on his cheek, she'd be able to face them and warn them not to mess with the marshal again unless they wanted to answer to her.

Instead, she'd heard something she was pretty sure she didn't want to know.

When the reporter had asked her if she'd betrayed the Daltons, she'd been too upset really to think. She'd been angry for herself. How could anyone imagine that she'd do something like that? She was loyal. She knew how to keep her mouth shut. She hadn't thought that someone had actually betrayed them.

How could she have been so stupid!

Of course she hadn't tipped off the law.

But someone had. Bert Ayers had confirmed the reporter's story.

Someone had tipped the law that the Daltons were coming. Grat, young Emmett, and Bob had ridden into a trap. She thrust her fist against her mouth to keep the cry of anger from escaping.

Who?

She'd like to look the dirty rat in the eye and tell him what for. To her way of thinking, he'd caused the death of eight men. The four townsmen, including poor George Cubine, so handsome and young, had died when they'd tried to shoot the Daltons. And the Daltons had died, when they'd probably have surrendered if Marshal Connelly and some of his men had formed a posse in a hurry and ridden them down.

She wanted to know who had blabbed. Even though Bert Ayers had said he didn't know, he probably did. He'd been one of the defenders. He'd been told to keep his mouth shut.

She'd started back down the steps and into the dark dining room, when a powerful hand closed over her wrist. The other clapped itself over her mouth. She was jolted back against a man's chest.

"Have you lost your mind?"

Will Wesley clamped her so strongly against him that she couldn't move, could barely breathe. With strength that she couldn't oppose, he hustled her across the empty dining room and out onto the side porch.

Above their heads a coach lamp smoked dimly, its kerosene almost exhausted. The wind was cold and bore all sorts of noises, shouts, and singing, the sawing of a fiddle, and the plunking of a piano over at the saloon across the tracks. Dimly, men's voices carried on it also. Their words were unintelligible, but their drunken revelry was loud and coarse.

Concealed by the darkness, he slowly lowered his hand from her mouth and turned her to face him. "What did you think you were going to do?"

For a second she didn't answer. When she finally caught her breath, her voice was shaking. "Oh, goodness. You scared me nearly to death."

"You scared *me* nearly to death. I'd told you not to come down into the saloon tonight. Those men were drunk and crazy. What did you think you were going to do?"

She wrapped her arms across her chest, but her voice was steadier. "If you must know, I started out to find Lee Ketcham and Corny Dahlerheidt and tell them to leave you alone. They wouldn't have hurt me in front of everybody because they'd have been ashamed. They'd have slunk out and they wouldn't try to hurt you again."

He was flabbergasted. He'd never considered that she might be thinking about him. He couldn't think of a thing to say.

While he stammered and stuttered like an idiot, she hurried on, her voice gathering strength and quivering with anger. "Instead, I think I'm going to find out the name of the dirty, low-down coward who snitched to the marshal. He ought to be shot."

For the space of several shocked seconds, Will Wesley

didn't say a thing. She looked up at him from under her eyelashes.

"Where'd you get an idea like that?"

Suddenly, she was crying, but her tears were furious rather than sorrowful. "Don't you realize that they didn't have to die? Nobody had to die."

"When a bunch of trigger-happy galoots come charging into a bank—"

"They could have been arrested right then and there," she interrupted. "If Marshal Connelly was so smart, why didn't he form a posse and wait for them inside the banks? He could have hidden in the vault or in the back room with his deputies. You could have been in one bank, and he could have been in the other."

Will cursed under his breath, but she caught the words. She'd never heard him use vulgar language before. He was really angry. But so was she. "Well, couldn't you?"

"You've been reading too many dime novels. Stuff like that doesn't work. Lots of people get killed."

"A lot of people did get killed," she reminded him sarcastically.

"That they did, but four of 'em deserved to die." His drawl was slow and cool now.

She clenched her fists. "You're wrong. Wrong. Wrong. Nobody deserved to die. Not for a handful of paper money. Not Bob Dalton."

He swooped over her and caught her by the shoulders. She gasped as he lifted her up on her toes. His face was inches from hers, his eyes glittering in the lamplight. "Especially Bob Dalton. This was all his damned idea."

"He could—"

"He was a punk," he pronounced through clenched teeth. "He didn't want to make his money like an honest man. He didn't want to work. He was as bad as they come, and getting badder."

She had to stay mad. Otherwise she'd start crying real

tears. She knew Will was right, but she just couldn't admit it. A snitch was so low. He was less than a man.

Toe to toe, they stared into each other's eyes. Then something like heat lightning arced between them. She caught her breath. Her teeth closed over her lower lip. He frowned. Quite suddenly, his hands relaxed. He lowered her to stand flat-footed. And stepped back.

She stepped back too and rubbed her arms.

Two men strolled by on the main boardwalk in front of the hotel. Neither looked down the side porch.

"Will," Peach said earnestly. "I've got twenty-nine dollars and fifty cents."

He hooked his right thumb into his belt loop and slouched against the porch rail. "Where'd you get that?"

She thrust her chin out. "Believe it or not, I've got almost twice that much in the—well, in the cookshack. I've earned nearly twenty-five dollars since the Daltons died. It makes me feel bad. But this twenty-nine fifty was money that B-Bob left with me."

Will waited while she got herself under control.

She cleared her throat. "So I think I ought to use it to do something for him, don't you?"

"No."

She didn't ignore his quick negative. In fact, it spurred her to a new resolve. An idea took shape in her mind. "I'm going to use it for him."

He reached for her arm. "Let me take you up to the room. You need to get to sleep. You've had a rough night."

She pulled away. "No rougher than any other Saturday night in Scurlock's."

"You've had a shock. You've still got a job here. You need to be able to do it in the morning."

"Will. I want to pay you."

He folded his arms. "Not for the room. Scurlock's still giving it to me for free."

"I want to pay you to find out who told the marshal that the Daltons were coming."

He stared at her as if she'd lost her mind. Then he shook his head sadly. "You're crazy."

"No. Listen—"

But he grabbed her arm, this time with a grip she was coming to recognize as his lawman's grip. "You come with me."

"Will you wait a minute—"

He led her protesting down off the side porch and in through the back of the building. Up the stairs he hustled her, and into the little room that she'd spent the night in not too long before.

He pushed her inside and glared down at her. "Now, go to bed. And stay there!"

Before she could object, he slammed the door and was gone.

So Bob Dalton had left money with her. He'd listened and now he bared his teeth in a satisfied grin. She was a little whore after all!

Dalton had told her where the gang had buried the forty thousand dollars. He must have. She was just waiting till the excitement died down to slip off and get it.

If Emmett Dalton died, or if he didn't heal up pretty fast, she'd be the one to go to.

Unfortunately, the marshal was watching both of them.

But if he was lucky, he'd have two chances. If Emmett lived, the marshal couldn't be in two places at once.

"Will!"

He didn't bother to light the lamp. She watched his silhouette go through the motions of turning down the bed. "Get undressed."

"I will not."

"I'm tired of fooling with you." He didn't sound like himself. Certainly he didn't sound like the genial drunk she'd come to know and trust. A hard note lanced through his voice. She could sense a controlled violence about him.

She thought about running away, but he was right about her being exhausted. She could feel the heaviness in her limbs. Her arms hung limply at her sides.

He took her arm and led her to the window. He raised the shade so moonlight and the new electric streetlight close to the depot shone in on them. Slowly, he began to unbutton her dress.

"Will," she protested faintly, but she didn't really care. In some secret part of her, she always wished for someone to take care of her. That same secret part welcomed Will's attentions, his hands at her throat. She welcomed the brush of his fingers down the front of her body as he unfastened the dress and slipped it down off her shoulders.

He didn't say a word as it fell to the floor. His face was shaded by his hat. She would have welcomed a kiss right at that minute.

Her conscience prodded her. She was a terrible person. With the memory of Bob Dalton's last kiss still in her mind, she wanted Will Wesley to kiss her. Sister Agnes Mary would say she'd fallen far. She should be doing for herself instead of—

He untied the petticoat at her waist and let it drop on top of the dress. She stepped out of the circle of material and he knelt to untie her shoes and slip them off.

Rising, he led her to the bed and put his hands on her shoulders. Before he could push her down, she rose on tiptoe. Sister Agnes Mary or no, she had to thank him somehow. He'd had a hard day too. He'd taken a beating for her.

She put the tips of her fingers on his cheeks. They were

only faintly prickly. She guided him down to her mouth, placing a kiss on the corner of his lips.

"Thank you, Will. I am awfully tired."

She sank down on the bed and tucked her feet under the covers. In the same motion, she pulled the quilts up over her shoulders. "Good night."

Will turned on his heel and strode to the door. Without so much as a "you're welcome," he went out, and closed and locked the door behind him.

She sighed. She'd ask Will again tomorrow. Probably, he'd think better when he wasn't so tired.

She turned over and stared out the lighted rectangle of window. Who could have done it?

Her first guess was John Kloehr, the livery stableman. He'd been the one who'd accused her. He knew about the Daltons' meeting in his stable, about her going there. He'd probably been sneaking around.

She sighed. Yes, Kloehr was the place to begin. Tomorrow she'd start asking questions.

Chapter Five

"No. N-O spells no. Give the money to the Catholic Church if it bothers you." Will clutched his fork in one hand, his knife in the other. His knuckles showed white around their handles planked down on either side of his plate.

"I don't think Bob was Catholic."

Color rose in Will's cheeks.

Peach could see she wasn't going to get any help from him. Even in the bright light of a new day with a special breakfast in front of him, he clearly wasn't cottoning to the idea of helping her track down the man who'd snitched on the Dalton gang.

She closed her mouth and thrust her tray under her arm.

He waited.

"Will there be anything else, sir?"

He slumped. "Aw, Peach."

She lifted her chin. "If not, then enjoy your breakfast."

"Peach, wait a minute."

"I've got a million things to do." She tossed the words over her shoulder as she bustled over to the sideboard to get the coffeepot.

As she moved among Scurlock's patrons, she looked at every man in the place except Will. Outwardly, she smiled and greeted everyone with extra cordiality. Inwardly, she was fuming. Some lawman he was. A citizen came to him with a legitimate concern and he told 'em no.

Six drummers had taken the table farthest from the kitchen. They all required coffee refills. One of them wanted another steak. She carried his empty platter to the kitchen.

When she came back, Will's table was empty. His plate she noted was barely touched. He'd drunk his coffee and thrown down a silver dollar.

And good enough for him, she thought. She'd return his dollar later.

The morning wore on. She served gallons of coffee, smiled at all the men, drummers, railroaders, cowboys, and tradesmen without letting a single one know how upset she was. She cleared table after table, collecting her dime and nickel tips, carrying the dishes into the kitchen for old Neddy to wash.

Because of the added business, he'd had to take over that part of her job as well as swamp out the dining room and the saloon. He'd grumbled a lot about it, but Luke had raised him a quarter. She, on the other hand, was still waiting for the raise she'd asked about.

While Neddy slopped around in the sudsy water, Peach prepared the noon meal for the free lunch in the saloon and chalked up the menu for the lunch plates to be served in the dining room.

Even as she cut and pounded, peeled and diced, she thought about Bob's money and what to do with it.

Will's attitude had made her more determined than ever. She'd expose the dirty, no-good snitch and at the same she'd make the town realize that every single person had lost a lot by what had been done.

By the middle of the afternoon, after she'd finished making all the beds and sweeping the rooms, she tucked Bob's purse into her pocket and sidled out the front door onto the porch. Several men were seated in rocking chairs in the warm afternoon sun.

One was the young reporter from the *Dodge City Democrat*. Cautiously, she approached him. She didn't want anyone to get a hint of what she was planning to do.

After all, she didn't know who had known and who had tipped the marshal. That man might be listening. She put her hand on the young reporter's shoulder.

He started. His feet came down from the porch railing. His heels hit the floor with a loud thwack. Everyone jumped and turned to look. She felt like a bug in a bowl of soup.

"Er—may—can—" Her courage nearly failed her. He rose slowly, straightening his spine. "There's a message for you at the desk."

He didn't say anything. His eyes searched her face. A slow smile curved his mouth. He was so young, his sideburns hardly showed. "Lead the way."

In the empty dining room she faced him. "I need some advice."

His expression altered from eager to puzzled. "What kind?"

"I want to find out the name of that man."

"What man?" He cocked his head to one side, considering her, his puzzlement growing. "And more to the point, what do you think I can do?"

"You can tell me whom to talk to."

He looked bored.

She leaned forward. "Someone tipped them off. You told me that. Do you remember?"

"Yeah. But the guy won't come forward. No story if he won't come forward." He looked aside.

"Someone could find out who did it. A detective." She had a bright idea herself. "A Pinkerton detective."

"Good luck," the reporter told her. "Those guys cost money."

"I've got money."

Again he stared at her appraisingly. "Not enough." He started back onto the porch. "If you find out, let me know. I'll still pay a little. But I'm going to be gone tomorrow. Story's over."

She hurried to bar his way. "Just tell me where to find a Pinkerton detective."

He shrugged. "I imagine they'd be over at Condon's Bank. There's still some business with dividing the money between it and the First National."

She cupped her hands around her eyes and peered through the window. Sure enough, the tellers were counting stacks of bills on a table. The presidents of both banks stood at either end, watching every bill as it was laid down and scanning the men doing it.

Two strange men watched too. One lounged against the teller's cage, the other sat in a small straight chair beside a damaged rubber plant.

She couldn't just go in and interrupt. Nothing she'd ever done had prepared her for this. Even though she was used to talking to men, she was the waitress. They paid for her services. Now she wanted to pay for theirs. This problem was getting bigger and more complicated by the minute.

She scrutinized the features of the two men. She'd recognize them when next she saw them.

The clock in the plaza chimed four. She was going to have to get back to start supper.

At that moment the tellers finished. As she watched, each one wrapped the last stacks of paper money and brushed the coins off into two bags. The two bankers shook hands.

The banker for the First National gathered up his bags while the teller walked in front of him. The Pinkerton men brought up the rear.

They were walking right by her. She could stop one of them and ask for a minute of his time. She held her breath. She didn't dare. Maybe she wouldn't get a better chance.

She reached out and touched the elbow of the one closest to her.

Felix Hough swung around, hand on his pistol butt. His eyes blazed. His handlebar mustaches fairly bristled.

Peach stumbled back against the bank window.

He watched her as she righted herself. "I—I have a job if you're interested."

He let his hand relax and slip down the side of his leg. "I'm busy right now." He glanced toward the other men as they went on across the street. "What sort of a job?"

Will Wesley was just starting on his rounds when Felix gave him the word. Will shook his head and cursed.

"Just thought you'd like to know." The detective grinned at the lawman's disgust. "My partner and I are catchin' the mornin' train. We wouldn't take the job anyway. Any man can see why your source don't want his name blabbed. At least one Dalton's still alive, plus a bunch of brothers out in California. No tellin' which one might get to feelin' lucky some night and decide he'd like to even the score."

Will nodded. "The whole thing'll die down if she'll just let it."

"Sure 'nough," Felix agreed. He held out his hand.

"Take it easy, Will. It's good to see you back behind that desk."

"I say 'Amen' to that."

Both men looked around. U.S. Marshal Jeptha Hughes stood in the doorway. He nodded to the Pinkerton agent. " 'Bout to get things wound up?"

"Leavin' in the morning." Felix stopped in the doorway while Hughes advanced to Will's desk.

"Son, there's a little girl runnin' around town askin' the derndest questions—"

Peach had just settled down and pulled the covers around her ears, when Will's knock disturbed her. "I'm in bed," she called.

"Covered up?"

"Yes. Go away."

"Not till we've had this out." His key turned in the lock. Before she could protest any further, he strode in.

"Damn you." She sat bolt upright in bed. It was way after midnight and she was dead tired. "I'm going to Luke first thing in the morning and asking him to buy me a new cot."

Will loomed over her in the dark. He made a big shadow. His tone of voice was gruff and threatening. "Then I wouldn't even have to unlock the door. I could just come right in."

She gulped. "This isn't right."

He stepped closer. His shoulders blocked out the glow of the streetlight. "I'll tell you what isn't right. It isn't right for you to be talking to men all over town, trying to find a gun to hire."

"I'm not hiring a gun. I'm hiring a detective."

"You're hiring a gun. What are you going to do if and when you find out what you want to know? Will the rest of the job be murder?"

"No!"

"Oh? You're planning to give him a medal, then? He kept the Daltons from making off with more than half Coffeyville's assets."

"If it had been handled right, the Daltons wouldn't have died. Nobody would have died."

"That's not his fault!" He dropped down on the bed beside her. The springs creaked under his body. He grabbed her by the shoulders. His hands dug in so deeply, she could feel her bones shifting. "That's not his fault."

"Ow! You're hurting me."

He didn't let up one bit. "Listen to me," he hissed. "You're a fool if you keep this up."

"Bob Dal—"

"Bob Dalton was a murderer." His voice rose. "He shot Charlie Montgomery over Minnie Johnson. I let him get by with it because Charlie wasn't one of the pillars of the Methodist Church himself. But I shouldn't have. I should have run him in, and that'd been the end of this."

She could hardly believe softspoken Will Wesley was sitting on her bed, manhandling her by the shoulders, and yelling at her in the dark.

Their faces only inches apart, she shouted back at him. "Then why didn't you?"

Abruptly he let her go, almost flinging her down on the bed. In the same motion, he rose and started for the door.

She bounced right back up and scrambled after him. "Help me!" She caught at his coattails. "Help me find who the traitor is. Or let me find someone who will."

He turned around so fast, he pulled the coattails out of her hands. "The Daltons weren't a damned nation. The man who tipped the marshal is no traitor."

She stood her ground in the dark. "Help me, Will." She could feel the floor under her bare feet, could feel the cold air circulating around her body under her billowing nightgown. Her teeth began to chatter. "Help me find the man. At least let me tell him to his face what I think of him."

He stood silent for a minute. Then he tipped his hat back on his head and heaved a sigh. "I'll go out and look around for just a couple of days."

"A week," she insisted.

"No."

"Yes. What if you get really close? You wouldn't want to stop looking when you're about to find out the truth."

The silence hung in the air between them. "A week," he finally agreed. "But if we don't find out who did it, I want you to throw Bob Dalton's purse in the Neosho River and forget about him."

Face impassive, Will watched as Peach opened the pinch purse and selected two greenbacks and a five-dollar gold piece. She was frowning. Her lips moved as she counted. "Here's one week's pay in advance."

He could feel the muscle jump in his jaw. God! He hated for her to do this. And he hated Bob Dalton more. Bob Dalton hadn't had much sense, but what he'd had he'd used. Will had to hand him that. Giving Peach that little purse along with a sad story was the smartest thing he'd ever heard of.

She'd fallen for it—hook, line, and sinker—when Dalton probably had ten times that much—the Katy robbery for instance—stashed away somewhere, probably buried under some rock, lost and gone forever. But Bob had bought Peach's loyalty, and now the outlaw was reaching out from his grave to cause her more trouble.

He considered telling her again what a smooth-talking louse Dalton was, but she probably wouldn't believe the outlaw had robbed the train. Instead, he said, "You don't need to pay me. I'll just ask around while I'm doing my job."

Her pretty jaw was set. She jabbed the money toward him. "You've got to work harder than that. The reporters and such here in town have been asking questions all over. They can't find out who did it.''

"Maybe nobody did it," he suggested, still not taking the money. "Those fake beards didn't fool anybody. Not for a minute.''

"Bert Ayers told everybody in the saloon that Marshal Connelly had been warned. I heard him.''

She shook her head. The long mane of blond hair shimmered and waved down her back. She sure was pretty since she'd started taking baths regular. Bob Dalton had been the first to see something beneath that dirt and grime. Will grimaced at the thought. He didn't want to credit the outlaw with anything.

In a way, he and Peach both owed something to the dead man.

Coffeyville was still full of people. The alley behind Kloehr's Livery Stable had been christened Death Alley. People came and looked up at the bullet holes in the bricks of the Lang and Lapp Furniture building. The photographs of the dead Daltons had been reprinted many times over and sold at premium prices. The hotels were full every night with sightseers.

The town council had ordered Will to hire himself a deputy of his own. While he rested during the day, Bert Ayers sat in the office and answered questions. At dusk Will patrolled the streets and saloons and kept the jail full with mostly drunks and drifters.

Luke Scurlock had had to break down and hire a cook and send the sheets to the Chinese laundry and bathhouse. Peach now merely changed the beds, swept the rooms, served the breakfast and lunch crowd, and waited tables in the saloon at night. She was making more money from tips than she'd ever made in her life. He'd seen her pick up a two-dollar gold piece the other night.

Now she pushed the money across the table to Will. He took the five-dollar gold piece but pushed the two paper ones back. "I've got too much work to do on Fridays and Saturdays. I can't spend time with something like this."

She looked a little relieved. He'd bet she'd never handed over so much money in her life.

When the bills were safely tucked away, she folded her hands and smiled. "Where are we going to start?"

He frowned. "We?"

"I bet it's John Kloehr." She leaned forward eagerly.

"He says not," Will said carefully. "All he's done since they died is pose with his rifle."

"And say nasty things about you," she added loyally. "We'll tackle him together."

He grimaced. "You can't go with me." He rose from the table. Tugging his hat down tight on his head, he walked out of the dining room.

As he crossed the plaza, he caught sight of her in the new glass windows of Condon's Bank. When he turned around, she stopped, shrugged, and caught up with him.

"What did I tell you?"

She looked off down the street toward the railroad tracks. Her reply was a mumble. "I just wanted to see his face when you—"

He caught her by the elbow.

"Will—"

She had no choice. He was all but dragging her down the street. His long strides ate up the ground, so she was forced to skip and run.

She dug in her heels, but he didn't slow. "Will Wesley, this is a free country. I can walk down any street in this town. If I just happen to be in the livery stable the same time you are— Where are we going?"

Into the Episcopal church he marched her, down the aisle between the pews.

"What do you think you're doing?" Her voice was shrill with amazement. He supposed the last place in the world she would have expected him to take her was to a church. "What are we doing here?"

Up to the altar he steered her. He opened the chancel rail and brought her inside. "Now. You are not going to follow me anywhere."

"I am too. I hired you."

He pulled the gold piece out of his pocket and planked it down on the altar. "Now you didn't. You just contributed it to the church, where the rest of it ought to be."

Her teeth champed together. He could see the scarlet blush rising in her cheeks. At the same time, her eyes watered. She looked about to cry. He almost took the money back. He couldn't stand for a woman to cry.

He reached for the gold piece, then stopped his hand. She was probably angry because now she had five dollars less to spend for Bob.

"I'll just have to hire someone else."

He rolled his eyes to the vaulted ceiling as if he were praying for strength. Then he looked down at her. His exasperation faded.

His gaze moved to her hair, then down over her. He wasn't angry with her any longer. All he could think of was how pretty she looked. And how he was holding her by the arm.

The church was empty, silent, and cold. Dim light shafted down on them through the windows. Bob Dalton's little gold piece gleamed. They were in front of the altar. Awareness skittered up his spine. He'd forgotten how long he'd stayed away from churches, but his mother had taken him regularly. This was not a place where a promise could be made lightly. Here it meant something.

He let her go and stepped back quickly. Standing with her in front of this altar made him downright uncomfortable.

"Let's get out of here" was all he could think of to say.

* * *

Peach stared after him. He was down the aisle and opening the church door before she unfroze and hurried after him.

Standing in front of the altar, she'd suddenly gotten a peculiar feeling. She realized she didn't know this Will Wesley with the silver star on his chest. He wasn't the familiar drunk whose beer she'd topped off from others' pitchers.

His face was downright handsome since he shaved every morning. Now that he patrolled the streets instead of hiding out in the bar, his skin had tanned and his color was good. He looked like a real lawman.

The door to the narthex swung to behind her and the doors to the porch were shut as well. They were alone in the dim, narrow space. He took her hand. "Peach, listen to me. I'll take care of it," he promised solemnly. "I swear."

As if he were a magnet, she leaned toward him. No one had ever made her a solemn promise before. It meant so much. She wanted to thank him. She parted her lips. What to say?

He put his hands on her shoulders gently. The pressure of his fingers tilted her. She stared into his eyes, trying to read his thoughts.

He shook his head. "You'd better stop me, Peach."

What had he said? *Stop me?* Why should she want to stop him? At that moment she'd never wanted anything more in her life.

His mouth was warm. His lips covered hers. She began to tremble. He lifted his mouth, but she couldn't let him stop. She'd never been kissed like this. She wanted more.

She clasped his arms and hung on, opening her mouth. She was going to say please, but his tongue got in the way.

She could taste him in a way she hadn't tasted Bob Dalton. She hadn't realized that people tasted like themselves. But of course they did. While she was thinking about that, he tilted his head to one side, fitting his mouth across hers.

She opened her eyes. The dimness didn't register. Nothing registered except his kiss. They were kissing in the church.

She could feel the heat building in her. His hands slipped around her shoulders and folded her to him. She could feel his heart beat. Her breasts flattened against his chest. She wondered about that. Wondered if he thought that was all right. Wondered if her breasts should do that.

Then she couldn't think anymore. She was trying so hard to savor all the wonderful sensations. They swirled around in her brain mixed with admonitions from the convent and her own too-long-suppressed desires. Her body— Her body—

She wrapped her arms around Will's neck and rose on tiptoe. He groaned against her mouth. She stiffened. Was she not supposed to do that? No. He was holding her tighter.

She wanted to get closer. She leaned against his chest. He must want it too. He didn't draw back. Her heart was pounding faster. She couldn't seem to get enough breath in her lungs. She had to open her mouth—had to, but he wouldn't let her.

Abruptly, he raised his head. His chest expanded as he sucked in a deep breath. "You'd better step back, little girl."

She started at the sound of his voice—deeper, huskier than she'd ever heard it. Instantly, she drew back. He let her go.

She stared at him, her heartbeat slowly returning to normal, the heated excitement fading. She couldn't read his thoughts. His lean, deeply tanned face had a guarded expression. His dark eyes were hooded.

"Let's go." After a minute he held out his hand. She took

it and they walked out into the bright morning sunlight together.

"Let's hang the dirty son of a bitch!"

"Get a rope!"

"Kill the last dadblasted one of 'em, and we'll be shed of 'em!"

The crowd had formed at Pearl Bridger's, a whorehouse just beyond the Coffeyville town limits. It had a reputation for bad whiskey and worse women.

At nearly two o'clock in the morning, the men were drunk and steaming, pouring alcohol down their throats and sweating it out through their pores. Swinging bottles and a rope, they marched across the railroad tracks and onto Main Street.

Foremost in the van was Corny Dahlerheidt. He wasn't quite sure how he'd gotten there. He couldn't remember who'd first suggested that they lynch Emmett Dalton. He'd been drunk enough to like the idea. He took a reassuring swig from his bottle and yelled, "I hope that damned marshal sticks his nose in our way! C'mon, Lee!"

Lee Ketcham wasn't having second thoughts exactly. He was just hanging back because his nose still ached. When he'd looked at it in the mirror, he'd seen it spread all over his face. While he didn't relish getting hurt again, he hoped the marshal would get his. Then they'd get that gal and run her out of town.

"Hurry up," Corny called again.

"Right behind you."

Will had borrowed a farmer's horse and galloped to the jail from the far end of town. He made it into the jail and locked the door against the loud talk and curses when the crowd was still in front of Scurlock's.

Emmett Dalton had climbed to his feet and was hanging on to the bars of his cell. The doctors had released him to Wesley's custody, even though he was still too weak to do more than creep around.

He stared between the bars, his eyes glittering with terror in the dim lamplight. He was barely twenty-one years old, but he looked about fifteen. His skin was drawn tight across his cheekbones and flushed with a low-grade fever he hadn't been able to get rid of.

The local girls had heard the stories of how he'd gotten shot riding into the fray to save his brothers. They'd brought flowers to his cell. The photographer had taken a picture of him in it with all the jars and vases. Now he thought maybe they were for his funeral.

"What're you going to do, Marshal?" His voice quavered and broke.

Will set about loading the pair of shotguns with buckshot. "What I'm supposed to."

Emmett shuddered at the sight. He'd lain on his belly on the doctor's cot for more than a month. His back was still dotted by scabs, some still breaking loose to ooze pus and infected matter. He was in pain every minute, but he didn't want to die.

"Let me make a run for it, Marshal," he begged. "I swear I'll come back when this has all died down. I don't ever want to get crossways with the law again."

Will shook his head as he reached up to turn down the lamp. "You'd never make it."

Luke Scurlock stepped out onto the porch of his saloon. His few remaining patrons straggled out after him. "Better give it up, fellas," he called. "This'll look pretty stupid in the morning."

"We're gonna get that murdering bastard and hang him

from the tree in front of Cubine's." Corny brandished the rope above his head.

"That's right!"

"Lynch him."

"Put poor ol' George to rest!"

As the **twenty or so** rowdies swept by, Peach darted out onto the porch. She would have yelled at them, but Luke caught her around the waist. "Keep your mouth shut, or you'll be hurt."

"But, Will—"

Luke chuckled grimly. "Will Wesley'll do what he's paid to do. He used to be pretty damn good at it. They won't know what a tiger they've got until they try to pull his tail."

From inside the jail, Will watched them come. He allowed himself a bit of a smile as he watched two men at the back of the pack lagging behind. One peeled off into the alley and the other followed. Some of the mob were already having second thoughts.

But he didn't fool himself. One bullet was enough. One blast. How well he knew. One drunk with a gun and a rope was more than enough.

In the street in front of the dark jail, the mob halted.

"Bring 'im out, Marshal!" Corny yelled. "He's a murderin' skunk. We gotta necktie fer 'im."

A few raucous yells of agreement followed, but generally the men fell to muttering among themselves.

Will stood just to the side of the light spill from the streetlamp on the corner. He cradled one shotgun in the crook of his arm. The second he had placed on the desk along with a Winchester repeater. He didn't expect to have to use either of them.

"Marshal!" Corny yelled again.

Some of them echoed him. One even called his name. Mostly they shuffled their feet and passed bottles among themselves.

Will noted with grim satisfaction that his silence in the dark had made them uneasy. They knew he was in there. They were imagining all sorts of things, including the feel of the guns trained on them. Their enthusiasm was swiftly waning.

Corny gestured toward the porch. "Couple of you fellers get on up there and bust that door down."

"Marshal?" Emmett whimpered behind him.

"Shhh."

In the street, nobody moved. Some of the men standing alongside Corny shuffled their feet, but no one actually mounted the steps.

The sharp November bite in the air had already begun to sober some of his mob. If they'd had an early snow, none of this would have happened.

"God dang!" Corny looked around. He cursed. Then, lowering his head, he exploded up the steps and hit the door with his shoulder.

The seasoned oak didn't budge. Instead, it threw him back. He grunted and rubbed his shoulder as he teetered on the edge of the porch.

"Er—maybe—" Lee sounded as if both nasal passages were completely blocked. His voice came rasping out over vocal cords obviously strained and chilled from having to breathe through his mouth.

Corny cursed again. He tugged his pistol from its holster and pounded on the door.

Will held his breath. He glanced over his shoulder. Emmett Dalton had a death grip on the bars of his cell.

"Shoot the damn lock, Corny!" someone yelled. "Hell! Will Wesley's probably lying drunk somewhere over behind

Scurlock's. Nobody's there but the prisoner. Let's get him and get this job done.''

"Right!"

"Come on. Let's get this over with. I'm freezin'.''

Corny reversed the pistol and stepped back off the porch. He draped the rope over his shoulder and took a two-handed grip on his weapon.

"Put it back on your hip, Dahlerheidt," Will called. He purposefully deepened his voice and pronounced each word with extra force, so they'd all hear him. "You might hurt somebody."

A silence followed. Corny froze, then lowered the pistol fractionally.

"He's in there," someone muttered unnecessarily.

"Get on home, boys.''

Nobody moved. As one, they stared at the dark rectangle behind which the marshal was standing. Uncertainty racked them. Nobody wanted to die for Emmett Dalton.

Suddenly, Corny let out a howl of rage. The pistol swept up and orange flame flashed from its barrel. The boom shocked everybody.

Will flattened himself against the wall as the door jerked. He shook his head as Corny fired again and again, fanning the hammer. The second .45 slug shivered the door. Metal spanged again. The third swung the door open.

Will knew Corny hadn't been able to see to shoot accurately into the lock mechanism. He had blazed away and had an instance of pure dumb luck.

Corny howled in triumph. "Let's go get 'em."

He cleared the steps in one leap. Will stepped out to meet him. The double barrels were trained on Corny's belly.

His howl changed to fear. He'd never recover from a twelve-gauge blast at close range. He stumbled back off the porch, falling over his own feet and sitting down hard on his butt.

Will moved into the light. He swept the mob with his weapon. As one, they shrank back.

"Get on home, boys," he said. "Nobody dies tonight."

Shouts came from both sides of the porch. Footsteps sounded. The two men who'd ducked into the alley a few minutes before leapt toward him.

Chapter Six

Will swung his weapon toward the figure coming at him on the right. As it crossed his sight, he squeezed the trigger. The shotgun boomed. The man screamed.

At that instant the second man hit Will in the back, catapulting him forward. He sprawled on the porch, the shotgun beneath him.

His elbow hit the floor. He thought the weight of his whole body must have jolted through his bad shoulder. Agonizing pain weakened him. His vision blurred, then blackened.

If the mob had rushed him at that moment, they would have won. They would have held him down, taken his keys, and taken Emmett Dalton. But they had no real leader, no one to give orders. They were drunk and confused.

Then the wounded man filled their ears with his shrieks. They knew the shotgun had one more charge.

As his assailant tumbled over Will's feet, Will managed to twist around. He sat up and cracked the barrel of the shotgun against the side of the man's head. The fellow collapsed in the act of trying to get to his hands and knees.

The wounded man kept shrieking fit to wake the dead.

Cursing and muttering, the mob was already falling back when Will rose. He could hear his knees crack, feel the pain in his joints and tendons, but he managed to come up despite it all.

His pain and weakness made him angry. He hated the way he was, hated the wound that had never healed properly. All his disappointment and frustration boiled over into an angry roar. "Come on, boys!" he shouted. "I've got one barrel left."

"For God's sake, he shot me. Oh, he shot me. For God's sake—" The shrieks became pleas. "I'm bleedin'! I'm bleedin' bad! Oh, Christ Jesus!"

As if they were deaf to the cries, the mob of men stared at Will.

Corny Dahlerheidt licked his lips and shot a glance over his shoulder, looking for support. He still had his pistol with at least three shots in it. He had only to raise it a few inches. But when he looked back, the shotgun was pointed straight at him.

Will took two catlike sidesteps. They brought him back into the doorway, the darkness all around him. "Come on," he challenged. A grim mirth tinged his voice. "Come on! Who's willing to bet he can get me before I squeeze off this load, duck inside, and get my other shotgun?"

He was frightening. At least four men, including Lee, who'd already had a run-in with the marshal, were already loping back down the dark street.

"Help me," the wounded man sobbed. "I can't see a damn thing. My face! Oh, my face! Help me, Gus! Gus!"

The man he addressed as Gus edged forward out of the crowd. He bent over his friend.

"Better take him over to the doc's," Will suggested.

"Why don't a couple more of you help him? He might have a shot in the eye."

Four sprang to follow Gus. Glad of an excuse to leave the scene, they gathered the wounded man up by his arms and legs. With Gus supporting his head, they bore him off.

Will nodded. "Dahlerheidt, it looks like it's going to be you and me. Want to make your play?"

Corny cringed. A shootout with the marshal wasn't what he wanted at all. He let his arms fall to his sides, the pistol in his right hand.

Will nodded approvingly. "Now ease that hammer down and drop it on the ground."

"Hey! It's my pistol."

"It's the property of the Coffeyville marshal's office and the town council. You can talk to them about it." Will hefted the shotgun to his shoulder. He wouldn't have fired it that way, but Dahlerheidt didn't know that. "Now!"

With a filthy curse, Corny dropped his weapon in the dust. As he turned, the noose fell off his shoulder. He left it and lumbered off into the night.

Will sat behind his desk listening to Emmett Dalton pace the narrow confines of his cell. Will wasn't surprised. If he had as many regrets and fears, he'd be pacing too.

Except that he couldn't. He laid his right arm along the desktop to relieve some of the strain on it. Solemnly, he faced the fact that a marshal needed a good right arm. In the month and a half since the raid, he'd been hurting bad more nights than not.

After tonight's jolt he was light-headed from the throbbing agony that wouldn't quit. As he massaged his shoulder, he felt the heat rising through his thick wool shirt. He pictured the steel pellets embedded in his muscles and bone, pictured them rolling around, doing further

damage, as he was forced to use the arm in the perform-
ance of his duties.

Emmett Dalton didn't know how lucky he was. He'd
been shot from a fair distance. The force had dissipated
and the scatter pattern had spread. The doctors had taken
out many shot, but not the whole load, and they hadn't
had to dig deep.

He, on the other hand— He shook his head. The memory of Tal Karnes standing in the doorway, teeth bared in
a vicious grin as he squeezed the trigger, would stay with
Will for the rest of his life.

He let his head drop on his chest, then raised it. Whiskey
would cut the pain. He hated the idea of going down that
trail again, not after he'd been handed this second chance.
But he was dying of pain, shaking with need. How was he
going to live with this?

At last Emmett Dalton dropped down on the bunk. It
squeaked under his weight. He sighed heavily, then was
still.

Will pulled the desk drawer open and lifted out the
bottle. Taking a swig, he shuddered violently. The next
went down with hardly a cringe. Hating himself, he faced
the dawn alone, his face drawn, perspiration drying on his
forehead. Gradually, the pain subsided to a bearable level.

Will was dozing when Lemuel Mungerson, de facto head
of the city council, burst in. The man had hurried so fast
that he was actually sweating although the temperature at
sunrise was well below freezing.

"Marshal! I understand you protected your prisoner
against a lynch mob last night. I'm here to express the
appreciation of the council for your efforts."

Will blinked and wiped his hand across his mouth. Mungerson had never had a kind word for him. Why the turn-
about? "Thanks."

"We need men like you, men who'll do their duty," Mungerson continued. He looked through the open door into the cellblock. Emmett Dalton was still rolled up in his blankets, his face to the wall.

Will waited.

"Er— The town needs money to go on with their projects. We've started a memorial to the men who lost their lives—the Coffeyville Defenders. We're taking up a collection for their mothers and widows."

Will started to dig in his pocket.

"Oh, no. No. No. Not you." Mungerson waved his hand nervously. "The fact is—" He leaned forward. "Well, it's generally believed that the Daltons buried most of their loot."

Will winced as he leaned back in his chair. He could guess what was coming.

"We'd like you to question Emmett Dalton. Put the fear of God in him if you have to. The—er—town needs that money. It's ours."

"How'd you figure that?" Will asked laconically. "The banks got back all but maybe twenty dollars."

"But the loss of life. The loss of life." Mungerson leaned forward. "Find that money, Marshal, and when I'm mayor, I'll remember you."

Will shook his head. "There probably isn't any money."

"Of course there is!" Mungerson looked outraged. "They were cousins of the James brothers. Everyone knows they buried—"

Will smiled through clenched teeth. All this arguing was bringing the ache back again. "Nobody every found any money that Jesse buried. That's all tall tales, Councilman. None of those boys ever had more than a few dollars in their pants."

"But—but—"

"Outlaws don't rob very often. The first thing they've got to do is split it up. Then they've got to take it home to pay the bills because it costs them and their wives and children just as much to live as anybody else."

When the councilman would have protested further, Will held up his hand. "Remember, they're not smart enough to have jobs like decent people."

Mungerson looked as if he'd bitten down on a sour pickle. He stared from Will to Emmett's blanketed form and back again. "You'll do your job," he ordered, "or we'll get someone who can."

"If the mayor and the rest of the council want me out, let them vote." Will spotted Bert Ayers hurrying down the street. "Here comes my deputy. If you'll excuse me, I'll head on back to Scurlock's for a bath and a bed."

Leaving Mungerson fuming, he hooked his thumb in his belt loop and limped out.

Peach was up before dawn to heat the water for Will to have a hot bath. When he came in, she wanted everything to be ready for him. He deserved the very best this town had to offer. He'd saved Emmett Dalton's life last night and probably the lives of several other men as well.

Two of the mob hadn't made it back to Pearl Bridger's. They'd stopped off at Scurlock's to split a bottle. Their hands were shaking so badly, they could hardly pour.

As they drank, they'd told all and sundry about "Pore ol' Billy Joe Lockerby dang near gettin' his eye put out by birdshot." Then they'd opined that as far as they were concerned, "Emmett Dalton was better off rottin' in jail."

When Peach had asked about the marshal, they'd hunched their shoulders and shaken their heads.

"Tiger by the tail." Luke Scurlock had winked knowingly.

As the steam rose from the bathwater, Peach hurried out to fetch a fresh pot of coffee and crashed into Will as he opened the door.

She righted herself and stared. "Will?"

His face was pale under his tan and glistening with perspiration. He had his hand braced against the wall.

"Oh, Will. Here. Let me help you." She put her arm around his waist and helped him through the door. "They said you weren't hurt. Were they wrong?"

She guided him to the only chair in the room and steadied him while he lowered himself into it.

"I'm all right. Just a little bunged up and a lot tired. This job's got terrible hours." He tipped back his head. His little attempt at humor didn't fool her.

She smelled the whiskey on his breath, but not so much. He certainly wasn't drunk.

She hung his hat on the bedpost and brought him a cup of coffee. He took a sip, then managed a smile although she thought it seemed forced. He looked around, spotted the bath, and nodded. "Peach, thank you. I can't tell you how good that looks to me."

"I thought you'd be needing it. Some of those fools came into Luke's last night. You must have fixed them good. They were too scared even to tell lies." She grinned. "If they hadn't told the truth, I'd have bashed them both with my tray."

"Wish you had. They both needed it." He chuckled as he drank more coffee and sighed. She'd fixed it with sugar and cream, just the way he liked it. Studying him with her head cocked to one side, she could see a fine trembling in his hands. She was sure that being cold didn't help his wound.

"You're right about that." She clasped her hands in front of her, hesitating. Then she took a deep breath. Now or never! "Shall I help you undress?"

He shot her a quick look. What was he thinking?

"That is, do you need any help? Just with the—er—top part? I know your"—she fumbled for a proper way to say

"I don't think this is right," she rasped. Her voice was back even though her throat was dry as dust.

He put his palms flat against the insides of her thighs. "It's right. The only mistake you made—" He stopped and took a deep breath. Then he leaned over her. He came so close, she couldn't take him all in. She had to close her eyes.

He kissed them. He actually kissed her eyes. Then her temple, her cheekbone, the corner of her mouth. Every kiss was so gentle, so soft.

She sighed and turned her head. Somehow she'd moved her face so their mouths came together. They kissed each other. In the middle of the kiss, she gasped. Her eyes flew open.

One of his hands had slid up her thigh. His fingers probed and parted her hair, the private parts of her body that the nuns had told her to wash with a rag beneath her nightgown.

"Oh, my—"

She felt rather than heard him chuckle as he trailed his kisses down the side of her throat.

While his fingers stroked her in those terribly exciting places, his thumb began a gentle circling and rubbing. In a rush of feeling, she could see why she hadn't been allowed to touch herself there.

She was trembling all over. He was tearing her apart with his hands, building pressure and pain and excitement in her belly.

She couldn't stand it. She arched her back and pushed against him. "Will—Will Weslee-ee-ee!"

Something gave way inside her, and she did come apart. Desperate, she bucked up against him.

"Shhh." He covered her mouth with his. She couldn't stop screaming and moaning. She'd never felt anything like it in her whole life. He kept his hand moving, never letting the feelings slack off. Each one built on the next.

She caught hold of his shoulders and pushed. She tore her mouth out from under his. "Stop it! Stop it, Will Wesley! You'll k-kill me."

But he kept right on.

Only after she couldn't find the strength to try to push him away did he stop.

Cool air rushed across her body when he sat back on his calves. She opened her eyes in time to see him lift his forearm and wipe the perspiration from his forehead.

He grinned at her. "Well. Are you dead?"

She had all she could do to manage a smile. "Pretty near."

"Are you happy now?"

She couldn't answer him until she'd wiggled her fingers and toes. Everything seemed to be there, only it felt so much better. "Happier than I've ever been."

He frowned. "Why are you doing this, Peach? You're no fancy woman. And you sure aren't planning to turn to whoring."

"No! I just—" She hoped this was the right thing to say. "I just thought—we were both so alone."

He sucked in his breath. His eyes closed as if he didn't want her to see what he was feeling. Had she struck a nerve?

"Am I wrong?" she whispered.

"No. No, you're not wrong." He ran his hands over her thighs. "The next question is: Do you want me?"

"What do you mean?"

"I mean there's more if you want to."

She stirred her hips. "If it's as good as the first part, I'm all for it." Goodness! She sounded like a cat having her belly scratched.

He smiled at the sound of her voice. "There's lots more." He slid his hands under her bottom and lifted her hips. "Lots more."

"This is the part that hurts, isn't it?"

"Not if you relax."

Despite her best efforts, she tensed.

"Easy." He soothed her.

"It's all right," she whispered.

And it was. With only a little trouble he slid right into her.

"Goodness!" she exclaimed softly. "Oh, my goodness."

He pulled her tight up against him, staring into her eyes, waiting. She began to get nervous. She shifted and pulled her legs up.

"All right?" he asked.

Had he been waiting for her? "Y-yes."

She was surprised at how little time he took. Just a couple of strokes and he was clutching her as if he were going to pull her right into his body. She opened her eyes so she could watch his face.

He gritted his teeth. The tendons in his neck corded. His eyes were slitted, but she didn't think he was looking at her. He was looking inside himself. He was feeling the same thing she'd felt a few minutes before. She put her arms around him and held him tight while he shook and groaned.

When he was through, he put his left arm down and hefted himself out and over. He fell beside her, his body limp as hers had been.

He looked at her and managed a weak, slow smile.

As they pulled the covers over themselves, she knew she was as happy as she'd ever been.

In the street below, some men yelled at one another as they galloped their horses. She opened her eyes but closed them as the strong mid-morning light filled the room.

The lunch crowd would be coming in. She needed to be up and about, but she felt so comfortable. What a pleasure to wake up with warmth surrounding her.

She wasn't alone either. Will Wesley lay on his side facing away from her. He was breathing heavily—not exactly snoring—just breathing heavily. His big body gave off heat like a cast iron stove. She raised herself on her elbow to look at him.

He'd pushed the covers down to his waist, and his right arm lay on top of them. Feeling a little guilty, she took the chance to study him.

His whole elbow was one huge bruise swelled out like a pump knot. While it looked pretty bad, his poor shoulder looked even worse by light of day. His chin and jawline were sprouting black stubble. Every line and crease in his face was stark in the light. He looked really old.

She reached out her hand to trace the angle, not touching it, just following the line an inch above the bone. Still not touching him, she traced the line of his shoulder. As she looked closely, she decided the damage looked less horrible than she'd first thought. She could see what had happened. Among reddened holes with slices like the tails of tadpoles were nearly as many reddened bumps.

How he must have suffered while the doctor had removed the shot. How many shot were still in there, like steel splinters under the skin, hurting every time he moved?

She supposed the doctor had done as much as he could, or as much as Will could stand. He'd been bandaged up. After days and weeks, he'd healed and left this mess. What surprised her was why he hadn't gone back to a doctor and had it fixed.

No wonder he drank. He had to have something to kill the pain that came every time he tried to move his right arm. She felt a sympathetic pain deep in her belly. She wondered if a good doctor could do anything for him after all this time.

She decided he wasn't so old-looking as he was worn out. She realized she didn't mind. He might not be so handsome as Bob Dalton, but at least she didn't have to worry about whether or not Will was going to rob a train or a bank. Gently, she covered him back up again and snuggled down against him, enjoying the warmth of his body. She'd close her eyes and give herself a minute more to enjoy it. Then she'd get up and go serve the lunch crowd.

Peach couldn't believe the mid-afternoon sun was heating up the room. She'd missed the lunch crowd. A sick dread made her shiver. Her first impulse was to spring from the bed, throw on her clothes, and hurry down to the dining room.

She'd never make it. She was too late. She'd failed Luke Scurlock, who'd been so good to her, and now he was probably mad enough to fire her. Even if he asked for an explanation before he fired her, what could she say?

I was giving the marshal a bath. Then we made love and fell asleep. She dreaded going downstairs.

The man beside her shifted his weight and muttered something. She turned her head to look at him. He'd turned over on his back while he slept.

She'd better be quiet. He didn't have to go to work yet. She slipped out of bed naked as a jaybird and bent to scoop up her clothing.

She was struggling to get her things sorted out, when Will cleared his throat. She threw an embarrassed look over her shoulder. He was awake, propped up on his good elbow, and staring at her.

"Just you turn your back and let me get dressed," she demanded. "I'll be out and you can go on with your sleep."

He shaded his eyes against the sun and sat up in bed. "Might as well come back to bed," he opined. "You've missed lunch."

She caught her toe in her drawers and had to hop on

one foot until she could get it loose. She heard some threads pop. "Oh, Lord, yes. Luke'll probably fire me."

Will made a negative sound. "Don't worry about that." Unconsciously, he clasped his injured shoulder and massaged it. "Luke's a pretty understanding guy. He's also real practical. He knows a lot of his customers don't come in because he waters his whiskey less than anybody else."

She'd run her arms through her camisole and stepped into her petticoats. "You mean they come for me? Not much! He can get a girl anywhere. I missed the lunch today. He's likely to send me packing."

Will shook his head. "He's no fool."

Stuffing her stockings into her pocket, she thrust her feet into her shoes and sat down to tie them.

"If he does—" He left his thought unfinished. Instead, he lifted his right arm, winced, then lowered it to his lap.

She looked up. A crazy feeling swept her. Had he been about to say something important? "If he does—what?"

His gaze shifted to the sunlit window. "You come back and tell me."

She tied the bowknots in her shoes with more force than necessary and jumped up. "Oh, sure. That would finish my reputation for sure."

He flushed.

She scanned the room. The remains of the bath needed to be carried away. The sheets would have to be changed and washed. This room was going to take a thorough cleaning. So much to do. She was so far behind in everything.

Suddenly, she realized she was mad and getting madder. She'd made a mess of everything last night. And Will Wesley hadn't even said one word of thanks. Bob Dalton would be having a laugh right now if he knew.

She dreaded facing Luke Scurlock. She might as well forget her raise. If she could get back in his good graces, she was going to have to work extra hard and extra long. As soon as she dared, she was going to have to ask that he replace her cot in the kitchen. At least there she'd be certain to wake up and get on the job on time. It was the very least he could do.

Will Wesley rose from the bed, wrapping the sheet around him. He came toward her, but she fumbled behind her, found the doorknob, and slipped out.

He caught the door before she could close it. "What's the matter?"

She looked right and left. Fortunately, the hall was empty. "I'm late," she told him pretending urgency. "I don't have a minute." She tugged at the door. "Please."

He only opened the door wider.

She stopped her efforts. Let him stand there practically naked if he wanted to. She had to get to her job. She turned and ran down the hall.

Chapter Seven

Will Wesley ran his hand around the back of his neck and stared at the closed door.

For one crazy minute there, when he'd said Peach didn't need to worry about getting fired, he'd been about to commit himself. He wasn't so bad off that he didn't know that he was going to have to be responsible for last night.

On the other hand, he knew what he was. He hung his head and cursed fervently. She'd felt sorry for him.

Damn it all to hell and gone! She'd felt sorry for him. She saw him as some old shot-up drunk who'd done a good thing for the town. And so she'd given him a present.

If he'd said he'd take care of her, she'd probably have been embarrassed. She might have laughed and treated him as if he were joking.

He squeezed his right arm again. It felt pretty good just then—after a nice hot bath and a good sleep, but he knew it'd be back tearing him apart as soon as the cold wind hit it.

He'd just wait and see what happened with Peach Smith.

Maybe they'd get lucky and they could both go on with their lives.

"Have you asked Emmett Dalton?"

Will blinked at Peach's question. "Asked Emmett Dalton what?"

She'd just served his second cup of coffee. He was about ready to go on down to the jail and check on everything before he started making his rounds. He'd taken his time getting out of bed after she'd left. He'd stretched and worked the muscles in his shoulder. He'd emptied the bathwater out the back, fetched hot water, and shaved. He'd put on clean clothes.

All things considered, he hadn't felt better since before he'd taken that shotgun blast.

He looked up at Peach. She wasn't just pretty. Darned if she didn't look pretty nigh to beautiful. Her hair was combed smooth as silk and her skin fairly glowed. He gave her a big smile. He was pretty sure she felt just as good as he did.

"Did you ask Emmett Dalton if he knows who might have told Marshal Connelly?"

Her question let the wind out of his sails.

He rustled his copy of the *Montgomery County Times*. The reporter had written a small account of the incident at the jail. It named him as the steadfast hero of the occasion.

She didn't go away. "I think you should. He was with Bob and Grat every minute. If he thought back about it, he could probably remember who was around when Bob was shooting off his mouth."

Will folded his paper and planked down a dollar. "I've got to be going."

"Will you?" she asked after him.

"Sure," he threw over his shoulder.

* * *

Bert Ayers leaned back in the marshal's chair, his feet on the desk, his fingers laced over his belly. He might not be completely asleep in the late afternoon. But he wasn't completely awake either.

Will stood in the door, taking in the scene with a mental shrug. If any Dalton brothers had been around to break Emmett out of jail, he'd be long gone.

He felt a little prick of sympathy. Emmett Dalton had been one of a big family of fifteen brothers and sisters. The others had managed to stay on the straight and narrow. He'd followed Bob and Grat everywhere. Now he was probably going to prison for the rest of his life.

Of course, his life might be very short indeed after he was brought to trial, but Will doubted that a judge would sentence Emmett to hang. His youth and the fact that it was his first offense were extenuating circumstances.

Moreover, the newspapers had written stories of Emmett's mounting his horse and riding to his brothers' rescue. They'd portrayed him as some sort of hero who'd ended up shot in the back. They'd done stories on the flowers that girls had brought to his cell.

Will's best guess was that Emmett would end up like his cousins the Youngers, who'd been at hard labor for sixteen years in the Minnesota penitentiary. And that would be his own fault. He was just another in a long string of footloose young men led into a life of crime by bad companions. The jails were full of them.

Will slammed the door behind him.

''Awk!'' Bert jerked upright with such violence that he toppled over backward out of the desk chair. His legs and arms entangled with it. His hat slipped down over his eyes. With much thumping and banging around, he struggled to extricate himself and draw his weapon.

Will thrust the barrel of his pistol under Bert's nose. "Gimme them keys, sonny boy."

Bert froze except for his squeal of terror. His eyes crossed, staring down at the hammer mechanism.

"Slow and easy," Will growled.

Cautiously, Bert pushed his hat back off his forehead and saw the man behind the gun. He almost collapsed with relief. A kid's scowl spread over his reddened face. "Lord, Marshal Wesley, you scared the fool out of me."

Will slid the pistol back into its holster and stepped back so Bert could get himself untangled. "I don't have much hope of that unless you stop sleeping on the job."

Bert pushed the chair back and stood up. His face stayed red with embarrassment. He shuffled his feet. "I didn't—"

Will gestured toward the cells. "Do you know where you'd be if I'd been one of the Daltons' friends come to set Emmett free?"

"Aw, Marshal—"

"The very best you could hope for was a lump and a headache. The worst would be a slit throat or a bullet that you never heard coming."

"Yes, sir." Bert swallowed, waiting miserably while Will checked Emmett's cell and let out the two drunks in the cell next to his. He hung the key back on the peg and walked back behind the desk. Bert gravitated to stand in front of it.

"I'm going to make my first rounds." Will pointed at his deputy. "You! Stay awake. Don't lean back in the chair and get comfortable. Sit up straight at the desk. If you get sleepy, get up and walk around. But don't fall asleep."

He punctuated each sentence with a jab of his index finger.

"Yes, sir. I promise, sir." Bert hung his head. His mouth compressed into a tight line. He looked as if he were about to burst into tears.

Will tugged his hat down tight on his head and went out into the twilight.

Peach hurried in with the plate of food for Emmett Dalton. She'd had to plead with Neddy Barnes to let her come, and then she'd had to wait and shiver in the shadows until Will disappeared down the street. Darn Will Wesley anyway! He'd told Luke Scurlock she mustn't come to the jail anymore.

Bert Ayers was sitting upright at the desk in the posture of a schoolboy in front of a strict master. He looked at her suspiciously. "I didn't think you were bringing the grub no more."

"Just for tonight," she assured him with a bright smile. Will had said it was dangerous for her to be around there, especially after dark. He'd talked Luke into giving her a little raise to make up for it. Of course, it wasn't the raise she'd asked for.

And after Luke had scowled at her all through supper, she wasn't going to push that. Anyway, the tips she earned as she waited the tables at night were pretty good. She was putting more away in the bean barrel every day. She'd had to buy another purse, and she'd begun to think seriously about a bank account. She could almost feel rich. "We're so busy over at the hotel. The cook didn't have time tonight."

Bert stared at the red and white checkered napkin that covered the plate. His stomach rumbled. "What you got there? I'm getting pretty hungry myself."

"This is for the prisoner." Peach put her hand protectively over it. "I don't get paid for bringing meals to guards. You might ask Marshal Wesley about it though."

Bert scowled. Then his forehead smoothed out. He rose and leaned across the desk. Holding out his hands, he tried to take the plate from her. "You can run on back, Peach, afore it gets any darker. I'll take it in to him."

She held the plate back out of his reach. "You don't fool me one bit, Bert Ayers. You're going to peek the minute I leave, and then you'll eat half of it."

His ears turned red. He dropped back down in the chair and pretended to shuffle through the papers on the desk. "I don't have time to fool with that anyway. Marshal Wesley gives me too much to do."

"I tell you what I'll do. I'll bake you a plate of cookies next time I come. How will that be?" She smiled her best smile. Bert was a good boy, and if she did him a favor, he'd be likely to do one for her.

He merely grunted, but she could see a little smile play across his face.

Peach pulled the key off the peg and unlocked the inner door as if it were her usual routine rather than something she had never done before. Once inside the cellblock, she closed the door behind her.

The order Will had left at Scurlock's was for one supper only. Emmett Dalton was by himself tonight.

She stood for an instant for her eyes to become accustomed to the near darkness. The dim light spilling from the marshal's office kept the cells in deep shadows. When she was able to see around her, she felt a little disappointed.

The cellblock was nothing more imposing than another big room, longer than it was wide, with only one narrow barred window facing out onto the alley. Just a few feet in front of her, bars rose from floor to ceiling with crosspieces bisecting them every two feet. Running down the center, another row of bars divided the area in two. Against the far wall were several old army cots made of cast iron. Each of them had a thin mattress and a thinner blanket.

Although a stove stood in the corner to her left, it wasn't lighted. The room was as cold as the out-of-doors. It also stank of human waste.

This dark, cold, odorous place was what jail was like. Her shivering started in the pit of her stomach and swelled until she had to clench her teeth to keep them from chattering. Now that she knew, she wanted to forget. This was awful.

Gradually, her eyes adjusted so she saw Emmett Dalton. Bob's baby brother lay on his side with one arm folded under his head. He paid no attention as she came up to the bars.

"I brought your supper."

He didn't move.

"I'll just set it down here."

Again he didn't answer.

"Mr. Dalton." She wet her lips. "Emmett. It's Peach."

He raised his head off his arm. "Peach?"

"Peach Smith." She mentally crossed her fingers. "Bob's girlfriend. Don't you remember me?"

He sat up like an old, old man, catching his breath in a little gasp as he swung his legs over the edge of the bunk. She remembered how terribly he'd been wounded. He still had a long way to go before he'd be well. "I remember."

"That's right. I work at Scurlock's."

"Yes." He waited staring at her.

"I brought your meal."

"I'm not hungry."

His sad, slow reply momentarily diverted her from her purpose. Clearly, Emmett Dalton needed cheering up. Before she could question him about who Bob might have talked to, she needed to be his friend. She could imagine how terrible he must be feeling. She'd been depressed for weeks because of what happened to Bob. And she hadn't even been in on the raid.

She passed the plate under the bars in a space provided next to the floor. "I'm sure you'll feel better if you eat," she suggested. "You'll begin to gain strength."

"So they can hang me."

She had almost forgotten that possibility. How could she have been so callous! She couldn't think of a thing to say except "I'm sorry."

He grunted.

She couldn't stay much longer. She had to ask her question and get out before Bert Ayers began to wonder what was taking so long—before Will Wesley came back in and found her.

"Emmett"—she rose up on her knees and caught the bars in her hands—"who told?"

"Told?" He raised his head. His voice had a faint note of interest.

"Someone told, Emmett." She looked over her shoulder, then back at him. "The marshal, the men at Isham's, the people at both banks—they all knew you were coming. They'd been laying in guns at the hardware store for over a week. Marshal Connelly and John Kloehr were waiting for you in the alley."

He drew in a breath and let it out slowly. The words came out with it. "The hell you say."

"I swear. What I want to know is who told? Who was around when Bob and Grat were spouting off?"

He was silent for a minute.

Both of them jumped when Bert Ayers yelled, "Hey, Peach, you don't have to wait around for him to eat it."

She scrambled to her feet. "I've got to go, but you think about it. I'll come back again tomorrow. You can tell me then."

"Wait." He limped across the cell and grasped the bars. "What difference does it make?"

She came back to him. "Bob was nice to me. You know he was. I—I cried to think of him shot down like a dog. And Grat and Billy Powers and you. They could have arrested all of you if they'd planned it right. No one would have gotten killed. You might have gone to jail for a few years, but you'd have reformed and gotten out and lived useful lives."

Emmett rolled his forehead against the bars. "Oh, Lord, don't I wish."

"The way I figure it is that skunk that told laid a trap and the whole town fell into it and eight good men died. I want everyone to know who it was. I want him to be sneered at and censured for what he did." She glanced over her shoulder at the door.

"Why?"

She could feel a lump swelling in her throat. Her voice wavered. "It's the last thing I can do for Bob."

"Peach!" Bert hollered. This time he peered through the little barred window in the door. "You all right?"

"I've got to go." With that she ducked out.

Luke Scurlock motioned Will Wesley over to his old end of the bar and uncorked him a bottle of sarsaparilla. "I'd make it beer, but I understand why you don't want to drink much."

"I'm trying not to drink at all." Will took a swig of the sweet stuff and shuddered. "But I'm not having too much luck with it." The sarsaparilla was wet and took an edge off his thirst, but that was all it had going for it.

Will stared hard at the whiskey bottle. His shoulder ached as if the devil were jabbing his pitchfork into it. He knew from experience how a shot of whiskey would take the edge off. At last he sighed. "Just one shot."

Reluctantly, Luke poured one.

Will pulled a dollar out of his pocket.

The innkeeper swept it up. "Sarsaparilla's free."

Will waited while the whiskey burned his stomach. He lifted his right elbow onto the bar and took the weight of his arm off the shoulder. A little sheepishly, he drank some more of the sarsaparilla. Gradually, the pain eased.

He was going to have to do something about his shoulder. He needed to figure out some way to support it without it showing. The town council sure wouldn't go for their marshal parading around with his arm in a sling. It would make the town a laughingstock.

Luke came back with a second bottle. He placed it on the bar and leaned across so his next comment reached Will's ears only. "I've always had a lot of respect for you, Will Wesley."

Will cocked his eyebrow at Scurlock. "Thanks."

"Until now."

Will studied the label on the bottle. "Uh-huh?"

"You're taking advantage of my best cook and waitress." Luke's eyes were steely. "And you've got to stop it. If it ain't already too late."

Will shifted his weight. He turned his shoulder to the bar and gave the saloon his full attention.

Luke wouldn't go away. "That little girl has always tried to do right. And you're letting her do wrong when you know better."

"I don't reckon this is any of your business."

"I reckon what goes on in my hotel is my business. This is a decent house. If I'd wanted to run a whore-tel, I'd have set up shop across the railroad tracks."

Will tucked his head. Luke was way off base. Peach wasn't a whore. That hadn't been the way the night had gone at all.

He flexed his fist, thinking how much he'd like to shove it into Luke's face. He knew he'd done wrong, but he wasn't in any position to do anything about it.

Anyone could see he was no prospect for marriage. For starters, he was a cripple. Then, his job wasn't any too certain. Most important, Peach Smith was too young for him. Even as that thought crossed his mind, he could feel the color climb into his cheeks.

Aw, hell!

Luke Scurlock was right as rain. Will had been over all this with himself already. He knew he should have pushed her out into the hall, but damned if he'd been able to. He'd turned back a dozen armed citizens, a lynch mob, for heaven's sake. He was strung tighter than a player piano. He needed to blow off a little steam.

Luke leaned forward to practically spit in his ear. "I'm asking you, as the father she doesn't have, Deputy Marshal Will Wesley, what are you going to do about her? Are you going to be a snake or a man?"

At that minute the subject of their conversation entered the room, her tray tucked under her arm like a shield. She was rosy-cheeked, her smile wide as she moved from table to table, collecting the empty glasses and pitchers and taking orders for more.

Luke nudged Will. "Look at that pretty smile. And all that blond hair. Now, don't she brighten the old place up? A man could do a lot worse than that, let me tell you."

Will moved his shoulder out of Luke's way, but the hotelkeeper wouldn't leave it alone.

His face was grim. "If you're not going to do the right thing, then I want you to swear you won't bother her no more. Maybe that one stint didn't take. But we both know it can. Just takes one time for a mare or a cow—"

"Goddammit!" Will snarled.

"We can both hope it didn't, but I suggest you keep a close eye on her for the next few weeks."

Will planked the bottle down on the bar with unnecessary force and strode out into the bitter night.

Peach finished wiping the last of the tables and straightened. She rolled her shoulders and tilted her head from side to side. Luke had locked the doors and turned out the lights. He approached her carrying two small lamps, one of which he handed to her.

"Before you go, I'd like a word, Peach."

She braced herself. *Here it comes,* she thought. *He's going to fire me.*

She wasn't particularly tired since she'd slept till the middle of the afternoon. Tonight she'd helped him close up. She'd never done that before, but she was trying to make up for not showing up for the lunch business.

"I'm sorry as I can be, Mr. Scurlock."

He nodded. "You should be."

"I really wish you wouldn't fire me. It'll never happen again. I promise."

"Fire you?" He chuckled. "Why would I fire you?"

"Well, I missed lunch."

"Oh, that." He shook his head. "We missed you all right, but I wouldn't fire the best help I've got over one little slip-up."

She closed her eyes and said a swift prayer of thanksgiving. When she opened her eyes, he was staring at her, his forehead creased in a frown.

"Mr. Scurlock."

"Peach."

They said the words together, then she chuckled nervously. "Let me just ask this. Could you please replace my cot?"

His brow cleared. He smiled as if he were positively happy. "Glad to. Glad to. I'll do it first thing in the morning. I'd been thinking about that."

"Oh, thank you. Thank you." She took a step backward. "Good night, sir."

She'd already thought of a place to spend the night. There was a linen closet on the first floor where they kept extra pillows and sheets and blankets. She could curl up under the shelves and be asleep in minutes.

"There's a room up on the second floor at the back," Luke said. He held out a key. "I thought you might sleep there just for tonight."

"A room?" She stared at the key. Luke Scurlock had

never offered her a room before. A sudden fear and a flush of shame darkened her cheeks. She bowed her head so he wouldn't see it. Did he suspect what she'd done last night? Did he know? Had Will Wesley told him?

She knew men talked about the girls they'd had. She'd watched them laugh and punch each other while they said nasty things. Her mind was whirling. Had Will Wesley done something like that? She felt sick at her stomach, and she knew her cheeks must have been red as fire.

"Come on. Take it." When she made no move, he pressed it into her hand. "Go on, little girl. Second floor at the back." He waited. "Scoot."

She was mortified to the bottom of her soul, but she had her orders. She hurried through the dining room, past the clerk in the lobby, and dashed up the stairs.

When she reached the room, she locked herself in and dropped down on the bed. Wrapping her arms around herself, she rocked back and forth. She'd never in her life been so ashamed.

"What's this about someone telling?" Emmett Dalton's hands clenched around the bars of his cell. His jaw was set, his expression murderous.

Will frowned. "I don't know what you're talking about."

"Sure you do." Emmett thrust his face between the bars. He flexed his shoulders as if he were going to push right through. "Peach was in here. Bob's girl. She told me all about it. Somebody told. Who the hell was it?"

Will closed his eyes and sucked in a deep breath. In his heart he prayed for strength—to keep from catching Peach and giving her a sound whipping.

"Goddammit!" Emmett all but yelled. "Tell me!"

Will let his breath out slow and easy. He shook his head and gave his best rendition of a marshal's sneer. "Now I know you're going plumb crazy."

Emmett blinked. He relaxed slightly. "I ain't crazy."

"Well, you sure aren't thinking worth a hoot. Both your brothers shot their mouths off all over Coffeyville, not to speak of Montgomery County. Probably more than a dozen citizens heard them."

Emmett cursed again, but his expression reflected uncertainty. "I ain't crazy," he muttered again.

Mentally, Will congratulated himself. "Maybe not. But you need to think about what you believe." He shook his head. "Where you're going you're going to hear a lot of lies. Big lies. Little lies. But everybody in prison lies."

"Peach Smith ain't no liar."

Will smiled. "You're right. She's not. But she might have heard a lie and believed it. She's an awful nice girl. Innocent and such."

Emmett let go of the bars. "I guess so." His feet dragging, he trudged backward the few steps. The cot creaked and groaned when he dropped down on it. He slumped back against the pockmarked wall. "What difference does it make to me anyway? I can't do anything about it."

Will nodded. "You best concentrate on what you're going to say to the judge. Plead how your brothers led you astray. Remind him of how you just wanted to be like Frank, but he was killed and you didn't know what to do. You might get lucky."

Back in the office, Will blistered Bert Ayers's ears. "You don't let anybody in that cellblock but me and you," he raged. He dangled the keys in front of Bert's nose. "Nobody puts his hands on these but you and me. Can you remember that? Do I have to take the keys with me to keep people out of the cellblock?"

"I thought she always took the meals in to 'em," Bert whined.

Will didn't bother to argue with him. "The sheriff and his deputy go in the cellblock. Nobody else."

"Yes, sir." The young man was beginning to regret taking this job. He blinked at the force of the door slamming as Will strode out.

Their bed hadn't been slept in.

Will didn't wonder at the chill that went through him. Neither did he wonder at his thinking in the plural. Even though they'd made love only the one night, he'd come to think of this bed as theirs. He wanted her in it.

Something had happened to her. She was always in it or just getting out of it as he entered. Maybe she'd gotten up early. That was it. She was already down the hall.

Maybe she was taking a bath. Luke had installed a brand-new bathroom on the second floor. It had a hot water heater and a deep porcelain tub, just like Kansas City hotels.

If Peach got up early enough, she could take a bath in it. That's where she was. Will raked his fingers through his hair.

He didn't know what to do. Should he go tromping up there and break in on her, or should he wait?

She might not come back. She might go straight on to work. She might go back to the jail—take Emmett his breakfast and try to get him to remember who'd tipped Marshal Connelly.

He had to find her and tell her to stay out of the jail. The situation was still dangerous. If she kept on asking fool questions all over town again, she was going to get herself in trouble.

He stared around him. He had to find her. Best check the bathroom first. And if she wasn't there— And if she wasn't in the kitchen— And if she wasn't at the jail—

—Cornelius Dahlerheidt was going to get a visit he'd never forget.

The morning light was just breaking when Peach hurried past the alley on her way to the jail.

She couldn't bear to look to either side. The alley was too awful, too heartbreaking. Four men had died there. Two others had been wounded. One had ridden away until he'd fallen dead. And Emmett had survived only by a miracle.

Someone had taken a paintbrush and a can of red paint and had painted circles around the bullet holes in the bricks. She couldn't bear to look.

She put her hand over the red and white checked napkin and walked faster. Her heart was thudding in her chest and her palms were sweaty. Emmett Dalton had had all night to think about what happened. When she'd asked him, she was sure he hadn't had the slightest suspicion until that moment.

She turned the corner. She'd use the front door and walk right into the jail. She was pretty sure Will was asleep by this time.

Will! She felt a surge of feeling. A hot blush swept through her body. He must know she'd slept in a different room last night. She'd cleared her stuff out of his and put it back in the cookshack after the saloon closed.

She'd lectured herself to forget all about Will Wesley and his problems and devote herself to finding out who'd snitched on poor Bob Dalton.

She was close. And getting closer. Even if Emmett didn't know for sure, he'd have a list. She'd bet John Kloehr's name was at the top of it. The livery stable owner had profited in every way from the Daltons' death. Some citizens had even collected a little pot of money and given him a reward.

She'd been trembling with fury the day she saw him in the alley. He was posing for a photographer with the rifle he'd used to kill Bob in the crook of his arm.

He'd scowled when he'd seen her. And everyone had heard him try to get the crowd to run her out of town. He knew she was after him all right.

Emmett just had to remember.

She lifted her skirts to climb the step. The door to the jail opened. She gulped. She was face-to-face with Will Wesley.

The first glance told her he wasn't happy. His face was gaunt. He had dark circles under his eyes. He hadn't shaved. He had his right thumb hooked into his belt loop. That meant his arm was hurting him. That always made him crabby.

"Where've you been?" he demanded.

"Er—at work."

"You know what I mean? Where were you last night?"

She wasn't going to answer that question. He was at least six inches taller than she was when they stood on the same level. Now with him staring down at her from the porch, she had a strong desire to thrust the plate into his hands and run for her life. "I—er—I've brought the breakfast."

"You don't do that anymore." His voice was heavy with menace.

She flinched. She couldn't tell a good lie. It made her feel like a criminal, and she started blushing and stammering. She gulped. "Neddy's still asleep."

Will stepped forward. He was standing so close to the edge that his boot toes were over. He looked like God on high. A very, very angry God. "That's a damn lie. He's working away. I saw him half an hour ago."

She shuddered. "Well, I've been helping him."

"I want to know where you spent the night."

She realized he didn't know that Luke had offered her another room. That must be what was making him so angry. He was furious that she wasn't sleeping with him.

Well, what did he expect? Still, she was more than a little disappointed. He should have reasoned that she couldn't keep on doing it. Suddenly, she didn't want to tell him.

"It's none of your business, Will Wesley." She lifted her chin.

He drew his dark brows together in a ferocious scowl, but he snapped his mouth closed like steel trap. He dropped his gaze, staring down at the weathered step. He kicked his boot heel against a board. "It's my business if you come in the jail at night and start stirring up my prisoner."

So he knew. She supposed Bert Ayers had told on her. "I brought him his supper."

"You came to question him about his brothers."

"Well, someone has to. You're not doing it." She could feel her throat tightening. She was going to start crying if she didn't start working herself into a fit of righteous indignation. The nuns had always said that righteous indignation was no sin.

"You took my money, but you haven't been asking questions. Some man's feeling mighty proud of himself, and he doesn't have any right—"

"You gave your money to the church," he snarled, interrupting her. "I'm busy right now. When I get time—"

This arguing was getting them absolutely nowhere. She didn't want to argue with Will. If the truth were known, she wanted to cuddle up to him. There sure wasn't any chance of that ever again. He was angry with her and she was getting cold. Besides, she needed to get back over to Scurlock's to serve breakfast.

Luke had been good to her. She wanted to make up

for missing lunch yesterday. She could make contact with Emmett Dalton later.

"Here!" She shoved the plate into Will's chest and spun on her heel. While he fumbled to keep from spilling it, she bolted down the steps and ran back down the street.

Chapter Eight

Will unlocked the door to his hotel room. He figured he'd let Peach cool down. In the afternoon, after he'd had a good day's sleep, he'd be able to hold his temper.

He shook his head over the way he'd waded into Bert Ayers. The kid's ears must be blistered down to the drums. But if he wanted to keep his job, Peach Smith had better not come any farther than the door of the jailhouse.

He looked around "their room." She hadn't left a trace of herself. Not a trace. The wave of loneliness shocked him. Sighing, he ran his hand around the back of his neck.

For the first time since he'd been shot, he thought about getting married again. Not that Peach Smith was the girl to marry, especially after Netta had hurt him the way she had.

He still had that broken-down ranch house and the section that went with it across the Missouri border. He had a job. He might be able to make a go of it. He shook his head.

Don't even think about it, old son! he advised himself. *It'll just make you start drinking again.*

That outlaw's bullet had changed everything in his life in a second. He'd been sick a long time. He'd lost his job. His expenses had mounted and his wife had left him.

He closed his eyes and tentatively rolled his right shoulder. The pain lanced through him. It wasn't getting any better. In fact, it was so bad that he had to work constantly to ignore it. Just the effort to push it out of his mind and function as a whole man was exhausting.

He couldn't be a husband to a pretty young girl. He wasn't that much of a fool yet.

One side of his mouth lifted at his reflection in the mirror. He reckoned she hadn't had anything to complain about last night. He'd sure been a whole man then. He felt his body surge at the memory of pounding desire and exquisite pleasure.

Plenty whole.

He admitted he wanted her there because he wanted her sweet, giving body again.

He also wanted her with him because he was afraid for her. If she so much as went near Emmett Dalton, someone was going to get the idea that she was trying to help him escape.

She needed to be set straight on a lot of things.

He'd checked the cookshack. No sign of a new cot. Her precious trunk was there with her left-behinds. At least she wasn't sleeping there.

Luke Scurlock probably knew where she was. But he didn't think Luke would tell him. Luke didn't think any too highly of him right about then.

A third reason niggled at his mind. It was the most important reason of all. He wanted Peach with him because she was important to him. He liked damn near everything about her. Just purely loved some things.

He sighed as he hung his hat on the bedpost and stripped off his clothes. In the mirror he stared at the scar. *Hell of an ugly thing!* He let his arm fall to his side. It hurt all the way from his fingertips to his neck. Dropping to a crouch, he snapped it up in imitation of a quick draw. "Damn!" He set his teeth as he clasped his elbow. So much pain and that without the weight of the gun. Still staring at himself, he massaged the screaming muscles.

Intense regret struck him. Who knew how much longer he could keep this job? He had it now through happenstance. Connelly's bad luck. The Daltons' bad luck. The town's bad luck.

No, he didn't really have any future. Even if the town council didn't ask for his badge back, he might have to give it up.

Gingerly, he stretched out on the bed, arranged his arm carefully across his midriff, and stared upward at the ceiling. Gradually the throbbing eased, then ceased altogether as he drifted off into sleep.

"I hear you've been over at the jail, talking to Emmett Dalton."

Peach almost spilled hot coffee on her last customer of the afternoon. As it was, she slopped it over into the saucer. Lemuel Mungerson peered up at her through his little wire-rimmed glasses.

She looked around nervously. The dining room was practically empty. But just through the swinging doors, Luke was at work polishing the glasses. "I just wanted to find out how he was doing?"

"You wouldn't be planning to help him escape, would you?" The councilman lowered his voice, even though no other customers were near enough to hear.

"Of course not." She was so surprised, she almost dropped the pot. "I wouldn't do such a thing." Nervously, she changed the subject. "What'll you have? The steak's really good today. Cook puts lots of pepper on it."

Mungerson drummed his fingers on the table once—a quick, impatient flick of his hand. "The steak's fine."

"Coming right up."

His hand closed on her wrist. "What'd Dalton say?"

She gasped. "Who do you think you are? Let go."

"You talked to Emmett Dalton. You're probably planning to help him escape. The treasure split two ways would be a lot of money." His eyes never wavered behind the pair of gold-rimmed lenses. Their expressions were colder than the norther ripping down Main Street right that moment.

"We didn't talk about escape. And besides, there isn't any treasure." Twisting her wrist was useless. He merely tightened his grasp. Even though his hand was soft and flabby, she was sure to have a bruise. She tried to back away.

"It belongs to the town," Mungerson insisted. "If Dalton tells you where it is, you should come directly to me."

"If you don't let go of me, I'll yell," Peach threatened. "Mr. Scurlock is just in there behind the bar. He'll be in here in a second."

"I'll say you were propositioning me. Everybody knows you were Bob Dalton's woman. Now it looks like you've taken up with the marshal." Mungerson leered nastily. "Scurlock'll have to fire you."

Peach froze. Then she lifted her chin. "I'm going to scream right now."

He released her so suddenly, she staggered back. Pushing back his chair, he rose and tossed a quarter on the table. Even though he was not much taller than she, he was stocky. She didn't fool herself. He could hurt her if he wanted to, but that wasn't his way. He was a skunk. Her reputation was gone for good.

He thrust his face forward until it was only inches from

hers. "You find out where that treasure is, you hear? And next time I ask, you give me an answer."

She could feel a trembling begin inside her belly and spread downward to her limbs. She wanted to sit down before she collapsed, but she stood her ground, cradling her wrist.

For the benefit of anyone who might see, he tipped his hat in a show of politeness. "I think I'll pass on that steak."

As he walked out, she turned to see old Neddy Barnes staring after him. The old man's face was a study in anger.

She rubbed her wrist and shrugged, but Neddy's scowl only deepened. Shaking his head, he spat on the floor, then deliberately swiped it up with his sour mop.

"Well, look what the cat dragged in. Howdy, Marshal." Luke Scurlock gave the shiny walnut bar an unnecessary swipe.

Peach saw him too. She had all she could do to keep from flinging herself into his arms. All during the long afternoon, she had alternated between shaking with anger and shaking with fear.

As Will walked toward her, his dark brows drawn together in a scowl, she knew she couldn't tell him what had happened. He'd warned her, told her, ordered her in no uncertain terms to leave the Daltons' murder alone. She'd actually been threatened. And by a member of the town council.

Now her meddling had attracted Lemuel Mungerson's attention. She wouldn't accomplish a thing by telling the marshal. Mungerson was his boss after all.

She'd just be stirring up trouble for her lawman. For another very personal reason, she hated to. She would be admitting she was wrong and Will was right. The Daltons should be forgotten.

She wasn't prepared to do that. After all, she wasn't

asking the questions Mungerson wanted the answers to. If he said any more to her, she'd just tell him what she knew to be the truth: The Daltons hadn't buried any treasure because they'd never had any to bury.

She clenched her fingers in alarm as Will approached. He'd hooked his thumb into his belt loop. His palm rested on the hilt of his pistol, so he looked ready to draw. His height and the stern set of his jaw cleared the way for him. Only she knew how bad that shoulder really was.

No, she couldn't tell him about Mungerson. She'd handle it herself if there were anything to handle.

Before the Daltons had ridden into town, Coffeyville hadn't witnessed anything more unlawful than the occasional crew of drunken trail drivers to be corraled and herded off to jail to spend the night. Now the town had plenty of strangers. Most were just curious to see where the Daltons died, but they'd be gone soon enough.

Then everything would quiet down.

Will could handle the old Coffeyville. No need to tell him anything.

She smiled inwardly. She could see Sister Agnes Mary shaking her head. She had neatly reasoned herself out of her guilt. She'd twisted things around to suit herself. She was making herself right to keep from giving Will Wesley the satisfaction of saying "I told you so."

She plastered a cool smile on her face. "Evening, Marshal."

He surveyed her up and down. His scowl deepened.

Luke looked from one to the other, then reached beneath the bar and pulled out a sarsaparilla. He sent Will a look that spoke volumes. "Here you go, Marshal Wesley."

Peach couldn't figure out what was going on. Luke had such a funny expression on his face. Will's scowl got blacker and blacker.

Around them the rumble of voices continued. The piano player thumped out the ending of "The Camptown Races" and picked right up on "Ring, Ring de Banjo." Someone banged his mug on the bar and called for the bartender.

Reluctantly, Luke unstoppered the sarsaparilla and edged it nearer to Will's hand. "Be right back," he said.

Neither Peach nor Will looked in his direction.

Suddenly, Will relaxed. He blinked and managed a half-smile. "Where'd you go?"

She looked away. She'd been prepared to fight. She didn't know how to deal with a simple question uttered in a low voice. "Luke's getting me a new cot."

She could hear the quick intake of breath. "Don't be silly, Peach. You can't stay out there anymore."

"Of course I can. It's the only place I can stay."

At that moment Luke came back. He drew a pitcher of beer and set it on her tray along with four mugs. "Take these over to the table in the corner."

Thankfully, she made her escape. For the next half hour she hurried back and forth among the tables, carrying beer to the men, collecting their money, carrying back their change. When she finally paused for a breather, Will was gone.

She wasn't surprised. And she told herself she wasn't disappointed.

Still, after that, the night was busy. She wasn't able to get a minute to run Emmett's supper over to him. In a way, she wasn't sorry. No sense drawing more attention to herself and to him. Better to let things die down. She wasn't a fool after all.

At midnight only the most dedicated drinkers remained. She surveyed them with a shudder. At least half were married. How did their wives tolerate them?

She wanted to cheer when Luke came around the bar and started herding them out. She hurried to swipe the tables behind them and turn off the lamps.

Luke was just closing the door, when Will pushed it open.

"We're closed," the bartender protested.

"I know," came the reply. "Let's go, Peach."

She shook her head. "Please, Will. No."

"She's got a place to stay," Luke told him.

"She's not sleeping in that cookshack. We've got an arrangement worked out."

Luke glared at him.

Will tucked his head. "I'm not going near her. Never again."

Peach wanted to die. She clapped a hand over her mouth to keep from screeching at him. How could he ruin her like that! She turned away so she wouldn't see Luke's expression. Now his and everyone else's suspicions were confirmed.

"God! Wesley!" Luke exclaimed. "You haven't got a lick of sense about some things. You don't need to worry about Peach sleeping in the cookshack. I've given her a room up on the second floor."

Will took her elbow. "Good. Then I'll take her up there."

He took the stairs two at a time, dragging her with him. She was puffing when they got to her door, but his breathing was steady. Nothing wrong with his lungs or his legs.

The hall was dark except for one smoking lamp at the head of the stairs. Will backed her up against the wall next to the door and put both hands on either side of her head. "Now, I want you to listen to me."

She ducked her head. She didn't want to hear this.

"I can't marry you. I would if I could. You've got to believe me about that." He ducked his head to try to see her face. "Do you?"

She flung up her head. "Who asked you to? As for whether I believe you or not—what difference does that make?"

He sighed. "You were the sweetest thing that's happened to me in a long time, but I can't do the right thing by you."

"You don't have to do anything." She had to clench her fists to keep from hitting him.

He lowered his head until his forehead touched the top of her head. "Don't take it like that. I just hope to hell I haven't messed you up, because I don't have a future. The right thing would be the wrong thing for me, Peach."

She jerked her head up, bumping his nose and forcing him to back away. "You sure got that right. Except that the right thing would have been the wrong thing for *me*. Any man who'd tell everybody in town what he did is real low."

"I didn't tell anybody." He flushed as he remembered Luke Scurlock's comments. He lowered his head. "He's— er—just guessing."

"Funny how Mr. Mungerson said the same thing."

Will's head snapped up. "I didn't tell anybody anything."

She folded her arms. "If everybody thought I was bad, then nobody would think any less of you."

His temper boiled over. He caught her shoulders and shook her hard. "Get this through your thick head. I'm more than ten years older than you are. Hell! You need somebody like Bert. You could grow up together. I'm in a dangerous job and"—he shook her again—"you've seen my shoulder. You and I both know, there's a better than fifty-fifty chance I won't survive it."

"I know."

His hands relaxed fractionally.

"Do you think I'm so different from every woman who marries?"

"Well"—he allowed his hands to slide down her arms—"no. You're just young."

"So was Marshal Connelly's wife once. She had a lot of good years."

"She's a widow now." He gestured to emphasize his point.

"But she's got her sons and daughters. And her grandchild. And another one on the way. She's got all that love."

He stepped back, raising one arm as if to ward her off. "I was just thinking of you."

"No, you were thinking about getting killed. But your death is no excuse. Men die every day. If not by gunshots, then they're thrown by a horse or gored by a steer or poisoned with lockjaw. If death was an excuse, nobody'd ever get married."

"Oh, hell, Peach." He used his good hand to lift her chin. In the near darkness, she couldn't see his eyes, but she could see his Adam's apple bob as he swallowed. Then he lowered his head.

She didn't want him to kiss her. She wrapped her hands around his wrist to push him away, but somehow she couldn't do it. His lips touched hers and the fire of righteous indignation turned to something totally different.

In the pitch-black alley beside Scurlock's, he waited for the marshal to come out. When the last customer wandered off and Luke turned out the lamps and locked the door, he doubled up his fists and slammed one of them into the side of the building.

He wanted that money. He needed that money. The attempt to break Emmett out of jail hadn't worked. And Emmett hadn't talked to anybody except that girl.

He'd thought he might get ahold of her when she took the supper to Emmett. But she hadn't done that tonight.

Maybe he needed to scare Emmett. That might work. Scare him into talking. He knew just the thing. He loped off in the direction of the jail.

Their lips met in the darkness. His were warm and infinitely tender. She felt a stab of misery. She wanted this man so very much. She couldn't fight her own body. She opened her mouth beneath his.

His kiss turned passionate. His tongue locked with hers. He groaned as she lifted her arms and passed them around his neck, kissing him with all the passion she was capable of, trying to send a message of respect that would get past the silver badge on his chest and overcome the pain in his shoulder.

Distinctly, they both heard the far-off crack of a pistol. Will jerked his mouth away from hers.

It came again. And then another.

She whimpered. She could have bitten her tongue, but she couldn't help the tiny cry of pain and fear.

He shook his head even as he pulled her tight against him. "Listen. Hear that? That could be the last shot I ever hear. You just remember what I said if that's what it is."

"Oh, Will." She rose on tiptoe to kiss him, but he set her aside.

"Good night, Peach."

* * *

The street was dark outside the jail. The door gaped open.

"Bert! Bert Ayers! Answer me, kid."

Will knew a moment of agony as the silence stretched.

"Marshal! Is that you?"

"I'm coming in." Suiting action to words, Will bolted up the steps. Just inside the door, his foot struck a metal object that spanged across the room into the corner with a loud clanking. It was the water bucket. "Hellfire! Bert. What's going on here?"

"Damned if I know." The voice came from beneath the desk.

Will chuckled. He usually had better control of himself than that, but he was so relieved. He'd put a kid in a dangerous position. He'd have to let Bert go. He couldn't face the boy's mother if he got killed. "Climb out from under there and tell me what's going on."

With a thudding and scraping of furniture, Bert climbed to his feet. "Someone shot through the window in back," he explained. "Emmett was complaining that he was thirsty, and I was just going to get him some water." He made a helpless gesture with his hands. "And then bang."

Will strode to the door of the cellblock. "You're all right. What about Dalton?"

Bert came after him protesting. "I swear he's all right. I cut the lamp fast—"

"Dalton!" The keys were still in the lock. "Emmett Dalton."

No answer.

"Emmett. It's Will Wesley."

"Here." Dalton's voice was a dry whisper.

"You okay?"

"Yeah."

They heard the rustle of clothing, the clump of boots.

"Shall I light the lamp, Marshal Wesley?" Bert offered.

"No. Dammit."

The cot creaked as Emmett's body dropped onto it. "You do a damn poor job of protecting your prisoner, Wesley."

Will came into the cellblock. His eyes were thoroughly accustomed to the dark. He could see Emmett as a dark figure hunched on one end of the cot, his back in the corner. "You're still alive, aren't you? Looks like I'm doing pretty good."

His prisoner didn't reply.

"Bring some of that water, Bert."

"Yes, sir." The bucket clanked. Bert headed out for the pump in the alley.

"Before you go," Will called, "bring that bottle out of the desk drawer."

Bert's enthusiastic "yes, sir" let Will know that the deputy had checked the contents of the desk. He hoped there was some left. In a minute Bert came stomping in with a bottle of whiskey.

Will uncorked it. The smell assailed his senses immediately. He closed his eyes against the temptation. The icy night air, so cold that occasional tiny flakes of snow sifted onto his cheeks, had set his shoulder to throbbing. He turned it up and took a long swig.

"Here you go, Emmett." He passed it through the bars.

The youngest Dalton hoisted himself off the bunk. "Much obliged." He turned the bottle up and swallowed once. He gagged but managed to hold it. "Damn! That's good stuff," he wheezed. He passed it back to Will. "I'd just about forgotten what it tastes like."

Will turned it up again. "Nothing like it for killing all kinds of pain."

Bert Ayers returned with the water and cleared his throat. "I was pretty scared too, Marshal."

Will chuckled. "Go on home, Bert. I'll take it from here."

"Er—I don't mind—"

"Good night."

Emmett took another swig. Both men waited until Bert closed the office door behind him.

Then Will lighted the lamp and pulled a chair in front of Emmett's cell. "I figure whoever fired those shots is gone by now. So tell me. Who do you figure?"

The last surviving Dalton shook his head. He sat back down on his cot, the bottle between his legs. "Could be just about anybody."

"Give me a name or two."

Emmett took another drink. He belched softly. "I wish I could help you, but I can't. I've thought about those last few weeks. Bob and Grat were both shooting off their mouths."

Will stirred. "I'm not asking you about that. Give me some idea of who might have shot at you tonight."

Emmett grunted. "Could have been half the citizens of this fair town. Or another half a hundred from Kansas City down to Fort Smith." He took another drink. "We haven't made any friends in a long time. Didn't seem so important while there were the three of us. But now—"

"You can't think of a single name."

Emmett shook his head. His voice was low with passion. "They want the last of us dead. Good riddance to bad rubbish. God! Sometimes I wish I'd've died with them."

Will said nothing. He could sympathize with the man. Emmett Dalton was not yet twenty-one years old. He had a long time to live to be sorry.

The whiskey was relaxing him as he ran his hand around the back of his neck. His gaze dropped to the floor. He blinked. Beside his foot was a bullet hole. Curiously, he stuck the tip of his finger into it. About a yard away was another. Both were well outside the cell. Whoever had done the shooting had wanted to be sure that Emmett was scared but not dead.

"It's just like they say." Emmett shook his head wearily. He slid lower onto his cot. "Crime doesn't pay."

Will started to ask for the bottle back, but he didn't have the heart. At least if Peach should get a chance to talk to Emmett Dalton, she wouldn't get any information out of him.

Peach was sorely disappointed. Emmett had told her he couldn't remember anything. He also had a splitting headache. Now, as she hurried through the alley, she tried to think what her next move was going to be. She hated to admit it, but unless Will could find out something—fat chance—she was defeated.

The snow had stopped and most of it had blown away, but the alley was frozen solid. At six-thirty in the evening it was pitch dark. She couldn't see where she was going. Her ankle turned as her shoe slid off a frozen clod. She stumbled.

A man sprang out of the shadows and flung himself upon her. Already off balance, she fell hard with him on top. The tin plate clattered against the side of the building. It set up a racket in the still darkness. The breath whooshed out of her lungs. She whimpered in pain, but his weight kept her from drawing breath.

Silently, frightened, she felt him pull her arms behind her. Like a roper tying a calf, he twisted the rawhide around her wrists. She bucked upward and sucked in a deep breath.

"No, you don't," he whispered.

He stuffed a bandanna into her open mouth. It turned her scream into a puling cry like a baby beneath a blanket. She twisted and kicked, but he jerked her to her feet, spun her around, and set his shoulder at her waist. A tug of his hand toppled her forward and he rose beneath her weight.

She looked around desperately as he bore her off through the black alleys.

"Got 'er?"

"Yeah. Nothin' to it."

Her captor had to be Corny Dahlerheidt. She recognized his voice. The second man had to be Lee Ketcham. Will had been right. She shouldn't have brought food to the jail any longer.

Together her captors jogged across the railroad tracks, her body jouncing painfully with every step Corny took. There, four more men joined them. At least she thought she counted four.

Dahlerheidt dropped her to the ground. The fall shocked the breath from her body. She stared up helplessly at the circle that formed above her. She could see faintly the silhouette of hats and heavy shoulders. They were black against darkness that hid their faces and disguised the shapes of their bodies.

"Man, oh, man. I'm first. I been dying to sample some of what Bob Dalton got before we send her on her way." Corny bent over her, groping for her breasts. His whiskey breath made her gag.

The silence that followed his drunken enthusiasm made her hope. Perhaps these weren't really bad men. Just cronies.

The one she identified as Lee whined and shifted from foot to foot. He still snuffled as he spoke. "Damn, Corny, I ain't sure I can get it up out here in this cold."

"Well, I can. I been—"

Pushing with all the strength of her tongue and opening her jaws wide, Peach managed to expel the nasty handkerchief. She took a deep breath.

"The marshal will be after you if you don't let me go." She stammered the first three words, but then her voice steadied. "You'll be the first one he looks at, Corny Dahlerheidt."

One man's breath hissed out between his teeth. She could smell the whiskey on his too. Drunks, every one of them. They stirred and grumbled. The shapes shifted.

"What's she talking about?" one wanted to know. "I thought the marshal was dead."

These men must be strangers. They were way behind the times. "Marshal Will Wesley," Peach told him loudly and clearly. "He'll be after you—"

"Shut your trap!" Corny drew back his foot and kicked her in the hip.

She cried out in pain and rolled half over.

"Easy there," Lee cautioned. He stepped out of the circle. "We don't want no trouble."

"Trouble." She was gasping for breath against the pain. "You don't know what trouble is. Marshal Will Wesley is one of the best. He used to work for Judge Parker's court in Fort Smith. He's purely dangerous."

"He's a drunk," a hoarse voice sneered.

She couldn't be sure, but she thought it sounded familiar. It was someone she knew. But who?

"The marshal could be trouble," Lee whined.

"He won't be trouble," the hoarse voice insisted.

"He hardly drinks at all," she argued. "Not nearly as much as you all must have done. 'Specially you, Corny."

"That ain't sayin' much." Surprisingly, Lee spoke. He chuckled a little as he said it.

"Shut up," Corny snapped.

She struggled to a sitting position. "The marshal's taken over the town. You'd better let me go."

"Shut up!" Corny drew back his leg to kick her again.

"Leave her be," the hoarse voice warned.

"She's Will Wesley's whore," Corny argued. "And most likely she's Luke Scurlock's too. Afore that she was Bob

Dalton's. We're gonna run her out of town afore she can take up with Emmett and help him break out."

The general rumble of agreement was not quite so strong.

Peach raised her voice above it. "You'd better let me go. You're the ones who tried to break Emmett out of jail. I'm just doing my job—taking the meals to the jail. The town council pays me to do it."

"She's been talking to Emmett Dalton at the jail. What'd he tell her?"

Who was that? Who? He certainly seemed to know a lot about what she did. She thought of Mungerson, of Scurlock, of poor old Neddy Barnes. She was losing her mind.

"What the hell difference does that make?" Corny cursed vilely. He stomped his feet and kicked at the ground. Peach would have laughed if she hadn't been so cold and scared. Her kidnapper was losing control of the situation.

"I'm getting out of here," one man muttered. "I don't want no more trouble with the law."

"Hey!" Corny protested.

Peach heard the footsteps thudding away into the night.

A man knelt at her side. He had no odor of whiskey on his breath. His voice reached her ear in a whisper as a scratchy beard brushed against her cheek. "What'd Emmett say?"

"He didn't know anything. He didn't remember."

"Where'd they been?"

"Hey!" Corny swung his fist into the man's shoulder, toppling him to the side. "I got this deal goin'. You get your own—"

A savage growl was cut off by a revolver's explosion. Peach screamed as the noise nearly deafened her. The circle broke like a bevy of quail.

"Goddamn!"

Corny screamed too, high-pitched, terrified. He spun and staggered away into the darkness.

"What the hell's happenin'?"

Peach screamed again, and the men scrambled to get away.

"Lemme outa here!"

"You and me too!"

Peach could hear Corny's heavy body stumbling, falling, getting up.

"Leeeeee!" he screamed. "Leeee!"

"What about the money?" The hoarse voice spoke within inches of her ear. She could smell the acrid gunpowder and his sweat, feel the heat emanating from the barrel.

"What money?" She was shaking with fear. "The Daltons didn't get any money. The bank didn't lose but a few dollars. I swear. Emmett doesn't know anything about it."

"Then you do." He laid the hot barrel against her cheek. "Tell me."

"I don't have any money. Are you crazy? They didn't have any money. That's why they were trying to rob the banks. They'd been cheated of their bounty money. They were going to Brazil." She could feel the tears start. She was so afraid.

"You're lying." He caught her arm in a painful grip and jerked her to her feet. "Come on!"

The sound of running footsteps reached her ears. "Peach!"

"Don't answer—"

Too late. She let out a shriek to wake the dead. "Will! Will! Here!"

"Bitch!" He hit her alongside the head. The blow knocked her over, but it was a short chop. She kicked at him and twisted away.

"Peach!"

She ran toward the sound of his voice. "Here! Here I am! Oh, Will."

He had to skid to a stop, so swiftly did she barrel out of the darkness. He threw his arms around her. "Are you all right? Are you all right?"

"Yes." She found she was crying now. She didn't know how the tears had started, but suddenly she couldn't stop. She buried her face in his neck and bawled.

"Are you hurt?"

"No." Her tears kept coming. Even after her sobs stopped, the tears kept trickling. All she could think of was the hot gun barrel against her cheek.

Will holstered his gun and ran his hands down her arms. He found the roping string and released her.

She groaned as she pulled her hands around in front of her. "Oh, Will. I'm so glad you're here. I was so scared."

"You're safe now, Peach." He cupped her face between his palms. Her cheeks were wet with tears.

"Someone wanted to know about the Daltons' money. I didn't know anything about it. I didn't." She shook her head desperately. Somehow she had to convince Will that she didn't know. "I didn't."

He got one foot under him and lifted her gently to her feet. "I know. I know."

"You saved me. They were going to r-rape me and then run me out of town." She couldn't quite stifle a sob. "But I told them you'd come."

What would have happened to her if Will hadn't come and found her didn't bear thinking about. Her lawman had saved her. She'd known. She tried to stand on her own but lost her balance. "Give me a minute."

"Put your arms around my neck."

She didn't know what he intended until he'd slipped his left arm under her knees and lifted her. She felt the quick intake of his breath, felt his chest swell with the effort. "Oh, Will. You'll hurt your shoulder."

"Not if you hang on tight."

She put her head against his shoulder and tried to hold herself stiff so her weight wouldn't sag against his right arm. Evidently, what she was doing worked.

His breathing was natural and easy as he carried her down the dark street.

Chapter Nine

On the other side of the railroad tracks, Peach put her mouth to Will's ear. "You can put me down now. Please, Will. I can walk from now on. I don't want to hurt your shoulder."

"My shoulder's all right," he said gruffly, but he stopped and let his arm slide from under her knees. As his right arm relaxed beneath her, she felt him let out a deep breath. It shuddered slightly at the end as his arm stretched out.

Her own nerves quivered in sympathetic pain. Wanting to offer comfort, she kept her arms around his neck as her body straightened out along the same plane as his. She turned against him and hugged him tenderly.

"Peach," he groaned.

Suddenly, his thighs hardened against her. His chest swelled. Her own body tensed in recognition.

Tenderness gave way to desire. Her nerves strung tight by terror tingled with response to his nearness. She closed her eyes and pressed herself against him. He was so warm.

She was so glad to be alive. She had been so cold and so afraid, and Will had rescued her.

Her sigh of pleasure moved her breasts against his chest.

"Careful, Peach," he whispered.

Why be careful? She'd almost died. When Corny and his gang had finished with her, she didn't doubt they would have killed her if for no other reason than to put her out of her misery. "Hold me, Will."

His hands came to rest on the curve of her hips. He made a sound deep in his throat. He took a step forward, opening his legs so her legs were between his thighs.

She could feel the swelling hardness pressing against her belly. She welcomed it. She was so glad to be feeling it. She lifted her mouth and tried to reach his lips. "Kiss me."

"Good Lord, girl!" He jerked his head back. His piercing gaze swept the darkness. "We're smack-dab in the middle of town. It's cold enough to snow."

She gave a nervous laugh. Exhilaration beyond anything she could ever have imagined pulsed through her. Her belly trembled because she wanted him so much. She was as far from the convent as the cold stars above. "Then no one's going to see us."

"Good Lord," he repeated through clenched teeth.

"You saved my life, Will Wesley. I was a goner for sure."

She could feel the negative tension in his body. He shook his head. "I was doing my job, Peach. I didn't do it so you'd make love to me."

"No, you didn't. I know that." She caressed his cheek. "Please, Will. Please." Her stroking fingers found his earlobe and tugged gently.

"You were mad as hell at me just a few minutes ago."

"I'm not mad anymore."

"You are the beat of any woman I ever saw."

His lips were cold when they met hers in the darkness.

His arms left her waist and encircled her body, lifting her tight against his chest. Her feet left the ground.

As his lips warmed, they opened. She opened hers too, and he thrust his tongue between them. She gasped in ecstasy. The darkness swam with flashes of color beneath her eyelids and the sound of their breathing.

His manhood was a steel rod covered by the wool of his trousers. It was hard between his belly and the cleft of her body. The pressure was powerful, insistent.

She wriggled her body. She wanted more. More. She groped for the ground, found it with the tip of her shoe. It was enough to allow her to push upward. Her right leg wrapped over the top of his hip. When she tried to raise her left leg, he scooped one big warm hand under her thigh and guided her around him.

He straightened with a sigh and a groan. The sensitive parts of her body were hot against the rough wool and his male shape. He arched his back. She cried out. His strength hurt her, but it hardly felt like pain.

It felt good, so good, it sent signals to all parts of her body. It forced her back in his grasp. She crossed her ankles in the small of his back and pulled herself tighter against him. Now that he'd taught her what would happen, she wanted it desperately.

"Peach," he muttered. "Girl."

"Yes, Will! Oh, yes." It came roaring through her body like a freight train. She tossed her head back, sending a high, keening cry into the icy blackness.

He held her while she writhed, exciting him till he was sure he'd burst.

But he couldn't allow himself to lose control. Never once in all the passion and distraction, all the hugging and kissing, had he closed his eyes or ceased sweeping the

4 BESTSELLING HISTORICAL ROMANCES BY YOUR FAVORITE AUTHORS CAN BE YOURS, FREE!

Kensington Choice brings you historical romances by your favorite bestselling authors including Janelle Taylor, Shannon Drake, Bertrice Small, Jo Goodman, and Georgina Gentry, just to name a few! Each book is filled with passion, adventure and the excitement of bygone times!

To introduce you to this great club which is part of Zebra Home Subscription Service, we'd like to send you your first 4 bestselling historical romances, absolutely free! And once you get these 4 free books to savor at home, we'll rush you the next 4 brand-new books at the lowest prices available, as soon as they are published.

The way the club works is that after your initial FREE shipment, you will get our 4 newest bestselling historical romances delivered to your

doorstep each month at the preferred subscriber's rate of only $4.20 per book, a savings of up to $8.16 per month (since these titles sell in bookstores for $4.99-$6.99)! All books are sent on a 10-day free examination basis and there is no minimum number of books to buy. (A postage and handling charge of $1.50 is added to each shipment.) Plus as a regular subscriber, you'll receive our FREE monthly newsletter, *Zebra/Pinnacle Romance News*, which features author profiles, subscriber benefits, book previews and more!

*We have 4 FREE BOOKS for you
as your introduction to
KENSINGTON CHOICE!
To get your FREE BOOKS, worth
up to $24.96, mail the card below.*

FREE BOOK CERTIFICATE

Yes! Please send me 4 Kensington Choice (the best of Zebra and Pinnacle Books) Historical Romances without cost or obligation (worth up to $24.96). As a Kensington Choice subscriber, I will then receive 4 brand-new romances to preview each month for 10 days FREE. I can return any books I decide not to keep and owe nothing. The publisher's prices for Kensington Choice romances range from $4.99-$6.99, but as a preferred subscriber I will get these books for only $4.20 per book or $16.80 for all four titles. There is no minimum number of books to buy and I may cancel my subscription at any time. A $1.50 postage and handling charge is added to each shipment. No matter what I decide to do, my first 4 books are mine to keep, absolutely FREE!

Name _____

Address _____ Apt. _____

City _____ State _____ Zip _____

Telephone ( ) _____

Signature _____

(If under 18, parent or guardian must sign)

Subscription subject to acceptance. Terms and prices subject to change.

KC1198

4 FREE
Historical
Romances
are waiting
for you to
claim them!

(worth up to
$24.96)

See details
inside....

KENSINGTON CHOICE
Zebra Home Subscription Service, Inc.
120 Brighton Road
P.O.Box 5214
Clifton, NJ 07015-5214

area with his searching gaze. At the same time, his desire matched her own.

His mind yelled at him to put a damper on his male organ. The practical, no-nonsense-marshal's brain reminded him that the street was colder than a well-digger's toe in Alaska. That she wasn't a whore to be backed up against the side of a building. That he'd taught her what to want and she was a healthy young girl bound on getting it.

Moreover, he knew she was going through the same sort of thing that all youngsters went through when they'd been in deadly danger and come out alive. And finally, they were in the middle of downtown Coffeyville.

While his mind lectured him on all those things, he fastened onto her gasping mouth and ran his tongue inside it. He was throbbing so hard against the fly of his trousers, he couldn't believe he hadn't burst his buttons.

She whimpered beneath his mouth. Then she uncoiled herself from his body and found her footing. Her hands flashed to undo his buttons.

''Peach—''

''Oh, Will, you have to. You just have to.''

She was right. Dimly he thought she was the sweetest, most considerate little thing. He was a lucky dog. The last button slipped through the hole. She pushed aside his longjohns and lifted her skirts.

He pushed into her. One powerful thrust into the hot, moist folds of her body. He lifted her off her feet and carried her into an alley. Back against the side of the building he pushed her. She gasped and murmured something. He didn't think he'd hurt her. She pushed his hat off his head and wrapped her fingers in his hair.

He pulled back and thrust again—and exploded. As he filled her, he completed them both—penis in her body, tongue in her mouth. His heart thundered in his ears. His chest heaved like a bellows.

He kissed her again and again, drinking her. She'd given herself to him. The act was the best thing that had ever happened to him. He'd never expected to have pleasure like that again. After his life fell apart, he'd resigned himself to misery and drink.

For just a second he thought anything was possible. He could have a future. Then a horseman trotted through the street. He tried to put her aside and his right arm sent a shaft of pain through his chest that almost brought him to his knees.

Stifling a groan, he stepped away from her and put his clothing to rights.

When he looked up at her, she had let her arms fall to her sides. Her face was turned away from him.

"You ready?" The minute the question was out of his mouth, he wished he hadn't said it like that. He held out his hand.

Instead of taking it, she walked ahead of him down the alley to the street.

In profound silence they walked, their arms at their sides, so close to touching, so far away. A snowflake settled on her eyelash. Another joined it on her cheek. And another.

She looked up to see them wafting down. Snow had always seemed like a benediction to her. She liked to think of God sending pure white blessings down upon her, upon Will, upon the turbulent town.

Then she thought of Sister Agnes Mary and wondered if God was covering her sin so no shame would fall on the convent that had taken her in.

She'd sinned tonight. She knew she had. Will knew it too. She'd grabbed him. She'd climbed up his body for goodness' sake. She was so ashamed. She'd been weak, but that was no excuse.

She couldn't think about that anymore. She had to think of something else. Her mind skipped to something even less pleasant.

The snow was falling on Bob Dalton's grave too. It was snowing in the alley where he died.

When they'd decided to rob the banks, they set something in motion. It wasn't over. Sometimes she didn't think it ever would be. It seemed to grow bigger and blacker, needing more and more snow.

She didn't want to break the silence, but Will needed to know. "A man was shot tonight."

He stopped dead in his tracks. "Shot dead?"

"I don't know. I don't think so. He ran away screaming. It was Cornelius Dahlerheidt." The memory made her sick to her stomach. It had been so fast, so ruthless.

Will took her arm and hurried her along. Scurlock's hotel was just in the next block. He moved purposefully now, increasing his stride until she had to skip to keep up.

He was all lawman now, lover and compassionate rescuer displaced by the man of action. He led her up the stairs and into the room they'd shared. She didn't have the strength to object. After what had happened to her, she was glad to be back with Will. At least with him beside her, she'd be safe.

He set her on the bed, lit the lamp, and pulled up a chair so they were knee to knee. "Now, tell me exactly what happened." As she opened her mouth, he held up his index finger. "The whole truth."

Lee Ketcham had a one-room shack and shed for his horse out beyond the Coffeyville town limit.

As Will pulled his livery stable mount up in the front, he noted the streaks of lantern light shining between the crude one-by-twelve siding. Instead of Lee putting up his horse, he'd tied the animal to the tree outside.

Will approached and ran his hand over the saddlebow. It and the horse's flank were still sticky. He thought about knocking on the shed door, but then changed his mind.

Corny might be dying. He was a drunken brute and a fool. No great loss to the community, but the whole Dalton affair had suddenly taken a new turn. Will didn't want the man to die without answering some important questions.

He pushed the door open.

Corny Dahlerheidt lay groaning on a pile of hay. A kerosene lantern hung on a peg above him. The mound of his stomach glistened red.

Gut shot.

Will shook his head. Of course, with Corny's gut, the wound might not be serious. He turned at the sound of footsteps trudging up behind him.

Lee froze. His homely face looked tired. He was still bruised and swollen around the nose and under the eyes. He cast a guilty look at the wounded man, then shrugged. "Marshal. Glad you're here."

"How bad is he?" Will held the door.

Poor Lee shook his head. "I don't know." He carried a bottle of whiskey in one hand and had thrown a thin blanket over his arm. "I ain't no doctor. I begged Corny let's get 'im to the doc, but he said no."

Will took the whiskey and led the way to Corny's side. The wounded man's eyes were closed, his face contorted in pain. His breathing was shallow. As Will knelt, Corny's eyelids fluttered. He lifted his head.

"Damn you, Lee," he wheezed. "I tol' you—"

"I didn't call 'im." Lee leaned over Will's shoulder. "Swear to God. He musta followed the blood or somethin'."

Will didn't bother to point out that it was pitch black outside and snowing. Lee's explanation seemed to satisfy his friend, who sank back with a groan.

Will marked the entry hole. The bullet must have been

a .38 caliber. A .45 would have done more damage. The wound was still bleeding sluggishly, but the wound smelled clean. No bowel odor tainted the air. He guessed the slug must be lodged in a layer of fat.

"Who shot you?"

Corny slitted his eyes. "Yore galfriend, Marshal. She's part of Dalton's gang. Ought to be run—"

His accusation ended in a squeal as Will caught hold of his earlobe and twisted. "You're crazy as a loon, Dahlerheidt. You know that girl didn't shoot you. Who did it?"

"I don't know," came the sullen reply. "Could I have some of that whiskey?"

Will ignored the request. "You had a bunch of men with you. Which one of them did it?"

Corny sighed. "Tol' you. I don't know. We was just standing around at the bar, talking about how the town was being cheated, and how that whore— Ow! Ow!"

Will twisted his ear again. "You mean you picked up some barflies and one of them bit you."

"That's about th' size of it." Lee was leaning back against the wall, the picture of dejection. He shoved his hands deep into the pockets of his bloodstained overalls and kicked at a clod of dirt. "Hell, Corny, you could mebbe die. You better let me go get the doc."

Will let go of the wounded man's ear. "Just as soon as your friend answers my questions, you can go get the doctor, Lee. He's not bleedin' too bad."

"Hey!" Corny raised his head and tried to stare down his body. "Am I still bleedin'? Let Lee go right now."

Will shook his head. "You're liable to pass out and forget everything."

"Hey!" Corny tried to turn over. "Hey!"

Will pushed him back. "What'd this guy look like?"

"I don't 'member. He was jus' standin' down at the far end of the bar. We decided we'd—" Here Corny swallowed and winced. He looked hard at Lee, who shrugged. "When

we decided we'd—er—throw a scare into Bob Dalton's
wh—er—galfriend.''

Will looked at Lee. "What'd he look like?"

"If he's the one I'm thinkin', he had a brown beard.
All hairy, all over his face. Bushy. An' his hair was all down
in his eyes."

"That's right," Corny agreed. He winced again and tried
to move. "Listen, I'm beginning to hurt pretty bad."

"In a minute. Where were you?"

The two men exchanged shamed looks. "Pearl
Bridger's."

Will made a tsking sound with his tongue and lips. "Now,
boys, don't you know your mothers wouldn't be happy to
know you went to a place like that. Not to mention you
might get a dose of something that'd leave you blind and
crazy."

Neither spoke.

Will rose. "Go on, Lee, and get the doctor. Tell him
I'm waiting for him. Otherwise he's not likely to come for
Corny here."

"Hey." Corny's protest was halfhearted. The fat man
looked exhausted. His face looked pinched and drained
of color.

Lee bolted out the door. Will uncorked the whiskey.
Thrusting his hand under Corny's sweaty neck, he helped
the man to drink. Corny managed one good swig and had
his mouth set for another, but Will pulled it back.

Holding the whiskey where Corny couldn't quite reach
it, he leaned forward. "I'm giving you the word, Dahlerheidt. I want you to pay attention and remember. Peach
Smith didn't have anything to do with the Dalton raid.
She didn't have any truck with Bob Dalton or his sorry
brothers, or his crazy friends. Got that?"

Corny's bloodshot eyes met Will's steely ones. "Yeah."

"She's a good, hardworking orphan girl who's making
her own way and living a decent life. If you want to go

pick on someone, find someone your own size. There are more bums around Coffeyville than ever. You found one tonight, and look what it got you."

Corny grunted.

"Now, I'm giving you this whiskey for you to nurse until Doc gets here. He's going to have to take that bullet out, and that's not going to be a picnic. I've been there, and I can tell you for sure."

More sweat popped out on Corny's face. He took a liberal drink.

"While you're lying there, I want you to practice saying Peach Smith is a lady through and through."

"Aw, Marshal."

"Peach Smith is a lady through and through."

"Peach Smith is a lady through and through. Peach Smith is a lady through and through."

"That's good." Will pulled his hat down tighter over his forehead and strolled to the door. "If I hear anything else from your mouth, I'll arrest you. Kidnapping and attempted rape'll keep you in jail for a long time." He closed the door softly, leaving Corny to contemplate his sins.

Peach was still dressed and seated in the room's single chair when Will unlocked the door. The sheets were smoothed, the pillows plumped, the bed turned down. She had stirred up the fire in the small iron stove.

He made straight for it, holding out his palms, then rubbing them together. His lips were chapped, his cheeks bright red.

"Did you find Corny?"

"Yep." He warmed his hands again, then clapped them to his cheeks. "The temperature must have dropped twenty degrees tonight. Snow's six inches deep in the streets."

"Is he dead?"

"No." One side of his mouth quirked up. "Only the good die young. Doc's probably got him patched up by now. He'll be back on his feet in a couple of days if the wound doesn't turn putrid on him."

"Did you find out who shot him?" She couldn't keep the eagerness from her voice. Corny would tell who shot him. He'd be mad as fire at the man with the scratchy beard. Will would arrest him or run him out of town. She'd be safe.

"That's what I can't quite figure." Will turned to the fire and looked at her speculatively. "Corny didn't exactly keep a muster list on his recruits. Just like with his necktie party, he claimed they were all hanging around the bar in Pearl Bridger's, when assaulting a female suddenly seemed like a good idea. He doesn't know."

He dropped down on the bed. Its springs creaked in protest. Frowning, he ran his hand around the back of his neck. "This is more than just a bunch of drunks going off half cocked. Someone fired three shots through the window of the cellblock the other night. Emmett wasn't hit, but he's mighty scared."

With a sigh he hauled his right arm across his lap and stared thoughtfully at Peach. "Something funny's going on here. This doesn't add up. This is the second time Corny has come after you in an alley. The first time you'd opened your mouth before the mayor and the town council about who tipped them off. This time was out of the blue. You'd been minding your own business."

She narrowed her eyes. "Don't you see? It must be the man who did it. He knows he's done wrong and he doesn't want to be discovered—"

Will shook his head wearily. "Peach. Listen to me. Number one. If someone tipped off the marshal—and I say if—he doesn't have anything to be ashamed of."

She curled her mouth in a sarcastic sneer. "Eight people dead's something to be ashamed of."

He leaned forward. "The Daltons might have shot that many riding out of town. While they were getting away with the town's money. Most people owe him their life savings. Number two—"

"You can't know that would have happened."

"You can't know it wouldn't," he snapped back. "Number two. Why come after you a second time? The trail was cold. You didn't have anywhere to go. You hadn't been going around town asking more questions." He looked at her questioningly.

She folded her arms across her chest. "I talked to Emmett Dalton at the jail."

"And that got you exactly nowhere. He can't remember anything for the simple reason that he probably didn't know anything to begin with."

"He was with them the whole time," Peach argued.

"They let him tag along," Will declared in a flat voice. "They should have sent him home. He's what they talk about when a boy falls in with bad companions. In this case bad brothers. If Frank had lived instead of Grat—" He shrugged. "Who knows? Anyway, more than half of what those other two were going to do and how they were going about it went in one ear and out the other."

Peach felt a little guilty. Will was absolutely right about Emmett. He was right almost all the time. But she wasn't going to tell him so. The least said about her visits to the jail, the best mended. Emmett Dalton was a miserable boy.

"There've been two attempts to get to Emmett Dalton," Will went on. He held up his index and then his third finger. "First, they tried to get him out in the streets so they could hang him. Second, someone shot through the bars of the cellblock."

"So they're trying to kill him?"

"Maybe the mob was, but I'm not so sure about that. A drunk, disorganized crowd might be easy to get a prisoner away from. Somebody might have been waiting till they got Emmett in the streets to run with him.''

"But someone shot at him.''

"If you want to shoot someone in a jail cell, you can do it.'' Will spread his hands in an eloquent shrug. "It's just like shooting fish in a barrel. The prisoner's got nowhere to hide. Just aim for the bunks. Both of them are against the wall.''

"Bert ran him off,'' Peach suggested.

Will looked disgusted. "Bert Ayers can't run off anything except his mouth. He was hiding under the desk when I walked in.''

Peach couldn't stop herself. She sniggered.

Will himself grinned. "Most people aren't up to law enforcement. Bert's just one of a crowd. No. If someone had meant to kill Emmett, he'd have been a goner. If you need more proof, I found the bullet holes in the floor outside the bars.''

Peach couldn't repress a shudder. "Why doesn't whoever's doing this just break him out? If Bert Ayers is as scared as you say, he'd be hiding under the desk the whole time?''

"Maybe he doesn't know that about Bert. But I know two things. I can't endanger that kid's life anymore. Nor Emmett's life. So I've got to move Emmett to somewhere safer.''

"That would be best,'' Peach agreed.

"This business with Corny Dahlerheidt is the big tipoff. Maybe the first time he and his buddy Lee went after you, they were just using you as an excuse to raise a little general and particular hell. They weren't among the men who stopped the Daltons. They weren't even related to them. They wanted to be part of the show, so they thought they'd run you out of town.''

"But that's stupid.''

The sarcastic look he shot her spoke more than a thousand words.

She shrugged meekly. "Well, it is."

"Dahlerheidt figured he could knock you around, scare you, run you out of town, and nobody would do anything about it. You didn't have a family to stand up for you, and he'd get to brag. Maybe a reporter would listen to his story. Maybe he'd get his name in the paper."

Will stood up and began to pace. He held on to his right arm to keep it from swinging against his body. "But the second time was something else again. The show's mostly over. The reporters have left town. He didn't have any particular reason for persecuting you. Since he picked up his gang in a whorehouse, I can't believe he's trying to rid the town of immorality."

She touched her hand to her cheek. The redness from the hot gun barrel had disappeared, but the memory was fresh. She opened her mouth to tell Will about the question, then closed it again. The man who'd shot Corny and threatened her had been drunk. She'd smelled the whiskey. He'd known that she'd visited Emmett in the jail. He'd wanted to know about money. Who?

Lemuel Mungerson!

A hard lump of ice formed in her stomach. She could scarcely breathe. The town councilman. She couldn't tell Will about him. For one thing, he couldn't do anything about Lemuel Mungerson. He'd probably lose his job if he tried to. Will was talking about moving Emmett. When that happened, Mungerson wouldn't have any reason to keep bothering her.

She'd just watch her step till then.

She just needed to talk to Emmett one more time. Surely, if he thought hard, he'd remember someone who had heard Bob and Grat talking.

If she could only find out who, she could telegraph the reporter from the *Dodge City Democrat*. He'd come back for that story. At the same time, she could reveal what she knew to be the truth—that the Daltons had gotten four thousand from the Katy, not forty. That they'd split it six ways nearly six months before the Coffeyville raid.

She'd show Will Wesley she'd been right all along. And most important—Bob Dalton could rest in peace.

The man who'd scared her and shot Corny was probably someone the gang knew slightly. He wasn't a friend. Of that she was certain. If he broke Emmett out of jail, he was likely planning to torture him. Her mind was flying when Will snapped his fingers in front of her face.

"Where are you?"

She blinked and started. "I'm right here." She smiled. "I'm just tired."

"The first thing I've got to do is get you out of town," Will announced.

"What're you talking about?" She couldn't have heard him correctly. Nervously, she rose, smoothing her wrinkled dress. It was torn and dirty. Her left-behind clothes had been having a hard time lately. If it continued, she was going to have to break down and buy herself something to wear.

"I said, you've got to get out of town for a while. You're the focal point of some of this, and Emmett's the other. I'll get you out of town first. You'll be easier."

"Wait." She shook her head. "Wait just a minute."

He went on as if he hadn't heard her. "Then I'll be able to concentrate on Emmett. The U.S. marshal will be here pretty soon to take him to Independence. He'll stand trial there. Everything will settle down."

"I can't leave town," she cried, her voice rising. She had to talk to Emmett again. She was sure she was so close to finding the man who'd betrayed them. "I've got a job. I've got to work to make a living."

"I can get you another job."

"No. No. No." Peach couldn't believe he was saying

this. She didn't want to give up her good job at Scurlock's for who knew what. "I've worked here for years. I'm making good money. You can't ask me to give it up."

He glanced at her with a vague smile. His face was tired and gaunt. Pain had deepened its lines. "It would just be for a few months. Maybe just till the winter's over."

"The winter!"

He didn't understand. He had no idea how hard it was for a girl to find a job that paid this much, that provided her a safe place to live. Because he had no idea, he couldn't conceive of how other bosses would take advantage of her. Luke Scurlock had never tried to lay a finger on her. She owed him her undying loyalty.

She crossed her arms over her chest. "I can't leave Luke."

"You'll be all right. I'll take care of it."

A wave of anger and disgust swept her. "You don't have the slightest idea how to do it."

She started for the door.

He caught her by the wrist. "Where do you think you're going?"

She twisted her wrist free. "You don't own me, Will Wesley. You don't pay me to do a job. You don't have any say in my life."

"I care about you," he protested.

"You've said that before, and I say, talk's cheap! Just because we've—" She didn't know what to say, didn't know what to call it. The very thought of her passion made her ashamed of herself.

She could feel the sting of disappointed tears. Will Wesley did things to her body, made her want things she mustn't have, made her lose control. If he hadn't made her so angry, she'd probably be mooning after him right then.

And he didn't want her. Why, he wanted her out of town! He was going to get her another job somewhere.

And she could just bet she knew what kind of job that would be. "You don't have any right to tell me what to do just because I've let you—er—take liberties with my person."

She lifted her chin. That was the way to tell him. She was proud that she'd remembered the phrase from several of the dime novels people had left in the hotel rooms.

One corner of his handsome mouth lifted in what she was sure was a sneer. "I didn't take anything that wasn't given."

He couldn't have hurt her more if he'd slapped her. She almost wished he had slapped her instead of throwing her passion in her face like that. There wasn't anything to say except, "Can I go now?"

He nodded. "You think about this. You'll see I'm right. Coffeyville is bad for you right now. It's dangerous. The next time, I might not be able to keep you from—"

She closed the door on his predictions.

"That's just about the damnedest thing I ever heard, Will. Have you lost your mind?"

He was startled at Luke Scurlock's reaction, puzzled. Didn't anybody understand the seriousness of Peach Smith's situation? He'd had to rescue her twice now. He said as much to Luke.

The innkeeper shook his head. "Listen. She can stay here in the hotel. We'll work out a schedule for her."

"Dammit. I've got to marshal this town. I can't be standing guard over her. If I get her out of town—"

Will broke off his sentence in the middle as Peach came to the bar to collect a pitcher of beer and some more mugs. She had to stand next to him while Luke filled it. She looked right through him.

When she walked away, Luke grinned. "Brrr. Colder in here than it is outside."

"If I get her out of town—" Will repeated.

"Where you planning on taking her?"

Will hadn't really thought about it too much. "Er— Oswego, or maybe across the state line in Missouri. Carthage is a big town. Lots of opportunity there."

"Good idea." Luke nodded sarcastically. "Everybody in Missouri just loves Kansas Jayhawkers dropping their discarded girlfriends off."

"No! I'll buy her a train ticket. She'll get a job."

"How? And where's she going to work?"

"She can get a job working like she works here."

"Oh, can she?" Luke's sneer was palpable. "Can she really?"

"Well, sure." Will could feel his ears beginning to turn red. Dammit! Luke wasn't cooperating. "You could write her a recommendation."

Luke folded his arms across his chest. "After she quit me flat in the busiest time of the year."

"That wouldn't be true," Will protested.

Luke looked around him at the bar. It was full. Peach was running to keep everybody satisfied. "Anybody who runs a place like this would be just as busy. He'd know something was fishy when Peach came in."

"I could write her a recommendation."

"They'd spot that a mile off. A recommendation from the marshal to get her out of town. Guess what they'd think." He looked Will dead center in the eye. "I'm a happily married man. Myrtle would just about take my head off if she got even the barest idea that I was messing around with Peach. But not every other man's like me."

"Now, just a minute."

"I'm guessing you'd take her over there yourself. Sort of set her up in business?" Luke raised one eyebrow and stroked his full mustache.

In a flash of understanding, Will saw how that would look. He couldn't take Peach to another town and tell somebody to hire her. They'd think she was bad. They'd think she'd been run out of town. A hotelman with a wandering eye would be on her before Will's dust settled in the street.

Even if he talked to the marshal of Oswego or whoever the law was in Carthage, they wouldn't believe him. They'd think he was lying to get rid of her. They'd probably suggest that she move on.

He felt his insides turn to stone as he saw the impossibility of the plan he'd outlined. Peach didn't want to go. He couldn't make her or take her without ruining everything for her.

He watched her waiting tables. The men liked her and respected her because of Luke Scurlock and because of him. Why, even dour old Neddy Barnes watched her like a hawk. Together the three of them made working there safe and pleasant for Peach. She was innocent—never mind her little slips with him. She was a good girl. Hell! She wasn't even a girl. She was a beautiful woman.

Wherever he took her, they'd turn her into a whore too quick to talk about. He couldn't do that to her.

She looked up at that moment and caught him staring at her. She kept her face impassive. Her eyes looked right through him, but he saw the blush rise in her cheeks. She was thinking about him, just as he was thinking about her. He could feel a little increase in his heart rate.

"What am I going to do?" he muttered.

"I suggest you act like a lawman," Luke responded immediately. "Find out who's doing this stuff. It don't make sense."

Will shook his head. He leaned against the bar, contemplating the problem. Luke uncorked another sarsaparilla and handed it to him. So distracted was he that he drank it without a shudder.

Luke polished the bar in front of him.

The two shared a morose silence.

Finally, Will set the bottle down on the bar with unnecessary force. He fished a nickel from his watch pocket, but Luke shook his head. "On the house."

"Much obliged." Will lifted his hat and ran his hand over his hair. "There's just no help for it," he said softly. "I've got to take care of her. It's just got to be."

Chapter Ten

Peach tucked a checkered napkin around the plate of food. On top of that she stacked a dozen fresh-baked molasses cookies protected by another napkin. Not that she had much chance to get anything to the jail while it was even slightly warm. The weather was terrible. The temperature had dipped below freezing during the night. The sunless morning had done nothing to raise it.

She wrapped a woolen muffler twice around her head and neck, tied it, and tucked the ends inside her coat. When she opened the door, the cold air rushed up her skirt. She shivered.

Poor Emmett Dalton! The cellblock didn't have a stove.

Will Wesley had come back to the hotel early that morning, nearly frozen. She'd served him a hot breakfast. While he was eating, she'd put hot bricks in his bed. He should sleep until the middle of the afternoon.

Turning her cheek away from the north wind, she hurried as fast as she dared across the frozen street. Even as cold as it was, she was determined to make one more try.

Surely, if she and Emmett put their heads together, he would remember something.

At the door of the jail, she put on what she hoped was a cheery if blue-lipped smile.

Bert Ayers had moved the desk chair close to the stove and smuggled in a quilt he brought from home. He was just getting comfortable when Peach walked in.

"I brought breakfast," she trilled. "Kind of late, but we had a busy morning."

He jumped to his feet, letting the quilt fall, and smiled as if he were not quite sure what to do. "That's good, Peach. Er—I've got to take it in."

"And something special for you." She handed him the napkin tied up like a hobo's bundle. "Molasses cookies. You'd better eat them while they're still the least bit warm. The weather's so cold, I'm afraid they cooled off."

He grinned like the kid he was as he sat down again and opened the napkin on his lap. His youthful face lit up. "Much obliged, Peach." He selected one and took the first bite. "Golly, these are good."

She took the keys off the hook and had the door unlocked while his mouth was too full of cookie to protest. "Enjoy them all."

He mumbled something, but he didn't rise and follow her. She closed the door behind her. "Here's your breakfast, Mr. Dalton," she announced loudly. "Come and get it while it's hot."

The room was terribly cold. A small drift of snow lay on the plank floor beneath the barred window. The prisoner must be nearly frozen to death. "Emmett," she whispered to the blanket-wrapped figure in the cell. "Emmett, it's me. Peach."

He stirred, but he didn't sit up and face her.

She crossed to the bars and set the plate down. "Emmett. Wake up. You've got to listen to me. You've got trouble. Do you remember a bearded man with a hoarse voice?"

He grunted and hunched his shoulder.

"Emmett. Think. A man with a thick, scratchy beard. The voice might have been disguised, so it might be someone we both know. He wanted me to find out where you all buried your money. But you didn't have any money. At least, Bob said you never did. What does he mean?"

"Damned if I know, and I don't think Emmett will either." Will Wesley swung his long legs over the bunk and sat up.

Peach toppled over backward in shock. "Where's Emmett?"

"I took him over to Doc's to spend the night. Last night was too cold in here for anybody, much less a man recovering from serious wounds." He opened the unlocked cell door and strolled out.

Looking up at him from flat on her back on the floor made her a little dizzy. He seemed taller than ever.

The way he was glaring down at her let her know she was in for a tough lecture. She scrambled toward the door. He held out his hand. "Come on. Let's get back in the office before Bert gets all the cookies eaten."

"You tricked me." She said it even though she realized how foolish it sounded.

"That's right. Figured you were too stubborn not to make one more try. Especially when I told you I was going to move Emmett."

She was too mad to take his hand, so he stooped to place it under her arm and haul her to her feet.

She tried to shrug him off, but he held her firmly and guided her back into the warm office. "Stay gone about an hour, Bert. When you come back, you're marshal for the next day and a half."

"Yes, sir."

"Wait." Peach called too late.

With the rest of his cookies wrapped in the napkin, Bert Ayers was disappearing out the jailhouse door.

Will led her over beside the stove. "Sit down."

She tried to bolt, but he pushed her down into the chair. "I said, sit down!"

She clasped her hands in front of her, the way she'd sat in front of Sister Agnes Mary. The marshal was going to deliver a lecture, and she wasn't going to like it at all.

He pulled up the only other chair across the room and sat opposite her. "Now. Tell me about this man with the hoarse voice and scratchy beard."

She should have told him last night. He wouldn't have been so mad. One glance into his fierce eyes and she dropped her gaze to concentrate on her hands clasped in her lap. She could see why Will had been a successful marshal before he'd been hurt. If she'd been his prisoner, she'd have broken down and confessed.

"He whispered in my ear last night. Right after Corny got shot." She cleared her throat and glanced up.

Will's brows drew together. His scowl was frightening. "He got close enough to you to whisper in your ear."

"Y-yes."

"What else?"

She hesitated. This was the unforgivable part. "I think he was the one who shot Corny."

Will came out of his chair like a shot. His face darkened like a thundercloud. "And you didn't tell me about this? Have you lost your mind, girl? You were a material witness to what could have been a murder."

She hunched her shoulders against the anger in his voice. "No, I wasn't. I didn't actually see him shoot Corny. It was dark, so I only heard the shot. I would have told you. I swear I would. I just wanted to warn Emmett first." She straightened her spine and laced her fingers together in her lap. "And anyway. I thought—that is—I have an idea who this man might be."

"What?" He was hanging over her now. He was simply

furious. "You know who he might be and you didn't tell me?"

"I—I don't *know*. I only *think* I know. And anyway, you can't do anything about it."

"The hell I can't. Who is it?"

Why couldn't she make him understand? "I don't know," she repeated with the emphasis on the last word.

"Tell me," he grated out.

She hunched her shoulders as high as they would go. "Mr. M-Mungerson."

"Lemuel Mungerson." Will dropped into his chair. His face relaxed.

"That's right."

He ran his hand around the back of his neck. "Why'd you think he'd hang out with the likes of Corny Dahlerheidt?"

"Well, he wanted me to ask Emmett where the Daltons buried their money."

Will shook his head again. "He ordered me to find out. But I can't believe he'd do anything more than order and bluster. He's just not the type."

"But—"

"He thinks too much of his skin to take a chance on getting shot. And he thinks too much of his reputation to take a chance on being recognized."

She digested this piece of information. It made sense at least from Will's point of view. She wasn't convinced.

"Tell me exactly what happened," he prompted.

Quickly she told the story. When she came to the part where the man held a smoking gun barrel against her cheek, Will growled low in his throat. At last, she faltered to a halt. Still staring at her hands, she wondered if he was about to arrest her.

Instead, Will dropped down in the chair and laid his hand over hers. His voice was gentle. "Why didn't you tell me all this last night?"

She hesitated some more. "I wish I had. But I thought I had to warn Emmett. And then, when I thought about Mungerson, I—er—I didn't want you to know."

He looked amazed. "Why not?"

"Because if you went after him, you'd lose your job."

"Lord, girl." He breathed softly. "Don't ever do anything like that again. Peach Smith, you've taken a terrible chance. You withheld information that endangered yourself because"—he reared back in his chair as if he couldn't take all of her in—"because you were protecting my job."

She kept staring at her hands. The silence grew in the office.

At last he leaned forward in the chair, his elbows on his knees, his hands hanging between them. Then he raised his left arm and touched her cheek. Uncertain, she looked at him. He didn't look angry anymore. Instead, he looked sad.

At last he gave himself a shake. "Let's go."

She drew back too slowly. His hand locked around her wrist. He pulled her to her feet. "What? Where?"

"You can't stay here any longer. And you won't go somewhere safe of your own accord." He put his arm around her shoulders and hurried her out the door. The wind blew the sign above the marshal's office. It creaked as it swung.

"Wait! You can't— Where are you taking me?"

She looked around her frantically. At that moment the streets were totally empty. Despite her protests, he turned her down the alley where the Daltons had died. The wind whistled like an angry spirit between the buildings. Into Kloehr's Livery Stable he guided her.

"Too bad the day's so cold. I'd sure rather take you on a nice warm day."

"Then don't take me today," she protested, hanging back against his arm. "Don't take me." Another thought struck her. "Where? Where are you taking me?"

"You'll see."

In the dimness she made out the shapes of three horses waiting patiently in the shed row. Two were saddled and bridled. The third was loaded like a prospector's mule.

"No."

He led her up on the left side of the smallest animal. "Climb aboard."

"No!" His left arm snaked around her middle, his right across her breasts. He lifted her off her feet.

She kicked out once, then stopped as she narrowly missed the horse. She couldn't kick it. It wasn't the poor thing's fault that she was being kidnapped.

She was being kidnapped. "You're kidnapping me," she raged indignantly. "This is against the law."

"Report me to the marshal." He held her twisting against his chest until she finally stopped. Then he put his mouth against her ear. "You can go out of here in the saddle, upright and comfortable, or you can go out belly down for a mile or two. But believe me, Peach, you're going."

"I'll hate you forever."

"There's more than one that has." He squeezed her extra hard. "Your choice. Say which it's to be."

"Upright." She forced the word out between clenched teeth.

"Good girl." He dragged in a deep breath.

She remembered his shoulder. "Don't. I'll get on by myself."

He stopped in mid-motion and set her on her feet.

She spun in his arms in time to see the relief in his face.

He hooked his right thumb into his belt loop as he stepped back. "Climb aboard. We're wasting daylight."

She scrambled awkwardly into the saddle. Where her bare legs touched, the leather made her shudder. "I'm not dressed to ride."

"If you don't make a fuss, we won't be in the saddle too

long." He gathered the lead lines on her mount and the packhorse and swung up on his own.

"I'll get the door for you, Marshal." Neither of them had seen John Kloehr standing in the shadows. The livery stable owner ambled down the shedrow.

Had he been there all along?

The hair rose on the back of Peach's neck and on her arms. As he passed, he leered up at her from under his hat brim. She narrowed her eyes and stared down accusingly. She didn't care what he thought.

She was nearly sure that Kloehr was the one who'd told Marshal Connelly. He could have been hiding there in the stable the night the Daltons had made their plans. He'd made a lot of extra money posing for photographers with his rifle and selling pieces of horses' manes and tails, claiming that they'd come from the Daltons' dead mounts. Maybe he also believed the Daltons had buried money.

She pulled her horse back when it would have followed Will's out of the stable at a trot.

"You did it, didn't you?" she whispered to Kloehr.

The stableman's head snapped up. Narrowing her eyes, she tried to imagine what he would look like with a heavy, scratchy beard. Would anyone recognize him?

"Did what?" Kloehr's mouth spread underneath his thick mustache. "Shot your fancy Dalton. Damn right I did."

"No, I mean—"

Kloehr struck her horse a sharp slap on the hindquarters. "Get on outa hyar."

She heard the stable door rattle closed behind them.

All of Coffeyville seemed to have retreated indoors. The lowering steel-gray sky looked as if it would drop a foot of snow at any minute. Here and there, a tiny early flake wafted down.

She'd be lucky if she didn't catch pneumonia. On the

other hand, the choppy trot was jarring her teeth. She had to concentrate to stay on.

As they crossed the railroad tracks, she caught hold of the saddle horn. She wasn't a good rider. She'd been on a horse only a few times in her life. The orphanage hadn't had mounts for the children to ride and now she worked all day.

As they rode past Pearl Bridger's, Will urged his horse into a canter and then a gallop. Peach bit her tongue as her mount stretched out. From there on, she had to hang on for dear life.

He watched her ride out behind the marshal. She was bouncing all over the saddle. He grinned. She was going to be sore. She didn't have any idea how sore.

His hand caressed the butt of his gun as he sighted it between the marshal's shoulder blades. *Shoot him. Shoot him now!*

But they were hitting a pretty good clip now. And suppose he didn't kill the marshal. Suppose he didn't fall out of the saddle dead, but got up and came after him, wound and all.

They'd made about a mile when Will glanced back over his shoulder. He almost called a halt right then and there.

He'd never seen anything like the expression on Peach's face. It was a cross between pain and fear. He'd never thought about how little chance she had to ride. Instantly, he eased down to a lope.

He'd ridden horses since he was big enough to climb up the corral fence and slip aboard. He'd never thought about how a girl—or boy for that matter—city born and bred might not know how to ride.

He'd never thought much about the whole business, but

he guessed fewer and fewer people rode horses anymore. If they wanted to travel great distances, they rode the trains. They rode in wagons and carriages, buckboards and gigs, along roads that were smoother and better planed, although some still had deep ruts. In large towns the streets were even being paved with bricks. The whole state of Kansas was becoming a civilized place.

He should have rented a gig and driven her, although the way it was starting to snow, he doubted he could make it back to town with wheels.

He regretted his mistake, and Peach was suffering for his stupidity. The wind had picked up and the snow was coming down fast enough to drift into the ruts in the road. He hated to do it, but he increased the pace of the horses.

Peach was numb everywhere except her bottom and the insides of her thighs when a farmhouse took shape among the swirling flakes.

Will turned in the saddle. His hat brim was full of snow. The shoulders of his sheepskin jacket were covered with it. His eyelashes and the stubble on his cheeks were dotted with snowflakes. "We're here."

"Thank you, dear Lord!" Peach prayed reverently. "Where's here?"

Instead of answering, he swung down and came back for her. He pulled her out of the saddle, bore her up the frozen steps, and set her down on a wide wooden porch. He had to hold her upright while she keened through her teeth as blood coursed through her numbed feet.

"Stomp around a bit," he said in an apologetic tone. "You'll be warm soon. I promise."

"Stomping around on a front porch isn't going to get me warm," she sneered. She couldn't ever remember being so cold.

"Come on in and make yourself at home. I'll build a fire."

The front door had carvings around an oval pane of beveled glass and a glass doorknob. He swung it open.

She shot him a withering look before she limped across the threshold.

The house was dark and dank. The only difference she could feel between the indoors and outdoors was the wind didn't blow and the snow didn't fall on her.

Will closed the door and headed on through the archway into what must be the parlor.

Peach followed him, taking in everything with bleak eyes. "Who lives here?"

"I do. That is, I used to. I haven't in a long time."

He knelt before a small pot-bellied stove. It stood out from one corner of the room on a metal plate. Against the wall behind it, a large open woodbox was filled to the top of the lid. He stripped off his gloves and set about starting the fire.

She stood in the middle of the room, her arms wrapped around her body. She was almost too cold and too miserable to be angry. Almost. "Why did you bring me here?"

The flame caught instantly. He closed the grate and stood up. He smiled a little diffidently. "I brought you here to live. You can live here."

She shook her head incredulously. "Why?"

"I wanted to keep you safe."

"Why didn't you just send me to jail?"

"Aw, Peach—"

"Now, you listen to me, Will Wesley." She started for him, her fists clenched at her sides. "You might as well send me to jail as set me down out here in the big middle of nowhere. I didn't do anything really wrong. You know that. I only said a man with a beard *might* have shot Corny Dahlerheidt."

"This doesn't have anything to do with that."

"It doesn't?"

"No." He brushed by her.

As she followed him out into the hall, he increased the length of his stride. Before she could say more, he was out in the yard, stripping the packs off the third horse. One at a time, he slung them up onto the porch.

"Here's food and"—he hesitated —"other things. Things you'll need."

"For what?" She couldn't believe the marshal of Coffeyville, Kansas, had brought her out in the big middle of nowhere to leave her.

He pulled his gloves back on and swung up into his saddle. "I've got to go back to town. If I ride real hard, I'll get back in time to catch the train."

"Train? What train?" She came to the railing on the porch and grasped it. "You can't leave me here."

"You'll be fine. I've got you taken care of. Now I've got to take Emmett Dalton to Independence, Missouri. The U.S. marshals are going to take him into federal custody there, and he'll be out of danger."

She shook her head. "You're leaving me out here." She looked up into the thickly falling snow. "I'll die, Will. Oh, please. Don't go. Oh, Will."

He urged the horse forward. "You've got a fire. The sheets on the bed are clean. There's plenty of blankets. Here's more than enough food."

"Will Wesl—"

He leaned out of the saddle and caught her around the back of the neck. The brim of his hat brushed her forehead as he kissed her. Once. Twice, a bit harder. Then a third time, softly and tenderly. Then he let her go.

"I've taken care of everything, Peach. Stay in. Stay warm. I'll be back in four days, five at the most."

He reined his horse in a circle. The other two followed. They were moving away into the whiteness.

"Will! Don't you leave me! Will! I'll lose my job! Will!

I hate you!'' She came down the steps. Her shoes slipped.
Only a quick grab for the railing saved herself a hard fall.

"I hate you!"

He slapped the reins across the animal's neck. It stepped
out smartly. In less than a minute they had disappeared.

With a grim smile on his face, Luke Scurlock set a bottle
of sarsaparilla on the bar in front of Will Wesley.

The marshal looked at it with loathing. "Got any
coffee?"

"Yeah, but it's strong enough to float horseshoes."

"Sounds about right."

While Luke went for the coffee, Will stripped off his
gloves and slapped them on the bar. His burning gaze
roved over the bottles of whiskey, rum, and gin lined up
on the shelf in front of the mirror.

He ached all over from his bruising ride. Twenty miles
to the farm and twenty miles back even in a snow had once
been nothing. Now he wanted only to buy one of those
bottles and curl up with it until his shoulder in particular
and the rest of his body in general stopped throbbing.

Until he couldn't hear Peach screaming "I hate you!"

He clenched his hand. It itched to curve around one of
those bottles. His shoulder throbbed as if pitchforks
stabbed him again and again. He closed his eyes.

When he opened them, he was staring at himself in the
mirror. God! He looked fifty, maybe sixty years old if he
looked a day. His graying hair was tangled in his eyebrows.
He hadn't shaved in a week. His eyes were sunk so far back
in his head, they looked like two burnt holes in a blanket.

If a man rode into town looking the way he did, he'd
have to arrest him. His hand twitched. He wanted a bottle
the worst way.

Luke set the cup of coffee in front of him. It was black

as hell and oily. Steam rose from it. "Did you get the job done?"

"Yep!" Will held out the coffee. "One jigger of sweetener."

Without comment, Luke added a dollop of whiskey to it.

Will drank it down with barely a shudder.

"Good enough." Luke polished a spot on the walnut bar.

Through the early evening, the mournful three-note whistle of a distant train called. Time to get Emmett Dalton.

"Much obliged." He fished in his vest pocket.

"Keep it," Luke advised. "As bad off as you look right now, a drink isn't going to make any difference."

Will pulled on his gloves and walked out. The snow had stopped and the wind had died. He took a deep breath. At least he hadn't bought a bottle of whiskey. He took comfort in that. Just a jigger mixed with the coffee had warmed him a little.

With a sense of resolve he headed toward Doc's. When he got Emmett Dalton out of the town, things would settle down. There'd be nothing to keep the strangers there. Two weeks, three at the most he could bring Peach back into town.

In the meantime he could visit her several times a week. He smiled at that idea. Almost as if he were courting her. His smile faded. He mustn't think thoughts like that. She was a young, pretty girl. He was a burned-out case.

He opened the door of the doctor's office.

"Ready, Emmett," he called.

He watched the marshal leave, cursing his luck.

No, he cursed the marshal. The man hadn't breathed a word to anybody about what he was planning to do with

Emmett Dalton. Too late, he'd discovered that Emmett wasn't going to be returned to the jail.

Instead, the outlaw was being taken out of state by train.

On the other hand, this might be his best chance. He could buy a ticket and get close to the outlaw, close enough to free him. Then he could take him to someplace quiet, where Emmett would tell where the Dalton brothers had buried all the gold they stole.

Emmett would tell him out of gratitude, he thought. If he didn't, then maybe the last Dalton would lead the way to the gold to save his life. Of course, he couldn't let Emmett go free after they'd dug it up. He consoled himself with the knowledge that the outlaw was a murderer.

He smiled. He'd be doing the state of Kansas a favor.

He waited until Scurlock squatted behind the bar to line up his clean glasses, then eeled through the swinging doors into the dark dining room. Silently, he moved down the narrow hall and out through the back door.

In the yard he stared at the cookshack. The glow from the big stove shone through the cracks in the door.

If this didn't work, he still had one more chance. If Bob Dalton had told one other person, Peach Smith had to be the one. He was pretty sure she knew. She'd be the easiest, but he didn't know where the marshal had taken her. He couldn't kill the marshal, because then he might never find Peach.

Think about that later, he advised himself. Emmett Dalton was out of the jail. He hurried across the frozen ground toward the depot.

Peach wrapped her arms around her body and shuddered. Not with cold. She sat with her knees barely a foot from the grate of the pot-bellied stove. Its warmth surrounded her and made her feel wonderful.

No, she wasn't cold. The chair that she'd dragged up

to sit in was a big leather one with wings, so all the heat stayed around her.

She wasn't hungry either. Will knew how to pack good things to eat. In fact, she'd been amazed at the variety of canned goods, so many expensive things she'd never tasted before. She'd eaten half a can of sardines on crackers spread with yellow mustard. She'd made herself a pot of tea. Then, for dessert, she'd opened a can of peaches in heavy syrup. With a mental snap of her fingers in Mr. Wesley's direction, she'd eaten half of them right out of the can.

Her stomach was pooched out, she'd made such a pig of herself. For breakfast in the morning, she intended to have the rest. That'd teach him.

Truth to tell, she couldn't imagine being more comfortable. Except she was so alone. And she'd never been alone in her life. Every so often the wind rattled the panes. She didn't dare go to the window because outside was ghostly whiteness.

Here she had no orphans like herself in beds next to hers. No people in the rooms in the hotel. No town around her. She was alone, miles and miles from nowhere. She was scared to death.

"We never had much more'n a few dollars ahead," Emmett Dalton mourned. With his wrist handcuffed to the iron seat frame, he stared out the window into the darkness. The interior of the coach was nearly dark as well. The kerosene lamps at each end had been turned low. Across the aisle a man snored lustily.

The youngest Dalton gave something suspiciously like a sob. "God! I wish I could turn back the clock."

Will smiled faintly at the poetic turn of phrase. Emmett Dalton had evidently spent more time in school than Grat or Bob. Will believed that the older Daltons, especially

Bob, had gotten about what they deserved—a place in the same cemetery where they'd put four good men. Emmett, unfortunately, had been dealt a bad hand that he was going to have play for the rest of his life.

"Can you think of anybody who might have gotten the idea you'd buried a lot of money?"

Emmett sighed. "Bob used to talk about the James gang's buried loot. Jesse's treasure." He shook his head. "Grat pretty much believed in it, but I didn't. That's a laugh. I didn't believe in it, and now I'm having to run because of it."

Will nodded. He knew what was coming next, but he waited to hear Emmett say it.

"Every member of the gang gets a split," the surviving Dalton recounted mournfully. "And you know Jesse and Frank had wives and babies to support. That takes lots of money. They spent it pretty fast too. Just like Bob and Grat did. They never really knew how much they had in their pockets until it was gone."

"Bob gave Peach a little purse," Will said softly. "He told her it was all he had."

Emmett looked at him curiously, then nodded as though he didn't care. "Must have been pretty little, 'cause—let me tell you, Marshal—people lie about how much got stolen."

He directed a penetrating stare at Will. "You know how you'll read in the paper that fifty thousand dollars was stolen from the Wells Fargo safe. Some crook is just trying to cheat his insurance company. There probably wasn't five thousand all told on the whole damn train."

The surviving Dalton used his free hand to smooth his longish hair. "Bob was kind of jealous of Jesse and Cole, us all being cousins, don't you know? He shot off his mouth a lot. He liked the gals to think he was a whole lot smarter and richer than he was."

"Someone believed him."

Emmett shrugged. "I could give you a list long as my arm of people he'd bragged to, but anybody who was around Bob longer than five minutes could figure him out."

"You didn't."

Emmett's mouth snapped shut. He returned his gaze to the darkness. The train chugged on, the wheels clackety-clacking over the rails. When he spoke finally, his voice quivered. "Do you think they'll hang me, Marshal?"

Will pulled his hat over his face and settled down. "Four citizens died, Emmett. One of them was unarmed. What do you think?"

"Yoo-hoo!"

Someone was knocking at the door and stamping his feet at the same time. Or so Peach thought as she tripped on the quilt and tumbled out of the chair.

"Yoo-hoo!" Someone opened the front door.

Peach rolled over and staggered to her feet. Thank heaven, she'd slept in her clothes. Otherwise, she'd be caught by a perfect stranger—

"Hy-dee-do." A woman came round the archway. "Will said he was a-bringin' you out."

"Hello."

"I'm Narcissey Jellicoe." She clumped into the room and extended a hand wrapped in wool rags.

"Pleased to meet you." Peach couldn't keep from staring.

Narcissey was a picture. She looked huge until Peach realized that the woman was wearing layer upon layer of garments. Men's trousers hung out from under at least one petticoat and several skirts. The top of a union suit showed above the V necks of at least two shirts, a knitted vest, a sweater, and a coat.

Narcissey made straight for the fire, turned around and

hiked up her skirts. "It's blowin' out there. Wouldn't o' come over just for anybody, you ken. But Will Wesley's a good boy."

Peach hardly thought of him as a boy. She smiled as much about that as about the sight of the older woman switching her bottom back and forth in front of the grate.

"I just wanted to be sure you got everything you need." She twitched her bottom again. "But if you got a fire and somethin' to eat, ever'thing's all right." She cackled as if she'd said something funny.

Peach stood in the center of the parlor and looked around. Two chairs, a small round table, and a lamp comprised the furniture. Substitute a bed for one chair and it would look like a hotel room rather than a parlor. She guessed she had everything she needed.

"I brung you some poultry. Left it on the front porch. It's fresh kilt, so ain't no hurry."

"Thank you so much." Peach smiled graciously. "If you'd like to sit down by the fire, I could cook us some lunch. I'm a good cook."

The old woman looked around one more time. "No, thanks. Can't stand it long." Her eyes glistened. "I see Netta ever'where I look."

Peach knew better than to pry.

Narcissey stopped in the archway. "Never had a lick of sense. Hurt Will somethin' fierce."

A second later Peach heard the door slam and the heavy boots clomp across the porch. She was left wondering.

Chapter Eleven

The whistle shrieked. The coach shuddered and jolted to a stop for the engine to take on water and fuel. Will's neck protested vilely as he tried to straighten it.

The lamps at each end of the coach had smoked out. Likewise, the stoves were giving off hardly any heat. The middle of the car, where he and Emmett sat, was so cold, his breath fogged in front of his face when he yawned.

He glanced at his prisoner. Wedged in the corner made by the seat and the window, Emmett slept on.

Will stretched so far as his right shoulder would allow. It was paining him like the dickens. Cautiously, he put his hand under his clothing to feel. His mouth tightened in a harsh line. The gnarled flesh still felt like someone else's body. And when he exerted pressure in certain spots, it hurt like a poisoned tooth.

He felt a gust of cold air as the door at the back of the coach opened and closed. Pity the poor conductor. Thank heavens, he didn't have to go out on the platforms at each stop.

He held his fingers against a particularly painful knob of flesh, less than an inch in diameter but throbbing like blazes. Was it more swollen than usual? Did it feel hot?

He took his hand away and tilted his head back. He was bothering himself needlessly. He couldn't do anything about his shoulder on a train headed for Independence.

He heard a noise behind him. Loud snoring broke off with a snort. Feet shuffled. Someone mumbled a soft apology.

Will didn't bother to turn. Almost immediately the snoring resumed. A second later, the train jerked forward. It shuddered through its length as the engineer tested its couplings. Distinctly, he heard a thud and then more hesitant footsteps.

The fellow was taking his own good time getting down the aisle. Will half turned in his seat. A dark shape loomed behind him.

The train jerked again, harder this time, as the iron wheels began to roll forward.

Will heard a whistling through the air. Out of the blackness, iron caught the brim of his hat, missing his head but landing squarely on his shoulder.

He screamed.

Later he would think he hadn't known he was capable of the sound that he made. But the pain was intense, so devastating, so like a lightning bolt racing through every part of his body that he lost all control.

"What the hell?" a man's voice roared.

"What happened?" A woman's voice came high and shrill.

"Goddamn! A man can't sleep fer nothin'."

"Somebody turn on the light."

All around him, passengers were jolted out of sound sleeps. A woman called her husband's name. A child began to cry.

"Marshal! What's wrong?" Emmett Dalton's left arm caught Will as he rolled off the bench onto his knees.

He heard himself grunting like a pig. He tried to set his teeth against it, but the pain was too intense. He tried to answer, but all he could do was gasp for air.

"Somebody turn on the goddamn light!"

Bodies brushed past. People milled around, bumping into one another in the aisle. The train was picking up speed.

"This one's outa kerosene," came the report.

"Same back here."

Doors at both ends of the coach opened. Light flashed down the aisle from the back of the train. Everyone froze where they stood.

The conductor flashed his lantern up and down the aisle, trying to figure out what was going on. From behind him, his brakeman stepped into the light. "What's going on here? Settle down! Now, just settle down! Please. Please, ma'am. The train's moving. Everybody, please get back to your seats."

Less than an hour later, Will and Emmett were stretched out on benches in the caboose. The stove was blazing and the warmth was beginning to ease Will's shoulder.

"Was he after you or me?"

Will squinched his eyes tightly closed as the train took a curve and swayed him toward the right. "Both of us."

"You reckon?" The youngest Dalton's voice cracked a little on the last syllable. The last two months had been an agony for him. Like a man in a runaway stagecoach, he'd been helpless to do anything but hang on.

"I figure he was out to knock me unconscious. If he hadn't made so much noise coming down the aisle, he'd probably have killed me. As hard as he hit, I imagine he would have caved in my skull. I'd have dropped like a stone.''

''I was still handcuffed.''

''It wouldn't have taken him long to fish the key out of my pocket and unlock you.''

Emmett kept his eyes focused on the swaying shadows created by the lamp hanging from the roof. ''I wouldn't have gone.''

Will snorted. ''Sure you would. You'd have been a fool not to. You didn't know who it was. Still don't. It could have been one of your brothers.''

''Them. Not much. Haven't heard a word from anybody named Dalton. Not even Ma,'' he commented bitterly. ''They didn't even take Bob and Grat back home to bury.''

''One of your gang?''

''Indian Territory last time I heard. There never was a Dalton gang like Jesse and Cole had. Charley Pierce and that skunk Bill Doolin didn't think we oughta rob them banks.'' He groaned as he adjusted his position. ''They was sure right.''

''So—'' Will had to ask, although he already knew the answer.

''Someone looking for the 'Dalton treasure.' '' Emmett snorted. ''God! If they just don't kill me, I'll do my time. This is like some nightmare, only I can't wake up. He about killed you. If he'd done it, he'd've killed me when he found out there wasn't any treasure.''

Will didn't answer. He was trying to get into a comfortable position. He was dead for sleep and sick with pain. He needed to rest.

As the train rumbled on, Emmett muttered, ''Crime just doesn't pay.''

He'd missed. He couldn't believe his luck. He clamped his fist against his bared teeth to keep from cursing. Before he realized what he'd done, he tasted blood. He'd bitten his knuckle. He forced himself to relax. He was just lucky that he'd knocked all the ambition out of the marshal. Otherwise, he'd have had to jump off the train.

Emmett Dalton was beyond his reach. He'd never be able to get to the man in the caboose because he couldn't move around in the dark. The conductor and brakeman had gone through the coaches and filled each lamp well. The lights burned now.

Many people were awake, too upset to settle back down. A card game had started across the aisle. He'd been asked to join.

He'd refused. He didn't trust his luck anymore.

He looked around the car again. Was one of the poker players staring at him?

He coughed deeply, using his clenched fist to smother the sound. Then he forced himself to clear his throat and lower his hand slowly, slowly relaxing it. He didn't think the man noticed the blood.

Closing his eyes, he sat very, very still, letting every muscle in his face relax until his eyelids drooped. He pretended to go to sleep.

When he opened his eyes after a few minutes, the man across the aisle was playing a card.

He directed his attention to the lamp flame by the door. When he closed his eyelids, it glowed red through the thin skin. It made him smile a little, thinking of blood and fire.

Peach plucked the plump guinea hen Narcissey Jellicoe had brought, but her mind was on the woman's last statement. Who was Netta? And more important, what had she done to Will?

Peach felt depressed. Of course, the marshal was much older than she was. Naturally, he'd had his share of women.

He might even have been married. Might *be* married. Or maybe he was widowed.

Was Narcissey Jellicoe his mother-in-law? Had her daughter died of some terrible wasting illness that had destroyed Will's happiness forever?

"Stop it," she told herself sternly. "Stop right there."

She didn't know any of this. Not any. Netta could be his mother. Or no kin at all. This house could have belonged to Narcissey Jellicoe's best friend. Will could have bought it.

She put the hen into a pot of water to which she added some onions and carrots. The bird was plump. She'd make dumplings and later have a stew.

It was too much for one person to eat. She heard the silence of the house. Even the wind had died down. She couldn't hear a solitary sound.

With a cry she thumped her fist against the washed oak of the drainboard. Will Wesley was a skunk. She couldn't wait until he showed up there. She'd give him a tongue-lashing that would set him back on his ear.

She couldn't believe how much she missed working at Scurlock's. She'd been making good money. She had her regulars that she joshed with every day. She had drummers who came through town regularly and tipped well when she put extra helpings on their plates.

Darn him! She was a city girl.

She missed her weekly bath. Now that Luke had put in a bathroom on the second floor, she'd gotten used to being warm and clean.

She wrapped her hand around her hair and pulled it forward over her shoulder. It needed to be washed. Funny how she'd gotten used to things like that.

Will Wesley was a good marshal. Everybody was settling down and coming to that realization. But he didn't have to take his job so seriously. He'd practically kidnapped her and hidden her out here.

She wasn't that important and she certainly didn't know anything. If she could have just talked to Emmett, especially about the man with the scratchy beard—

Her eyes narrowed as she thought of the man who'd brought her there. Sometimes she felt so tender toward him. He'd been so good to her in so many ways. Her nipples prickled as she thought of the man who'd taught her the feelings her body was capable of. She felt warm all over.

Sometimes she could believe she loved him even when she knew he couldn't ever love her.

And others—like now. He made her so angry, she wanted to bash his head in.

Anger was good. She'd used it before to get past the bad times. She looked around her. She'd take her mind off her troubles by exploring the house, not that she had much to explore. Later the sun would come out and she could go for a walk. Perhaps she could find where Narcissey Jellicoe lived and learn more about Will Wesley.

She was surprised to find the house was nicer than anything she'd ever been in, except that it had almost no furniture. One bedroom contained only a tall mahogany four-poster sitting in solitary splendor on a red and blue turkey carpet. Otherwise, the room was bare. It contained no armoire, no dressing table, no nightstand.

The bed was made up with embroidered sheets and pillowcases covered by a beautiful quilt that hung almost to the floor. She looked around for the stepstool to climb into it, but in the end she had to scramble up without one.

The pattern was the flower garden, hundreds of bright-colored hexagons sewn together with tiny careful stitches. It was the kind of work the nuns had tried to teach her to do, the kind of work for which she'd never had the patience.

Feeling guilty to be sitting on it, she climbed down and moved on to the other bedroom. Its hardwood floor had four large dents, indicating that a big bed had sat there. Along the wall were the dents of an armoire. Someone had taken a whole room of furniture. She wondered who, wondered about Netta.

What must have been the dining room was empty except for a mahogany sideboard with a missing drawer. It must have been the partitioned drawer for the silver, because she couldn't find one. The heavy red velvet drapes were somewhat faded from the sun. Curtain rods that would have supported lace or sheers lay on the floor beneath the windows as if someone had carelessly dropped them. Had Netta taken what she wanted with her when she left?

Only the kitchen retained its furnishings, the big iron stove, the cupboard, the center table with its butcher-block corner that carried the scars of knives and cleavers.

Peach didn't know what to think, but she decided that she was going to have to control her imagination. The simplest explanation was that Will Wesley had bought the house without furniture and had moved in only what he absolutely needed.

Still, she hated the emptiness of the place. It made her feel sorry for Will. Perhaps that explained—

"Stop that!" she commanded herself. The sound of her voice startled her.

She had to get out of there. She had to get back to town. She pulled on her coat and went out onto the porch.

They'd traveled east. She was sure of that, because they'd crossed the railroad tracks as they rode out of Coffeyville. She squinted up at the sun. If she walked with it at her back until it passed overhead, she should be able eventually to find the railroad tracks. From there she could—

A gust of icy wind rattled the branches of the dormant oak in the front yard.

She wrapped her arms around her middle and turned her cheek away from it. She was no fool. She didn't have any idea how far she'd come. The shortest day of the year was approaching. The ground was icy hard and slippery. She could walk for ten miles and be caught out at night, then she would freeze to death.

"Damn you, Will Wesley," she called to the empty yard. "You'd better get on back here soon. The longer I stay, the madder I'm going to be."

"The longer I put it off, the madder she's going to be." Will downed his sarsaparilla as if it were quinine and stared morosely at himself in the mirror above the bar in Scurlock's.

He'd spent the past three days in bed with a cold so bad, he was sure it was going to turn into pneumonia. He'd begun to get sick in Independence. The train ride back had been a nightmare. His shoulder had swollen to twice its size, and it was now so sore that he couldn't move his arm above his chest.

Coughs racked him because his ribs were somehow involved. He would bet even money his collarbone was cracked, but he didn't bother to go to the doctor. It was so swollen by the time he'd turned Emmett over to U.S. Marshal Jeptha Hughes that the best doctor in the territory wouldn't have been able to tell.

He dreaded doctors anyway. He wouldn't let them punch and prod him when he was pretty sure they couldn't do a thing for him.

Now he stared into Luke Scurlock's sympathetic eyes and wished he could go back upstairs and go to bed.

"I didn't mean to leave her out there this long," he sighed. "I'd planned to be back on the next train and maybe go out and spend the week getting acquainted. Instead, she's been out there nearly a week alone."

"You thought about marrying that girl, Will?"

"Thought, yeah. But then I look at my shoulder in the shaving mirror and that's as far as it goes."

Luke polished the bar in long, slow swipes. Will waited for the innkeeper to argue, but Luke was silent.

Will finished the last of his drink and stalked out.

"Um-um, Miss Peach Smith. You sure do make good biscuits." Narcissey helped herself to another and swiped it through the melted butter on her plate. "Makin' biscuits is a gift. There's most that can't do it. Like me. My biscuits'd kill a dog if'n one happened to fall on the pore thing's head."

They chuckled together. Yesterday, when the sun had come out for a few minutes, Peach had found the old woman's house by simply backtracking her through the ankle-deep snow.

She'd knocked on the door and been invited in for dinner. Now she was returning the favor.

Narcissey popped the last of the biscuits into her mouth, chewed reflectively, and leaned back in her chair. "I'm real pleased to see you here," she opined. "I don't guess you're best pleased to see me."

Peach's eyes widened. "I can't think why you'd say that." She looked around her at the warm kitchen that was so much warmer because Narcissey was there. Just beyond the windows the day was bluish-gray with fine mist that would probably turn to sleet if the temperature dropped. "I'm alone out here and you're really good company."

"Yeah, but I'm the skeleton in the closet." Narcissey tilted her head to one side. "He ain't told you, has he?"

Peach didn't pretend not to understand. "No. He hasn't told me anything."

"My Netta was married to Will until he got hurt." Narcissey stirred the sugar in her coffee as if it hadn't dissolved five minutes before.

Right on the very first guess. "I didn't know he was married."

Narcissey put the spoon down and tasted and sighed. "He ain't. No more. Netta was always crazy for what she didn't have no business havin'."

Peach didn't know what to say.

"When Will got shot, she went down to Fort Smith to take care of him"—Narcissey's eyes brimmed with tears; she blinked hard—"as well she should. But she took one look and left him flat." The old woman sank back in her chair, nursing her coffee cup.

"Oh, poor Will," Peach whispered.

Narcissey nodded. "Come through here with a fella in some kind of starched-front shirt and a derby. They loaded the bedroom stuff that come from St. Louis in the wagon and whatever else they could steal and took off."

Peach was speechless remembering the gaping hole in the sideboard and the curtain rods tossed on the floor. She couldn't imagine how a woman could do something like that. No wonder Will stayed drunk. He was suffering two kinds of pain. She shook her head.

Narcissey straightened in her chair. Her mouth quivered. "I seen 'em and come runnin' over. 'What you doin'?' I yelled.

"Netta wasn't gonna answer me, but I grabbed her by the shoulders and shook her till her teeth rattled. 'Where's your husband?' I yelled.

" 'He's dead.'

"But I could tell right off she was lyin'. 'Not Will Wesley,' I says.

"Well, she didn't answer. Just jerked herself away and climbed in the wagon. I just didn't know what to do. I just stood there like a dumb cluck and watched 'em drive off. I should've run for my varmint rifle," she mourned.

Peach reached across the table and put her hand over Narcissey's. "I'm so sorry."

Narcissey squinched her eyes so tightly, her eyelashes disappeared beneath the wrinkled folds of skin. She made a snubbing sound as she tried to control her tears. When she opened them, she looked directly at Peach. "I sure do hope you're here for that boy. He's had a terrible time these past two years. You look like you could be a good wife to him."

Peach didn't say a word. Instead, she poured herself another cup of coffee and drank it black. Chalk up another black mark for Will Wesley. She felt terrible. She was embarrassed to tell this sweet old woman what had gone on between them. Narcissey was thinking one thing, when the truth was the marshal wasn't about to ask her to marry him.

And he'd probably cost her her good job as well.

What a skunk!

He had his horse already saddled. All he had to do was tighten the cinches, slip the bit between its teeth, and climb aboard.

He couldn't resist the thrill of excitement that lanced through him as he followed the marshal's tracks out of town.

He let his right hand drift down to the butt of the shotgun sheathed in the boot strapped to the saddle. He'd chosen the scattergun because his aim might not be good enough to stop the marshal with a rifle. If he didn't put Will Wesley out of commission on the first round, he'd be finished.

Also, he figured that since the marshal had been shot once with one of them, he'd be scared to death of them. He might even ride off and leave Peach Smith alone.

"Peach!" Will opened the front door cautiously. Peach was a demon with a serving tray. He'd called from the front porch, but she hadn't come out. He'd knocked. Still she hadn't answered.

She'd be sure to have an ambush planned for him somewhere. "Peach! I'm back."

He stepped into the entryway. At least the house wasn't cold and dank. As he hung his hat on the coat tree, he peered around the archway into the living room. It was empty, but a cheerful fire blazed behind the grate.

She hadn't been gone long.

"Peach, where are you?" He sniffed the air. A delightful aroma wafted his way from the kitchen. It smelled like chicken. He could feel his mouth water. He guessed it must be about noontime.

He pictured her standing over the stove, stirring something delicious in a big iron pot and smiling at him. He felt a wave of longing hard to suppress. At the same time, he moved his right arm.

The pain that lanced out of his shoulder made his whole body clench. This was a farm. He couldn't farm. He didn't know how long he'd be able to marshal. This shoulder could have incurred more permanent damage. He might never be able to lift his arm over his head again.

"Peach!"

He started toward the bedroom.

Just as he reached the door, he heard the hoofbeats.

"Damn!"

Cursing like a trooper, he raced down the hall, burst through the front door, and plunged out onto the porch. The hindquarters of his horse were just disappearing among the trees that hid the road.

"Peach!" He leapt to the ground and ran after her. "Peach! Don't go!" In the middle of the road he cupped his hands around his mouth and gave all the power of his lungs. "Peach! You're going to get yourself killed."

* * *

Peach laughed aloud as she let the gelding slow to a walk. She'd tricked Will for sure. Just see how he liked being left afoot and alone in a practically empty house.

Of course, he wouldn't stay out there long. He knew where Narcissey Jellicoe lived. He could borrow a horse or a mule from her and be back in Coffeyville almost as soon as she was. She shouldn't count any chickens.

She wrapped her clothing more tightly around her.

The day was just as cold as it had been when he'd brought her out. A raw breeze blew from the northwest. She really was a town girl. She didn't see how she could ever be happy living on a farm or a ranch where no buildings stopped that wind.

She patted her horse's shoulder. He was a dark reddish animal with black mane and tail. As he walked, his head bobbed up and down and his forelock flopped. His horsey smell made her wrinkle her nose, but he had a nice, smooth walk. She wasn't jouncing around.

On a rise, she pulled him to a halt and tried to see above the trees to some familiar landmark. Nothing but more trees.

She sighed. "Get up, horse!"

He flicked back an ear. He swung his head and stared at the copse of trees to the right of the road ahead.

"Get up!" She jabbed her heels into his sides, the way she'd seen the cowboys do.

He took one step.

"Get up, I said!" She jabbed again, then held her breath until he started off.

A horseman pulled into the road. He had a hat pulled low over his eyes and a bandanna covering his mouth and nose.

She gaped, then shrieked. With all her strength she pulled on the right rein. Slowly, too slowly, her horse's head came around. "Get up! Get up!" she screamed. She drummed her heels into his sides with all her strength.

He lumbered into a gallop—

—too late. Another horse's head thrust itself into her line of vision. A man's arm shot forward to grab hold of her horse's rein just behind the bit.

Her mount twisted around and buck-jumped as the man hauled backward.

Her thighs slipped on the saddle. She grabbed for the horn but missed. She screamed as her body flew sideways through the cold air and slammed down on the icy road. The breath whooshed from her lungs. Her temple cracked against a rock.

As if someone had blown out a candle, the day went black. She blinked frantically. Gradually objects reappeared bathed in unnatural yellow light.

Get up! Get up! Her mind screamed.

She struggled to clear it away, struggled to rise. She could feel the ground vibrate close to her head. She rolled over. Out of the yellow haze appeared the masked face.

He spoke. At least she thought he spoke, but his words were an unintelligible roar. His hand closed over her shoulder. He shook her.

The shaking hurt her head the worst. She closed her eyes, cringing against the pain. He must be banging her temple against the same rock she'd struck when she fell. He had to stop. He was going to kill her.

"Stop!" she thought she said.

"—all right?"

Had she heard those words? She opened her eyes.

"Don't you die on me."

Good. He sounded anxious and also vaguely familiar. He had forgotten to speak as if he had a frog in his throat.

Also good because he didn't want her to die. He didn't want her dead. Rather than try to be brave, she gave a heartfelt groan and slumped back. She rolled her eyes up into her head the way she'd seen a lady do when she had an epileptic fit right in the middle of the dining room.

The shaking stopped instantly. His hand left her shoulder.

She slumped, letting her body sprawl on the icy ground, trying to think what to do. But her head hurt too much. The ground was too cold. The pain too intense. She tried to fill her lungs, but all she managed was a gasp. The roaring in her ears grew louder.

She let herself slip into the painless darkness.

Will flung his hat down in the middle of the road and cursed. Peach Smith was the damnedest girl for making a fellow lose his temper.

When he'd cussed around for a minute or two, he picked up his hat and slapped it with extra force against the side of his leg. He should have been expecting she'd do something like that. He was probably lucky she hadn't hit him over the head with the iron skillet before she took off on his horse.

That's what he got for trying to help somebody.

For two cents he'd let her ride on back to town and take what came. Unfortunately, the ferocious ache in his shoulder wouldn't let him. She needed protection now more than ever.

Emmett Dalton was beyond the reach of whoever was looking for this imaginary treasure. Peach Smith was the fellow's only hope. He'd be coming for her.

Will was pretty sure he hadn't been followed, but there were other ways for a smart man to find out about this place: an inquiry to anyone of several people in Condon's Bank, where he'd made the loan; a question to John Kloehr at the livery stable. Hell! Bert Ayers knew where he was going. And he'd talk to anybody.

He clapped his hat back on his head and made tracks

for Narcissey Jellicoe's. He'd borrow a horse there and catch Peach before she got back to town.

He hadn't jogged more than twenty yards before a fit of coughing bent him over. *Damn!* He hated himself. He was so old and sick and out of condition.

He knelt in the melting mud on the road and cursed. Had he killed her? Damn his luck! He couldn't have killed her. He couldn't lose all that beautiful gold.

She lay in a crumpled heap, her legs drawn up nearly to her chest. Maybe something was broken. He needed to straighten her out.

Carefully, he turned her on her back and arranged her arms and legs. During the process he whistled between his teeth. It was his way of calming himself. He didn't care about tunes, didn't know any music, but the sound comforted him because he was so afraid she was seriously hurt.

He really didn't want to hurt her if he didn't have to. For that reason, he'd worn his mask and his beard underneath it. He'd mussed up his hair and pulled it down over his forehead. If he could scare her into talking, and if she didn't figure out who he was, he wouldn't have to kill her.

She hadn't moved, hadn't made a sound except one, when he'd straightened out her leg, and that was a funny kind of gasp.

He studied her face. Her color was good. She seemed like she was breathing pretty evenly.

Suddenly, he smiled. He'd bet anything she was playing possum.

Allowing himself a superior grin, he got to his feet and slipped and slid over the ruts to the side of the road, where some trees had protected a big drift of snow.

Scooping up the snow in both hands, he strode back to her side and pushed it in her face.

She came awake as if he'd stuck a pin in her. She sat up, spitting and trying to brush the snow away.

He laughed. He was too clever for her.

She had been playing possum, but she hadn't been able to fool him. He waved his finger in her face as he drew a length of stout twine from his pocket to wrap around her wrists.

"You ain't got the sense God gave a goose, Will Wesley." Narcissey Jellicoe shook her finger in his face.

He tried to get on with saddling her old mare, but the woman he still thought of as Ma was making the task impossible.

"So far as I can tell, that's a sweet girl," Narcissey continued. "And can she cook? Um-um. Those biscuits were just about the best things I'd ever put in my mouth."

"She's one of the best cooks in Coffeyville," he agreed. He managed to reach under the old mare's belly and pull up the cinch strap.

"Well, then—" Narcissey put her hands on her hips. "Why don't you hitch up with her? There's many a spat or a squabble done been forgot over a good meal."

He set the bit between the old mare's teeth and buckled the cheek strap. "Narcissey, I need to get after her. She's liable to get herself into serious trouble."

He swung up into the saddle, but the old woman stayed him with her hand on his knee. "Why don't you, son?"

He looked straight down into her faded eyes. She was his best friend in the world and his staunchest defender. She loved him almost as much as he loved her. "Who'd want me, Ma? I'm an old, used-up lawman. I could hardly get old Jess here saddled. I'm trying not to drink so much now, but who knows how long it'll be before I fall off the wagon. She's young and she's a comer."

Shaking her head, Narcissey put her hand over her

mouth. Her eyes glistened. ''You are too, Will. You just don't believe it no more.''

Will smiled down at her as he backed the old mare out of the stall and laid himself down on her neck to ride out under the barn door. Once in the yard, he urged her into an easy lope. He couldn't afford to let her spend herself too soon.

''You bring her back, Will!'' Narcissey called after him. ''You hear me!''

Her captor had been leading them in a circle. Ever so often he would stop and stand in the stirrups and look all around him at the trees. He was hopelessly lost.

When it got dark, Peach prayed he was going to have to stop to build a fire. She was nearly frozen to death.

She'd finished chastizing herself because she'd ridden away from Will. She owed him an apology. Of course, she was pretty sure that the reason her captor had found her was that he'd followed Will.

She'd long ago made a list of everything she could see that might help Will to catch him. He was smallish to middle-sized in the saddle. A cheap yellow slicker that looked as if it had seen better days covered him completely.

His face was hidden to his eyes by an ordinary red bandanna. She couldn't even tell what color his eyes were. He'd swiped his hair down over them and pulled a battered black hat down low.

The only hope she had was that hat. One side of the brim had a strange-looking hole in it. It looked as if someone had taken a bite out of it. She could identify the hat. It was all she could hope for.

And that was probably nothing. The hat was most likely part of a disguise. What if this were someone well off, someone like John Kloehr, pretending to be poor?

She had to get him to stop for the night. Will couldn't find them if they kept moving.

"Hey," she called. "Listen. I'm hungry."

He rode on as if he hadn't heard.

"I'm hungry and freezing."

Still no response.

"And I have to go to the bathroom." She said the last before she thought, but it was the proper thing.

He turned in the saddle. "Huh?"

She managed a pleasant smile, although her wrists hurt so badly that she wanted to cry. "We have to stop for the night."

She knew she was taking a chance. She could be dealing with a desperate criminal who was trying to find a place to torture her. But nothing could torture her worse than the bagging twine wrapped around her wrists until in some places it had disappeared into her swollen flesh.

"Please," she called.

He looked around and behind him. He looked at the ground and at the darkening sky. As if his own body were stiff, he climbed down from the horse. "Here?"

She closed her eyes. They were in the middle of nowhere with the temperature already below freezing. She grasped the horn between her numb hands and managed to dismount. "Here is good."

He came to her and pushed her down on the ground. "Don't do nothing," he said in a deep gruff voice obviously disguised. "I got to think a minute what I need to do."

She stared hard at him, trying to find his shape under the slicker. She was certain now that she knew him. But who could he be?

Frustrated and miserable, she sat, shivering. She had nothing left to help her except her own wits. She'd better use them well.

"You need to pick up some firewood," she suggested in her most reasonable voice. "We need to build a fire."

"No fire!" He shook his head adamantly.

She smiled even though he couldn't see her in the dark. In her friendliest voice she insisted. "Just a little one wouldn't hurt. I can cook you a meal. You know how good I can cook."

"No!" he growled. "I don't know you. You don't know me."

"Oh, that's right. Well, I'm a good cook," she said sweetly. "And there's all kinds of supplies on the back of the horse."

"Supplies?"

"Food and such. I'll cook if you can find some firewood," she urged. "You're cold too. We need to get warm."

He stood over her for a long while. She closed her eyes and gritted her teeth to keep from screaming at him. They were both miserable. And for what? The promise of the Daltons' loot. Once again she had reason to wish she'd never heard of Bob Dalton.

"I'll take the horses with me," he told her at last. "Don't try to run off. You could freeze to death out here." He gathered the reins together in his fist and moved off, scanning the ground.

She watched him as he went. He was crazy, but he wasn't stupid. He was also deadly determined. She couldn't forget the shots fired in the jail at Emmett. She couldn't forget Corny Dahlerheidt.

She lifted her wrists to her mouth and began to pick at the knots with her teeth.

Chapter Twelve

Will found the spot where someone had caught up with Peach. Until that minute her horse's hoofprints had made a clear straight track in the road. The warm sun had turned ground frozen in the night into soggy, dark clods.

There, in the middle of road, the ground was churned up. Two horses had circled, stamped, and pitched. Here a man in boots had sprung from his horse. His heels had left deep indentations. Here were the shallower but unmistakable prints of Peach's small work shoes.

He knelt beside the impression left by her body when she'd been thrown. With a curse he touched his gloved fingertips to it. Anger mixed with desperation as he looked around. She could be badly hurt. Even though the ground was fairly soft, she could have landed wrong and broken an arm or an ankle.

Sick helplessness made him catch his breath as he thought of several terrible things the brute could do to her—could already have done to her.

Will damned Bob Dalton to eternal fires. All that boasting with nary a word of truth, and now Peach was suffering for it.

He had to find her fast. Rising, he circled the area. Clearly, he could see where she'd turned her horse and tried to gallop away. Her kidnapper had been too fast for her. She'd have had better luck charging straight at him with the hope of knocking him and his horse off the road.

Innocent little Peach! She didn't know anything about that. He'd been a damned idiot for bringing her out there. She was a town girl. He could picture her miserable and frightened, maybe crying, away from all she knew.

Farther on down the trail he found the place where two horses, one after the other, turned off into the woods. At least following them was going to be simple. Partially melted snow and darkly disturbed humus marked every hoofprint clearly. He urged the old mare forward. The faster he traveled, the sooner he'd catch up with them.

The trail meandered off to the right almost immediately. His quarry was traveling in a circle. Obviously, the man had neither compass nor trail sense. That and all the other mistakes he'd made comforted Will. The man would be pathetic if he weren't dangerous and hadn't shot one man, kidnapped a girl, and tried to murder a law officer.

The old mare blew a roller through her nose. She was sweating lightly, but Will had kept her pace even and rested her at intervals. He leaned over and patted her neck.

"Good old girl," he complimented her. "Nobody can say you don't give your best."

Her ear flicked back at the sound of his voice. She shook her head vigorously, making her tack jingle.

"Ready to move on?" He made a clicking sound with his tongue and she stepped out willingly.

The trail kept bearing northwest. He reckoned they were getting close to the trail back to Coffeyville. He doubted that his quarry noticed what was happening. Sometimes he meandered off at a tangent for no reason that Will could see. What was he looking for? What was he thinking?

No question about it. The damned fool was completely lost. He must be town born and reared too, like Peach. A real outlaw would have better sense.

The sun came out behind a blue haze. Big as a mountain, it glowed with sullen fire just before it sank below the horizon. In an open space among the trees, Will spotted their silhouettes.

Reacting instantly, he swung down and went to the head of his mare to place his hand over her nose and lead her into a small grove. He wasn't a moment too soon. One of the horses ahead of him looked around and whickered a greeting. The mare's ears flicked forward, but he kept her quiet.

Neither of the two riders looked back to see if anybody was behind, another testimony to their ignorance on the beasts they rode. Silently, Will waited until their silhouettes disappeared.

He was close. Better to wait until darkness fell. He didn't want to risk a meeting face-to-face, where the kidnapper could use Peach for a hostage. Neither did he want to start a gunfight where who knew where a stray shot might strike.

Before long, they'd build a fire. Twice while he was marshaling for Judge Parker, he'd walked right up and stuck a gun in the back of an outlaw sitting dazed and exhausted in front of a little campfire. Once, he'd waited until three of them had settled down for the night. They'd been easy to catch wrapped up in their bedrolls.

The kidnapper moved on, meandering aimlessly, sometimes standing in the saddle trying to locate a familiar landmark, always bearing more and more back to the right, as right-handed people invariably did.

Will mounted and rode after them. Now and then he caught a glimpse of Peach and her kidnapper through the trees. Always, he stayed carefully back.

* * *

Peach slid from her horse without any assistance. She had to be quick. She didn't want her captor to think to check the twine around her wrists. While it gave the appearance of being wrapped and tied, she could set herself free with a flip of her wrist. Sitting as still as possible, she flexed her fingers to get the circulation going. She had to bite down hard on the inside of her cheek to keep from laughing at his efforts to build a fire.

After he'd collected some sticks, some so damp they had leaf mold clinging to them, he arranged them in a haphazard fashion. Next, he pulled some matches from his shirt pocket. The first he tried to strike on the sole of his boot.

She had to duck her head to keep her amazement from showing. He hadn't given a thought to the fact that his boot was caked with mud from tramping about the woods. The match head disintegrated after a single ineffectual stroke.

He cast it aside and tried another with the same result. This time he held it up to study it and solve the problem. Out of the corner of his eye he caught her looking at him.

Hastily, she ducked her head. She didn't want to give him the idea that she was on the alert, watching his every move.

"Everything's too wet," he declared angrily. "Can't burn wet wood."

He rose and pulled the pack off her saddle. Muttering to himself, he began to root through it, holding up one item after another and turning it to catch the dying light. The supplies Will had brought did not please him, and he cast each item aside in disgust.

Careful to hold her body still, she stretched out her hand. Her fingers closed around the end of the largest of the fallen branches. Inch by inch she pulled it out of the haphazard pile.

"Peaches," he announced.

She jumped and dropped the branch.

He didn't notice. Instead, he held up the can for her inspection. "I like peaches. You can eat 'em right out of the can."

The gray evening had turned to full dark. Beneath the trees he was only a bulky figure squatting over the packs, rooting through them, searching for something to eat. She heard paper ripping.

She gathered her legs under her.

Now or never!

With a defiant screech she launched herself at him. He flung up his arms. She brought the branch crashing down with all her strength. It smashed his arms back into his face.

"Ow! Ow!"

She changed her aim and swung at his head. Her blow connected solidly. His hat went flying off into the darkness.

"Ow! Stop it! Stop!" He toppled over on his side.

She hit him again across the shoulders as he rolled over and came up on his hands and knees. Like a panicky child, he tried to crawl away.

"Stop! Stop! Stop!"

"Not much!" she screamed. "I'm mad enough to beat you to death!"

"Ow-woo-o-o!"

"You'll never kidnap anybody again." Yelling made the blood pound in her veins, so she kept yelling. "You skunk! I'll teach you to kidnap girls." She was sure the blows were getting harder and harder.

Both of them heard a horse come crashing through the underbrush at full gallop. Her screaming captor rolled over on his hands and knees and scrambled away. While

Peach turned to face whoever was coming, he staggered to his feet and dashed for his horse.

"Peach! Peach!"

"Will! Oh, Will! Here!" She dropped the piece of wood. "Get him!"

The marshal of Coffeyville came galloping into the campsite, a cavalry charge of one, riding to her rescue.

She swung around in time to see her kidnapper spring into the saddle and spur his horse into a mad gallop. "There he goes."

"Don't stop!" she screamed at Will. "Don't stop! Get him!"

He swung down and caught her in his arms. "Are you all right?"

"Yes! Yes! Oh, yes. But he's getting away." She pointed frantically, trying to urge Will to remount.

He shook his head. "It's full dark. No chance now that we'll find him."

"You should have gone on," she mourned.

"I might not have been able to find you when I tried to come back." He ran his hands down her arms and over her body. "Are you sure you're all right."

"Not a scratch," she vowed. "I'm just fine."

"He didn't try to hurt you? To make you tell where the treasure was?"

"We never got around to that. I'm pretty sure we were lost."

"He's a city slicker born and bred," Will agreed.

"What's more, I don't think he's very smart," she volunteered.

"Just because he doesn't know his way around out here doesn't mean he isn't dangerous as a rattler." He stepped away from her and took a deep breath. "Corny Dahlerheidt's not ever going to be the same. And the fellow from the lynch mob's lost an eye."

Now it was Peach's turn to be scared. "Suppose he comes back."

Will shook his head. "He's a sneak. He'd never attack me when I'm ready for him. Right now he's headed back to Coffeyville. That's if he can find the way. In any case, I doubt if he could find us again."

She had to agree with him.

"What was all the screaming and yelling about? I'd made my plans to sneak up as soon as you got settled down for the night."

She realized she was really safe. Her legs turned to water. She sat down abruptly and clapped her hands to her cheeks. Hot, salty tears started from her eyes. She didn't want Will to know. She was too embarrassed.

"Here." He dropped down beside her. "What's wrong?"

"Weak." She took a deep breath after the shuddering word slipped out. "I just feel weak. From hunger and cold."

He put his hand on her shoulder. "Of course you are."

"He collected some wood over there for a fire," she whispered, "but he couldn't get it lighted. He said everything was too wet."

Will left her and found the pile. Hunkering down, he rearranged it and pulled out his own matches from his striker box. In less than a minute he had coaxed a tiny flame. He moved to settle his back against a small tree.

"Come over here," he called.

Eagerly, she scooted into his arms. They closed around her like a warm blanket. Despite her resolve, she could feel the emotional tide breaking. She turned her face into his shoulder and began to weep.

"Peach," he whispered. "Aw, Peach. Don't take on so."

"I wasn't scared, Will," she declared.

He rubbed her back some more. "No. You sure weren't."

She shuddered and sniffled. "I really wasn't."

He pulled her legs over across his lap and tucked her skirt around them. "You? Not you. I know that."

"I got myself untied and—and—" She hiccuped. Her voice sounded high and thin, like a child's. "I hit him hard."

He chuckled. "That's my girl. Swinging that tray in Scurlock's was good experience. You did a good job. You had him on the run. He was lucky I came along to rescue him."

He rubbed her back and kissed the top of her head. She could feel his lips. No one had ever kissed the top of her head before. It should have comforted her, but instead, it made her even sadder. She really should push herself away.

"He tied me up with bagging twine."

"Bagging twine!"

"You know—like they use in the g-general store—" The memories of the pain in her wrists and arms, of the feelings of helplessness, swept over her. She started to cry again. Instead of being able to push herself away, she clutched Will even tighter.

"I know what bagging twine is." Will's voice sounded puzzled. "That beats everything I've ever heard of. I can't feature a kidnapper bringing along bagging twine."

She didn't know what to say, but she didn't know how to stop crying. She could feel the tears pouring down her face. She put her hand to her cheeks. They were wet all right, but not as a real lady's would have been. Quite suddenly, she realized that she'd messed up Will's coat.

That did it for her.

"Oh, I'm sorry." She tried to sit up, but he shifted his weight and gathered her more comfortably against him. "I've gotten you—er—wet."

"Doesn't matter," he muttered. He used the heel of his boot to push a good-sized branch closer to the center of the fire. "Bagging twine." He made a humming sound through his teeth. "Did he have it on a ball?"

"No. He just had some of it wound up in his pocket."

"I'll be damned."

"That means something, doesn't it?"

"Maybe. Maybe not. I need to think about it."

Will's warm arms and lap and the even rise and fall of his chest began to lull Peach. Her eyes stared into the flames; she drifted farther away from her troubles.

At last, he sighed. "I've got to disturb you."

"All right."

While he rose to unsaddle the horses and stake them out where they could forage, Peach scooted closer to the fire and held her hands out to it. The small flame had ignited the rest of the branches. Now a good-sized fire cast a circle of light and warmth.

She looked up into Will's face as he returned with the gear. He spread the blankets out and laid the saddles at the ends. They could lie with their shoulders against the saddles and their feet to the fire. She hoisted herself onto the bed as he dropped down beside her and put his arm around her.

The warmth along with the beating of his heart beneath her ear lulled her. She began to doze.

When he spoke, he spoke slowly, as if he were putting together a puzzle in his mind. "He can't be a rancher or a farmer or have access to ropes. He probably doesn't even think about ropes."

"Maybe he owns a general store."

"Or works in one."

She told him about the slicker and the hat and the mask. "I couldn't tell anything about him. But I'm sure I would know him. There's something about his voice. Maybe it's somebody I've waited on in the dining room or the saloon."

He patted her shoulder. "Don't worry about it. He's probably on his way to Texas by now."

"I don't think so," she murmured. "He's tried too many times. He won't give up."

The fire popped. One branch burned through and collapsed. She noticed Will didn't argue with her.

At last he sighed. "Peach."

She tilted her head back. "What?"

"This." He caressed her cheek, then lowered his head. The fire lighted one side of his face. His expression was as serious as she'd ever seen it. Then he kissed her.

His lips were gentle at first, little brushes of tenderness on her lips, at the corner of her mouth, over her cheekbone, over her temple.

She sighed and pressed herself closer. She was surprised at herself. She'd missed his lovemaking as she'd never missed anything in her life. When she'd moved out of his room, she'd felt a wrench. She hadn't wanted to leave. She tightened her arms around his waist and rubbed her breasts against his chest.

With a groan he returned to her mouth. His lips were eager now. He kissed her for a long while, searching for her response.

She gave it, opening her mouth, taking in his tongue, caressing it with her own. Pleasure knifed through her. She could feel its sharp claws in her belly. She pushed her knee in between his knees, straddling his thigh, arching against him, kissing him.

She wanted him! Desire set her on fire. Her clothes were too hot, too constricting. She wanted him to kiss her, kiss her breasts.

"Will—" she begged. "Will—"

He lifted his head only an inch. His breath blew against her face. "What do you want?"

"You." She pushed against him, rubbed herself against his thigh, felt the powerful muscle jump. Against her belly she could feel him tighten hard as iron.

"You." She scrambled up to her knees and caught his

face between her hands. She kissed him, this time demanding, sucking on his tongue.

He moaned deep in his throat. His hands clutched her waist, held her. "Here? Now?"

"Yes." She couldn't bear the heat any longer. She pulled at the buttons on her clothes. She didn't care about the material. She jerked at them until her breasts were bare. Desperate, she thrust them against his face. "Please, Will. Please, kiss me."

"Yes, ma'am. Anything to oblige a lady." His voice deepened until his southern drawl sounded warm as honey. It slid over her just before his hot, wet mouth slid across her breast.

He growled deep in his throat, the way he did when he was excited.

She hauled his head up. "That's right, Will. Oblige me. That's what I've always wanted. No one's ever obliged me." She planted her mouth on his and held his head even though she was sure he wouldn't pull back. His silky hair wrapped tight around her fingers gave her a sense of power. She wanted his kiss, his hot tongue, his hot mouth.

She was on fire. She writhed her hips, bumping against him. She wanted him. She wanted an end to unbearable tension, to fear, to anger, to the pain of the day. Suddenly, she realized she was panting. Between her efforts to take in more air, little sounds of pleasure that began deep in her throat were coming from her lips. They sounded like laughter.

"Are you happy, girl?" Will nibbled his way down the side of her throat on to her other breast, laving it with his tongue. At the same time, he closed his hand over the other. He squeezed and flicked her nipple.

She shuddered. Her pleasure increased. She ground herself against his belly.

He bit her, not hard, but sharply.

The pain went through her and her back arched. A

keening cry tore out of her throat and lost itself in the silent woods.

He held her tightly until she wasn't shivering anymore. Raising her to her feet, he leaned her back against the tree. Through half-closed lids she watched him. The fire's red glow surrounded his dark figure as he unbuttoned his pants and freed himself.

He reached beneath her skirts, found the slit in her soft woolen drawers.

His efficient movements, his touch, his rapid breathing, set her own heart to beating again. At the same time, her muscles refused to tighten. She felt as if even her bones were limp. Barely able to stand, she knew what he was about to do, but she couldn't help him.

Her head fell back and skidded up the tree trunk as he put his hands under her thighs and lifted her.

"Hold on tight."

"Me. Not much. There's not a bone left in my body." She couldn't believe that the next sound out of her mouth was a giggle.

Will chuckled too as he guided her legs around him. His mouth was against her shoulder; his hot breath brushed her neck. She could feel him, velvety hard, hot and slick. As surely as he slid his pistol into the dark polished leather of his holster, he slid himself into her.

"Um." Her giggle turned to a gurgle. "Um-um-um."

All she was doing was feeling. He was so long, so big. Was he too big? "I don't think this is going to work."

His hips moved back and forward, pushing her higher—and sure enough, she found herself pressed tight against his belly.

"You feel just right to me," he breathed in her ear. "Am I hurting you?"

She shook her head against his shoulder, inhaling his scent—heady, masculine, a hint of bay rum, a touch of leather.

"You feel right to me too."

He began to move, pushing up, pulling out, pushing up again. She tensed. She'd never realized how strong he was. Each time he drew back and let her slip down, she braced herself for the upward thrust. Each time it came harder than before. Each time she was sure it would hurt her, but she only wanted more and more.

With his left arm he reached up to catch the branch above their heads. He sucked in his breath. Then he reared himself upward.

"Yes, Will, yes."

He pressed his forehead against her shoulder. She was aware that he was gasping for breath and shuddering.

His whole body swelled as he sucked air into his lungs and drove his hips forward and up. The pressure drove her over the edge again. She clutched at his shoulders, she pleaded for mercy, she screamed at him to stop.

In her mind.

The words that came from her mouth were "Yes, Will, yes. Oh, please. Oh."

She whispered the words on his skin. If he couldn't hear them, he could at least feel how grateful she was with every caress. If she died at that moment, she knew she'd die happy.

"You'll have to go somewhere else."

They lay side by side, their feet to the fire, the saddle blankets pulled up around their shoulders.

"I have to go back to Coffeyville."

"You can't."

She pulled a little away from him and folded her arms tight across her chest. "I won't ask for another thing. You don't need to worry about me."

He heaved a sigh. "Peach, I'm too tired to fight right now."

"Then don't." She tightened her mouth against a string of reasons why she couldn't go back to his house. He knew those as well as she did. What he didn't understand was why she couldn't go anywhere else.

They lay in silence, both of them stiff as statues, forbidding each other to speak. An errant breeze stirred the flame as it cooled and coated a glowing branch with a fine film of gray ash.

At last, he sighed. "I can't protect you in Coffeyville."

"You didn't protect me out here either. He was following you out to your farm. Chances are he'd have waited till you left to come in and get me. So I'll be just as safe in town as anywhere. Whoever tried to kidnap me tonight wants to know where the Daltons buried their loot. He can't get it through his head that there isn't any loot."

"Exactly. That's why you have to go away."

She didn't move. "I'm not going."

He sat up. Clasping his right wrist with his left hand, he positioned his arm on his drawn-up knees. "You're going to get yourself killed."

She shook her head. "I can't leave Coffeyville. I've got to make a living." She hesitated. *Speak the truth and dare the devil.* "I can't depend on anyone else to support me. I understand, so you needn't worry about that."

"Peach," he chided. "I never—"

"I've got a good job," she interrupted. "I do still have a job, don't I?"

He nodded.

"And anyway, where would I go?"

He turned to stare into her eyes. "I thought maybe you could go to—er—Fort Smith."

"Fort Smith." She made a rude noise. "I don't know a soul in Fort Smith. I'd have to find work."

"Luke Scurlock said he'd write you a good recommendation."

She pressed her palms against her cheeks as she could

feel a blush rising in them. "Oh, no. Don't tell me that you've discussed me with Luke Scurlock? Oh, no."

"It's all right—"

"All right!" Not just her cheeks, but her ears were getting hot. "All right!"

"I told him what I was going to do, so you wouldn't lose your job."

"Oh, good. You tell my boss that we're—that you're—ooooh!"

He cleared his throat. "Well, he already knew."

She closed her mouth and closed her eyes. It was the end. The very end.

"Peach. Everything will be all right. He'll write you a good recommendation. And I'll write you one."

She crossed her arms over her chest and flounced back. "And what could you recommend me for?"

"Peach," he reprimanded sharply. "Don't. Don't put yourself down. We both want what's best for you."

She groaned and clenched her fists in frustration. "I should be the one to decide what's best for me. And you might trust me. I didn't let Bob Dalton talk me into doing something bad. Don't you think—"

"Peach." He held up his hand. "This isn't a matter of your knowing right from wrong. This is a matter of you—you—being hunted down like a rabbit or—"

"I am not a rabbit." She sat bolt upright. How could he insult her like that! "Just remember that when you came galloping in here, I had him screaming and crawling for—"

He raked his hands through his hair. "My God. I can't reason with you. I can't even finish a sentence."

"Well, neither can I." She crossed her arms over her chest.

"Peach." He reached out for her. "Peach, sweetheart—"

"Ooh! Now you call me sweetheart."

She could hear him grit his teeth. "Peach. Don't you

see. It scares me for you to be in Coffeyville all unprotected. It's not the same town. The Daltons changed all that. In Fort Smith you'll be safe.''

"For how long?"

"What?"

"For how long?"

He didn't miss her meaning. He shrugged his good shoulder. "Until I catch this fella."

"And how long will that be?" She wished the look she fastened on him would stab him to the heart.

He shifted uncomfortably. "Not too long."

"Two months? You've had two months to find the man who snitched on them. I wouldn't be surprised if he's the one who's caused all the trouble. He most likely warned the town, because he was mad when they wouldn't give him a share of the treasure. He didn't know they'd all be killed except Emmett. Doesn't that make sense?"

He didn't answer.

She flounced back down against the saddle. "Are you going to take another two months to find him?"

He shook his head angrily. "It shouldn't take that long."

She didn't believe him. "Or it might take six months. Or never." She had another thought. "Is Emmett still in the jail?"

"He's gone. Turned over to the U.S. marshals in Independence. I took him while you were at the farm."

"Then if I leave, there's no one for this fellow to go after. Who are you going to look for? A man with a mask? A man with a beard? A man with a hoarse voice?"

"Well, I—I'll ask around," he promised lamely. "All those men who were in the lynch mob. Somebody's got to know something."

"While I spend Christmas in a strange place without a friend."

He closed his eyes. He'd forgotten Christmas. His lips

moved. She had to bend forward to catch the noise. "I could come visit you."

His suggestion was more like an admission. She felt a little start of happiness. If he were willing to come to see her, what else would he be willing to do?

Then she straightened her thoughts out. She couldn't let her hopes obliterate her good sense. He wouldn't come. Or if he came, he'd come only once. He'd never find the man. Probably he wouldn't even look for him very hard.

No. If she left Coffeyville, she'd never return. She'd have to start all over again. Who knew whether she'd have so good a job?

"I'd give you some money," he was promising.

"Give me money. Not much! I'd throw it on the altar of the Episcopal church so fast, it'd make your head swim."

"It wouldn't be like that. It's for a new start."

"It's to get me out of town," she corrected him. "He'd find where I was and follow me. Or he'd follow you, just like he did this time. I'd never be safe."

"It would be a new life," he pleaded.

"I like my old life pretty well, for your information."

She reached across and put her hand on his knee. With all the earnestness she could command, she leaned toward him. "Would you quit when the going got tough, Will Wesley? Would you run off and leave the only home and the only true friends you've ever had because someone was giving you trouble?"

"I'm a man. It's different with men."

"And I'm an orphan. And orphans are a whole lot different. I've found a place for myself. I won't give it up. I've got to take a stand too."

"You're a girl."

"But I'm not helpless."

"It's a matter of strength and experience. I'm a law-man—"

She took his hands. "Then for just a few days be my

lawman. Be with me. He'll come after me if I go back to town. It'll be your chance to catch him once and for all. If I go away, you'll never have a chance."

Even as he was shaking his head, she was nodding hers. "Don't you see? It's the only way. You have to take me back."

He shook his head.

"You have to."

Will and Peach rode into Coffeyville at noon the following day. She'd been away less than a week, but somehow things felt different. A spot between her shoulder blades tickled. She could imagine someone staring hard at her.

She rolled her shoulders and let her gaze travel up one side of the street and down the other. In front of Scurlock's they dismounted and tied their horses. Again she had the feeling of eyes looking at her. It made her skin crawl.

She tried to put a light tone in her voice. "I hope Luke hasn't given my job away."

"I doubt it. And if he did, he'd hire you back anyway. You're good for business."

At that minute the door opened. "Peach!" Luke Scurlock had spotted her through the window. "Lord, girl! I'm glad he brought you back."

"Hello, Luke."

"Did you catch him, Will?"

The marshal shook his head. "He found her, and then he got away."

"Aw, hell. Bad luck!" Scurlock reached out his long arms and gathered Peach into a bear hug. Then he opened the door wide. The place was crowded with the regular customers drinking beer and eating the free lunch. "But you got a good look at him."

Will raised his voice a little louder than necesary. "Sure did. Got him pegged for real. But I want to do some more investigating before I arrest him. I've got to take a ride up to Independence and talk to Emmett, see if he can shed some light on this treasure.''

The usual noontime chatter had broken off. By the end of Will's last sentence, she could have heard a pin drop.

She shot him a wide-eyed look. He'd told a lie. They hadn't said a thing about any treasure. Then she realized what he was doing. He wanted people to think he did.

A cold chill shook her. He was drawing the attention away from her, making whoever had done these things believe that he had to get rid of the marshal first. Will Wesley was doing his best to protect her. Suddenly, she felt ashamed of herself. Maybe she should have gone to Fort Smith.

She put her hand on his arm.

He frowned a warning. Then his gaze lifted. Slowly he stared around, sweeping the room, his piercing lawman's stare searching every man's face.

More than one dropped his head or turned halfway around in his chair.

Luke took her arm. ''Ready to go back to work, Peach?''

She smiled gratefully up at him. ''I sure am, Luke. I've missed you.'' She spotted several very familiar faces. ''And my regulars.''

One old man grinned around a boiled egg he was stuffing into his mouth. ''I need 'nother beer here, Peach. Damn stuff tastes bitter when Luke serves it.''

Everybody laughed. Some of the others agreed loudly.

Peach could have hugged them all singly and in a bunch. ''Coming right up, fellas.''

She hung up her hat, coat, and muffler and slipped behind the bar. The laughing and talking resumed.

Will watched for a moment, then jerked his head toward the door. Luke followed him out.

What they said, Peach didn't know. She was too busy, too happy. As she passed among them, men were smiling at her, greeting her, telling her how glad they were to see her.

Bert Ayers was there. And John Cubine, with a tinge of sadness still in his eyes, but nodding to her. And Henry Isham.

She was glad she hadn't gone to Fort Smith. No matter how dangerous this was, she was still glad she'd come back.

At that moment Scurlock's felt like home.

Chapter Thirteen

From the shadows of the dining room, he watched the marshal and the innkeeper talk. Though he strained to hear their words, they were too far away.

He clenched his fists and gritted his teeth. If the marshal was going to Independence to talk to Emmett Dalton again, he must believe in the treasure. That was bad. The more people who believed in it, the faster he was going to have to work.

The girl had known about it all along. She must have been able to convince the marshal. He couldn't believe they rode back into town bold as brass. He had been so sure the marshal would have hidden her away somewhere.

Maybe they'd made a deal to wait until things cooled down and then dig it up and leave. That was it! He shouldn't have underestimated her. She'd been Bob Dalton's woman. She hadn't had any trouble getting the marshal to do what she wanted.

She was the key. She knew, and he could make her tell. A terrifying thought struck him. Maybe they'd already dug up the treasure and had come back to town just so people wouldn't be suspicious.

He gritted his teeth. He had to hurry. Just the thought of them spending any of it made him furious. After all he'd done, he'd earned it. No one else had really believed it existed except Emmett Dalton and her—and now maybe the marshal.

He stared at the marshal as he talked to Luke. Did he look happier? Did he look as if he had a fortune somewhere around?

He couldn't tell.

Maybe he was getting upset for nothing. Maybe nothing had happened.

But it would. It would.

Will shook hands with Luke and pulled the reins free of the hitching post. Swinging into the saddle, he headed down the street to Kloehr's livery. He'd go ahead and pay John's stable boy to take Narcissey Jellicoe's mare back to her, but not that day. The old horse needed at least two days' rest and hot mash.

He patted her neck. She was game as they came. Just like Narcissey. Just like Peach. None of them knew the meaning of the word "quit."

A prickling feeling trickled down the back of his neck. It began like the stroke of a cat's paw, its claws barely out of their sheathes. In a way, he welcomed it. It had been a long time since he'd felt it. He thought he'd never feel it again.

Several lonesome midnights in the streets of Carthage, Missouri, and Fort Smith, Arkansas, marshaling for Judge Parker, he'd felt the gunslingers before he'd seen them.

The last time was on a platform in Fayetteville as he climbed down from the train. That afternoon, he'd taken the Tal Karnes shotgun blast in his shoulder.

A particularly hard twinge racked him. He set his jaw.

Still patting the old horse, he moved casually around her rump. She flicked an ear backward and whickered. Over the saddle back he pretended to inspect something on the horn. Beneath his lashes he swept the scene. He could still feel the eyes. But he couldn't spot a single person loitering or even looking in his direction.

"Come on," he whispered through bared teeth. "Come on. I know you're around here close. Show yourself. Make your play."

The plaza and the two streets that converged on it were busy. Dozens of people were walking in and out of the stores, taking advantage of the break in the weather before winter came down hard again.

A trio of horsemen came out of the First National Bank and swung up. As one, they wheeled their horses and loped out of town. An old man, the stick he'd been whittling fallen from his hand, dozed in a sunny spot on a bench near the bandstand.

Everything was ordinary, quiet, peaceful.

But he could feel the eyes.

Dare the devil!

He stepped out from behind the mare with his hand resting on his gun butt.

Instantly, the eyes were gone. As if a shadow had lifted, the feeling ceased.

He surveyed the street again, particularly the windows and doorways. No one appeared to loiter there. No curtains rippled; no shades moved. Everything looked exactly as it should be.

Sliding his hand off his gun butt, he hooked his thumb in his belt loop. Gathering the reins, he led the horses down the alley. Though Dalton blood had long ago washed into the dirt, he imagined he could still see the wet, dark red.

Damn Bob Dalton! He'd started this whole thing with his reckless plans and his wild talk.

At that moment John Kloehr strolled out of the stables. The liveryman swung open the wide gate, moving without the least hint of concern over the spot where Marshal Connelly had bled to death.

"Glad to have you back, Marshal."

"Glad to be back, John." He judged the man's friendly smile to be sincere. Kloehr ran his hand over his rented gelding and then stood back a little to appraise the mare.

"Good saddle horse," he said.

"Very good saddle horse. Give her a good rubdown, hot mash along with her feed. Let her rest a couple of nights. Then send someone to return her to Narcissey Jellicoe at her place over near the Missouri line. I'll give him directions when he gets ready to go."

"Will do, Marshal."

Will strode out of the alley certain that at least one of Peach's theories had been wrong. Kloehr hadn't been the one staring at him. The man couldn't be in two places at once. Kloehr had had the opportunity to hear about the raid since the Daltons had planned it in the stable, but he would also have heard the Brazil plans.

He wouldn't have heard about any buried loot. Of course, he could believe that the Daltons had stashed the Katy holdup money. As that story made the rounds, more and more people had gossiped about it.

Out in the street once more, Will saw Bert Ayers hurrying to meet him.

"Marshal," the youth called, "I'm sure glad you're back." He grinned like a puppy as he rocked back on his heels on the boardwalk.

"Any problems?"

"Naw." Bert shook his head and took a swipe at his deputy's badge with his cuff. "Nothing I couldn't handle."

"Any drunks?"

Again the vehement shake of his head. "It ain't Saturday yet and it's gettin' too cold for lyin' in the gutter. Everything was real quiet."

Will patted his deputy on the back. "You did a good job, Bert. The measure of a marshal or his deputy is how quiet the town is."

The youth beamed.

"Why don't you take yourself on home now? Or go on over to Scurlock's if you want. Peach came back with me. She'll have hot molasses cookies before too much longer."

"I think I'll do that. That's good news for sure." He swept off his battered hat and slapped it against his pant leg. "She bakes better cookies than my mother. I purely wish there was somebody else in jail for her to talk to."

With new respect, Will watched his deputy lope away. He hadn't given the boy credit for figuring out that he was being bribed. He'd bet that Peach hadn't either. Bert would probably get more molasses cookies from her before she figured what he'd figured.

The first thing Peach did was check her store of money. It was there. She grinned to herself. Even though Luke had hired a cook, he hadn't hired an ambitious one. The man hadn't touched the stack of dirty pots and pans pushed back in one corner behind the washtub.

Peach congratulated herself. She'd taken the purses—hers and Bob's—out of the bean barrel and hidden them in a narrow gap between the wall and the cabinet. While her store grew steadily, Bob's stayed the same except for the money she'd given Will. And he'd promptly given it to the church.

She tried to imagine Bob's amazement if he knew. He'd probably be provoked.

When she tried to call his face to mind, she found she couldn't. In just two months the sharpness of his expressions was fading from her memory. She clutched his purse. She wasn't ready to give up yet, but she had to admit she wasn't likely to find the snitch.

The skunk had probably left town with the rest of the sightseers. By the new year 1893, Coffeyville would be back to normal. Except for the fool who was riding around trying to find the imaginary Dalton gold.

Peach shuddered as she pushed the money back in her hidey-hole and restacked the dirty pots and pans. She looked around her at the kitchen. She could be happy here if only she could be safe.

Enough of thinking. She flung herself into her work. She'd show Luke he really needed her. She stirred up a batch of cookies as well as set out the usual bowls of pickles, boiled eggs, and such for the free lunch. When the cook came in, she helped him get started on the specials. While the cookies were baking, she ran up to her room to wash and change clothes.

He watched her hurry back and forth across the alley from cookshack to hotel, carrying trays and bowls. She was sure a pretty girl. It was a shame really. He hoped he didn't have to hurt her too bad. But whatever it took to make her tell, he was ready to do it.

The best time would be while the marshal was gone. Let him take the train back to Independence and talk to Emmett Dalton.

He'd have the gold and be gone before he got back. He'd scare the life out of her. He'd tell her exactly how she could save her life, because if she didn't tell him, she was going to be a dead woman.

He pulled his note from his pocket and unfolded it. It ought to put the fear of God in her. Now all he had to do was wait for the cook to leave the shack. He'd slip in and tack it up where she couldn't miss it. And while he was at it, he'd throw a bigger scare into her so she'd know he meant business.

He read the note again. It was a real scary threat. No, it wasn't a threat. It was a promise.

With a heartfelt sigh Peach sank into the bathtub. How funny that she'd never thought much about baths until she'd started taking them regularly. Now the difference between clean and dirty was clear as rainwater. Clean skin and hair felt good and looked good. Dirty skin and hair itched and looked bad.

With clean skin and hair she felt like a lady even though she was just a waitress and barmaid for Luke Scurlock. With dirty skin and hair she looked like a waitress and barmaid even though she knew she was a lady.

She flushed. Looking at her face in the mirror, she wondered if every man in Scurlock's knew what she was doing with the town marshal. She closed her eyes as shame rolled over her in waves. She knew right from wrong. Sister Agnes Mary had taught her that. She had no excuse.

She didn't expect God to understand or forgive. She was what she was. But she didn't have to slip any further down that slippery slope. At least, Will didn't seem to treat her like a tramp.

She lifted the warm washcloth to her face and blocked out her unhappy expression and flushed cheeks. Breathing the warm, damp air between the threads, she turned her mind to other thoughts.

Then she cleaned herself, scrubbing the washcloth over her arms, shoulders, and breasts. She'd been knocked about by a crazy man. She'd been dragged through the brush. She'd been rescued and made love to.

She stepped out of the water. Instantly, the cold air gave her goose bumps. Luke's bathroom couldn't hold a candle to the hot water and warm rooms at the bathhouse.

When she had the time, she'd give herself a treat.

Dried off and dressed, she thought of her customers and the money they'd give her. She was happy to be back even with the threat hanging over her. She was looking forward to bringing in a big plate of cookies for the people in the dining room.

While she was at it, she'd take a few over the marshal's office for Bert. He surely loved her molasses cookies.

She pushed through the door into the cookshack and uttered a cry of disbelief.

The place was a shambles. Someone had turned the pie safe over on its face. Its contents, the flour and cornmeal as well as the pots and pans and utensils, spilled out on the floor. The pantry had been turned out as well, the root vegetables, eggs, and canned goods rolled in the dirt. The wood box had been dumped out last, crushing and damaging things that might have been saved.

Only the stove, hot to the touch from its fiery oven, cooked on. The scent of fresh molasses cookies wafted above the chaos.

Moving in a daze, Peach wadded her skirt to protect her hands and pulled the tin baking sheets from the oven. When she had to look, she had no place to set them down. Two legs had broken off the enamel-topped table when the pie safe crashed down on it.

She began to shake. Such wanton destruction made her ill. In the orphanage the smallest thing had been saved. From time to time, the sisters hadn't had money to purchase supplies. Everyone had to make do.

Paralyzed, she felt in another part of her mind the heat from the metal penetrating the cloth and blistering her hands.

A sound behind her sent prickles up her arms and raised the hair on the back of her neck. In a panic she spun around.

"Lord," Will Wesley breathed.

"I—I—" She couldn't think what to say. She looked at him helplessly.

The marshal crossed the room in two swift strides. With his gloved hands he took the hot baking sheets away and righted a chair to set them on.

She remained standing helplessly, aghast at the waste and the anger that she couldn't help but feel. The man who did this was crazy and desperate. She couldn't doubt it.

She thought of Corny Dahlerheidt. He had torn up her cot before, but Corny was laid up with fever and infection. Some said he might not live.

When Will held out his arms, she went into them, grateful for a haven against the shudders that racked her.

"How could anybody do this?" she whispered at last.

"Somebody who's getting mighty desperate to have that imaginary forty thousand dollars." His lips moved against her temple as he spoke. "Somebody who's gotten to the point where he thinks it's his. Somebody that we all know."

She looked up at him. "Somebody we all know?"

Will nodded. "It took him only about a minute to do this. He couldn't wait around to be recognized."

She pushed out of Will's arms. Slowly, she turned in a circle, surveying the destruction. "A minute? Only a minute."

"Maybe less. One—pie safe. Two—pantry. Three—wood box." Will dropped to one knee, put his left shoulder under the pie safe, and lifted. Crockery and tinware rattled as he pushed it back upright. She stepped forward to help him wrestle the wide wooden breadboard back into its slot beneath the enamel cabinet top.

At the same instant, they both saw the piece of paper attached to the metal clip that held the recipe card for the cook.

Peach gasped and reached for it, but Will was closer.

He plucked the note from the clip and read it at a glance. His mouth tightened and his eyes narrowed.

"Let me see."

Grimly, he passed it to her. "So now we know."

> You tell me what I want to know and I won't hert
> you. You don't and you'll be dead when I'm finishd.
> Don't tell the marshel.

The writer had drawn a crude knife in place of a signature.

"I guess we do." She passed the note back to him to fold and slip into his pocket. Again she turned in a slow circle. This time she felt the anger boil and roil inside her with a life of its own.

This destruction didn't hurt her. This hit Luke Scurlock, who was her good friend. This wasted food and destroyed property. She saw half the flour and cornmeal had fallen out of the bins in the pie safe. Supplies for a week spilled out into the greasy dirt.

She didn't remember how many dozen eggs she had, but they'd been crushed and trampled underfoot. Coffee, cream, and sugar were ruined, all the fine items that Luke kept for his dining room, to make it one of the best places in Coffeyville for a man to eat breakfast.

She stooped beside the broken table. The force of the overturned pie safe had cracked the enamel. Even though the legs could probably be replaced, it could never be the same because now food could slip into the cracks, where it would be impossible to clean out.

She clenched her fist as she looked up into Will's sympathetic eyes. "I'm so angry, I want to hit him."

The marshal blinked, then a humorless grin spread over his face. "That's good, Peach. That's real good."

"He didn't hurt me with this. All this belongs to my boss."

"That's right," Will agreed soberly. "You've just figured out one of the big reasons why outlaws are just scum."

"Because they don't think?"

"Or care. They just want what they want. Never mind that someone else worked hard for it. Never mind that they waste and ruin more than they ever steal." He swept his arm in a semicircle. "How much stuff you figure Luke lost?"

She shook her head. "A lot." The color rose in her cheeks. "Because of me."

He caught her by the shoulders. "Don't blame yourself. This didn't have anything to do with you. Except that you just happened to be smiling and looking pretty when the Daltons rode by. Bob Dalton set the whole thing in motion. Don't you ever forget that."

"But—"

"Is Luke to blame for letting them drink in his saloon?"

She saw his point instantly. "No. Of course not."

"Then forget about blaming yourself."

"Whee-oooo. What done happened here?" Neddy Barnes had peeked around the doorway. Now he came in, squinting in the dimness, then blinking owlishly at the mess. "Lor-dee, girl, what'd you do?"

Peach gasped in horror as the old man headed for the flour piled up in the middle of the floor. She could still save some of that if she scooped it carefully.

Will headed him off. "Looks like some bad boys came in here and hurrawed the place, Neddy. Peach is real upset about it."

"Well, I don't wonder." He scratched his grizzled chin. "Boys, y' say? Lor-dee. What's this world coming to?"

He allowed Will to herd him outside, but there he balked. "I done come for one of her molasses cookies. Smelt 'em all the way from the hotel."

Will stepped back in and scooped up two from the pan.

"Here you are. Now, go on, and don't come back until she gets the place cleaned up."

"But that's my job," Neddy protested, scattering crumbs from his beard. "I'll swamp it out in no time a-tall." He headed doggedly back in.

Peach waved helplessly at Will as she tried to direct the old man to clean where he wouldn't ruin what could be saved.

The marshal left her to talk to the men still lingering in Scurlock's dining room. Maybe somebody had seen something.

Peach didn't wait for Will to come to the hotel. In the marshal's office she faced him across his scarred desk. "We have to do something."

He nodded. "I agree. This has gone far enough. He's getting his nerve up now. Somebody's going to get hurt."

From his chair by the stove Bert peered into the checkered napkin he held in his hand. "Maybe there really is a treasure."

Both of them looked at the youth, then back at each other. Will shook his head.

Bert stopped with a molasses cookie halfway to his mouth. "All right. All right. So it's crazy, but everybody's saying it now. These are sure good, Peach."

"Glad you enjoy them. I'm surprised whoever tore up the cookshack didn't pull them out of the oven and trample them too."

Bert looked astonished. "Nobody'd do that. These are too good."

"Why don't you go on home, Bert?" Will suggested. "I'll take it from here."

The deputy hesitated, then nodded. He folded the napkin around the rest of the cookies. "I'm real glad you're back, Peach."

"I couldn't stay away long."

When the door had closed behind him, Will and Peach looked at each other. He chuckled. She smiled and shook her head. "He's a good boy."

"Yes, he is."

Her expression changed. "What can we do, Will? What can I do?"

He came from behind the desk and took her hand in both of his. "Let me handle it," he said earnestly. "Just let me do my job."

She looked at him directly. She wished she didn't have doubts about Will's ability. He'd come charging in to back her escape attempt when she'd been captured. She thought she'd had things under control, but she couldn't be sure.

The man she was beating might have grabbed her stick and turned it on her. No, Will's charge had driven him off.

On the other hand, he hadn't had much luck in finding the man who'd ratted on the Daltons. Of course, he hadn't had much time. And he probably hadn't spent much time trying. He'd been too busy getting Coffeyville to settle down.

Still, she couldn't keep the plea locked behind her lips. "Let me help you."

He was in the act of shaking his head when she placed her other hand on top of his. "We can set a trap."

He snorted. "You've been reading too many dime novels."

"No, we can. Let them all know that you're going out of town. Let me go on about my business, except you sneak back into town and watch me. You'll see him and can stop him."

"You'd be in danger."

"He's not going to kill me. He needs me alive. Without me he'll never find the Daltons' gold."

"This is crazy. You're crazy."

She rose and drew his hands around her waist. When he'd pulled her against him, all the time shaking his head, she put her hand over his mouth. "We can do it. We can make this whole thing go away. You can find out who shot Corny Dahlerheidt and tried to break Emmett Dalton out of jail and tried to kill you. He would have killed you on the train if the train hadn't lurched and he missed your head."

He closed his eyes.

She took her hand away. She had him now. "It's probably some stranger. I'll bet it's a man who rode with the Daltons. Maybe he told on them because he thought he was supposed to have a share of the loot from the Katy. Maybe we'll find the man who caused the death of eight men, including the town marshal right here on the streets of Coffeyville."

He opened his eyes. "You are—amazing."

She'd never heard the word before. Of course, she'd read it, but she couldn't believe it came from his lips. It was the most wonderful compliment she'd ever been paid.

"I love you." She kissed him.

Neither really noticed the words. Just because she'd never said them before didn't mean that they both didn't know them.

"You take the office today, Bert."

"Yes, sir, Marshal." The youth grinned. His step held a decided hint of a swagger as he strode around the desk.

"If anybody asks, tell them I'm taking Narcissey Jellicoe's horse back to her. I'll be gone nearly all day." Will went to the door and scanned the street. Everything looked normal.

A norther had blown in during the night. The temperature was dropping steadily, but it held no hint of snow. A blue haze dimmed the sun, but otherwise, the air was crystal clear. Tonight they would have a hard freeze.

He hated to treat the old mare like that, but she had a thick winter coat. A couple of days in the livery stable hadn't softened her. He'd blanket her and she'd be fine.

He set his hat low on his brow. "Take care of everything, Bert."

He rented his usual mount from John Kloehr. He told him the same story.

"No need for you to go, Marshal. I can send a boy," the stableman offered.

"I need to check on Narcissey. She's sort of my responsibility." Just the opposite was true. Ever since his injury, she'd felt as if he were hers.

"Take it easy." John gave the mare's rump a pat as the old horse obediently followed the livery mount out into the alley.

In front of Scurlock's he tied both horses to the hitching post. Peach saw him when he came into the dining room and bustled forward with coffee.

He could tell she was a little nervous. She splashed a bit into his saucer. "Sorry, Will."

He caught her wrist as she reached forward to wipe it out. "Stay in these two rooms all day," he whispered. Then out loud he said, "Can you fix me some in a canteen, Peach? I've got to ride out to Miz Jellicoe's to return her horse."

"Sure thing. Be right back with one."

While she was gone, he surveyed the place. Several townsmen finishing their breakfasts nodded to him. Neddy Barnes was collecting dirty dishes from the tables. Of course, Neddy gave no sign that he had heard Will's remark, but the way the old man's rag had slowed as he'd wiped the tables told the marshal all he needed to know.

Not that he thought Neddy might be the one. The old man was a gossip. He heard everything that was said in the dining room and in the saloon. He'd thought about asking Neddy to keep his eyes and ears open, but he knew Neddy would tell everybody he was working for the marshal, and that would be the end of that.

"Here you are, Will." Peach placed a canteen on the table. She'd wrapped it in a towel and slipped it in a burlap sack to keep it warm. "Can I get you breakfast now?"

"Much obliged, but I need to be moving." He finished his coffee and strolled into the saloon.

Luke pulled out a bottle of sarsaparilla, but Will shook his head.

"I'm taking Narcissey Jellicoe's mare back to her today," he explained for the fourth time.

Luke set the bottle down with a little too much force. "Are you taking Peach with you?"

"No sense putting her through the cold. She'll be here with you. She'll be safe."

The innkeeper stared at him. Will returned his stare. The hair on the back of his neck prickled. He'd never considered Luke Scurlock. Never thought the man was anything but all wool and a yard wide. Now he realized everyone was a suspect.

Luke had certainly been behind the bar most nights when the Daltons were drinking. He'd heard the boasting and bragging. This hotel was making good money, but did anyone ever have enough money?

"She'll be safe."

Luke shook his head. He leaned across the bar. "Wesley, you are the—"

Will's eyes narrowed. He braced himself for some defamation of character, when Lemuel Mungerson hurried in through the swinging doors.

"Glad I caught you, Wesley. I understand you're going to Independence tomorrow to take another crack at Emmett Dalton." He was using his speechmaking voice. He probably regretted that he hadn't caught Will in the dining room, but he wasn't going to let that stop him. "That's a fine idea."

"Thank you."

"Fine. Fine. Bring the gold home to Coffeyville."

Will stared at the little politician. Had the man lost his mind? "The money belongs to the Katy railroad."

"Can they prove it?" Mungerson gestured broadly, as if he were addressing a crowd of constituents. "I don't think so. If you bring the treasure here, it can go into the town banks until such time as its ownership can be proven."

He rubbed his hands in anticipation. "Think of the people who'll come to town this time. You'll be famous, Marshal Wesley. The town will be famous because of you. The man who found the Daltons' treasure."

Will shared a meaningful look with Luke Scurlock. Mungerson was an idiot. The U.S. marshals would be there too quickly to talk about, as well as the railroad detectives and the officers from the insurance company—if such a treasure existed.

But it didn't.

While the councilman postured and talked on and on, Will took his measure. Could this be the man who'd ridden after him to kidnap Peach?

Both of them agreed that the attacker didn't know anything about finding his way in the woods. So far as Will knew, Mungerson was born in Kansas City. He and his wife had moved here some ten years before, and he'd hung out a law shingle.

His practice had led him to run for city council. He'd run unopposed. Council members had just gone on about their business except to have meetings three or four times a year, but Mungerson had turned it into a bully pulpit to air his views. He was critical of the mayor whenever he had the chance to be.

Did he want that job? And maybe later the Kansas legislature?

Did he have enough money to realize those ambitions? He certainly dressed modestly. Will bet $40,000 would be mighty tempting. What's more, Mungerson had no use for Peach. He'd spoken out against her.

Will lowered his head and took a deep breath to keep from blurting out something that he'd be sorry for.

When he had himself under complete control and Mungerson had begun to wind down, he raised his head. "I'll do what I can," he promised. "I'm going up there tomorrow."

Placing a dime on the bar, he strode out.

"Bring it back for us, Marshal," Mungerson boomed for the benefit of the room. "The Daltons' treasure belongs to the grieving citizens of Coffeyville."

Chapter Fourteen

Exactly two miles out of Coffeyville, in a copse of trees fifty feet from the railroad track, Will tied Narcissey Jellicoe's mare. Tomorrow, when he took the train for Independence, he would watch out the window for C. N. Howard's windmill and water tank located on the other side of the track. They were impossible to miss. When he spotted them, he'd pull the emergency cord.

He and Peach had planned this to the minute. He'd be off the train almost before it came to a stop, have the saddle on the mare, and be headed back for Coffeyville at a gallop.

When Peach heard the train pulling out, she'd go to the bathhouse. That was the dangerous part. The kidnapper would come after her fast, thinking she was unprotected.

Will's palms got sweaty whenever he thought about what could happen if he couldn't get back in a few minutes.

He stared at the train rumbling past. Surely it wouldn't have time to break down over the two-mile stretch of straight track between Coffeyville and the farm.

He was pretty sure the mare would be safe out there. Howard was well known as a man who tolerated no trespassers. Also, she was well hidden in the copse. Will hung a feed bag over her head and over the head of the livery stable horse he'd rented to ride back on. Both fell to munching contentedly.

Just before he left, he'd fasten another feed bag to a handy tree, and tie a blanket over the mare against the chill. She'd be as safe as if she were in a stall.

For the time he had to pass, he unfastened the heavy blanket from the back of the mare's saddle and wrapped it around his shoulders. Sitting down in the sunshine, he thought about Peach working back at Scurlock's.

His palms began to sweat all over again. Suppose she forgot to stay in the hotel. Suppose Luke sent her off on an errand and then someone dragged her into an alley. Maybe Luke himself—

Lord! He was going to have to stop thinking. He was scaring himself to death.

He unstoppered the canteen. The coffee was still hot. Two miles was just a few minutes out of town. Just a few minutes back in. He took a drink.

The worst part was the waiting. He pulled his pocket watch out and studied it. He'd said four hours. He cursed himself for telling the truth.

Except that he had to. The man who wanted Peach's information so badly that he'd threatened to kill her for it knew approximately how long it took a man to ride to Narcissey Jellicoe's.

Will sighed morosely as he massaged his shoulder. At least he had some hot coffee he could nurse along for maybe the first hour.

All day long Peach had the distinct impression that someone was watching her.

The sensation had caused her to slop coffee onto table-tops and rattle dishes. Her fingers had been clumsy. She'd burned herself on a pot handle. She'd nicked herself with a paring knife. She'd been hot and cold by turns. Once she'd had the sensation that someone was moving just beyond the range of her vision.

Once, she'd turned around quickly, but the only person she saw was old Neddy Barnes, sweeping out from under the tables and humming under his breath.

Just before the dining room closed after lunch, Will strode in. Peach felt a rush of relief. It fused into a rush of love. His cheeks were red, his eyes bright from the chilly air. He'd pushed his hat back on his head, freeing a wave of brown hair, a few silver strands peppering it, onto his forehead. He smiled at her.

He was a bit early, but she was so glad to see him. Eagerly, she followed him to his customary table and poured him fresh hot coffee. When she set the cup beside his plate, he squeezed her hand.

Another thrill went through her, this one of sympathy so acute, it was almost pain. She could imagine how his shoulder must be aching because of the chill of his hand.

Mentally, she promised him a hot bath and a massage. The way she felt just then, she couldn't do enough for him. She didn't ever want to leave his side. With Will beside her, she was safe—at least for the time being. She couldn't help herself. She leaned her hip against his shoulder.

She wanted him to hug her. She wanted him to take her upstairs immediately. She wanted— She could feel the hot blood rising in her cheeks, the curl of hot longing between her legs.

"Steak and potatoes?" Her voice was so hoarse, she sounded like a man.

He smiled up at her. The backs of his fingers brushed against her thigh as he set his coffee cup down.

She almost dropped the pot. Her breath came hissing in between her teeth.

His smile became a knowing grin. "Steak and potatoes will be fine."

"Coming right up." She didn't want to leave the table, to break the contact. His hand had somehow slipped beneath her apron when he rubbed his knuckles up and down her thigh.

She sucked in another deep breath and shifted from one foot to the other. The usual noises in Scurlock's dining room dimmed beneath a roaring in her ears like the wind of a blue norther. Her heartbeat matched the insistent pressure of his knuckles. He had to stop. She had to step back. Otherwise, someone was going to see, and then they'd both be embarrassed, she in particular.

His hand didn't ease off. Instead, it moved higher and more intimately. Her breath caught in her throat. Her knees were trembling. She had to hold on to his shoulder to steady herself.

His hand dropped away. He nodded solemnly. "I think someone over there is trying to get your attention."

"What?" She was startled out of her daze.

"I said—"

"Never mind." She jerked away from him, feeling her body clench in defiance. She never wanted to end the contact with his hard, strong fingers.

As she carried the coffeepot from table to table, her sensual excitement mingled with her nervousness until she wanted to scream.

Replete, Will pushed his plate away. Since Peach always fixed his steak herself, it was exactly the way he liked it— not cooked to a cinder or charred on the outside and bloody on the inside, but done on the outside, faintly pink in the middle, and liberally sprinkled with black pepper.

He sat back, feeling pleasantly full as he finished his third cup of coffee. He would have carried it next door for a jigger of whiskey to sweeten it, but she didn't like him to do that. Now that he'd warmed up, his shoulder didn't ache nearly so badly.

The afternoon was waning. Most of the day had been spent in laying the groundwork for the plan. Even if Peach hadn't disliked his drinking, he wouldn't have drunk a drop now.

As he made his rounds tonight, he'd set up the blind. From then on he needed all his senses alert. If somebody acted too interested in where he was going, he needed to keep an eye out for him. If someone listened too closely, he needed to watch for him too.

Will rose and adjusted the gun at his hip. Time for the marshal to start making his rounds and casually letting the town know that he was heading for Independence the next day to question Emmett Dalton about the Katy gold his brothers had stolen.

The train pulled into the depot only half an hour late. The conductor didn't even bother to put down the step. Men much preferred to swing down and be on their separate ways. Two drummers hurried away toward the center of town. A cowboy with a saddle hooked over his shoulder stopped on the platform to look around before moseying in the direction of Pearl Bridger's.

Will eyed them suspiciously before turning to Bert. "The town's yours, son. Stay in the office and be available in case anybody needs you. You've got two prisoners you can check on at noon. If they're sober, let them out. If they're sleeping, just leave them alone. I'll take care of them when I get back tomorrow."

Bert pulled his hat tighter down on his head and thrust

his right thumb into his belt loop. "I'll take care of it, Marshal. You can trust me."

Will rolled his eyes heavenward. Bert had even picked up on the way he supported his injured shoulder. At the same time, he hoped that his youthful deputy didn't ever have to endure the pain of a serious wound. "Just keep your mind on what you're doing, son. You'll be all right."

As the train pulled out, he observed Bert swaggering down the middle of the street, looking over everything and everybody as if he owned the place. He shook his head. He really needed a man for the deputy job, but maybe Bert would grow into it. He hated to hurt the youth's feelings.

"You're welcome to take a bath upstairs." Luke shrugged his broad shoulders. "Half the time, nobody uses the bathroom anyway."

"But then I'd have to clean it up," Peach pointed out with a smile. "This way I can splash as much as I want. Besides, they have more hot water."

He looked a little disappointed. "That five-gallon hot water heater came all the way from Chicago. The copper tubing is guaranteed."

Suddenly, she wished she could tell him what she and Will were doing. She couldn't, or wouldn't, believe that Luke Scurlock, who'd acted more like her father than her boss, had threatened to kill her. He wouldn't have shot Corny Dahlerheidt. He wouldn't have set a mob on Emmett Dalton to scare him into talking.

She pushed her thoughts aside and forced herself to lie. "Thanks, but I promised myself a long soak. I'll be back in an hour."

She was sure her imagination was making the day colder than any December she'd ever known. Again she had the feeling that someone was watching her. In vain she looked in every direction as she crossed the street and climbed the steps to Haswell's Emporium.

Those five people who were on the street hurried from one errand to the next to get in out of the cold.

Nervously, she walked into the shop. She didn't often patronize the big general store because it was pretty expensive, but today she wanted to be seen by as many people as possible.

She wandered past several shoppers before she finally located the fancy soaps. In consternation she stared at the choices. Two bars were wrapped in pleated tissue paper and had fancy French names on the labels. The only one she really recognized was Pears, which, of course, everybody knew, even girls from convents.

She started to take a box, when a wild spirit overcame her. She picked up a bar called Fleurs de Printemps and held it to her nose. She didn't know what the words meant, but it smelled like flowers. She would have it. When she carried it up to the counter, the price turned her legs weak, but she bought it nevertheless, flashing a tiny dollar gold piece, collecting her change in silver, and taking care to tell everyone standing around that she was headed for the bathhouse.

". . . Dalton . . ." reached her ears as she opened the door. She flashed a look over her shoulder in time to see Mrs. Haswell leaning forward toward Edna Mungerson's ear.

Perhaps they thought she was spending some of the money Bob Dalton had given her. Perhaps they thought she had found the fabled treasure.

She smiled as she imagined Councilman Mungerson's expression when his wife trotted over to his law office and fed him that line of gossip.

As she started down the street, she walked a little slower than she would have ordinarily. She was waiting for the particular feeling of someone watching. It never came. She stopped in front of the window of Isham's Hardware and peered at the glass.

She could see the street behind her, including Condon's Bank and beyond it the alley where the Daltons had died. She could see the plaza and the bandstand. The street was just as it was before she'd gone into Haswell's.

She braced herself. She couldn't see anyone. She couldn't feel any eyes following her. The chances were good that someone was waiting for her. Cold chills that had nothing to do with the weather set her teeth to chattering. He might already be at the bathhouse.

She clutched the French soap and managed a half-smile. Everything was going to be fine. Will was probably already on his way back to town. Perhaps he was even waiting for her.

C. N. Howard's windmill spun so fast, the blades were a blur in the rising December wind. Will rose from his seat and pulled the emergency cord in one quick movement. Before the train had done much more than slow, he was out on the platform that connected the car to the caboose.

The conductor met him with a thunderous scowl, but Will flashed his badge and swung down. By the time the brakeman highballed the train on its way, he'd disappeared into the copse.

"All right, old girl." He gave the mare an affectionate slap on the rump and mounted. "Get me back to town."

The mare started off willingly, but before they'd gone more than a hundred yards, she stumbled and gave down in her hip. In a couple of yards she was limping badly.

His whole body clenched in apprehension as he swung off her back. Running his hands down her hind leg, he discovered her hock swollen around a scar running up from hoof to pastern.

He could have howled with frustration. When he needed

a fast horse, he'd laid his bets on a lame one. The cold night air had stiffened her leg, so she could barely keep her weight on it. She needed a poultice and a night in a warm barn.

He looked around desperately. Despite the proximity of the windmill, the Howard farm was more than half a mile in the opposite direction.

He'd gotten himself into a fix. Hastily, he led the mare back into the copse and tied her to the same tree. "Sorry, old girl, about a lot of things." He patted her neck. "But I promise I'll be back real soon."

He pulled his hat down tight on his head, stuck his right hand inside his belt, and began to run. The pounding of his heart had little to do with the speed he set himself.

He slammed the butt of his pistol down on the skull of the Chinese man who ran the bathhouse. Without a sound the man crumpled in the mud. He put his fingers under the man's nose and felt for the warm breath.

Still alive—but he'd wake up with a headache and never know what hit him.

He slipped in through the back door the man had come out of and closed it behind him. There he paused to press himself against the wall and listen. All he could hear was the beating of his heart. He was more excited than he'd ever been. He swiped his hand over his mouth, anticipating what was to come.

He wanted to give Peach plenty of time to strip and get settled down in the tub. He wanted to see her naked. Even though she was skinny, she had all that yellow hair. He wanted to see if she had it between her legs.

Some of the gals over at Pearl Bridger's had yellow hair on their heads, but it was black between their legs. He'd bet Peach's was yellow.

He pulled his mask up around his face. He planned to bust into the room with his gun drawn. He'd stride right over to the tub and look right down at her. With any luck, he'd scare her so much, she'd tell him what he wanted to know first off.

Either that, or she'd pee. He giggled nervously thinking about that.

Women were crazy about their modesty. She ought to be just about the craziest since she'd been brought up in a convent. He just hoped she wouldn't faint when he walked in on her.

Will leaned against a tree. Sweat dripped from his face. His chest heaved. His arms braced against his knees trembled. His heart was thudding like a trip-hammer, shaking his entire body. His feet in his new high-heeled Cubine boots felt as if he'd held them to a campfire.

He'd run more than a mile as fast as he could. Now he'd lost his wind. He couldn't drag any more into his lungs. Two years of abusing his body had left him crippled in more places than his shoulder.

The sweat on his face mixed with tears of pain and self-disgust and fear. His whole body felt wrenched apart and shoved back together again with every breath he drew.

He swiped at his face as the sweat ran into his eyes and stung like hell. He was terrified for Peach. She'd put herself into a trap because she had faith that he would rescue her.

He looked around desperately. Still a mile to the railroad tracks and some city blocks after that. He'd taken twenty minutes when he should have taken only ten. It'd be at least another thirty before he'd get there.

Dear Lord! If they both survived this, he swore he'd never touch another drop of whiskey so long as he lived.

* * *

Peach listened so hard, she could hear her own heart-beat. When she didn't hear anything, she splashed her hand in the clear warm water she'd used to half fill the big white porcelain tub.

She felt a particular irritation with the man who'd attacked her twice already. She hated to waste all this lovely bathwater. If not for him, she'd be sitting in the tub right now. She'd be lathering herself with her newly purchased Fleurs de Printemps and leaning back and squeezing her washcloth over and over herself.

Whoever the outlaw was, she hoped he came in soon. Wouldn't it be wonderful if Will could capture him and take him off to jail as soon as he burst in? Then she could have her bath just as she'd planned.

A floorboard creaked outside the door. She froze. Her heart stepped up its beat. He was there. She knew it. He was right outside.

She leaned over the tub and splashed harder. Let him think she was actually in the tub. Let him think—

Man, oh, man. He could hear her splashing around in the tub. She was naked as a jaybird, all that yellow hair hanging down her back or floating around in the water, or maybe pinned up on top of her head.

He'd get to see her pink, pointy titties and the hair between her legs. He rubbed his hand up and down his front, then clenched his fist and jerked his hand away. He was going to milk the chicken right there in his pants if he didn't quit it.

A cowboy on a piebald mare trotted toward him. If Will had had the breath, he would have cheered.

Instead, he dropped to his knees in the middle of the road and fought for breath. His lungs heaved, his chest pounded. He huddled over, trying to ease the pain in his side.

The cowboy pulled up the horse, and man and beast eyed the fallen man suspiciously.

"Help me—" Will was sure he was saying the words, but the awful wheeze of his breath made them unintelligible. He sucked in a full breath of icy air and tried again. "Horse—" He coughed up the word. He was sure the man couldn't understand him.

Indeed, the cowboy pulled back on the reins. The mare snorted and sidled nervously.

Desperately, Will pushed himself to his feet. He couldn't allow the fellow to get away. He'd lost way too much time. He pulled his heavy overcoat open and thumbed out his badge. "I need—"

"Hey, Marshal." The cowboy grinned as he guided the mare forward. "Lose yer horse?"

Will came up to the horse's neck and caught hold of the mane and rein. "Went lame—two miles back." He could feel his heartbeat slow even as the cold wind blew in through his open coat and chilled his sweat. "Got to get back—to town. Take me up."

"Golly, Marshal, I can't. I gotta—"

With a wordless yell, Will jerked him from the saddle. The cowboy went over in a heap, landing on his head. Too surprised to do more than roll over and sit up, he watched as Will sprang to the saddle, spun the mare on a dime, and spurred her back toward Coffeyville.

Quivering from head to toe, he flung the door open. It crashed back against the wall, shocking him with the noise it made. He lunged in, straight for the bathtub.

"Where's the gold?" he thundered. He almost collided

with the huge porcelain-coated cast iron vat. Then he gaped in disbelief. Clear water lapped against its sides.

Where was she?

He whirled around, his gun tracing his path.

At first he thought there was no one in the room. Then he spied the screen in the corner. Beneath his bandanna his mouth split in a grin. He sited along the barrel the exact center of the fabric. In the silence he could hear himself breathing, but he couldn't hear her.

Slowly, he raised the pistol until it was aimed at the wall a foot above the screen. He considered pulling the trigger. That would be the way to roust her out. The shot would probably scare her so bad, she'd knock the screen over. But then someone in town might hear and come to investigate.

Not likely, but someone might.

"Come on out," he growled. "If you don't, I'm going to put a hole right smack-dab in the middle of that there screen."

Peach huddled against the floor, peering through a tiny hole near the bottom of the screen. Her teeth were chattering so hard, she couldn't have answered if she'd wanted to. *Where was Will? This wasn't supposed to happen this way.*

She recognized the masked figure as the one who'd kidnapped her before. However, he seemed smaller, less imposing. Without the slicker covering him from shoulder to knee, she could tell more about his body.

She breathed a swift prayer of thanksgiving. Luke Scurlock, with his broad shoulders and comfortable girth of chest and belly, was innocent, just as she'd known all along.

She didn't have time to think about much else. The man lunged across the room and wrenched the screen aside.

As it crashed to the floor, Peach straightened up, keeping her back to the wall. She lifted her chin. "You're going to be so sorry."

"Oh, no. I don't think so," he growled.

Obviously, he was trying to disguise his voice, but the eyes that glared out at her from between the mask and the battered hat brim were so familiar.

He stabbed the gun toward her chest. "Where's the gold?"

She closed her eyes, praying that he wouldn't accidentally pull the trigger, praying for Will to appear in the doorway.

"Where'd them Daltons hide their gold?"

She shook her head. "There isn't any."

"Liar!"

She jumped. She couldn't help herself. She'd never been yelled at like that. Then he stabbed her with the gun barrel. The muzzle thudded against her breastbone. She gasped in pain and cringed. He'd bruised her.

Infinitely worse than that was the knowledge that if he made a mistake and squeezed the trigger, she'd be dead in a fraction of a second.

"I'm not lying." The tears started from her eyes. She was so afraid. "I'm not. There never was any gold."

"The—gold—from—the—Katy." He punctuated each word with a stab at her chest.

Just five words, but she had no breath left. She felt sick. "It was f-four thousand dollars. Not forty," she whispered.

"Liar!"

"No. Really. Four thousand dollars. That's all they got."

She thought the pressure on her chest eased fractionally.

"You're lying," he insisted, but his voice didn't sound so gruff. His eyes above the bandanna flickered. A frown appeared between them.

"No." She took a deep breath and smiled. "Bob told me. That's why they wanted to rob Condon's and the First National at once. They'd never gotten more than a few hundred dollars apiece. They were going to steal a lot of money and then escape to Brazil."

He stared at her.

She could feel the tension go out of his gun arm. He eased off. The muzzle retreated an inch from her chest. She took another deep breath. Could she convince him to go away?

She thought about Will and their carefully laid plans. Something had happened to him. She tapped down her panic. She had to save herself. Or at least she had to try.

She put her hand on her hip and tossed her head. "There isn't any gold. You don't think I'd have stuck around this two-bit town waiting tables and sleeping in the kitchen if I'd had a ticket out of here, do you?"

His eyes widened.

Where had she seen that expression before? She was certain now that she knew who her would-be assailant was. If she could just catch her breath and think a minute, if he'd just quit pointing that gun at her, she'd be able to place him.

"Not much," she hurried on. "If I knew where forty thousand dollars in gold was, I'd be halfway to San Francisco. My dust would have settled on Walnut Street a long time ago."

His eyes narrowed. "Maybe the marshal's keeping too close of an eye on you. He's real sweet on you. You've got him jumping through the same hoops you had for old Bob Dalton. But you know that."

She couldn't think of a thing to say. This person obviously knew about their relationship even though he was wrong about everything else. He didn't know anything about Bob Dalton. But he'd followed the marshal out of town to find her. He'd been watching them for a long time.

As she sought something to say, she saw the tension come back into his shoulders. "You'd better tell me where the Daltons hid their gold."

"I told you—"

"Yer lyin'. Maybe they didn't get much gold from the Katy, but they had a lot from before. They'd been outlaws for a long time. Everybody knew that. They were bad as the James gang."

"No." She was losing him again. She let her eyes drop to the gun. The barrel had swung down away from her chest for a moment. Now he raised it again. Her whole soul quaked as he brought the barrel alongside her cheek.

"Tell me," he snarled.

Even though the steel was icy cold, all she could remember was the fiery heat from the barrel that had shot Corny Dahlerheidt. The terror broke her. The tears flowed down her cheeks. "I don't know anything to tell you. Why won't you believe me? They didn't have any gold. They were just farm boys."

"The James gang—"

"They were cousins. That's all. Believe me."

Hoofbeats of a horse hard ridden sounded muffled in the street outside. Then both of them heard the animal pulled to a stop. Frozen, they stared into each other's eyes as boot heels hit the boardwalk and thundered into the outer room.

His eyes widened. "You tricked me."

His voice sounded high and frightened. It gave him away.

"Bert?"

He jerked the gun away as if a wasp had stung his hand. "Naw. What you talking about?"

"Bert Ayers!"

"No." He backed away from her, shaking his head.

She followed him, unable to believe her own ears and eyes. Her eyes swept him up and down. Her stare stripped him of his mask. How could she not recognize the pale eyes? His youthful, slighter figure wasn't filled out to man's size. She held out her hand. "Oh, Bert."

He shook his head.

They heard Will thudding from room to room, opening the doors, slamming them, calling, "Peach! Peach! God-dammit!"

"Keep your trap shut!" The young deputy swung his gun back into her face. "Just you keep quiet."

"He'll find us in another minute," she reminded him. "The Chinese man always puts the ladies in the last room, so they won't be walked in on, but Marshal Wesley will find us."

She thought she had never seen so much terror and anger combined in one man's eyes. Clearly, they had fooled him completely. Bert Ayers had never figured on being caught.

"Peach!"

"Here!" She dodged around the boy and darted for the door.

"Stop right there!" He caught her by her hair. She cried out as he twisted it around his fist and jerked her back against him.

At that instant Will flung the door open. His trained pistol led the way as he charged into the room.

Bert caught Peach around the waist and hauled her back against his chest. "I'll kill her, Marshal. You turn right around and walk back outa here, or I swear I'll shoot her."

Will blinked and gaped. "Bert?"

"Yes!" Peach exclaimed. She felt a rush of sorrow. This eager puppy of a young man corrupted by the dream of Dalton gold. Fool's gold. "Don't shoot him, Will."

The marshal of Coffeyville took only a few seconds to recognize the situation for what it was.

Peach could see his face change. Worry and concern for her smoothed away, to be replaced by an icy calm.

He let the gun swing down to his side. His left hand extended as if to shake hands. "Let her go, son. You haven't done anything to be too sorry for yet. Let her go and we'll talk."

The muscles in Bert Ayers's chest relaxed fractionally. He drew in a shuddering breath. Then he tensed again. "Naw. You're both wrong." He deepened his voice. "I ain't Bert Ayers."

Peach shook her head.

Will nodded. "Whatever you say, son. Just let the girl go. We'll talk. Maybe you could just walk on out of here."

"Naw." He was shaking all over. His heart was thudding. She could smell his sweat. "Naw!"

"Bert," she said softly. "You don't want to shoot anybody. Put the gun down."

"I ain't Bert!" he screamed.

She could feel his shoulders tense. Her eyes dropped to the gun thrust out in front of them, aimed at Will's chest. "No!"

The boom of the old .44 was deafening in the tiny room. She screamed as Will seemed to catapult back as if he'd been kicked by a horse.

"No!"

Bert's grasp on her hair fell slack. She threw herself out of the room in time to catch Will's body as it slid down the wall.

"Will! Will! Oh, my God. Heavenly angels, intercede. Pray for him." Blood blossomed like a deadly flower on his abused right shoulder. She put her hands over the wound. Blood flowed between her fingers like water from a pump.

Dimly, she was aware that Bert came slowly up behind her. She looked over her shoulder.

He pulled the kerchief down off his face. It was pasty gray. He shook his head.

"Get help," she cried. "Get help!"

He shook his head again, then turned and bolted down the hall. The last she saw of him was a silhouette in the back door.

Chapter Fifteen

"The bullet went clean through his shoulder. Just nicked the flesh and muscle out on the point. Didn't really touch anything vital. Couple of stitches was all it took. I'd say the marshal's a mighty lucky man. Mighty lucky." Doc Shandlin had donned the leather apron he used for operating and rolled his sleeves up above his elbows.

Peach unclenched her hands from her crystal rosary, Sister Agnes Mary's parting gift. She hadn't used it often, but sitting in the doctor's tiny waiting room, she had needed it as never before.

Doc Shandlin was staring at her from beneath hooded lids.

She slipped the rosary into her pocket and rose. "That's good. He's lucky to have you for a doctor."

The doctor harrumphed at the compliment, then tilted his head to one side. "How well do you know the marshal?"

She frowned. She didn't understand the question. *Was Doc going to deliver a lecture about morals?* "Er—he's been awfully good to me."

Shandlin nodded. "Maybe I didn't ask the right question. What do you know about his right shoulder?"

Peach wrapped her arms protectively across her middle. *Where was this leading?*

She hesitated. Was the doctor on the town council? "He was shot a couple of years ago. Buckshot." She didn't want to say anything that might cost Will his job. "He's been in pain ever since."

"Uh-huh. Well, I'm not surprised to hear that."

She tried to decide what else to say and how much. "He's—er—he sometimes has to—er—rest it."

"I'm surprised he can use it at all," the doctor said baldly. "If he ever fell in the lake, the lead he's carrying around with him would take him straight to the bottom."

She waited.

Shandlin continued to regard her. He was a slight man, stooped at the shoulders. He had a long beak of a nose on which he wore a pince-nez that squeezed tight a quarter of an inch deep into the flesh on either side. In Scurlock's she'd once heard him explain that he did it himself, so he could bend over a patient and be certain that his "eyes" wouldn't fall off.

He stared so long that she shifted uncomfortably and hung her head.

"Fact is," he said, "I was just wondering. So long as I've got him in here, I could give him a whiff of chloroform and clean some of that mess out."

Peach didn't even hesitate. Shandlin was one of the men who had worked all night long taking shot out of Emmett Dalton. "Would you?"

Shandlin smiled thinly. "Might not be able to get enough to do much good, but I guess every little bit'd help."

She pulled her rosary from her pocket in preparation for another session.

He raised a thin eyebrow at the sight of it, then looked

her full in the face. "I think I need a little bit more of an assist than prayer."

She gulped. "You mean me. You want me to help you."

He nodded. "You think you're up to it?"

She felt her stomach clench, not with nausea but with trepidation. Was she capable? She'd never done anything like this before. She'd never even had a man's blood on her hands until that day. And this was Will.

She looked down at her hands. Will needed to be able to use his arm again. If he were going to keep his marshal's job, he needed to be whole again. If he were going to stop drinking and stop feeling no good, he needed to be whole again. If he were going to love her as she loved him—

She looked straight into the doctor's steady gaze. "I think I'm up to it."

When Will started to protest, Shandlin clapped a chloroform cone over his nose and mouth. "Take a deep breath, son. When you wake up, you'll think you've just gone to sleep."

He motioned Peach forward and handed her a brown bottle containing a clear liquid. "Now, just take this and drip it over this cone."

"No." Will's voice was muffled "No way in hell, Doc. People die—"

"Not for someone who knows how to use it." Shandlin smiled his thin smile at Peach. He pulled the glass stopper from the bottle. A sweetish odor rose from the mouth. "Just a drop at a time. And count. Tell you what, Marshal Wesley. Why don't you count with her?"

Peach looked down into Will's eyes. "This is your chance, Will."

His dark eyes were glazed with pain. "You don't know—"

"He operated on Emmett."

Will closed his eyes. She could feel him still shaking his head, still protesting, but he didn't say anything more.

Peach looked at the doctor and then down. She put her hand on Will's forehead. It was wet with perspiration. He was hurting and afraid. She felt the huge weight of responsibility slide onto her shoulders. "I'll be right here with you," she promised. Of the doctor she asked, "What shall we do?"

"Count."

At that Will opened his eyes and looked directly into hers. "I'll count with you."

"Thirty drops," Doc Shandlin said as he turned away to wash his hands to the elbows in carbolic acid and rainwater.

"One—two—three—four—"

"Breathe deep," the doctor encouraged as he dried himself on a clean white linen towel.

"—five—six—seven—"

The first cut of the scalpel made Peach close her eyes. Blood welled around the blade, but the doctor's triumphant pronouncement made her open them. "Got it. Number one."

He flipped a tiny steel ball through the air. Blood spattered on Will's white skin. The shot pinged into the basin set between Will's arm and side.

Another tiny cut and another ball joined the first.

Maybe it was the chloroform, but Peach realized she wasn't sick, only a little dizzy. Otherwise, she stared intently at the badly scarred skin of Will's shoulder.

"Not very many are going to be that easy," Doc observed after four more had pinged into the pan. "Those were just the ones that the man who worked on him missed before."

"How could he?" Peach asked. "They're just under the skin."

"Probably they've worked their way up as the swelling's gone down." Shandlin dabbed at the area. "Remember, there's no telling how long this wound went without attention before a doctor got to it. If it was swollen, and infection had started, whoever did the work couldn't see much of what he was doing.''

Shandlin was working swiftly now, slicing with the scalpel wherever a nodule appeared, flicking out the ball and dabbing the area with a stiptic pencil such as a barber might use if he nicked a customer.

"Now for the hard part." He opened a section of bright red scar tissue in the joint. "Ah-ha! This is where the real damage is.''

Will's blood was running freely now. One stream ran over the top of his shoulder, narrowly missing the bandages from the bullet wound. The other ran down into his armpit. Both ran down through a channel at the edge of the steel table and into an enamel pan beneath the table.

"He's bleeding to death," Peach cried.

Shandlin smiled at her. She was getting used to that smile. It was his accompaniment for every answer. "It looks worse than it is. I sewed up his wound within a few minutes after he was shot. He didn't lose much there. He's all right. Ah—''

Fascinated, Peach watched as the doctor exposed the white muscle and extracted shot after shot.

"I don't see how he used this arm at all. I'll bet he was suffering the tortures of the damned every time he tried.'' He looked at her for confirmation.

She nodded. "It's why he drank.''

Again the mirthless smile. "At least he didn't turn to laudanum. So many do. And then they can't leave it alone.''

Will moaned softly beneath the cone.

"Another five drops," Shandlin directed. "And that ought to be enough to get us through.''

Will woke to the whistling of the December wind. It rattled the windows and blew sleet against the panes.

Slowly, he turned his head toward the sound. A shade had been drawn, but he could see that it was dark outside.

He turned back and tried to swallow. His mouth and throat were parched. His tongue felt swollen. His teeth felt grimy. He made another effort to summon up enough saliva to swallow. It came with a croak. "Water."

"Will?" a sleepy voice answered.

"Peach?"

She raised her head. Her hair was mussed. One side of her face was imprinted with the hobnails of the bedspread. Her eyes were bleary. "Do you want some water?"

"Yes." He didn't actually say the word. It came out in a dry hiss.

She scrambled to her knees, then tipped over backward and sat down again. "Sorry."

He shook his head as she pulled herself up, steadied herself with her hand on the iron bedstead, and found the ewer. He heard the water splash into the glass.

"You shouldn't be on the floor," he muttered. "Too cold."

"I've got a blanket." She slipped her hand under his head and lifted the glass to his lips. It was cold and fresh. He couldn't get enough. He drank it down, then another, and another.

"Careful," she whispered. "You'll make yourself sick."

His tongue came unstuck and his throat opened up. He could talk now. "I'm dry as a bone," he whispered. "All that blood—"

His head felt woozy. He could feel himself drifting. He didn't hurt. Probably the chloroform hadn't worn off yet. Doc had set a couple of stitches in his shoulder, but then—

Narcissey Jellicoe's horse! His eyes flashed open. "Kloehr," he whispered. "Get John Kloehr."

Peach frowned. "It's after midnight."

He could feel the darkness edging in around his consciousness. "Tell him. C. N. Howard's windmill. Two miles. Narcissey's mare. Lame. Went lame."

Peach nodded. "First thing in the morning."

He thought about getting up and going himself. How long had he been there? He wondered what they'd done to him, wondered about his shoulder. For a second, real panic streaked through him. Maybe he'd never be able to use it again.

Peach put her cool hand on his forehead. He must be getting a fever. He could see her lips moving, but he couldn't understand her.

He closed his eyes and drifted away.

"He's so hot." Peach still sat beside him. He could hear her voice.

"That's to be expected. Fever's not the worst thing that can happen to a body."

Will opened his eyes to stare into Doc Shandlin's, magnified by the pince-nez.

"It's bad," he tried to say, but his tongue was swollen again. "Water."

Again Peach lifted him, but he couldn't remember whether he drank or not before he drifted away.

The pain was bad. He tried to set his teeth against it, but a particularly severe twinge wrung a groan from him. He needed a drink, but when he tried to rise, he couldn't get more than his head off the pillow.

"Will?"

He tried again. This time he managed to roll to his left side. That didn't do him any good, since he faced the wall. He got his left arm under him and pushed himself to a sitting position.

"Will! What are you trying to do? Lie back down."

But he felt a sense of triumph even if his head swam sickeningly, and he had to swallow to keep from throwing up. He was going to get his strength back.

The room felt cold when he came out from under the blankets. "The mare," he croaked. "Did John Kloehr—?"

"I sent him out the next morning," Peach reassured him. "He brought her back in. The last time I checked, he'd put a poultice on her leg and she was coming along fine."

"Good." He felt a sense of relief. The mare hadn't suffered from cold or hunger. He wouldn't want to face Narcissey and tell her that the old creature had died.

Peach hovered over him. "Are you hungry?"

Surprisingly, he was. While she went for some food, he raised his left hand to feel his right shoulder. It was swathed in a thick bandage. He summoned up all his courage and tried to move it.

It was bandaged too tightly, and just flexing the muscle made it hurt like a son of a gun. He couldn't tell whether it had been further damaged by the pistol shot he'd taken.

When Peach came back in with a tray, he asked the question. "Bert Ayers?"

"He ran away. Left town. Nobody's started out to chase him. It's been too cold." Peach set the tray on the bedside table and laid a blanket across Will's shoulders.

He didn't want to ask the next question. "Who's marshaling?"

She shrugged. "Nobody. That is, everyone's waiting for you to get back on your feet."

"Damn." Will moved his legs restlessly. He could feel the soreness in his muscles. "How long have I been in bed?"

"A week." She set the tray across his thighs and pushed several pillows behind his back. Anticipating his next question, she said, "You're in our room at Scurlock's. Luke's gone down to the marshal's office twice and gotten the mail, but mostly everybody's agreed not to sell too much liquor to anybody and the town's stayed pretty quiet.''

Will dug into the bowl of thick potato soup. When he began, he thought he wouldn't ever get full, but he was able to eat only about half of it. Satisfied, he leaned back against the pillows.

Peach took away the tray and brought him a cup of hot coffee.

He felt drowsy and replete, but he had catching up to do and an explanation to make. "Did he hurt you? Did I get back in time?''

She nodded. "He didn't hurt me. Just scared me to death.''

"I'm sorry. I can't tell you how sorry.''

She looked at him reproachfully. "When you didn't come, I was more scared that something had happened to you. I knew you'd be charging through the door if you could.''

"You knew that, did you?" A warm pleasant feeling spread over him.

"Of course.'' Her smile was angelic. He thought it was the prettiest thing about her. "You're my lawman, aren't you? Dedicated to defend me and the town.''

"The mare went lame,'' he explained morosely. "Probably from the cold during the night. I should have picked a better horse. I couldn't ride her.''

"How far did you have to walk?''

"I didn't walk. I ran.''

She gaped at him. "Ran?''

He grinned. "I couldn't run all the way. I gave out after about a mile.''

"I shouldn't wonder.''

"But it did me good.'' His grin changed to a self-deprecatory sneer. "I found out what an idiot I'd been for the last two years. All that drinking. I was dying before I'd gone twenty yards.'' He looked at her soberly. "I swear to you right now, Peach Smith. If I never sleep another night, I'm not going to touch another drop of whiskey."

She reached for his hand. "Oh, Will."

"Swear to God, Peach."

She leaned over him and kissed him softly on the lips. "I believe you."

He raised his left arm to her shoulder. Her kiss stirred him. *My God,* he thought. *I want her—right here and now.*

Their lips clung. When she lifted hers away, he pulled her back down. Suddenly, he could feel her begin to tremble.

Abruptly, she wrenched herself away. Moving out of reach, she stared at him. "Will Wesley. That was mean."

He ducked his head. "I know. But you started it."

She took the tray away. She was gone a long time while he sipped his coffee and let his mind drift. When she came back, he held out his left hand. "I'm sorry."

She put her hand in his and sat down on the bed facing him. "You may be able to go for the rest of your life without needing any whiskey."

He glanced down at his shoulder. "What happened?"

"Do you remember when he had me give you the chloroform?"

Will closed his eyes. He couldn't remember anything much since Bert had shot him. "Vaguely."

Peach leaned forward. Excited color warmed her cheeks, and her lips were still a little flushed from his kiss. "Well, Doc Shandlin operated on your shoulder."

She opened the drawer in the bedside table. From it she pulled a pouch and placed it in his hand. "Here."

It clicked and rolled across his fingers. "What is it?"

"The shot from your shoulder. Seventeen in all."

He weighed it in his palm. No wonder he'd hurt so badly. "Tal must have had a choke on the shotgun," he muttered.

"Doc thinks he got it all. He worked a long time. I had

to give you five more drops of chloroform twice." She looked down at her hands. "I didn't get sick at all," she reported proudly. "Doc Shandlin wants to use me as his anesthetist every time he needs one. He says I have a steady hand."

Will poked his finger in the mouth of the pouch and looked inside. He had an intense desire to pour them out into his palm and see what had hurt him for so long. His right arm rested in a sling. He set his teeth to turn his right palm up. Pain flashed through him.

"Oh, Will, take it easy."

Sweat dotted his forehead. "If Doc did a good job, then I won't do any harm. I'll just be loosening things up some more." He held his fingers out straight in front of him and poured the shot into them.

Such little things to cause him so much pain.

He rolled them with his thumb. The pain was there in his shoulder and arm, but he could tell it was different. For the first time, he felt a surge of hope. He positioned the pouch beneath the tips of his index and third finger. With a sigh he let the shot roll into it.

He didn't spill a single one.

Peach was hanging over him, scarcely daring to breathe. He looked up at her with a smile. "I think it might be all right."

She laid her cheek against his. "Oh, Will. I hope so."

He let the pouch fall to the bed and reached for her. With his left arm he guided her down into his lap.

"Will!" she exclaimed. "Don't. You'll hurt yourself."

Actually, he was hurting himself, but he wanted her in his arms more than he wanted to avoid the pain. "Give me a kiss."

She tried to scramble away, but he wouldn't let her go. "No. You've been bending over me for a week now. Every time I woke up, there you'd be. Washing my forehead with cold water and snow, holding my head, giving me drinks—and kissing me.''

She turned her head away. "I did no such thing."

He bent low trying to see her face. "You did too. I was pretty much out some of the time, but some of the time I could feel your mouth on my forehead, or my cheek, or—"

"Stop it," she whispered.

"Why?"

"Because you weren't supposed to know anything about that. Those were s-stolen. I'm not proud of myself. I don't know why I did that."

She tried once more to pull free, but he settled her more firmly across his lap with the words, "Well, I'm proud of you. I'm pretty sure I'm on the mend because of you."

She tried to dig her elbow into his ribs.

"If you don't stop squirming around, you'll hurt me. You don't want to hurt me and undo all your good nursing."

Reluctantly, she subsided and relaxed against him. He hugged her against his chest. "Now, give me a smile."

He didn't wait for her to comply. Instead, he kissed her. He thought for an instant about his rough beard. A week's growth created quite a stubble. Then a faint humming began in his brain as he tasted her mouth. He licked her lips and slid his tongue across hers.

She pressed down a little harder in his lap, as if she'd arched her back.

He used his tongue again on the inside of her mouth. This time she made a soft sound.

His left hand insinuated itself along the outside curve of her breast until the tips of his fingers covered her nipple. It was easy to find, already erect and pushing against the fabric of her dress. Gently, he set up a circling motion, rubbing, rubbing.

She gave a moan of desire before she wrenched her

mouth away from his and hid her face against his chest. "You mustn't do this. You'll hurt yourself."

Even as she said the words of warning, she squirmed in the cradle of his thighs. She couldn't help but feel him erect and pushing against her. "Let me up."

She tried to sit straight in his lap. The movement drove her bottom harder against his erection. He groaned. "I'm hurting now."

She inclined her head, refusing to look at him. He searched her face in profile. Her cheek was red, her lips swollen from his kisses. He leaned forward, his mouth brushing her ear. He pursed his lips and blew into it. He could feel her tremble. Her hands clenched at her sides.

"Why don't you be nice," he whispered, punctuating his request with his tongue, "and put us both out of our misery."

She waited so long, he thought he was going to have to ask her again. At last she drew in a shuddering breath. "How?"

"That's my girl. Just hike up that dress and straddle me. Put your hand on my shoulder, and I'll put my hand on your breasts."

She whimpered then, but whether in pain or pleasure he couldn't tell.

"You can ride me just like riding a horse. Better, considering how you ride."

Like a woman in a dream, she pushed herself off his lap. Instead of hiking her dress up, she reached for the buttons. Her eyes met his. They glistened as if she were about to cry or laugh.

He pulled the sheet down and pulled his own nightshirt up. His manhood stood like a rod in his lap. He put his hand around it.

She closed her eyes as she slipped her dress down off her shoulders. One by one she pulled the straps of her camisole down past her elbows. At her waist she untied the ribbons of her petticoat and pantalettes.

She was just about perfect. Her white shoulders were rounded and shaped by the hollows of her bones. Her breasts were small, but not too small, each tipped by a rosy nipple. He swallowed hard as the temptation to kiss each one drove every ache and pain out of his body. For this time he was whole again.

She smiled at him as she slipped her thumbs beneath the various materials bunched at her waist. Then, with a sigh, she pushed everything down at once.

"Sweet Lord," he breathed as she stepped out of her slippers and put her knee on the bed.

"Are you sure, Will? I might hurt you."

He damned the wounds in his right shoulder. If ever a man needed two hands— As it was, he didn't know where to touch her first. Should he put his hand on her shoulder or at her waist? Should he run his palm down the inside of her thigh or over her breasts? Her skin was so fine. Her hair—

Her hair. Peach raised her arms and pulled the pins and combs from the heavy knot at the top of her head. It rolled down, a pale yellow fall like watered silk. She put her other knee on the bed to kneel in front of him.

She bit her lip. Her gaze flickered.

He reached out for her hair. Spreading his fingers, he combed them back from her temple and pulled the strands over her shoulder and down across her breast.

She set her teeth as his palm brushed her nipple.

"It's hard," he whispered hoarsely. "Just like I am. You want me as much as I want you."

She bowed her head. "That's no news," she sighed. "We've always wanted each other."

"Don't think about any of that. Please." He stroked her breast, then bent to kiss her nipple through her hair.

She arched her back as the sensation drove her mad.

To keep from falling against him, she slipped her knee over his thighs. His erection nudged the cleft at the base of her belly. She moaned and caught her lower lip between her teeth.

Still kissing her, he slid his hand over her buttock to clasp her thigh from behind. His fingers sought and found her wet, hot opening. She jerked and twisted, but she didn't pull away.

"You're ready," he muttered, transferring his attention to her other breast. "Come on. Please. Make it happen. I can't wait any longer."

"I can't either."

He wasn't sure whether she'd spoken the words or only thought them. But he braced himself as she rocked forward and slid down on him, sheathing him inside her in a single exquisite movement.

He clenched every muscle in his body to keep from exploding. He had to keep telling himself that he wasn't a boy. This wasn't his first sexual experience. He had a man's control.

He needed a man's control as she sat on his thighs and moved her knees forward, gluing herself to his belly. She leaned her forehead against his good shoulder and released a long, shuddering breath. "Am I hurting you?"

He chuckled. "Enough to die—if you don't go on."

She lifted her head. Her own smile answered his. "Then since I've been your nurse, I guess I have to go on."

"Kiss me first."

She leaned forward to brush his lips.

He wouldn't let her get by with that. "A real kiss," he demanded. "From a real woman. You're not a little girl any longer, Peach."

She opened her mouth and pushed her tongue into his. In what he was sure was an extension of the same motion, she rocked her hips forward.

He closed his eyes and let intense pleasure build and build. Her mouth sucked his, pushing and caressing with her tongue, nipping at his own tongue when he tried to return her caress.

Her hands rubbed his body. Her palms slid over his chest, across his nipples, and under his armpits, where his excitement had created heat and moisture. He'd always been ticklish. When she touched him where no woman had ever touched him before, he shivered, embarrassment adding another dimension to his pleasure.

He knew so much more than Peach. He'd a full fifteen years on her in years and a rough life to boot. He ought to be touching her and squeezing her, exciting her. But she turned him into a boy experiencing his first pleasure.

She was moving faster now. She needed him. She needed him.

That thought pleased him immeasurably. For months he'd never thought she really needed him. But now—

She was gasping for breath against his shoulder. "Will— too much."

He slid his good arm around her waist and held her as she let herself go, crying her pleasure. Her body clenched around him, and he exploded, gasping for breath, incapable of drawing enough air into his lungs.

Her shudders rippled all along his length, pulling him with her. *She's a perfect fit*, he thought. *A perfect fit*.

When they'd finished, he slid down from the pillows and she collapsed on top of him. Their bodies slick with sweat moved against each other as he turned on his side and she pulled the sheet over them both.

"I hope I didn't hurt you" was the last thing she murmured.

"You just about killed me," he replied. "But I'm dying happy."

* * *

When Peach awoke, her head was still cradled on Will's shoulder. He lay on his back, his arm around her, his face turned away from her.

His broad chest rose and fell rhythmically. His skin was cool. The fever must be gone. That was good. He was going to be well. Completely well.

She wondered what that would mean for her. She wondered about what they'd done last night. She'd really loved every single thing about it. She wanted to do it over and over again with Will.

Only with Will.

But she didn't dare. How was she going to stop this? He didn't promise anything. But they'd made love now four times. Suddenly, she wanted to cry. She could very well be having a baby. *Oh, sweet Jesus.*

She closed her eyes and tried to think of something else. When she opened them, she found Will smiling at her.

"Good morning."

She almost choked with pain. She wanted to hear those words from him for the rest of her life. "Good morning."

He brushed the top of her head with his lips. "My arm's gone to sleep."

"Oh!" She sat up. The sheet fell away, but she caught it and dragged it back across her breasts. Tucking it under her arms, she began to massage his shoulder.

"Don't bother. It'll be all right in a minute." He stretched it to demonstrate.

She reached over the side of the bed for her clothing. The room was cold. The fire in the stove had gone out. She pulled her dress over her head and swung her legs over the bed.

"You don't have to get up," he protested. "My arm's already better."

"Oh, yes, I do. I've got a job with Luke. I can't let him down. He's been too nice to both of us."

Will looked provoked. "Why don't you just poke up the fire and come back until it gets warm?"

She hitched up her petticoats and knelt to collect her hairpins and combs. "I'll start the fire for you. Then I've got to go. They'll be coming for breakfast any minute."

As efficiently as she could under his annoyed gaze, she set the room and her clothing to rights. "I'll bring you some breakfast in just a few minutes," she promised from the door. "Just take it easy."

"Peach," he called.

"What?"

"Come back and kiss me." He held out his arm.

She should refuse. She was already late.

She shook her head. Shaking her finger at him, she dashed across the room and kissed him hard on the mouth.

Then she ran for her life.

Chapter Sixteen

As soon as Peach left the room, Will eased his arm out of the sling. While beads of sweat stippled his forehead, he worked to straighten it out.

When he peeked under the bandages, his stomach turned so violently that he thought he was going to vomit. The only way he saved his breakfast was to start cussing Doc Shandlin for a butcher. He'd expected to see swelling and bruising, but the crosshatching of scabs and stitches made his head swim.

What had Doc done to him?

He thought about putting the arm back in the sling, about giving up. He could lie there like a slug until he lost his job and all hope. He wished for whiskey—a good, stiff drink to dull the pain. While his muscles trembled and pain streaked all the way down to his fingertips, he realized he needed half a bottle to handle this.

He'd gone that route before, and Peach had almost died. He'd sworn he'd never drink again.

He'd give the arm a try.

Will gritted his teeth to turn his howl into a thin keen. The tears welled over and ran down his cheeks. Sweat popped out on his forehead.

Nevertheless, he managed to lift his arm to shoulder height. He stared in amazement at his hand trembling a yard in front of his chin. He hadn't been able to do this for two years.

What *had* the doctor done?

Dimly, he remembered Peach holding a bottle of chloroform over a cone above his nose. He'd woke up that morning to discover he'd lost a week of his life.

He tried bending his arm and lowering it. He could feel the blood running out of his head as the pain built. Not just the muscles protested. The tendons and ligaments screamed at being forced to hold muscles and bones together to perform movements they'd almost forgotten how to perform.

When he tried rotating his arm in the shoulder socket, he had to give up. The agony was too intense. Still, he felt hopeful. Even if he didn't have any more use of the limb than he had just then, Shandlin had made some important improvements.

Moaning to himself, he maneuvered the sling back around his arm and waited for the flaming pain to ease down.

As he sat, he realized he couldn't stay in the room any longer. He needed to go downstairs and take his job back. Maybe they'd told Peach they were waiting for him, but he didn't believe it. Towns just didn't do things like that. Hell, he didn't even have Bert to cover for him.

Poor Bert Ayers had been the one who'd shot him—in the right shoulder.

He'd thought he was unlucky. Now, as he massaged his bicep, he was beginning to think Bert might have done him a favor. If he could just stave off the town council.

Led by Mungerson, they'd probably been making inquiries for a week for someone to replace him.

The doctor would have told them that he'd been wounded twice in the right shoulder. When he walked downstairs with his right arm in a sling, the job might be over.

He sighed. No sense putting off the inevitable. With much sitting down and resting between tasks, he managed to dress himself. He tried to stick his thumb through his belt loop, but the arm needed more support than that. He finally realized he had no choice. He had to put his arm in the damned sling and come downstairs.

When he walked into the saloon, Luke grinned.

"Hey, Marshal," he boomed, "welcome back to the land o' the living!"

Will nodded as he gingerly lowered himself at a table instead of standing in his usual place at the bar. Several men at the bar nodded and smiled. At the table across the room, the poker players raised their hands.

"Sarsaparilla?" Luke asked.

Will wanted whiskey. He could imagine the burn in his throat, the pleasant headiness that would numb his pain at the same time it eased his worry about his job. His mouth felt dry in anticipation.

Clear in his mind, however, was the staggering, panting fool who'd tried to make the run back to Coffeyville from C. N. Howard's windmill. One mile had almost killed him. He wasn't sure he wouldn't have fallen over dead of a heart attack if that cowboy hadn't come along and given up his horse.

Will made himself a promise to find the man and thank him and offer to pay him for his day.

No, he'd let whiskey take its toll on the rest of his body. Now he had to stop it. "Sarsaparilla," he called. "Cold if you've got it."

Luke grinned like a father pleased that his son had made the right choice. "Comin' right up."

As he waited, Will caught a glimpse of Peach passing among the customers in the dining room. She looked good even from a distance. She'd probably scold him when she caught him out of bed. Women were like that—women who cared.

A tinge of bitterness swept him. His first wife had left him the first time the doctor had changed the bandage. Peach had nursed him for a week. But Peach was like that. She had a good heart.

His brows drew together in a scowl. Probably Peach had made love to him that morning out of pity. She'd done it before. He'd never forget the shame he'd felt when she'd said they were both so lonely.

He needed to do something real nice for Peach. He hoped to hell they hadn't anything to be sorry for.

Luke set the bottle of cold sarsaparilla on the table.

Will raised his left hand out of habit, then lowered it. With studied care, he lifted his right. The sling draped off it as he closed his hand around the bottle and raised it to his mouth. He would have given all he owned right now if he'd been tipping up a slug of whiskey.

Instead, he drank the cold sarsaparilla and set the bottle down. When his arm was settled back in the sling, his gaze met Luke's. The innkeeper nodded, his grin growing impossibly wider.

Will's arm hurt all the way, but at least it worked. If the town council didn't fire him, then maybe—

The door opened letting in a blast of frigid air. Bundled up like an Eskimo, Lemuel Mungerson charged in.

Luke grimaced. He hoped he'd had a few more hours before the councilman lit into him. Plenty of signs had pointed to his being the man who'd caused all the trouble. He'd really expected him to be the one caught in the trap. Instead, he'd caught poor Bert Ayers. He shook his head faintly at the thought of the misguided, greedy boy. In their way, the Daltons had him to answer for too.

"Marshal!" Mungerson strode toward him like the December wind—cold and blustery. "Marshal! What's this about Bert Ayers?"

Will regarded the stocky man soberly. The question had several answers. He wondered which one was required. "He got away," Will said at last. "I'll be after him as soon as I'm back on my feet."

Mungerson hunched his shoulders. "There must be some mistake. Bert's always been a good boy. You can't go off half-cocked and assume someone's guilty of something."

The councilman had pitched his voice so that everyone in the room heard him. He pulled off his wool cap and ran a hand over his thinning hair to be sure it was in place.

Will instantly recognized this as a political speech. "I didn't assume anything," he replied evenly. "He had a gun aimed at a woman." He didn't say that she'd been in the bathhouse. Peach hadn't been naked, but that part of the story was nobody's business. "When I ordered him to put it down, he shot me."

"Maybe you scared him," Mungerson suggested. "A boy like that should never have been a deputy."

"You're right about that," Will admitted. "I'm pretty sure that he shot Corny Dahlerheidt and was party to the attempt to lynch Emmett Dalton. I never suspected him at any time."

Mungerson grinned knowingly as he looked around. Everyone was listening to him. "In other words, you made a mistake."

"I'd say so."

"You've made quite a few, I take it. So many that the town would be well within its rights to take back your badge." Again he looked around, expecting to see approval on the faces of the listeners. Their neutral expressions drew a frown from him.

"The *town*," Will said softly, "can take back my badge anytime it wants. Everything's pretty well settled down now. As soon as Emmett Dalton was safely transferred to the territorial prison, things got quiet real quick."

Mungerson folded his arms. "You did that without permission," he accused. "He was our prisoner. He was ours to try."

"And make another circus," Will suggested. "Get photographers and reporters hip-deep in here. Have people coming from miles around to collect souvenirs."

"It was good for business." Mungerson looked for confirmation to Luke.

The innkeeper shrugged. "Oh, I admit we did a land office business, but we had a lot of drunks. Lots of breakage. Lots of stuff stolen and torn up. I had to send for the marshal practically every night for a while."

"Some of 'em was real nasty," a customer at the next table observed. "Real nasty people."

"I was robbed one night," the man across from him said. "Some owlhoot stuck a gun up against my backbone and pulled my money right out of my pocket. Got dang nigh twenty dollars."

Mungerson scowled at the two. "That's my point. The marshal wasn't doing his job."

"Man can't be in more'n one place at a time. Guns were goin' off all over town some nights."

"Marshal Wesley's out every night all night," Luke Scurlock chimed in. "He's patrolled this town for more than two months now. We've got ourselves a real lawman, Mungerson."

Mungerson shifted from one foot to the other and glared at all and sundry, Luke in particular. "I wouldn't say that—"

"Why don't you go on about your business," Luke continued, "such as getting the town another couple of streetlights? The one over on Walnut across from the banks works real well, but the banks close at six in the afternoon. We need more than one down here by the railroad tracks, where people are coming and going at all hours.''

As if he'd been stabbed, Mungerson swung around to face the innkeeper. His ears turned red. He coughed and mumbled something.

''That's a good idea.'' A man at the bar agreed. ''Make things a damn sight safer in this end of town.''

''That's taxpayer money we'd be spending,'' Mungerson protested. He fumbled for his cap.

''I'm a taxpayer,'' Scurlock informed him.

''Me too.''

''Same here.''

The councilman pulled his cap down tight over his ears as he retreated to the door. ''The town will want more of an explanation than you've been able to give, Marshal.''

''I'll write a report,'' Will called. ''When's the next meeting.''

''Er—after Christmas—er—January.''

''I'll have it for them.''

Mungerson let in another cold blast of air on his way out.

Luke came out from behind the bar to bring another bottle to the table. ''How about another sarsaparilla, Marshal Wesley?'' Then he lowered his voice so only Will could hear. ''Now, why don't you do the right thing for you-know-who?''

Will hunched his good shoulder. ''The situation's still the same. Still broken up and old and—''

Luke leaned even closer. His lips brushed Will's ear. ''Bullshit.''

Will had been back at marshaling nearly a week when a gentle knock startled Peach. Her braid only half done, she stared at the door. She didn't remember anyone ever knocking at her door before. Not that it was just her door. It was hers and Will's.

So she'd have more room to nurse Will, Luke had moved them into the room at the front of the hotel. It was the closest to the railroad tracks, which meant that it was pretty noisy, but it was also one of two big rooms. Besides a bed and a chest of drawers, it had a table with two chairs, and a love seat. It had two lamps and a rug on the floor. Peach had never enjoyed such luxury.

The situation between her and Will had gone back to the way it was before. She slept in the bed at night while the marshal patrolled. He slept in the bed during the daytime. She never went to bed until he came down to work. He never went to bed until she'd served him breakfast. They tried not to look at each other if they passed in the halls.

At first, Peach thought she'd go quietly crazy, but when she discovered she wasn't going to have a baby, she managed to calm down and go on about her business as before.

Now she hesitated. It was nearly midnight. Was some stranger blundering around the halls, looking for his room? The knock came again.

She was about to ignore it, when Will's voice sounded through the panels. "Can I come in for just a minute, Peach?"

She didn't think it was a good idea, but this was Will's room too. She stepped back.

"I saw your light was still on before I came up," he explained. He pulled off his hat and gloves. "Can I sit down?"

Something was up. She felt a little thrill of trepidation. If he was getting unhappy with the way things were, that was just too bad. She wasn't going to go through another month of worrying for him. She'd been lucky, but next time she might not be.

He seated himself on the love seat.

She waited.

"You sit down too. Please." He patted the seat beside him. "I want you to look here." He held out a big book.

She stared at it. "That's the Sears and Roebuck catalogue?"

His smile reminded her of a little boy's. "That's right. Some folks call it the wish book."

She waved it away. "It is that. I took a look in there once. I can't even afford the stuff in the emporium. Sears, Roebuck is way too high for me to even think about."

"Well, let's see what we can find. Christmas is coming up pretty fast."

She couldn't believe what she was hearing. She wanted to say that he didn't have to buy her a Christmas present. Only that might be the wrong thing to say. It might sound as if she expected one, when he meant no such thing. He probably just wanted her to look at the catalogue to help him pick out something for his friend Narcissey.

He'd made it crystal clear the way he felt about her—the way they were supposed to feel about each other.

Carefully, he stretched his right arm across the back of the seat.

She noticed how he seemed to have pretty good use of it if he moved slowly. When he ate, he used it almost as much as he used his left. She felt a little curl of pleasure ripple through her. She'd told the doctor to go ahead and look how well it had turned out.

He opened the book to the pages with the dresses.

She stared at him while she bit her tongue to keep from asking him what this was all about. Did she dare hope?

"I figured you could help me pick out a dress for Narcissey," he explained. "After all, I did borrow her horse and practically kill it."

For Narcissey. Ah! That explained everything.

She sat down beside him, keeping her head bent so he

wouldn't guess she was even a little disappointed. She told herself she was actually relieved, because she couldn't have accepted the dress. No nice girls would accept clothes from men. She might not be a nice girl in the strict sense of the word, but she wouldn't have to turn a gift down to prove it.

Why did a secret part of her wish she'd have the chance to tell him no?

"What do you think about this one?" Will asked.

He pointed to a garment labeled a "Ladies Walking Suit." The picture showed a lady in a lovely fitted suit with wide lapels and leg-o'-mutton sleeves. The skirt was full, but when she bent over to read the description, she found it didn't require crinolines, nor did it have a bustle. The outfit included a small hat tilted low over the forehead and tied back with a veil. The parasol matched it.

It was wonderful. It made her left-behinds look worse than ever. She wished she didn't want it so badly for herself. It was five dollars and ninety-eight cents. Any woman would love to have it.

"I think Narcissey will love it," she said through stiff lips. "It'll be perfect for her to wear to church and for socials and such."

"That's what I thought," he agreed enthusiastically. "It's not too fancy."

"No." She ducked her head. She could feel heat rising in her cheeks.

"Good. I don't think Narcissey would want anything fancy." He bent lower to look into her face. "She's a pretty practical gal after all."

"Yes." She smiled. She knew she should be happy for Narcissey's wonderful gift. "She's pretty practical."

"What color?" Will urged.

Peach ran her finger down the description as she tried to remember the color of Narcissey's eyes. "I think navy blue would be nice. It says right here you can get it in black, brown, or navy blue faille.''

"Navy blue faille?"

She smiled. "You don't know what faille is, do you?"

"No. But I'll take your word for it."

She hesitated. "Were you planning on a hat too?"

He nodded. "Otherwise, Narcissey's liable to clap that old hat of hers on her head and go off to church without thinking."

"I like the hat that's shown here."

He regarded it with his head cocked to one side. "It looks awfully small."

Men! Narcissey wasn't going to wear it for protection from a snowstorm. She was going to wear it to look pretty. "It's perfect."

He frowned and tugged at his lower lip. Finally, he relented. "If you say so."

"It's forty-nine cents."

"That's okay." He studied the picture closely. "Since the hat's so small, she oughta have something to protect her head. How about the umbrella?"

"Parasol," she corrected him. "Oh, yes. You should get that too. It's only ninety-nine cents. That's not so much more."

"Right," he agreed heartily. "Shoot the works."

She nodded. Her finger traced the figure on the page. It was a wonderful present. Narcissey Jellicoe was lucky to have a friend like Will Wesley.

His hand closed over hers. His arm hugged her over against him. He kissed her temple. His lips moved to her ear. "Thank you."

She should pull away. If he kept hugging her and kissing her like this, he was going to make her cry. She wanted that suit so much even though she didn't want Will to buy it for her. She thought about her small store of money. It wasn't enough to squander nearly ten dollars on an outfit. Besides. Where would she wear it?

She tried to push away from him. "You're welcome."

He wouldn't let her go. Instead, he took the wish book off her lap and pulled her closer to him. With his chin against her hair, he murmured, "Doc Shandlin told me what you did for me. That's about the greatest thing that anyone ever did for me."

She pulled away so she could look him in the eye. "I didn't do so much. Doc did all the work. You should be thanking him."

"I did. He told me he couldn't have done it without you."

"I told him to do it."

"And he said you stood right over me and dripped the chloroform. A couple of times he said you passed him instruments and adjusted the light."

"That's not so much." She couldn't help being pleased. She'd been proud of what she'd done because to her it had seemed wonderful.

"I don't know of another woman who could have done it."

She remembered Sister Agnes Mary and the nuns at the orphanage. "I know several. What I did wasn't so special."

He caught her by the shoulders and turned her to face him. Leaning toward her, he kissed her long and tenderly. "Peach Smith, I'm fifteen years older than you are and pretty beat up, but my arm's feeling good, I swear I'll never take another drink of whiskey, and I've got a job. And it's all thanks to you. Will you marry me?"

A ringing set up in her ears. She felt dizzy and warm and cold all at once. She closed her eyes. She hadn't expected this. Never in a million years. He'd been so certain that he wouldn't marry her. She felt tears starting.

"Peach—" He shook her gently. "I'm asking you to marry me."

She whipped up her temper and opened her eyes. She had a good job too. She was able to take care of herself. "I thank you very much, Marshal Wesley, but you don't have to do this. You don't have to be this grateful."

She started to get up, but he caught her. "Now, don't you get on your high horse with me, Peach Smith. For your information, I don't *just* feel grateful the way somebody I remember said she did when she made love to me the first time."

Peach whipped her head around. "I never."

"You did."

"That was different."

He used his right arm to take her hand. The light in his eyes warmed her all the way to her toes. "You gave me the most important thing you had to give. I'm giving you the rest of my life. It's a fair trade."

She tried one more time. "But you don't want to marry me."

"Why not? I've been in love with you for weeks."

"You were trying to get me to leave town."

"And you know why. Peach, look. I can marry you now because I can take care of you." He let her go and rose. Standing in front of her, he demonstrated how he could move his arm, lift it straight out from his shoulder, lower it, bring it across his body, raise it above his shoulder level, although he still couldn't reach straight up with it.

"It's going to take time," he said thinly. The sweat had popped out on his forehead while he'd executed those movements. Once, he'd bitten down hard on his lower lip.

Now he held out both arms side by side to illustrate. "My left is a lot stronger than my right. You can see the difference. I'll have to exercise it and do some plain old heavy work to get it back into shape."

He dropped to his knees in front of her. "But I can do that. I'm grateful. I also think you're one of the sweetest girls I've ever known. You've given me back everything I ever wanted. And I think you want to marry me."

She felt all fire and ice. He was surely right about that last sentence. She loved him so much and she wanted to get married so desperately. She had been so afraid that she'd spoiled her chances. She didn't want to live alone all her life. And she wanted a baby. "I do want to marry you."

He smiled a joyous smile that made his face look ten years younger. Shaved and dressed in clean clothes, his badge polished to a high shine, he was as handsome as a dime novel hero. "Then let's do it. Let's do it tomorrow. Luke can give the bride away and be the best man too."

She hesitated. Happiness brimmed over inside her. She was dizzy with her. Her thoughts whirled. And out of the whirling thoughts came a ghost that cast a pall about her. It had no face, but she knew its name. She took a deep breath. "I want to ask a favor."

"Name it and it's yours."

"Let's get married in Fort Smith."

He rocked back on his heels to stare at her. "Why, for heaven's sake?"

"I want to talk to Judge Isaac Parker."

He looked frankly puzzled. "What do you want with him?"

She might regret this, but she had to do it. She had to put this thing to rest. "He's my last hope. If he doesn't know, then I guess nobody does."

Will bounced to his feet, shaking his head. He thrust a hand out in front of his body as if to ward off an attacker. "Don't say it. Don't say it."

Rising, she caught his hand between her own. "I have to, Will. Don't you see?"

"No!"

"Please."

"*No!*"

"This is very important to me."

"Forget it."

"Will, I have to try one last thing."

He ran his other hand around the back of his neck. "God damn! God damn Bob Dalton!" He stalked across the room to stare out the window. "If he's not burning in hell right this minute, he sure ought to be."

She came after him and put her hand over his mouth. "Don't say that. I'll just ask the judge if he knows who told the town they were coming. It was probably one of his marshals. They're the only ones left. But I have to know. I promise I won't do anything about it."

"Oh, sure. You travel three hundred miles and then you won't do anything about it."

She squirmed. "Well. Maybe I'll write the man a letter and tell him what I think of him. If he lives around here, maybe I'll just go up to him someday and look him in the face. That's all. But I have to know. Then I swear I'll let them rest in peace."

Peach bought two round-trip tickets out of the money Bob Dalton had left her. It took almost all of it. When she counted out the contents of the purse, she found she had only nine dollars left. Four of silver and a five-dollar gold piece.

Will watched her with his arms folded across his chest, his brow contorted in a scowl.

"You don't even remember what Bob Dalton looked like," he challenged darkly. "Go ahead. Describe him to me."

She tossed her head. "I remember how he died. I remember that he didn't have to. You were the only one in the entire town who didn't start shooting immediately."

Disapproval fairly radiated from his tall figure. His anger showed so clearly that a couple on the platform turned to stare at him. The woman edged nearer her husband and wrapped her gloved hand around his arm.

"We're on a wild-goose chase."

"It's not costing you anything."

"I should have taken that damned purse and thrown it in the river."

"But you didn't."

Toe to toe they faced each other.

The conductor stood by the step, staring. "Marshal?"

Peach put her hand on Will's chest. "Just this once. If nothing comes of this, we've had a honeymoon."

"I don't need Bob Dalton to pay for my honeymoon," Will snarled.

She slipped her hand under his arm. "Come on. We'll be back before you know it."

"All aboard."

She climbed into the coach. Cursing under his breath, he followed her. The conductor set the step up and swung up. He waved his arm to the fireman up ahead in the locomotive. The train began to roll. "All aboard."

"Will Wesley. Lord, son, you're a sight for sore eyes."

Judge Isaac Parker came around his big desk and caught Will's hand in a hearty grip. His usual stern face, with its lantern jaw, spread in a welcoming smile.

Will returned the judge's handshake and allowed himself to be pulled into his old friend's arms for a hug. "It's been a long time."

"Too long," Parker agreed. "Too damn long."

He eased his grip on Will's right hand. "How's the arm?"

Will's smile widened. "Better. Much better. Doc Shandlin in Coffeyville took seventeen more shot out of it last month. It's really on the mend."

"Great! Great! Modern medicine is great stuff." Isaac

stepped back when he saw Peach waiting in the doorway. He looked at Will expectantly.

Will came back to usher her forward. "This is my bride-to-be, Judge Parker. Miss Peach Smith. Peach, this is Judge Isaac Parker, the most honest man and the straightest shooter this side of the Mississippi."

Parker made a dismissive gesture, but he looked pleased. "Marrying too. Good for you, Will. Put all that behind you. You've got your arm back. You've got a good job. Now take a pretty wife."

He took Peach's gloved hand and looked her up and down. She was glad she had chosen to wear her new Christmas suit.

Again she felt the thrill she'd experienced when Will had presented her with a Christmas package. Her hands had trembled as she'd opened it because she'd never received a present before. When she saw it contained the suit she'd picked out of the Sears, Roebuck catalogue, she'd burst into tears. She thought he'd gotten her to pick it out for Narcissey.

Now she caught the admiring looks that passed between her husband-to-be and the most famous judge in five states.

"We came for you to marry us," Will said happily.

Parker's eyes widened, then he tightened his lips and swallowed hard. "I'd be pleased to do that, son." His voice had suddenly turned hoarse and developed a bit of a catch. "I'd be purely pleased."

Peach couldn't believe how fast it happened. The judge stepped to his door and called the bailiff to bring the Bible, his Bible, the one that he swore the witnesses in with.

It was well used, the black dye worn off the corners. The gilded letters on the top were darkly tarnished. Knowing what it was, she imagined the hundreds who'd touched it—guilty and innocent, criminals pleading for their lives and victims pleading for justice. It gave Peach an eerie feeling.

The bailiff was their witness. The judge pronounced the words. Will held the Bible and took his vow in a deep voice that made Peach shiver.

When her turn came, she found her throat was suddenly dry. Why was she afraid? This marriage was what she'd wanted. This was what she'd dreamed of. She swallowed and placed her hand on top of the Book.

When she'd said the words, Will placed his other hand over hers. It was his right hand. The hand that now moved so well and was gaining strength every day.

"Have you the ring?"

The question startled her. She certainly hadn't thought about jewelry.

Will smiled reassuringly. Reaching in his pocket, he handed a gold band to the judge. It was shiny and brand-new like the bands the newest sisters wore at the convent. Only she wasn't being married to God, she was being married to Will Wesley, the town marshal of Coffeyville, Kansas.

Her heart was so full, she wanted to sing and weep at the same time.

"You may kiss the bride," Judge Parker said.

Will passed the bailiff the Bible and took her in his arms. He was so handsome, so dear. She could feel a tear and then another slipping down her cheeks. Oh, this was so embarrassing. She didn't want Will to think that she didn't love him. That she didn't want to marry him.

He grinned at her and then at the judge. "I think you've made her cry."

Parker patted Peach's shoulder. "You're not the first, Mrs. Wesley. And you've got good reason. You're getting one of the best men I know."

The judge insisted on pouring Will a drop of whiskey to toast the nuptials.

Peach held her breath, but Will didn't waver. "I've just

come off that horse, Judge," he said offhandedly. "It nearly killed me. If you don't mind, I'll just be pleased for you to drink for me."

Parker nodded as he set Will's glass down. "I understand, son, and I'm glad for you. It's a bad habit, and it'll kill you. At the rate I'm going, I'll probably beat it, but not by much." He raised his drink to them both and tossed it off. "Long and happy lives and a baby the first year. Isaac's a good name."

They all laughed.

Peach cleared her throat. "Judge Parker, I have a question for you."

He inclined his head. "If I can answer it, I'll be glad to."

"Who was the man that tipped the town of Coffeyville that the Daltons were coming?"

The smile slipped off the judge's face. He glanced at Will, then shook his head. "I haven't the foggiest idea."

Peach let her breath out in a sigh. Her last chance was gone. Both men were standing ramrod straight, staring at her. She wondered. "Would you tell me if you knew?"

The jovial friend who had hugged Will and toasted their marriage was gone. In his place stood a stern, cold man with a jaw like granite. "If I knew, young woman, I would personally give the man a medal. He got rid of the last of a bad lot. The only Dalton worth knowing was Franklin. He worked for me and died in the line of duty, serving a warrant for this court.

"His brothers, alas, were a thoroughly reprehensible and dishonest lot. Grat, Bob, and Bill rampaged around Oklahoma, murdering and robbing. When Bill was killed, Bob and Grat recruited young Emmett. I understand he's still alive and will serve a long time in jail for his crimes. The other two—had they survived—would most assuredly have been hanged.

"This man, whoever he might have been, saved the state and the country a great deal of time and money."

Peach felt his words like blows. Even though Will and Luke had said as much, the sonorous pronouncements of the "hanging judge" were like a death knell. She slipped her hand into that of her new husband. "Thank you, Judge."

"You're quite welcome, Mrs. Wesley."

Bert Ayers watched them leave the courthouse.

He couldn't believe they'd come to Fort Smith. He'd hated to run, but he had to go somewhere he wasn't known to find a job. He'd tried to put them out of his mind, but the more he thought about how he'd been cheated out of that treasure, the more angry he'd become.

They'd set a trap for him. They'd caught him in it and made him look like a fool. He couldn't ever go back to Coffeyville again.

He stiffled a sob. He was homesick. He missed his maw and paw. He missed his friends.

He hated Marshal Wesley. But more than him, he hated Peach Smith.

Chapter Seventeen

"I want to go to church, Will." In front of the Catholic church on Garrison Avenue, Peach let her gaze rise with the spire to the cross on top.

He patted her hand. "Here we are."

Together they entered, but Will remained in the entrance.

As Sister Agnes Mary had taught her, Peach touched her fingertips to the basin and then walked slowly toward the altar. Halfway down the aisle, where a prayer bench was down, she knelt, then entered the pew.

She knelt on the bench, her eyes fixed on the altar. Candles flickered in banks on either side. With her heart full, she made her devotional.

She could hear Sister Agnes Mary's voice reminding her that all things in this vale of tears are fleeting. Yet here she was, happy as she had ever been with her life stretching before her, as perfect as life in this mortal world could be.

Except for the weight in her purse. It dragged on her

arm. It weighed on her soul. She had to lay it down. Fervently, she bent her head and prayed for Bob Dalton's soul.

For the first time in a long time, his face swirled out of the depths. He was smiling. Handsome Bob Dalton, smiling. His lips moved. "Brazil."

The day had been a turmoil of emotions. She could feel the tears starting again.

Stop it, she told herself. *There's no reason to cry.* She pulled a handkerchief out and dabbed at her eyes. Useless. A waterfall of emotions slipped out of her. She'd cried for Will today and for happiness. How dare Bob Dalton resurrect himself on her wedding day!

She opened her eyes wide and concentrated on the cross. She stuffed the handkerchief back in her purse. Her fingers touched the pinch purse. Bob's money. What was left of it. Her fingers were cold as she pulled it out.

She shook the coins out into her hand. A five-dollar gold piece and four silver dollars. She touched each in turn, moving them across her palm.

"Bob," she whispered. "I tried. I tried everything I knew to do. Will you ever forgive me?"

Almost before the words were out, she had her answer.

She didn't believe in ghosts. Bob Dalton's spirit wasn't about to blow down the church aisle to whisper in her ear. The words were from her. Would he have forgiven her? Could she forgive herself? The answer came to her out of her own logic. Wherever he was—hell or purgatory—Bob had other things on his mind right now. He'd put all this nonsense behind him.

She rose. Instead of coming back up the center aisle, she sidled across the row to the candles flickering before the station of St. Veronica wiping the blood from Christ's face as he struggled up Calvary.

Into the poor box she slipped the nine dollars. She took

a candle and lighted it. "For you, Bob Dalton. May you find forgiveness for your sins."

Then she hurried out to join her husband.

She didn't tell Will until they were back in their room at the hotel.

Her husband dropped down on the bed with a great creak of the springs. He closed his eyes and uttered his own prayer of thanks. When Parker couldn't help her, he'd been so afraid she'd keep on looking. Peach had a stubborn streak a mile wide.

"You're sure about this?" He took her hands and drew her down beside him. "You're really sure?"

"Really sure?" she said soberly. "I've done all I can. I have nowhere else to go. No one can tell me anything new." She smiled. "It's the new year. It's 1893. Judge Parker was right. The outlaw gangs are gone forever. And that's a good thing."

He could feel his eyes stinging. He couldn't imagine what was happening to him. He knew only a great surge of relief and happiness.

"Will." She leaned toward him. "Are you crying?"

He blinked rapidly and snorted. "Who? Me? Not much. I've been thinking I was about to take a cold."

She smiled as if she didn't believe him. That was all right. He wanted to be loved. He didn't need to be believed.

He drew her toward him and kissed her. Tonight was his wedding night. He wanted this to be a long one that they'd never forget.

They undressed together, looking at each other's bodies, touching them because now they had the right to do so. They had vowed to honor each other with their bodies. They belonged to each other.

When she ran her hand over his hipbone and down his belly, he just grinned and let her. When he came up behind her and thrust himself beneath her buttocks at the same time he squeezed both her breasts, she threw her arms up around the back of his head and arched against him.

He kissed her neck and tugged at her earlobe with his teeth.

"Will," she whispered. "Please. You're my husband. Let's—"

He pushed her down on the bed and caught her ankles. Doubling her knees against his chest, he drove into her. Her eyes closed as he tried his dead-level best to make her feel everything she was capable of. He grinned like a fool when she couldn't keep from screaming.

It wasn't ladylike, but there it was. He knew from past experience. Pure pleasure was harder to keep still about than any pain.

When they did it again, Will broke his promise to himself to take a long time. His excitement drove him faster and faster. Instead of taking care with her, he lost control like a boy. She was so hot, so wet, so tight.

They finished together in a burst of passion that left them with barely enough strength to crawl beneath the covers and wrap their arms around each other before they fell asleep.

Later in the dark he caressed her again, brought her to her pleasure, then did it again—and again. In the end he held her limp and purely satiated with pleasure while she begged for mercy but didn't mean a word of it.

The boom of a rifle followed by the crack of a pistol, once, twice, three times, brought Will to his feet.

Suddenly, Peach's lunch made her sick to her stomach. "This isn't your town—"

But he was already heading for the door.

The train had pulled into Joplin, Missouri, at five minutes to twelve. The train to Coffeyville wouldn't be pulling out for an hour. They should have bought a sandwich and gotten on. That way Will might not have heard the noise.

"Will." She sprang to her feet and hurried to the door. "Stay here."

She was a marshal's wife now. She clutched her napkin to her waist and thought how she was going to have to live with this for the rest of her life. Every time a shot was fired, Will was going to run toward it.

He was going to be in danger.

Another rifle shot boomed out, and then another.

She remembered the Daltons. They'd had pistols. The rifles had come from the defenders. She leaned against the wall and began to pray.

Three men in yellow slickers and red bandannas were backing out of the bank. Also wearing a yellow slicker, another man mounted on a skittish sorrel was trying to hold three horses for his fellows.

Will took all these things in at a glance. The sorrel was the key.

Drawing his pistol, he knelt behind the hitching post in the next block. He aimed at the ground under the animal's front hooves and squeezed off a shot.

Up the animal reared, whinnying in fear. The bank robber lost his seat and toppled from the saddle. At the same time, he lost his grasp on the reins. The other mounts broke free.

Will aimed again at the ground beneath the horses' feet. He squeezed off the shot, and the horses bolted.

The robbers tried to catch them. One actually caught the trailing rein and jerked his animal around. It reared up, fighting the bit and the bridle.

"Easy, boy, easy." The animal came down.

The rifle boomed. The man who'd caught his animal staggered. The horse whinnied, then backed away at the smell of blood. The robber fell to his knees, then face-forward in the dirt.

Keeping himself behind the post, Will shouted, "It's all over, boys! Drop your guns and raise your hands."

Two of them looked in his direction, while the third dived back into the bank.

When they looked as if they might try the same stunt, Will put a shot into the boardwalk in front of them. "I said, drop 'em!"

From behind them came another voice. "Much obliged, stranger." To the bank robbers he said, "We've got you in a cross fire, boys. Why don't you just lay those guns down and stretch out flat so you won't get hurt?"

When they didn't move, he lobbed a shot into the board a foot from the hole Will's had made. "Down!"

Obediently, clumsily, they dropped.

"Don't shoot no more!" One robber awkwardly raised his hands above his head, though he kept his face pressed to the boards. "I'm giving up. Don't shoot me!"

His partner did the same. The one who'd taken the rifle shot lay still in his blood in the street.

One robber still remained inside the bank. A woman began to scream.

The marshal of Joplin stepped from behind a building. He motioned to the man on the roof to keep him covered. Keeping low and close to the wall, he hurried along the street.

The woman's screaming stopped as if she'd been throttled.

Will stepped out too. At the same time, he pulled open his coat and flashed his badge. Better let the defenders see him than be mistaken for one of the gang and shot.

All along the street, men were stepping out of stores, some with guns, some profoundly curious even at the risk of their own lives. The robbery was far from over.

One of the robbers started to get up.

"Keep your face to that boardwalk if you don't want to get it shot off!" the marshal of Joplin yelled.

Will caught a flash of movement at the end of the alley to his right. Pivoting, he saw a man dragging a struggling woman behind a building. The robber had gone out the back door with a shield.

Will waved his arm. "He's out the back and going this way!"

His counterpart waved to his deputies. "Cover these two."

Will ran down the alley and halted at the corner of the building, from where he ducked low and stuck his head out.

The robber had his arm around the woman's waist. Clapped against his side, he was half carrying her along. She'd stopped screaming, probably under threat, but Will could tell she was dragging her feet. In her struggles she'd pulled the bandanna down, revealing the robber's face.

Will recognized him. A spurt of anger blazed through him. Tal Karnes.

He lined his pistol up, but the woman kept struggling, jostling the robber. Will couldn't get a clear shot. Farther up the alley was a rain barrel. He darted for it.

The robber must have heard him or looked back over his shoulder, because suddenly he turned, clutching the woman in front of him for a shield.

For more than two years Will had carried the memory of that load of double-ought buckshot slamming into his shoulder. For two years he'd been in hell because of it.

He stepped out into the alley. "It's all over. Drop it."

"Like hell I will!"

The robber must have tightened his grip convulsively, because the woman screamed again. In panic or fury she kicked back at her captor's shins. She clawed at his wrists with her fingernails.

Karnes slapped the barrel of his .44 against her temple.

"You wanna bullet through the head?"

She screamed again and stopped struggling.

"Come any closer and I'll shoot her! Swear to God I will!" the robber yelled.

"They're coming behind you now," Will called. "Your friends are already on their way to jail or the cemetery. You'll be joining them one place or the other."

Karnes threw an angry glance over his shoulder. The way was clear so far. He began to back along the alley. The woman was forced to match his steps, although she couldn't keep up.

"She's a drag on your arm," Will called. "Let her go. I'll let you get out of sight."

"Hell with you!" Karnes snapped his pistol toward Will.

Will dived behind the rain barrel.

The bullet slammed into the alley. Dirt flew.

The woman whimpered. She must be nearly deaf from the noise so close to her ear.

Aiming far to the left, Will fired back. The bullet clanged into a metal drum behind the feed store. Yellowish liquid spurted out in a stream.

Karnes glanced in that direction. His face split in a grin as he dragged the woman farther.

Behind him at the entrance to another alley, Will saw a figure step out, then duck back in again.

Cautiously, he rose and stepped out. He was careful to stay next to the barrel. If the shooting started, he wanted to be able to duck. "We can go on playing hide-and-seek all day, Karnes. Or you can give up and go quietly. You'll probably get out in a few years and come back. If we have to shoot you, you'll never come back."

"How'd you know my name?"

"I've met up with you before."

Karnes squinted. He backed another couple of steps. He was almost to the alley.

Will kept his weapon trained on the man's right shoulder. Even though he couldn't pull the trigger, his finger itched to give the criminal a taste of his own medicine. "I work for Judge Parker," he called.

"Wesley!"

Karnes recognized him. He snapped off another shot. But the pistol was pointed down. The bullet threw dirt halfway between them.

Will didn't bother to duck. Instead, he watched the marshal of Joplin step out of the alley and place the muzzle of his pistol against the back of Karnes's skull.

The robber froze.

A deputy followed the marshal and pulled the woman away. She fell into his arms and he carried her away.

At the marshal's prodding, Karnes slowly lowered his pistol.

Will started to stride toward them.

Suddenly, Karnes went berserk. He twisted his arm around and pointed the pistol back under his arm at the marshal's side.

Will's yell of warning was cut off by the explosion. The marshal fell straight over backward.

Karnes tried to bring his gun around to shoot again, but Will fired first. The bullet struck the outlaw dead center in the chest. He went down in the dust beside the man he'd shot.

Will hurried to the marshal's side. "Is it bad?"

The marshal managed a nod. "Burns like he set me afire." He grinned through his teeth. "But they tell me that's good."

"I think so." Will nodded. "If it hurts, you're still alive." He moved around to Karnes's head.

The outlaw's eyes were open. His mouth hung slack as he panted for breath. He recognized Will. "Should of used the second barrel."

As Will nodded, the blood bubbled out of the man's chest.

"Damn fool—"

Who the fool was and why he was damned were never revealed. Karnes's body went slack. His head rolled. The blood slowed to a sluggish stream.

As two deputies knelt by the marshal, Will rose and hurried from the alley. His wife would be worried to death. She'd begged him not to go.

When he hit the main street he was running, running toward the train station, his boot heels hitting the boardwalk like pistons.

He burst into the depot ready to comfort her, to reassure her. She wasn't there. He swung around, taking in the entire depot and the platform behind it. Then he turned to the ticketmaster, who shook his head. "She went with some feller. Young kid, but scruffy. She didn't look like she was too happy, but the marshal was busy."

A young kid! Will drew his gun, still hot from the bullet that had killed Karnes. "Which way?"

The ticketmaster threw his hands in the air. "Across the tracks. Into the stockyards."

Will plunged out the train side and leapt across iron rails. Heart pounding, he climbed through the bars of a cattle pen. He was agonizingly afraid he knew who the young kid was.

The devil's own luck had crossed their paths again. He prayed Peach would be safe. So long as Bert Ayers thought she knew where the Daltons had buried a treasure, she was certain of remaining alive.

He ran up the ramp of the chute where cattle were loaded into cars. From there he could see over the entire expanse of pens and barns.

He couldn't see any sign of them, but the horses in the

second corral over were circling. He leapt down the chute and headed for them.

"You'd better let me go." Peach tried to speak calmly, but she was shaking.

Bert was wild-eyed, spouting all sorts of threats, talking about gold and money and what he was going to do when he got it.

Her greatest fear was that he'd pull the trigger of the snub-nosed .22 he'd stuck in her ribs. Even now he kept gesturing with it. Sometimes the muzzle pointed at the sky, sometimes at her face, sometimes at the ground, sometimes at her heart.

She couldn't believe this was the boy she'd made molasses cookies for.

"Bert," she pleaded. "Don't keep on like this. Look at yourself. Your mother's crying, Bert."

He didn't care. He wanted the gold. "The marshal kept me from getting it. I shot him. I'll shoot you if you don't tell me."

"The marshal isn't dead, Bert. You can come back to Coffeyville. You can see your mother again. I'm sure you won't go to jail. Everyone will forgive you."

He wouldn't listen. "Shut up! Just shut your mouth!"

He dragged her into a stable and pulled a tiny notebook from his pocket. The stub of a pencil was stuck through the spiral. "Draw me a map."

She shook her head.

He struck her in the shoulder with the gun barrel. "Draw me a map!"

She cried out. The pain made her reel. He was completely crazy. Why hadn't anybody ever seen this before?

She took the little notebook and tried to think. This had to be good. What had she seen during the train ride from Coffeyville?

"Hurry up! Hurry up!" He crouched over her, his gun pointed down at the paper.

"It's not in Coffeyville," she said slowly.

" 'Course not." He laughed hysterically, as if she'd said something very funny.

"They buried it—er—just outside Poteau in the Oklahoma Territory. There's a mountain up there with a b-big scar on the side of it. It's a—er—um—slate ridge."

Bert frowned hard as he tried to concentrate.

She drew an inverted V on the page to indicate the mountain. She drew a wavy line to stand for the ridge.

She was drawing a road when she heard the footsteps.

Bert heard them too. He looked up.

Will Wesley stood silhouetted in the door, the light behind him, the darkness of the interior blinding him.

Bert recognized him instantly. He raised his gun. Peach caught his wrist and twisted it upward. He lost his balance and fell forward. The .22 popped in her ear like a Roman candle on the Fourth of July. The next instant, Will's .44 thundered.

Bert's weight dropped on her. He toppled forward and lay still.

"Will!" she screamed. "Will!"

He was beside her in an instant, rolling Bert's body off her, pulling her to her feet and into his arms.

They came together as if they had been apart for years. His arms clutched her and lifted her onto his chest. She wrapped her arms around his neck and kissed him with her mouth open. Her tongue stabbed into his mouth and locked with his.

The terror and pity for poor Bert Ayers were drowned in the ecstasy of love and life in his arms.

The town of Joplin paid for the bridal suite at their best hotel.

"Your money's no good here," the mayor declared. "You're our guest for as long as you want to stay."

When he learned that Peach had struggled with Bert and kept him from shooting her husband, the marshal asked whether the new bride was going to be a deputy.

"She already is," Will replied, hugging her against his side. "If she keeps catching outlaws, I may have to raise her pay."

"We'll be having a little presentation on Thursday," the mayor said. "We sure hope you all will stay." Then he looked Peach up and down. "I notice your bride's got a tear in her skirt. I'd be much obliged if she'd stop by my mercantile on main street. My wife can fix her up with a new one."

Clad in her new dress, Peach went with Will to Joplin's fine new stone courthouse. She was the only woman there when U. S. Marshal Jeptha Hughes arrived to take charge of the prisoners.

The mayor made a speech about ending lawlessness in Missouri. He thanked Will and gave him an envelope with two hundred dollars in it for saving the town's money and the life of the wife of one of its worthiest citizens.

Everyone applauded.

Peach was so proud of Will, she could feel tears prickling in her eyes. He looked so handsome and so happy as he returned to his seat on the dais.

Then Jeptha Hughes took his turn in front of the podium. "I've known Will Wesley since we marshaled together for Judge Parker. He's a square shooter if ever there was one. He's been taking some time off, but he's back in top form now. I'm thinking the U.S. Marshal Service is going to be tapping his shoulder before very long."

He smiled broadly.

"Specially when they learn that he was the one who

warned the town of Coffeyville that the Daltons were coming. He saved the citizens' money then just like he—"

His words were an arrow to Peach's heart. She didn't hear any more. A roaring began in her ears, sweeping everything away. The room went dark. Only the chair arms kept her from falling to the floor.

She blinked. The light came back brighter than before. Will was staring at her, his face white, his expression stricken.

The meeting was over. Men gathered around Will to congratulate him.

She couldn't stand it any longer. She sprang to her feet and ran from the room. She had to get away.

Will Wesley was the snitch. He'd deceived her. He'd lied to her. He'd taken Bob Dalton's money. No wonder he'd given it to the church that day. He never had any intention of searching for the man. He didn't need to investigate himself.

She pulled off her glove and stared at the gold band. So new, so bright, so tarnished.

Oo-oo-oh! She could just imagine him laughing at her behind her back. She was so furious, she wanted to smash and rip things. She wanted to get on the next train out of there and never see his lying, smirking face again.

"Peach!" Will caught up with her. "Peach, sweetheart."

"Don't!" She rounded on him, smashing her fist into his chest. "Don't say anything. There's nothing you can say."

He rocked back on his heels. His face was pasty white. His mouth looked as if it would never smile again. "It was my job, Peach."

The simple words stopped her for an instant, then made her angrier than before. On the streets of Joplin, Missouri, right there before God and everybody, she screamed at him. "You did a damned poor one. They were shot down on the street." Tears flowed down her cheeks. She didn't bother to wipe at them. "Down on the street like dogs! Eight men died! Died!"

He caught her shoulders and tried to pull her against his chest, but she fought him off.

"And you were laughing at me all the time. Behind my back. Pretending to hunt for the traitor when you were the traitor. You were the man who—"

"I was not a traitor," he interrupted harshly. "They were outlaws. They shot their mouths off. I was a deputy marshal. I did my job."

She couldn't deny anything he'd just said. That made her even angrier. She spun on her heel and continued striding toward the depot.

Will stared after her.

Jeptha Hughes, his face white, and part of the town council caught up to him. "I'm sure sorry, Will," the U.S. marshal apologized.

"It's all right. You didn't have any idea how she felt about that damned Bob Dalton."

His friend patted him on the back. He hurried after Peach. As she entered the depot, he came in behind her.

The ticketmaster saw them and stepped back from the grilled window. He looked a little scared.

"I'll take a ticket on the next train out." Peach slung her purse down on the counter. "I don't care where it's going."

Will came up behind her. "I never laughed at you," he said over her shoulder. "I never once laughed at you. You were the the bravest thing I'd ever seen. And so loyal. I never credited any of the Daltons with much sense, but Bob was sure right when he picked you. You'd have followed him to hell and back if you hadn't had sense enough not to love him."

Peach whirled. "I did love him."

Will shook his head. "You did not."

The ticketmaster caught his eye and suddenly remembered he had business in the back room. The town council had lined up in front of the building, peering in at the windows.

"You never loved him," Will said softly. "He was handsome. You were young."

"I'm not that much older now," she snapped.

"You're way too young for me. But I fell in love with you anyway."

She started. "You never loved me."

"I was mooning in my beer over you practically from the first day Luke hired you."

"You were not. You're a liar."

"No lie. When Bob Dalton finally started flirting with you, I was green jealous. Like a kid."

"You were not." She didn't shout quite so loudly that time. She could feel something that had been like a chip of ice letting go inside her. Then she hardened her heart and thought of Bob cut to pieces by gunfire. "I won't stay with a liar. I'm leaving."

"Here!" He pulled his gun from the holster, reversed it, and passed it over to her.

She stared at it as if she'd never see it before.

"If you're going to leave me, just put me out of my misery."

"What?"

"I was a crippled, self-pitying drunk when I first fell in love with you. Thanks to you, I pulled myself back together again."

"Thanks to Bob Dalton, don't you mean?" she countered coldly.

"No, ma'am. No thanks to Bob Dalton. He pulled a robbery and he murdered the marshal. And I got the job. I profited from Charlie Connelly's bad luck. Not Bob Dalton's generosity."

She shuddered. He was right.

He pressed the gun into her hand. "Thanks to you, I

got my self-respect back. I got the use of my arm. I got my life back.''

She let the gun's weight carry it down to her thigh so it no longer barred the way between them. She couldn't bear to look into his pleading eyes. She couldn't.

"I can't stay together without you," Will murmured. "Kill me quick or kill me slow."

She shook her head. "Oh, Will."

She dropped the gun and wrapped her arms around him. They were both in tears.

Outside on the platform, the members of the town council were cheering and congratulating themselves.

Will and Peach said their good-byes and took the train for Kansas.

While the iron wheels click-clacked away beneath them, they leaned against each other. Exhausted emotionally, Peach felt empty. Her husband sat with his arm around her shoulders. Now and again his fingers caressed her shoulder. Twice she felt his body grow heavy as he dozed. Then he'd jerk awake with his fists clenched, his muscles fighting.

As they rolled into Coffeyville, he took a deep breath. "Do you want to visit the cemetery?"

She shook her head. "I'm through with all that."

"No more ghosts."

"No." She rose and indulged her body in a ladylike stretch. He stood aside for her to enter the aisle, then followed her off the train.

The sun shone on the platform. The day was cold but fair, the sky bright blue without a single trace of cloud.

He handed a coin to the stationmaster to send the boy to the hotel with their bags. "Walk with me."

She unfurled her parasol and cocked it over her shoulder. He took her arm. Past Scurlock's they walked. They turned up Walnut Street past the bank. She didn't look down Death Alley. It was just an alley after all. There was nothing to see.

Another two blocks carried them out of the business district. Three narrow two-story houses stood together on a block. They were new houses, painted a muted buttercup yellow with white trim. They had picket fences around good-sized front yards.

Curiously, Peach admired them. Two holly bushes, green despite the freezing weather, grew on either side of the porch. The oak trees in the front yard were barren of leaves. Will opened the gate of the middle one.

"Who do we know that lives here?" Peach asked.

Will grinned like a boy. "Do you like it?"

She nodded. "Someday."

He led her up the steps. "What about today?"

She couldn't believe it. The house was too beautiful for the likes of her. "Oh, Will."

He opened the door and swept her up in his arms. On the threshold he kissed her long. What started as tender turned passionate. She hugged him tighter. When they were both breathless, he reared back his head and gave a cheer of pure joy.

"Will," she cautioned, looking in the direction of the neighbors.

He grinned. "I paid Luke to buy us a bed while we were gone. Let's go see if he did."

She pushed the door closed behind them.

AUTHOR'S NOTE

The 1892 raid foiled by the Coffeyville Defenders saw the end of the legendary outlaws that were the kith and kin of Jesse James.

Emmett Dalton served fourteen and a half years of a life sentence in the Kansas State Penitentiary. He married his childhood sweetheart and moved to Hollywood, California, where he wrote a book, *When the Daltons Rode*. He died in 1937 at the age of sixty-six, mumbling over and over what he had just cause to believe: "Crime doesn't pay." The movie based on his book premiered in Coffeyville in 1940.

In the end the true West belonged to the lawmen who triumphed over the outlaws. Allen Pinkerton and his men became world famous. To this day, the Texas Rangers remain a force for law and order in the Lone Star State. Pat Garrett, who shot Billy the Kid, was highly praised by President Teddy Roosevelt. After marshaling in Ellsworth, Wichita, and Dodge City, Kansas, Wyatt Earp went on to Tombstone, Arizona, where his fame reached national proportions. Bat Masterson, Wyatt's partner in so many of his adventures, left Tombstone to become a sports writer for the *New York Morning Telegram*. America still depends on its U.S. marshals.

Their names and others of their kind are as famous as the men they killed or captured. Even though America may glamorize its outlaws, it loves its lawmen too.

SAVAGE ROMANCE
FROM CASSIE EDWARDS!

#1: SAVAGE OBSESSION   (0-8217-5554-4, $5.99/$7.50)
Yellow Feather, Chief of the Chippewa, rescues Lorinda from an Indian attack and renames her Red Blossom. While they struggle through tribal wars they learn how to unleash their desires and commit to love.

#2: SAVAGE INNOCENCE   (0-8217-5578-1, $5.99/$7.50)
Tired of life in Minnesota, Danette leaves home to begin anew in the rugged frontier, where she meets the Chippewa warrior, Gray Wolf. Together they fight off enemies and begin on an adventure that will lead them to love.

#3: SAVAGE TORMENT   (0-8217-5581-1, $5.99/$7.50)
Judith McMahon is taken on a trip to visit Chippewa country, where she meets Strong Hawk and finds more than the land attractive. When love overcomes treachery and racial conflict, she is compelled to stay permanently and fulfill a new life.

#4: SAVAGE HEART   (0-8217-5635-4, $5.99/$7.50)
Traveling to Seattle, on a journey to riches, Christa and David lose their parents to cholera. Poverty-stricken, David forces Christa to marry a wealthy businessman against her will. Despite convention and a furious brother or a rival tribe, when she sets her eyes on the handsome Tall Cloud, chief of the Suquamish, she is joined to him forever.

#5: SAVAGE PARADISE   (0-8217-5637-0, $5.99/$7.50)
In the Minnesota territory, Marianna Fowler felt miserable and far from civilization. Then she meets Lone Hawk and the grass looks greener. Although they become outcasts, they both commit to a love that is taboo.

ALSO FROM CASSSIE EDWARDS . . .
PASSION'S WEB   (0-8217-5726-1, $5.99/$7.50)
Against the backdrop of sailing ships and tropical islands, a spoiled heiress named Natalie Palmer and a pirate named Bryce Fowler turn the Florida coast golden with the radiance of their forbidden love.

Available wherever paperbacks are sold, or order direct from the Publisher. Send cover price plus 50¢ per copy for mailing and handling to Kensington Publishing Corp., Consumer Orders, or call (toll free) 888-345-BOOK, to place your order using Mastercard or Visa. Residents of New York and Tennessee must include sales tax. DO NOT SEND CASH.

PASSIONATE ROMANCE
FROM BETINA KRAHN!

FROM ROSANNE BITTNER:
ZEBRA SAVAGE DESTINY ROMANCE!

#1: SWEET PRAIRIE PASSION   (0-8217-5342-8, $5.99)

#2: RIDE THE FREE WIND   (0-8217-5343-6, $5.99)

#3: RIVER OF LOVE   (0-8217-5344-4, $5.99)

#4: EMBRACE THE
    WILD LAND   (0-8217-5413-0, $5.99)

#7: EAGLE'S SONG   (0-8217-5326-6, $5.99)

ROMANCE FROM FERN MICHAELS

DEAR EMILY   (0-8217-4952-8, $5.99)

WISH LIST   (0-8217-5228-6, $6.99)

AND IN HARDCOVER:

VEGAS RICH   (1-57566-057-1, $25.00)

ROMANCE FROM JANELLE TAYLOR

ANYTHING FOR LOVE   (0-8217-4992-7, $5.99)

DESTINY MINE   (0-8217-5185-9, $5.99)

CHASE THE WIND   (0-8217-4740-1, $5.99)

MIDNIGHT SECRETS   (0-8217-5280-4, $5.99)

MOONBEAMS AND MAGIC (0-8217-0184-4, $5.99)

SWEET SAVAGE HEART   (0-8217-5276-6, $5.99)